The Corescu Chronicles Book One

ellen c. maze

The Judging
The Corescu Chronicles Book One
By Ellen C. Maze

2020 ANNIVERSARY EDITION
www.ellencmaze.com
©2010, 2020 by Ellen C. Maze

v.20.08.2020

Cover
Title Graphics: Elizabeth Little, www.hyliian.deviantart.com

Little Roni Publishers, LLC
ISBN: 978-1-7340474-1-7
Also available in eBook publication

The following is a work of fiction. Names, characters, places, and incidents are fictitious or used fictitiously. Any resemblance to real persons, living or dead, to factual events or to businesses is coincidental and unintentional.

All Bible verses have been taken from the New International Version (NIV).

PUBLISHED IN THE UNITED STATES OF AMERICA

The Judging and *Rabbit: Chasing Beth Rider* Connection

In Ellen C. Maze's *Rabbit: Chasing Beth Rider*, a bestselling novelist finds herself on the run from a bloodthirsty race of beings whose leaders despise the affect her novel, *The Judging,* has on their people. Here is what readers are saying about *Rabbit's* fascinating and unique look at the vampire mythos:

Praise for *Rabbit: Chasing Beth Rider*

"Maze's storytelling is fast and fun, overflowing with ideas and spiritual insight."

~ Eric Wilson, author of *Fireproof,* and *Valley of Bones* *(The Jerusalem Undead Trilogy)*

"What a great book! It kept me on the edge of my seat, waiting for what was going to happen next. With all the strange powers at work in this world, this book reveals the greatest Power of all."

~ Rabbi John Giddens, *www.ChavurahShalom.org*

"I absolutely love it when an author can take a myth or legend and weave them neatly and efficiently into a brilliant and original tale. This book is definitely not simplistic in nature. Ms. Maze gives us a fast-paced plot with many twists and turns, not just in the action, but also for the mind. *Rabbit: Chasing Beth Rider* will grab your attention from the first page and will not let go until the end, and maybe not even then. Enjoy the chase!"

~ Stephanie Nordkap, *Bestsellersworld.com*

Maze takes us on a vampire journey with a one-of-a-kind twist! Rabbit is a fast-paced, action-packed, exciting vampire thriller. As an avid reader of vampire fiction, this gem unexpectedly has become one of my very favorites.

~ Marcia Freespirit, CEO, *JimSam Inc. Publishing*

"Riveting and eye-opening…a powerful testament to the often overlooked spiritual strength within us all."

~ *Apex reviews*

From the Author:

Rabbit: Chasing Beth Rider and *The Judging* are tied in a very unique way. The title character of *Rabbit*, Beth Rider, is the author of a provocative and bestselling vampire series entitled the *Corescu Chronicles*. Her first two books, *The Judging* and *Damascus Road*, are the catalyst that sets the vampires (the Rakum) after her in *Rabbit: Chasing Beth Rider*. dive in to both series' today, and please watch your step. Things get mighty hairy in my imagination!
Enjoy and God bless you,

Ellen C. Maze

ALSO BY ELLEN C. MAZE

Rabbit: Chasing Beth Rider (Book One)
Rabbit Legacy (Book Two)
Rabbit Redemption (Book Three)
Anomaly: Beyond the Rabbit (Book Four)
Conundrum: The Lost Rabbit (Book Five)
The Vestige: Final Chapter (Book Six)

The Judging: The Corescu Chronicles Book One
Damascus Road: The Corescu Chronicles Book Two
Tree of Life: The Corescu Chronicles Book Three
Anathema: The Corescu Chronicles Book Four
Novus: The Corescu Chronicles Book Five

22 Sideways: Twenty-Two Bloodthirsty Tales
Loose Rabbits of the Rabbit Trilogy
Feckless Tales of Supernatural, Paranormal,
and Downright Presumptuous Ilk

Ellen's Links:
Email the author at ellenmaze@aol.com
Sign up for newsletter for freebies & project-related alerts at
www.ellencmaze.com

This book is dedicated to you, the reader.
Oh, how I have longed to put this book into your hands.
I hope you enjoy it.
~ Ellen

The Judging

The Corescu Chronicles Book One

ellen c. maze

Prologue

Arise O LORD! Deliver me, O my God!
Strike all my enemies on the jaw;
break the teeth of the wicked.
Psalm 3:7

Hungary, 1640

IT WAS THE DREAM OF A MADMAN; ECSTASY AND AGONY and nothing in between. The priest resisted the perverse imagery, still unable to escape the midnight terrors threatening to unhinge his mind.

A white horse trapped in a lake of sludge the color of blood, its taut musculature gleaming with sweat as it struggles to escape. The surrealistic steed grows darker as its body disappears, inch-by-inch, devoured by the sticky, red-black slime. It screams in terror once, but is quieted, soothed as the crimson mud approaches its long neck and fills its gaping mouth. And then there is silence. Like the silence of the grave.

CRASH!

The sharp sound ripped through the priest's subconscious, abruptly delivering him from the jealous bonds of sleep. Awake and alarmed, he bolted upright and listened to the night. Tiny slivers of light seeped into the Spartan bedroom through the shuttered window, while in the street outside a cacophony sounded. The priest threw off the bed linens and gained the window in two clumsy strides. Knocking the shutters wide, hell filled the courtyard.

Flames engulfed every structure, from the Spisak hostel on the north side of the main thoroughfare to the Trova Mercantile on the opposite end. The priest rubbed disbelief from his tear-filled eyes, the village burning alive. Orange-yellow tongues of fire licked the black sky turning it gray above with thick, lung-bursting smoke. His flock, the simple and precious villagers, scattered carrying their paltry treasures to safety. Still others dumped painfully small quantities of water on the carnivorous flames with buckets and cooking pots.

"God, help us!" he cried and yanked open his bedroom door. A deadly fog of black smoke rolled over him and in his panic, he

1

remembered the boy. "Miki!" he said aloud and stumbled toward the tiny alcove beyond the crucifix.

The boy's parents had abandoned him into the Father's care five years ago, and as he searched the inky darkness, his heart burst with love for the child.

"Miki! Miki!" he screamed into the doorway fearing the worst.

The violent heat pushed him back and forced him to his knees. Within a moment, he regained his feet and hurled into the gray rooms beyond. He barely took two steps before his lungs were unbearably singed by the smoke.

Three more steps, Lord! Please, help me!

The priest surged forward in the impossible abyss of moving shadow and fire. When he finally stumbled into the recess, his palms sought the child's sleeping form; Miki wasn't there. The priest thought to cry out, but instead a weak gasp issued from his tortured throat. Legs pumping, he lunged for the large pine doors at the front of the chapel. The smoke thinned as he reached the first row of carefully crafted pews and filled his lungs with the cleaner air before he hit the ground.

I must make it through those doors or I am finished!

He crawled for the shimmering image of the exit. The brass door handles glowed with unnatural appeal, but then... The priest's eyes jerked right. There had been movement. A spark of hope flared as he peered into a fluid vision of haze and shadow.

Miki?

Interrupting his retreat, the priest turned back.

"Save yourself! It is too late for the boy. Get out while you still can. There is danger here, even more dangerous than the flames of hell..."

Trained to recognize the voice of his God, the priest regarded the words he heard in his spirit. He thought to resume his progress to the exit when another flicker of movement caught his attention. Narrowing his eyes to focus, a scream welled in his throat. It was Miki! With a parched gasp, he crawled toward the boy, croaking to the demanding presence of God in his heart, "I told You! Look! It's Miki! I can save him!"

As he neared the boy, the gentle but adamant inner voice urged him to escape. *"Get out, get out..."*

The priest stubbornly continued, convinced he could rescue the boy he'd come to love as his own son. *I can save him. I won't let him die.*

"Why do you argue? There is danger here—"

Because I can save him, Lord. Please, help me!

2

Snarling now, the priest half-crawled, half-lunged toward the boy, seeing him dimly through thickening plumes of smoke. At first glance, Miki appeared to be napping on the coarse wooden pew, but his green eyes were open, glassy, and still. His shining black curls hovered halo-like above his brow and his tiny mouth was unnaturally agape. The boy's chest did not rise and fall with the breath of the living and his dead gaze penetrated the priest's very soul.

"Miki!"

No sound. The priest had lost his voice, his vocal cords seared. He pulled himself toward the boy, grief flooding his heart with madness. Then, as if only opening his eyes for the first time, he noticed the devil sitting upon the boy's chest. Materializing astride the child, the demon glared directly at the priest, a challenge in its gaze. The solidifying apparition had red, hate-filled eyes that pierced the priest as surely as a sword. He tried to look away, but the fierce eyes held him fast. For the first time in his thirty-three years, the priest truly believed in Satan.

As his heart fractured within him, the priest glared at the monster. It bore the hunched-over and misshapen semblance of a man, the smoke had blackened the demon's skin, and its wicked smile exposed sharp teeth. It wore no clothing on its featureless body and it stared into the priest's face. Bringing a gnarled claw of a hand to its mouth, it licked its lips. Growling appreciatively, it approached.

Oh, my God! Father, protect me! The room spun as the priest succumbed to asphyxiation. The dark monster came close, but with his eyes too heavy to remain open, and his brain too weary to resist, the priest lost consciousness.

ය⌘ා

Seconds later, with the priest thrown over its shoulder, the monster pulled him from the fire and spirited him off to the woods.

Its mission accomplished.

Its prize acquired.

One

Do not accept a ransom for the life of a murderer,
who deserves to die. He must surely be put to death.
Numbers 35:31

Present Day

THIS LAST ONE WOULDN'T SCREAM.

Tate rolled the corpse over for one last look. She was Emily all over again; it was uncanny. But why didn't she scream? That really sucked the fun out of the exercise. The original Emily had screamed, and oh, what a sound.

With the toe of his work boot, Tate shoved the body over the bridge edge. No one would find her. He'd chosen this spot three years ago and since weighted down and buried seven such Emilys. Deep in the Talladega National Forest, but no more than a mile from his granddaddy's farm, the traffic on the abandoned road was nil. Only equestrians and hikers ambled by these days, and with the recent summer flooding, not even they attempted the treacherous terrain surrounding the defeated wooden crossing.

The eighth Emily made a surprisingly small splash and disappeared. The water was twelve feet deep and hardly moved. Tate thought about the others down there, what they must look like, wrapped in ropes, chains, and shower curtains, with only their long brown hair free to wave at the fishes that happened by.

Snap.

Tate looked toward the noise, his flashlight dark for the moment. It was half-past midnight and he was alone. Maybe an animal?

Snap!

Tate switched on his halogen beam and it sliced into the dark tree line fifteen yards north. The noise was deeper in, snuggled into the way he was to go. It might've been a "woodland creature," as his mother Emily called them, but she'd been a whore—

4

Tate spat the bile that rose as his memory of her sharpened. Cursing under his breath, he puffed out his chest. The sound occurred again, but this time on the opposite side of the disrupted clay path that used to be a road.

"Who's there?" he whispered, unnerved the forest had fallen quiet. The only noise that filtered into his ears was the echo of the latest branch breaking. It wasn't an animal; someone was toying with him. Tate backed two steps from the last noise and swallowed. A list of possible suspects paraded past his consciousness as he worked to divine who might have followed him to his killing field. Whoever it was, they had to die. There were too many Emilys left to locate and destroy before his work was done. Tate opened his pocketknife and hid it in his palm. If somebody rushed him, he'd do what the Army trained him to do twenty years ago. He was an excellent killer.

"Tatian Murphy, you are being judged."

A raspy voice filled the clearing with no directional source. Tate whirled to his right and presented his blade with a stiff arm.

"Who's there?" he shouted, jerking to the left, behind, and then right again.

"You have killed for the last time. Repent of your murderous deeds and you will find forgiveness." The voice rumbled closer now, eerily emanating from the air itself.

Tate jabbed at nothing and sought a reply. Intending to scream curses, he ended up repeating, "Who's there?"

Strong hands from behind took hold of his shoulders and held him fast as Tate yelled out, this time in surprise and fear. Twisting backward to see, he caught a glimpse of a pale face floating in a sea of black, the mouth open and red. A hungry maw with the sharp teeth of an animal.

"Your sins have called me here and the time of judgment has come. Repent," the voice hissed into his ear.

Tate screamed and swiveled his upper body with all of his strength only to be pulled into the thing's wide chest. Twice more, his attacker whispered for him to repent, now speaking telepathically, penetrating his mind with icy fingers.

"Get off me! Help!" Tate shouted until his throat was raw, but did not expect rescue; he had chosen this desolate location well.

Still behind, his attacker repositioned to hold Tate immobile with one arm while the free hand yanked down the collars of his coat and T-Shirt. Tate's panic level rose as the monster's breath whispered across his bare skin. A sickly aroma accompanied and the watery sound of the monster licking his lips sent new shivers to Tate's spine.

"Once more, Tatian Murphy," the telepathic voice threatened, *"repent of the murder and violence you have perpetrated. Repent and be saved..."*

First, the undeniable touch of a tongue, molding itself to the curve of his throat, flattening, licking, one swipe. And then, his assailant's fang-like teeth touched his skin. Tate increased his struggle, accidentally pushing himself upward until blood trickled from the self-inflicted punctures. The monster inhaled, held him tighter, and sent him one last mental message.

"You should've repented."

With that, the fangs plunged into his jugular. Tate's eyes bulged as the fire that raged at the wound site was surpassed by the undeniable sensation of his life slipping away.

"I'm sorry! I'm sorry!" he shouted, his knuckles white where his fists grasped the attacker's sleeve. "God, help me! I'm sorry!" Did he make it in time? Who was God and was He listening?

The vampire drank deeply, squeezing Tate's chest until it was difficult to breathe. Whimpering, his knees buckled. The monster supported his weight and held him fast, still brutally draining his life.

"I don't want to die. No..."

Tate's pleas fell to a whisper and then became internal as a white fog encroached on his senses. Would God help him? He had worked hard to punish his mother for what she did. He was washing evil from the planet; wasn't that a good deed in itself? Should he have left that job to God?

Tate moaned and realized the *lub-dub* thump in his ears had become irregular. Soon, it would stop altogether.

"I'm sorry. I'm sorry."

He tried to say it, but he had no breath. Oh, but he was sorry.

6

Two

"Look at the nations and watch—and be utterly amazed.
For I am going to do something in your days that you
would not believe, even if you were told."
Habakkuk 1:5

DR. MARK CORESCU'S CHAMPAGNE-COLORED LEXUS FLEW down the interstate as if not touching the ground. He nodded his head in time with the classical music pouring from the speakers and slowed only to exit towards the hospital. A new billboard for the White Stallion Pub and Restaurant caught his eye and he frowned.

Didn't I dream recently about a white stallion? The doctor decelerated to enter the parking garage and as he wove his way to his assigned space, he went over the dream in his mind. *A stallion. A sad, shimmering animal, coated with mud; suffering the terrors of...* It wasn't clear.

Corescu parked and closed his eyes. What exactly happened to that horse? And the real question, Corescu furrowed his brow, what happened to the roses?

The mud-encrusted animal dragged itself across the riverbank, onto the shore, and into the grass. Roses sprouted along the edge of the river, and as the horse passed them, they wilted and died.

Corescu shook his head, puzzling over the possible implications. Lunacy or prophecy? He was familiar with both. After a few moments, he left the car scoffing, filing it away as a meaningless triviality of his subconscious. Corescu chuckled under his breath, his waking life was strange enough to keep him entertained.

Disdaining the elevator, the doctor took the stairs to his office, whistling. He smiled as his superior sense of smell picked up a whiff of the rose petals from his dream. He wasn't surprised; he'd experienced much stranger things than this.

Much stranger things, indeed.

ભ્રૹ

7

Hope Brannen checked her makeup in the rearview mirror and examined her teeth. A minimalist when it came to cosmetics, mascara and eye-liner were her mainstays. As long as she rode horses in the scorching Alabama sun, and tanned by the pool on weekends, foundation and rouge remained superfluous. If only she didn't have that mole half-way between her lip and nose. Shaking her head, she covered the small brown bump with her finger. When her stomach grumbled, she turned her mind to the meal ahead, happy for the mental subject change.

Her lunch date was a woman who kissed the Blarney Stone three times. Fran Booker, a former coworker from Hope's allergy-clinic days, was loud, brassy, and opinionated, with an easy smile and contagious laugh. An adult immigrant from Ireland, Fran had the thickest Irish brogue Hope had ever heard. Today, they were meeting for lunch to celebrate Fran's new position with a local star of the medical world. Fran had a better job with better pay and couldn't be happier. *Maybe it was God...*

Hope scoffed at the errant thought and slowed the Geo to the speed limit. Her closest friend, Anthony Agricola, told her she was "ripe for a great move of God." A part-time seminary student, Anthony recently counseled her that everyone suffered to some extent in his or her life. *But he is pretty dramatic for a man...*

Hope smirked; she had lived twenty-five years in relative bliss. Sure, her husband had been killed in an auto accident after only one year of marriage, but Hope persevered. Her parents passed soon after that, yet she handled their deaths with a stoicism that surprised everyone. *I grieve in my own way, that's all...*

At the last family reunion, one of her aunts accused her of being dead inside. Another aunt went so far as to imply she was insane, like poor old Uncle Joe, the loon her forefathers hid away in the attic. Hope chuckled. They didn't get it. Only her sister Glorie understood. Hope was self-actualized, which was extremely liberating.

"Not everyone suffers on a cross. You'll get your chance to prove yourself to God. I'm positive you're being prepared for something huge."

Ughh! Anthony's words came to her in the same tone with which there were delivered last Sunday – with all his goofy reverence to an unseen Boss. Hope shook her head and turned her mind to her lunch date. They were going to have a great visit and she wouldn't think about God or Anthony the whole time.

ক৪৪৩

The large font on the glossy cover of his newly-opened college directory read, "Dallas Theological Seminary, Atlanta Campus." Anthony Agricola, Tony, sat in his office and flipped through the course catalogue. The fee schedules made him cluck his tongue; seminary was expensive. He had taken his pre-requisites at Auburn University and planned to become a preacher like his father if he could manage it, but so far, it didn't look promising.

Dr. Tony Agricola, Sr., had pastored the fastest growing Presbyterian Church in the city before he passed away four years ago. Tony was twenty-eight when his father died, but he took the loss like a child. For three months, he moped around his apartment and shirked his church administrator duties until the day his mother stopped over and found him on the couch in the dark surrounded by dirty laundry.

"Come on, Tony," she'd said in her sweetest voice. "I loved your father, too, but it's time you got about God's work and stopped focusing on yourself."

The tough love worked. The next day, Tony picked himself up and got back to it.

It had always been his father's dream that his son follow his example and preach at Green Oaks Presbyterian, the church Grandfather Agricola founded in Whitford City a hundred years ago. But Tony was forced to maintain his full-time church job to pay the bills, and as he got older, school took a backseat. At the rate his savings account grew, Tony figured he'd be ready to move to Atlanta and attend seminary in a decade.

Resigned, Tony sighed and shook his head. For now, his mother would have to be content he at least *worked* in the family church. She could pray for him to fulfill his legacy and they would see what happened.

Another thing she prayed for was that he would find a wife among their one-thousand-plus members. Tony did his best to oblige, dating any woman who consented, but invariably, he came on too strong and ran them off. Not every woman wanted to settle down and have eight children after a first date. Enter Hope Brannen. Tony fell hard for the spunky blonde who politely blew him off. Somewhere out there was his chosen helpmate; he'd just have to let go and let God.

Tony groaned and remembered why he'd taken a seat at his desk in the first place. The elders had asked him to submit an article about faith for the weekly church periodical and he'd procrastinated himself into a corner.

"Life as a Christian," Tony read aloud, rubbing his face with his palms as the document pulled up. He read and re-read the few lines he had written so far. Taking a deep breath, he allowed his fingers to fly across the keyboard, writing anything and everything that came to mind. When he stopped to read it aloud, he sighed.

Life as a Christian is like being in that Matrix movie. The real world is not real at all, and only those who know the Truth realize the sleepers are simply batteries and food serving an alien race of demons...

Ridiculous drivel. Tony hit "delete" and scrounged for an old paper he could resurrect and serve the Elders' purpose

Three

*…I urge you, as aliens and strangers in the world,
to abstain from sinful desires, which war against your soul.*
1 Peter 2:11

IN THE DOCTOR'S TOWER, HOPE RODE THE ELEVATOR to the fifth floor and tugged on the hem of her baby-tee, which barely reached the waist of her low-rise Levi's. Heading down the hall to Suite Nine, Hope wrinkled her nose as a wall of aromas assaulted her senses. The recently refurbished offices smelled of fresh paint and latex gloves. Purple drapes and elaborate tapestries drew her attention to the lavish décor. Before she pondered further, she spotted a brass plaque:

*Made possible through the generous contributions
of the Howard H. Block Foundation.*

Bingo. The Blocks were the richest family in town, their philanthropy well-documented. Hope put her hand to the door as it jerked violently inward. At top speed, Fran tumbled into her and they both teetered to the side.

"Whoa! That was close!" Hope laughed. "Where's the fire?"

"Ouchy-wah-wah!" Fran grinned and patted down her short frosted hairdo. "'Bout got me a speedin' ticket!" Fran drawled in an accent thick enough to shame a leprechaun. She took Hope's arm and pulled her into the office. "Since you're here, come on. We have to hurry if I'm going to drop these files off before lunch. I'd be pleased to get gone before the boss arrives."

"I thought you said he was *wonn-derful,*" Hope teased and rolled her eyes, fluttering her eyelashes as she dragged out the syllables.

"Very funny," Fran said, fanning herself with the folders in her hand. "Oh, he's *grand.* I don't wanna be held up. Sometimes he gives

11

me a ton of filing before I've had me lunch!"

Hope laughed with her friend as they reached the door. An engraved plate at eye level stated smartly, DR. MARK CORESCU, a romantic name Hope repeated to herself. Fran barged in without knocking and froze. Surprise, surprise. The doctor was in.

A voice recorder at his mouth, Dr. Corescu pushed a button on the device and looked up. Fran cursed at her rude entrance while Hope simply blushed. Fran's new boss was *perfect*. Hope watched as the doctor stood, bemused as Fran stumbled over her apologies. Then he came around the desk and offered Hope his hand.

"Mrs. Booker," Corescu said in a rich baritone that filled the office with sound. His smile revealed perfect teeth. "Introduce me to your friend."

Hope swallowed as heat rushed again to her cheeks. Corescu had striking features with smooth cappuccino skin and jet black hair cut long on top and short on the sides. His deep set, dark brown eyes held her captive although she didn't try to look away. When Fran remained mum, Hope smiled demurely and grasped his offered fingers for a quick shake.

"Hope Brannen, nice to meet you," Hope said and his smile went to the side. *He's into me...* She latched onto the idea and added a giggle for effect. Her girlfriends hated it, but men? They were a different story. Then, Corescu released her hand and returned to his desk. Hope had expected anything but that and an odd sigh rippled across her mind at the severed contact.

Fran shuffled papers on the desk behind them and forced a laugh. "I apologize, Doc. I didn't expect you this early. Hope, meet me boss, Dr. Mark Corescu."

Hope clasped her hands behind her back and sent him another smile when he swiveled his face. He returned the gesture, but his eyes... she'd need a minute to decipher his signals.

"Corescu. Is that European?" she asked hoping to hear his lovely voice.

"I am from Maine," he said with a half-grin, daring her with his eyes to pry again. Hope was game.

"How long have you been in Georgia?"

He maintained his grin and the eye-contact, as if amused at her audacity. In lieu of a verbal response, he licked his lips and after three long seconds, flicked his gaze to her friend.

"After your lunch break, please stop by my office," he told her and when Fran grunted affirmative and returned his gaze to Hope with a sideways look. "You're welcome to come, too."

"Heh," she chuckled, her blush returning. As hard as she tried to maintain the upper hand, the man repeatedly snatched it away. Hope tried one more line. "Fran told me you are a *wonnn-derful* boss," she cooed, dragging out the word.

"I'm sure she's exaggerating." Corescu shrugged, still not flirting as she expected. She could be a matronly nun for all his reactions revealed. The room fell silent as Hope was at a loss for a reply, still locked in the man's gaze. With one more trick up her sleeve; Hope stepped close. She got her wish—his eyes widened with a quick inhale. Emboldened, Hope touched his lapel.

"Can I call you Mark?" Hope asked as being on a first-name basis would be the way to get to know him better.

With a tiny grin and in a casual manner, Corescu stepped out of reach. "I much prefer it."

Hope drew in her bottom lip and held it there before saying with a small grin, "great."

Fran groaned with drama. "Come on, wee one. I'm havin' roast beast, no matter how often it sends me to tha' jacks." Fran scooped the pile of folders and headed for the door. "I'm sure we'll be finding some salad or tofu for the likes of you."

Hope's smile dropped, suddenly concerned if the doctor would find her vegetarianism a turn-off. He didn't react, but remained sitting on the edge of his desk, regarding her with his eyes.

From out in the hall they both heard Fran call out with a comic retort. "If the good Lord didn't want us eating animals, why'd He make 'em out of meat?"

"That's my cue." Hope backed toward the door. "It was nice to meet you, Mark."

"Indeed," he said. With a sinking suspicion he didn't want to be the first to break eye-contact, Hope spun on her heel and stepped into the hall. Reaching Fran at the elevator, she grabbed her elbow.

"Indeed," she repeated, imitating his voice. Her friend sighed and punched the elevator button. "FRAN!" she hiss-whispered, "you could have warned me he was gorgeous!"

Her friend rolled her eyes and began discussing lunch food choices. Funnily, Hope was no longer hungry in the least.

$\mathcal{F}$our

There is no fear in love...
1 John 4:18

MARK HURRIED THROUGH HIS NOON PATIENT. AFTERWARDS, he breathed a sigh of relief and returned to his office. Once there, he crossed to his cupboard and yanked the stethoscope from his shoulders, his mind turning to Hope Brannen. Four centuries was a long time to wait for the fulfillment of God's promise. Mark had no use for the past and did not dwell on it, but he never forgot the promise. It was time; God had ordained it.

Decades ago, before Whitford City, before Paul, before he came to America, he had been given a vision that one day, a woman would come into his life and ease his burden. The particulars were vague, but Mark interpreted the hazy details to mean this special woman would take on his yoke and aid him in his calling. Thus, he watched for her as he trudged through the centuries. When he locked eyes with Fran Booker's young friend today, he was certain she had arrived.

This woman will ease the burden I bear to judge mankind, he mused, studying his long, manicured fingers that had ended more lives than he cared to count. It was time he had some help. Mark would make Hope his equal, her aesthetic beauty a delightful bonus. He pictured her, reticent to release the image. Heart-shaped face accentuated with smooth skin, a pouty mouth, and huge blue eyes, the woman was in the prime of her life, not a blemish or physical short-coming evident in the glimpses he had been afforded. The sight of her caused his head to buzz in much the way Paul did when he first laid eyes on the young man he chose as a companion a century ago. Mark chuckled. All of the signs pointed to Hope Brannen as the answer to his prayers.

I have to get home and tell Paul.

In a hurry to share his news with the only one he could, Mark shrugged off his lab coat as a knock sounded at the door. He barked a

14

curt welcome and Mrs. Booker entered carrying a mountain of file folders. She mumbled a greeting without meeting his eye and Mark smiled. He made her uncomfortable; which he enjoyed. Making a wide berth to cross behind her, he shut the door.

"Thank you, Mrs. Booker." Fran piled the folders on his desk with one small peek over her shoulder at the closed door. "Tell me about Miss Brannen," Mark said, encouraging the woman to elaborate.

"She's a good'n." Fran shifted her weight and tapped her foot on the carpet. "Wort wit 'er at me old job."

Mark sat on the edge of his desk, arms folded, hoping his casual stance would put the woman at ease. "Is she married?"

Fran's tight smile faded. "She's a widow, poor ting."

Mark focused his gaze and the woman loosened her tongue.

"Two years it's been since her Kevin passed on. She's okay; she's a well-adjusted lass. She stays busy."

The woman's heartrate increased and she looked at the door. Mark released her with a nod and she exited with a mumbled goodbye. Hope was single; those were the words he longed to hear.

ᭉᜆᝄ

"I'm not crazy about the color." Reuben leaned against the Jaguar and watched Paul look over the new Tahoe. He smoothed out a wrinkle in his white silk shirt and avoided Paul's gaze. Smirking, he offered another jab. "The boss would probably rather have black. White is boring as hell and twice as annoying."

Reuben's comments went ignored, but he wasn't surprised. Paul often dragged him away from his duties and today, he'd been compelled to drive the boss's lackey to the dealership. Officially, Reuben served as Dr. Corescu's driver and garage manager, but Paul had seniority. The doctor favored the blond geek and Reuben would not risk a real altercation, cowed enough by the boss that he didn't take chances with his pet. Still, irritating the slender puff was supremely entertaining.

"As a matter of fact, Mark said it is entirely my choice," Paul snapped without looking his way. "And I prefer white. It doesn't take long to get tired of anything black." Paul shut the truck's rear cargo door and headed toward the building to close the deal.

"Ass kisser," Reuben muttered under his breath.

"What?" Paul asked, turning to give Reuben a stern glare.

"Nothing," Reuben returned with a scowl. He let Paul get halfway across the lot before following, watching the man's ridiculously loose

15

shirt billow in the warm summer breeze. The guy was so slight that Reuben doubted they even made clothes to fit him. With his long stick-like legs and surfer's tan, he resembled an anorexic Ken doll. Reuben laughed aloud; the dork made a perfect houseboy. After tailing Paul onto the air-conditioned sales floor, Reuben assumed a quiet posture behind him.

Like a good little slave.

He sneered at the thought. Since he was a child, he had served alongside this jerk.

One day, one day soon, you're gonna pay. You're both gonna pay.

Reuben cleared his mind, his thoughts not his alone. Glancing at his watch, he tried to imagine where the boss might be at the moment. He grabbed a brochure to allow the images to dispel his inner monologue's treasonous thoughts. He schemed constantly against his overseers, for what slave worth his salt didn't at least dream of freedom?

"Here," Paul barked, pushing the Jaguar's keys into Reuben's hand. "I'll drive the truck home."

The portly salesman shook Paul's hand and walked them to the new vehicle. Paul waited until they reached the driver's side door before turning to Reuben with a final directive. "Drive straight home. I have more chores for you."

Reuben looked at the fat sales rep and hated what he saw there. It was written across his round, sunburned face as clear as crystal: *you just can't get good help these days, can you?* Inside, Reuben fumed with anger, but outwardly, he smiled—real wide.

"Yessah, massah, I'se gonna take real good care of yo cah. Yessah." Reuben, now thirty feet away, spoke louder over the wind. "And when weez get back to tha' plantation, I'se gonna help pick *all* da' cotton." Reuben tipped the imaginary brim of his imaginary hat and headed for the silver Jag. A job well done.

ive

He who does what is sinful is of the devil...
1 John 3:8

MARK OPENED THE FRONT DOOR OF HIS TWO-STORY home a little before six and listened to the quiet house. Standing in the foyer, his keen ears picked up even the minutest of sounds, from the steady hum of the kitchen appliances to the grandfather clock's tick-tock in the rear of the house. With little effort, he heard the disturbance in the air as the pendulum swung to and fro. Yet he was listening for Paul.

Usually introduced as Mark's personal assistant, the boy was more a brother or an adopted son. In the beginning, Paul was everything a manservant of the early twentieth century should be, but as the times changed, so did their relationship. Mark would always be his master, but over the decades, they found a middle ground that aided their day-to-day camaraderie.

Was that...?

Interrupted from his thoughts by a noise, Mark closed his eyes. Upstairs... the soft sound of cloth on cloth. Mark headed for the staircase and bounded up the carpeted steps without a sound. He crossed the landing and put his hand to the doorknob. Paul was just on the other side and Mark grinned. He would not be able to surprise him. They'd been together a hundred years and his companion eventually developed a form of telepathy all his own. Where Mark saw clear images and heard fully-formed words, Paul received glimpses, shadows, and sounds. At the same time, Mark turned the knob as Paul pulled the door open and met him with the same shy grin he held in 1915, eighteen years old and ready to take on the world.

"Hey," Paul said and backed when Mark moved into him.

Mark crossed to the center of the room and turned, not hiding his cheer at the thought of discussing Miss Brannen. Paul caught a whiff of his mischief and smiled wider.

17

"What?" he said laughing. "Why are you so happy?"

Mark sensed him working to divine an answer so instead of replying, he closed the distance and pulled Paul into an embrace. He wasn't a hugger and neither was Paul, but he held on, both arms wrapped tightly around the slender form of his only familiar. Chest to chest, he inhaled, taking in Paul's aroma—laundry detergent, dust from cleaning, a touch of perfumed shampoo, and a trace of sweat—all of it a delight in Mark's current mood. When the contact continued into five seconds, Paul squirmed and Mark opened his arms and grasped Paul's narrow shoulders.

"I have big news. Sit down." Mark pushed him to the armchairs parked against the wall. Paul took a seat and Mark remained standing. He took a deep breath releasing it with a new grin. "I met her today, the woman I have been waiting for." Paul raised his eyebrows with a slow, *Hmm*. It was no surprise that Paul was fearful of adding to the family since Reuben had been a thorn in their side from the beginning. "Don't pout," Mark continued in a defined nod. "You'll like her. Her name is Hope Brannen." He allowed his announcement to hang in the air awaiting a proper response.

"Oh…good," Paul stammered, his forced smile in place. "Congratulations."

"She's the one," Mark said and pictured the details of their meeting. The same odd feeling returned to his gut. He put a hand to Paul's blonde hair, delivering a single stroke. "She is blonde, blue-eyed, a very traditional American beauty." Paul nodded, but maintained the same paralyzed facial expression. "Just like you," Mark added with a half-grin.

"So what happens now? Where is she?" he asked in a soft voice.

Mark lowered his gaze to catch Paul's eye to say with dry humor, "Slow down. I can't abduct her off the street."

Paul offered a half-smile. "It's about time. I'm happy for you."

"For us," Mark chided and put one hand to Paul's inner shoulder, him still seated below. "As my burden is lessened, so shall be yours."

"Good. Let me know if there's anything I can do to help this come together." Paul intertwined his fingers in his lap.

Mark huffed. "I thank you. She tested me without shame. If I allow it, this might be an entertaining diversion, wooing a modern woman to my side."

"She tested you? How?" Paul asked quietly.

"Something moved in her, too, I saw it. But she's an attractive

18

young woman, accustomed to manipulating the opposite sex."

"Ah," Paul said without inflection. "I can't wait to meet her."

Paul swallowed hard on his last word and Mark narrowed his eyes, searching the man's mind. He wanted to please his master, but had no fondness for women. No matter what sexual or familial path he might have taken if he'd never met Mark, since they joined forces, he spent no time with females.

"You know how much I appreciate you, right?" Mark said and put out his hand for Paul to rise. He did and his shy smile said it all. To Paul, Mark was the sun and the moon. *That's as it should be,* he thought and waited for Paul to speak.

As if reading Mark once more, Paul's features lit up with a new topic. "Did you see the new truck? I parked it behind the house."

Mark formed a half-smile. "Is it nice?"

"Oh, yes. Thank you for getting it."

"You're welcome. Anything you want, just ask." Mark forced a more complete grin and pushed him toward the door. "For now, I have an appointment."

"Of course," he said and headed out of the room.

When the boy was gone, Mark exhaled and prepared to translate to the next judging. The timing was perfect; he was plenty hungry.

Six

An unfriendly man pursues selfish ends;
he defies all sound judgment.
Proverbs 18:1

"YOU'RE NOT IN LOVE, IDIOT!" GLORIE HERSHEY, HOPE'S identical twin, laughed in guffaws at Hope's claim.

"I am! What do you know!" Landline to her ear, Hope fell onto her overstuffed couch and smiled at the ceiling. Glorie lived several states away, so they kept in touch via social media, texting, and phone calls. Her sister lived in Maryland with an adoring yet workaholic husband, and three stair-stepped sons, ages two, three, and five, by three previous husbands.

Hope knew better than anyone the pain and suffering Glorie experienced over the years. She stood by her sister's side for the burial of a stillborn child, later a burial of a SIDS baby, and the funerals of two of her three past husbands. Even surviving her current life was a constant effort. Jim Hershey's health was good, but her boys baffled the doctors with unclear symptoms of various illnesses. Her sister faced life with great courage, especially considering the tough hand she'd been dealt.

"God, you're a nerd. What's he like?"

"You should see him… I mean, *damn.* I had that feeling, you know? My hair stood straight up on the back of my neck. There it goes again!" Hope rubbed the area and smiled.

"It's probably just fleas from your stupid cat."

Hope endured the taunting, too giddy to care. She twirled her fingers through her hair and closed her eyes as the recollection of Mark's dark gaze exhilarated and panicked her at the same time.

"He's married. All handsome doctors are married."

"I don't think so." Hope looked up to the ceiling and tried to remember a wedding ring. "He liked me, too. I can tell."

"That proves it! He's married, you dork!" Glorie laughed. "So, when do you see him again?"

20

"I don't know. I ran away." Hope's cat Spider hopped onto her belly and she rubbed his ears. "I'm not usually so stupid around men."

"Oh, you're stupid all right."

"I should call Fran. She could help me out." Hope looked at her watch; Fran would've left work by now. Maybe she could call her at home. Glorie grumbled to regain her attention.

"What does Doctor Feelgood look like?"

"Oh, God." Hope concentrated on the memory of his face, but only his eyes came to the forefront. She pushed Spider to the end of the couch and sat up. "He's tall, dark, and handsome, he looks like a king. A Gypsy King!"

"A Gypsy? Gross!" Glorie said disgusted.

"Bite me! I'll get a photo next time. You'll see."

"What does a Gypsy look like? I'm Googling it right now..."

"Stop. He looks foreign. European." Hope got to her feet, ready to close their call.

"Are you sure he's not Israeli? Lotsa doctors are Jewish. Momma always said, *marry a Jewish doctor and your life will always be kosher.*"

"Stop!" Hope parried back, prickling at her sister's bigoted mind-set.

"Sorry to trigger ya, snowflake. I was only joking."

"Screw you," Hope said laughing and was ready to move along. She made her goodbyes and hung up. Then she closed her eyes, hatching a plan to meet with the wonderful Dr. Mark Corescu, and soon.

Late Night was a rerun and Glorie changed the channel a few times before turning the TV off for good. She wanted a cigarette, but was too comfortable to cross the room to get one. If she wanted one now, Jim was gone, how would he know? He left for a month-long business trip to the Orient.

Glorie's nicotine craving grew and she trained her eyes to her purse hanging on the doorknob. After another moment hemming, she rolled out of bed and shuffled over to her handbag. Camels in hand, she locked the door and fell onto the soft mattress. Her oldest son, Brown, liked to show up the second his mom lit a smoke. He was supposed to be fast asleep, but he had an uncanny ability to sniff out mommy's shortcomings and run to daddy with a full report.

Little brat. Daddy ain't here, so go back to bed and cry about it.

Glorie took the first couple of drags, the acrid smoke filling her lungs. Everyone thought she'd quit and she loved being naughty. The truth of it was, being bad made her feel alive. Her doting husband and her goodie-goodie sister would never understand, but in her heart, Glorie was empty. She felt nothing. Never really had.

Glorie leaned back against the pillows and propped up her cigarette on the bedside table, calculating how much it would cost to fly down to Georgia and visit Hope. Wasn't there a brand new Visa card on the kitchen table? She could baptize it on Priceline.com and fly south to check out her twin's new beau.

There was a knock at the door by the time the first cigarette was crushed out. The second smoldered in her hand as Glorie awaited another knock. It came moments later.

In her sweetest voice she said, "Darlin', mommy's sleeping. Go back to bed." No child's voice answered from the darkness, but the knock came again, louder. "Look!" Glorie balled her fists and looked at the closed door. "I said mommy's asleep. Get back in bed before I tan your hide!" *If I have to get out of this bed for that brat, I'm going to explode!* The knock came again, louder still, and she cursed, dreading another knock. It followed very closely behind. *Dammit! He's going to wake his brothers at this rate!*

Glorie flipped the sheet off her torso and slammed her bare feet onto the carpet. She mumbled obscenities and stomped across the room, hoping to at least frighten the little imp. Unlocking the door, she yanked it open hard and fast.

"I told you—" Glorie stopped mid-sentence. The hallway was empty. Maybe she scared the little punk after all. *I should spank him good anyway. That'll teach him to ignore me in the first place.*

Glorie took two steps toward the oldest boy's room and stopped. The bathroom light flicked on and the door creaked inward. When the unmistakable sound of splashing reached her ears, she poked in her head to investigate. What she saw could not have been real. Glorie blinked several times in succession, but the image remained.

Her bathroom had become a river glade.

The tub had morphed into the edge of a wide river, and a miry bank separated Glorie from the brackish water. Lazy waves slapped against the mud and a leaf-strewn path came out of what used to be the vanity. Glorie huffed at the image of her sister riding up the trail on one of her ridiculous show horses. Even when dreaming, Glorie despised the giant hay burners.

"Glorie! Have you two met?" her sister asked and assumed a vacuous smile stroking her mount's sleek neck.

Glorie mouthed "no" and watched the duo descend into the mud. The beast's legs were black to its knees before her crazy sister noticed.

"Oh, my! Do you see that?" she said, her voice sing-song.

"Hope, you're sinking," Glorie's voice wavered.

"Don't be silly." Hope's steed was up to its neck in muck, yet continued blithely on, its eyes glassy and expressionless.

"Stop! Aren't you afraid?" Glorie had grown terrified, but why? It was a dream and dreams weren't dangerous, right?

"There's nothing to be afraid of. Here, take my hand and ride with me."

Dream-Hope extended her arm and it grew several feet to reach her sister. Glorie stifled a scream and shrunk into the hallway. For a terrifying moment, she feared the mirage would pull her to her death. Dream-Hope laughed then, loud and shrill. The last thing Glorie saw was her sister's pronounced wink before she disappeared under the wet earth.

Panicked, Glorie turned for her room and tripped over her feet. As her head slapped the rug, she peeked back at the bathroom door closing on its own, a murky liquid seeping into the hall.

Glorie screamed.

Knock, knock, knock. Glorie's eyes snapped open and she startled. She was in bed, her second cigarette reduced to a tube of loosely-packed ash between her fingers. *Knock, knock.* Glorie jumped again. Meekly, she answered, "What?"

"Mommy, you okay?"

It was Scotty, the middle boy. He was a good kid, just kind of stupid like his dad, Glorie's second husband.

"Yes, honey." Glorie's thoughts scampered. "What's wrong?"

"Uh, mommy…" His voice was small and pitiful.

Glorie sat up and crushed out her cigarette. "What is it, honey?"

"The potty, mommy, I broke it. I'm sorry." On the opposite side of the door, he was crying.

Glorie took a deep breath and unlocked the door. Sure enough, behind him, the carpet runner in front of the bathroom had turned black with water. In the dimly lit hallway, the water looked like mud. Glorie squelched a scream and put her hand to her chest.

23

 Seven

My lover spoke and said to me,
"Arise, my darling, my beautiful one, and come with me."
Song of Solomon 2:10

MARK TOOK THE STAIRS TO HIS FIFTH-FLOOR OFFICE two at a time. Switching the file folder from his right hand to reach for the doorknob, a written prescription slipped out and fluttered to the ground. He grunted with frustration, irritated to be at the office on his day off, and returned the colored paper to its place. His business today was diplomatic; a vacationing surgeon coerced Mark over the phone into doing him a favor. He generally avoided the other physicians but on occasion he was obliged to make political overtures.

Mark had been at home enjoying the deep dreamless sleep that occurred only at the new moon. He napped daily, but his true rest was found in the twelve euphoric hours the coma-like state provided. Waking him was an unfriendly task, but Paul had done his best. He shook Mark for several minutes before he roused and even then, he resisted. Nothing could possibly be important enough to leave the bliss of the deep sleep. Unless it had something to do with Hope Brannen. Which it didn't.

Mark pulled open the heavy steel door with a grunt and tromped down the hall. *Why do I do it? Why the pretense? I should retire.* But he knew better. He couldn't perform his other task when shut off from society. The regular influence of humanity kept him grounded in his work. His main work. *The Judging.* If he saw only the evil in mankind, how would he recognize the good? That knowledge compelled him to stay in circulation, to serve mankind, even though he'd been sent also to judge them. So today, he did a co-worker a favor. He would first hit Mrs. Booker's filing cabinet for the appropriate forms.

Mark turned the corner and smiled; a familiar form stood at his office door twenty yards ahead. It was Hope Brannen and like before, the sweet aroma of roses stroked his senses. Mark disguised his reaction and strolled up to the door.

24

From her position at Fran's office door, Hope spotted the doctor, straightened her hair, and sucked her teeth. She was hopeless. Officially, her presence was due to an art job she had accepted in the hospital nursery, but since the insurance policy her husband left her was nearly a million dollars, Hope didn't actively pursue work. When this job came in, she had to accept. What if she saw Mark Corescu while she was there? Fran's office only opened on Fridays for emergencies and Hope had a story ready. As the doctor neared, she rolled her eyes and feigned forgetfulness.

"Mark!" Hope stuck out her hand. "I came to see Fran and I forgot you guys are out today. But there you are!" Dr. Corescu shook her proffered fingers and smiled. Hope was lost.

"Good afternoon, Miss Brannen," he said, unlocking the office door. "How fortunate for me that you're so forgetful."

Hope blushed, thankful his gaze averted to enter the room. She took a deep breath to calm her nerves. "I can be pretty scatterbrained."

"I'm glad to see you. I only came in for a small chore, but what a happy coincidence." He rummaged through a filing cabinet and pulled out a large yellow folder.

Hope leaned on the wall. She watched him a few moments and tried to think of something to say. "Did somebody die?"

"No," he remarked flatly without looking up.

Hope made a small "huh" noise and watched him collate each sheet, marveling at the fluid way his fingers slid across the paper. The movement hypnotized her until he cleared his throat and looked her way. Hope smiled. "Sorry, I feel absolutely goofy today."

The doctor motioned for her to follow him to his inner office where he pointed to a chair. "Won't you have a seat?"

Hope sat and crossed her legs noticing for the first time she was dressed like a barn rat; her crummy black jeans were coated with horse hair and her T-shirt sported horse snot on one shoulder. Add to that, her long hair was pinned up tightly for riding and she smelled of hay and sweat. *Meet the real me,* she mused and came to her feet uncertain whether to go or stay.

"Been riding?" he asked without looking up.

Hope murmured yes and looked at her muddy shoes wondering if he was impressed or disgusted.

"I used to ride for pleasure," he said still working. "At one point,

25

I kept a stable of carriage horses."

"Oh? Carriage horses..." With a sudden urge to shower, she backed toward the door.

"Are you leaving?" Mark didn't look up, but continued to speak with his eyes on his work. "I thought you might have lunch with me." He raised his head to catch her eye and Hope exhaled.

"Sure," she said and laughed aloud. "That sounds nice."

Mark stepped around her toward the door. "Where shall we go, Ms. Brannen? You name it."

"Call me Hope," she said and followed him. "Don't laugh, but I have a hankering for Wendy's. Is that okay with you?"

"Of course. Anywhere you choose is fine." Mark ushered her into the hall to lock up. "Why don't we eat outdoors? The Wendy's on Festus Road is adjacent to the park."

Hope hugged herself to calm her butterflies. "That sounds terrific."

"Good." Mark led her to the elevator. "Give me a moment to drop off this file."

When they reached his supervisor's door, Hope excused herself to pop into a nearby ladies' room. Using her tiny folding brush, she fluffed her heavy hair and powdered her nose. For two whole minutes, she stared in the mirror debating whether or not to leave her hair down. Finally, she twisted it into a rope and fastened it up making a mental note to be better prepared in the future. The stains on her shirt weren't going anywhere, but she thought she might be able to do something about the earthy smell. She doused her arms and lathered them to the elbow, then washed her neck. As clean as she was going to be, Hope took a deep breath and headed for the door.

Mark awaited her in the hall and as they resumed their trek to the parking garage, he didn't take his eyes off her the entire way. Apparently he liked barn rats just fine.

☙❧

Reuben ran a new chamois over Dr. Corescu's bronze Porsche, clucking with approval. The boss might be a monster, but he had impeccable taste in cars. Corescu rarely needed a driver on Fridays, which freed up the day for Reuben to wash the entire collection. It was nearly noon and Reuben hadn't seen the doctor or his lackey all morning. He smiled at his reflection in the car's rear quarter panel, but as he stood, his grin fell. In the car's mirrored skin he caught a glimpse

26

of Paul posed behind him, arms crossed, his expression sour.

"I've been waiting for you to clean the truck. It's your responsibility. Do your job."

Reuben clenched his teeth, his chest tightening. Yet he had to obey. He passed the guy, purposefully bumping his shoulder, and collected his kit. Then he answered as calmly as possible, satisfied his ambivalence would be evident regardless.

"My mistake." Reuben pulled a clean sponge from the box and made his way to the Chevy parked outside the garage door. "I'll get right on it." Reuben mumbled curses and expected Paul to return to the house and mind his own business.

"Mark told you months ago to rotate the cars through the shop and I've never seen them leave the garage." Paul stood square, hands on his narrow hips and his chin down.

Reuben slapped the hood of the truck and took a deep breath. He was no doubt on probation for how he behaved toward Paul at the car lot. Balling his right fist around the sponge, he forced a smile.

"Well, Paul, that's because my schedule works so perfectly that every single vehicle is tuned-up and filled with gas all the time. You don't notice because I do my job." Reuben paused and realized with relief that his scarcely-bottled rage was dissipating.

"It's good that you do, because if you didn't, all I have to do is mention it to Mark, and—"

Reuben interrupted him, his voice edgy. "Enough, okay? I got this," he said waving his sponge in a circle over the hood. "Why don't you do us both a favor and trot back inside?" This time he bounced the dripping hand with the last phrase. "Go in the house. That's your domain. Make a cake, vacuum the floor, fluff some pillows. Do whatever it is that you do in there and leave me the hell alone."

Reuben met Paul's eyes. He had the jerk spooked and he waited for his slight superior to return to the kitchen where he belonged. Within moments, Paul turned and walked toward the side yard.

When he was out of eyesight, but still within earshot, he called to Reuben, "You're taking me to Lowe's in fifteen minutes."

Reuben kicked the truck hard and shouted obscenities across the lawn until his throat was raw.

~*~

Paul scooted inside and leaned against the closed front door. Reuben scared him, always had. He was a bully and getting meaner by the minute; it was time Mark reprimanded the man.

Unbidden, memories of life without Reuben filtered into his consciousness. Mark advised him many times to let the past stay forgotten, but things had been so much better then. Every sunrise found them in a different adventure, whether they were providing medical support to the soldiers coming home from one of the wars, or setting up house in any of the many cities they relocated to over the decades; life was better when it was the two of them, alone. No animosity, no conflict, no Reuben.

Paul reconsidered bringing Reuben on his errands and headed to his room. Perhaps Mark heard his suggestion regarding the insolent driver. Their telepathic link was strong, and soon enough, Reuben would get the scolding he deserved. Moments later, he telepathically heard the reply he expected.

"You will see your justice."

Paul smiled.

Eight

These men lie in wait for their own blood;
they waylay only themselves!
Proverbs 1:18

A LOUD CURSE AND A SHORT BUT VIOLENT DISPLAY OF his middle finger was the sum of Connie's reaction to his latest phone call. Slamming down the phone with enough force to crack the handset, he got to his feet and looked around his cluttered home office. The voice on the other end of the line had been full of bad news. But what else was new?

Try to bump my story...just wait until I get my hands on that asshole Grouper!

Craig O'Neal Nixon, Connie to his enemies and Craig only to his mom, had no qualms about dragging his editor through the mud if he didn't run his stories on demand. His fat drunk of a boss wasn't discreet with his after-hours playtime, and Connie had a hundred digital photographs and three hours of amateur video of the slob in several trysts to prove it. This leverage allowed him to write on any subject he desired, whenever the mood hit him.

Why had Grouper put his latest journalistic endeavor in the garbage? Grouper sure was bold; it'd only been six days since Connie last blackmailed him. The week before, the boss obediently ran his exposé on the Third Avenue Food Bank. In the *Feather Times* exclusive, Connie exposed the extortion of the bank's officials. He didn't particularly care that their greed adversely affected the city's poorest children, but he *did* care if the jerks in office profited from their schemes. Initially, Grouper didn't want to run the piece because it lacked substantial proof, but Connie handed the copy over to him anyway and reminded him of their "agreement." Grouper had said, "Are you gonna blackmail me every time I refuse to print your stupid articles?" Connie had replied simply, "Yep," and left the man's office.

So why was he ballsey enough to ignore Connie now? Did he

29

decide to come clean with his wife? Or did he simply not care if the world knew what a disgusting, perverted low-life he was? Connie decided he'd find out Monday morning when he got to the office.

Hitting print on his keyboard, Connie waited for the lurid photo to come out of his Hp Deskjet. He would take the 5 x 7 honey with him to taunt Grouper. This one the pick of the litter, a clear shot of Grouper, attended by not one, but two ladies of the night. Most disturbing, though, was that the fourth occupant in the room was Mrs. Grouper's twenty-something baby sister. This photo was the prize, all right. Connie tucked it into his brief case, retired to his messy bedroom, and turned on the twelve o'clock news.

Just as the all-too-jovial anchorman appeared on the screen, the telephone at his elbow rang again. Connie propped himself up and glared at the caller ID: *Snack Peters.*

The name was familiar enough, but Connie didn't pick up the receiver. He had several loser cousins and this one was the crème of the crop. The only relative lower than Snack was an obnoxious, redheaded, bleeding-heart, holier-than-thou chick related to him on his mother's side. Thankfully, she lived far away in Georgia with her giant Black bouncer husband. Cousin Opal was only good for one thing—research. More than once, she discovered obscure items of interest for Connie that in the end, padded his résumé. He paid her a few bucks and did that mostly for his mother who was afraid she was broke, not adequately supported by the "Negro-Mongoloid she married," as his mother described him.

Connie let the call go to the machine and turned up the news. Monday, everything would be worked out, once and for all. No more mister nice guy.

ᏗᏋᎨᎧ

Arriving at the Whitford City Park, Hope hugged herself as Mark tucked the Lexus into a shady space and turned off the ignition. He gestured for her to stay as he exited first to get her door. He then walked them to a picnic table tucked under an ancient oak and didn't sit until she was seated. The sun sat high among huge white clouds. With a smile, Hope sighed and he turned, catching her eye through his dark sunglasses.

"I'm glad you had the idea to eat outdoors. I haven't done this in forever," she said and opened her salad.

Mark crossed his arms and leaned upon the table top, sitting across and watching her every move. An errant piece of grilled chicken had made its way into her meal and she plucked it out with two fingers. That done, she peeked at his face and he shot her a new grin. He hadn't ordered saying he'd already eaten. Hope faced into the wind and enjoyed the breeze filtering through the strands of hair that had fallen from her clip. So far, her lunch date thrilled her to bits.

"Why did you become a vegetarian?" he asked, his side-smile in place. Hope had expected him to make a comment and she replied between bites.

"It's a silly story..."

"Do tell. I'll be the judge of that."

She gave a deprecating shrug. "When I was little, my favorite food was chicken nuggets. When I was seven, I was eating a kid's meal and one of my nuggets had something hard in it."

"A bone fragment?"

"I wish." Hope shuddered at the memory. "It was a *beak.*"

"That *is* disgusting," Mark agreed.

"And it wasn't just part of the beak but the whole thing." Hope took another bite of her salad. "My sister laughed so hard, Coke came out of her nose. Believe me, I was only seven, but I had an idea of what was funny. A chicken beak in my dinner was just plain *gross.*"

"I concur," Mark added. "So, you stopped eating meat?"

"You betcha. The restaurant made a big deal of it and I think mom and dad ate at Mickey D's free for six months. I made up my mind that I would never eat meat again. My mom labeled me a vegetarian and that was it. I thought it was kinda cool after that—none of the other kids were vegetarians so I felt really special. And it's been good for me—I never get sick. *Never.*" Hope smiled proudly and Mark nodded his head.

"Vegetarianism can be a very healthy way to live. But confess; you never, ever, ever eat meat?"

"Are you teasing me, Doctor Corescu?" Hope recognized his playful tone and she blushed, going along. "Okay, once a year, I'll have some steak."

"Red meat, no less. How barbaric!" Mark laughed. "And you like it rare, correct?"

"Yeah, but it's only once a year. A girl can indulge."

"If you're going to eat red meat, at least cook it medium or medium-well. It's packed with all manner of microscopic worms," he said grinning.

Hope stopped chewing. "No it's not." He nodded, still smiling.

31

Hope swallowed. "*Worm* worms?"

"Sure."

"Like put-them-on-a-hook-so-I-can-go-fishing worms?"

"That's right."

"There goes my once-a-year steak celebration."

"Not necessarily. Just cook it; that'll kill most of them." Mark put his elbows on the table and rested his chin in his hands.

Hope shook her head. "I'd rather go without." Hope resumed eating and stabbed her salad with her fork. "What about you, big doctor man? How do you take your steak?"

"I don't eat steak."

Hope was caught off-guard. "You're a weirdo like me?"

"No, not like you," he said, with a mysterious grin. "I'm my very own brand of weirdo with a highly specialized diet."

"Food allergies?"

Mark shrugged. "In a way."

"That stinks," Hope grimaced. Her thoughts went to Fran who had so many food allergies that she could only eat a total of five things without becoming ill. She shook her head. "I couldn't handle any kind of forced restrictions on my diet. I love food too much."

"Don't feel bad for me. What I do eat, I find very palatable."

The issue sounded settled and Hope shrugged. Mark was completely at ease and Hope wanted to feel the same way. She cleared her throat and thought it would be a good time to change the subject. Maybe he had a hobby.

"So, what do you do for fun?"

"For fun?" Mark's eyebrows went up and his smile faltered only to steady again. "My work keeps me busy."

"Come on—you don't just work, do you? You have to have fun. If there's a God up there, I don't think he put us on this planet to work ourselves to death."

"*If* there's a God? You aren't sure?" Mark looked genuinely interested and Hope prepared a flip reply.

"Sometimes I'm sure."

Mark made a *tsk* sound. "It's important to know."

Hope's face fell and then she smiled and nodded. "You sound like a friend of mine. He knows a lot about God." Hope shrugged, penitent. "I'm a work in progress."

Her date studied her a little longer and she stuffed lettuce into her mouth to pass the uncomfortable silence. She never had been very interested in religion, but found Christian men likable. Was Mark a Christian? In her silence, the doctor took up her slack.

"What do you do for fun?"

"I have lots of hobbies." Hope swallowed the last bit of her salad, saddened their date was coming to an end. "I paint horses, I ride horses, and I plant carrots in the garden for horses." She laughed. "I never work too much."

"It's good to know how to relax. I have considered retiring," he said as a large cumulous cloud crossed the sun, causing their shade to intensify. Mark removed his sunglasses and caught Hope's eye. "If I were to retire, what should I do for fun?"

Hope's stomach ached as she looked into his eyes, but she wasn't willing to look away. "You could travel. Everyone likes to travel."

"I have traveled extensively already. What else is there?"

"You can't have seen the whole world." Without breaking eye contact, Hope put her empty salad bowl into her sack for disposal. How could he be sick of exploring the planet? *He didn't have the right woman at his side…*

"You're probably right." Mark released her from his visual grip to glance at a couple on bicycles that zoomed by. "Perhaps with the right companion, this big old world would seem new again."

"I haven't been anywhere. It's pretty sad." She also looked to the cycling couple as they disappeared around the curve.

Mark shrugged. "You're very young. Give it time."

Hope blushed deeper and imagined skipping the globe with him—Paris, Stockholm, Dublin. All the places she dreamed of visiting one day, but doubted she ever would. He said she was young—how old was he? Should she ask? Hope stopped her mental wheels and said with snark, "How old am I? Give you a quarter if you guess right."

Mark grinned and replaced his dark lenses. "I don't have to guess. I know."

Hope's expression held as she worked out what he meant. When she made a couple of huffs of disbelief, her date shrugged one shoulder, adding, "You will eventually learn to believe anything I say."

Hope's smile hitched sideways, but she figured he had that right.

ॐ

Mark read her easily and wasn't ashamed to use his mental acuity toward his own end. "You're twenty-five and your birthday is November 1st."

Hope lowered her chin to whisper, "Are you psychic?"

Mark smiled, recognizing the wonder in her eyes.

"You like being mysterious," she said as a statement, rolling her paper sack closed. "Let's go out again so I can ask more questions that you won't answer." Hope's mischievous grin returned with power and Mark enjoyed seeing the twinkle in her bright eyes.

"Are you asking me out?" he asked and tossed her garbage into a nearby receptacle. When he returned, she put her hands to her hips.

"Wait. You looked my birthday up on the internet," she said, eyebrows raised. He gave her a tight grin and she stood firm. "Tell me how you knew that and I'll give you my phone number."

Mark's grin widened. "Fran already gave it to me."

"Fran wouldn't do that," Hope said with furrowed brow.

Wanting to see her reaction, Mark stepped close and gently cupped her cheeks in his palms. Besides widened eyes, she did not pull away.

"Ask me again," he said low, searching her eyes, her lips, and back again. Her heartrate doubled, but she was not afraid. She was exhilarated; another good sign she was the one.

"Okay, how did you know?" she asked this time in a whisper, holding his gaze.

The flutter was there, causing a longing in his spirit and a smaller one in his gut. *Her blood will be intoxicating.* A tiny grin met his mouth at the thought and whatever she read gave her a spook. She tensed and he answered, "Even Irish receptionists have difficulty resisting my will. I am very persuasive."

"I guess so," she said and fell silent.

Mark dropped his hands. Bending her to his will so far proved effortless, which only further convinced him that Hope Brannen was the one. When he put out his elbow, she took it and he walked them to the car.

The cloud cover parted and Mark adjusted his Ray Bans; the sun stabbed his eyes even through heavily-tinted sunglasses. *When did I become so sun-sensitive?* Twenty years ago, he went out without sunglasses altogether. Was he evolving? And if he was, what could it mean?

Mark forced the questions down, the internal search threatening to open files from his past he had long ago sealed. He allowed Hope's coquettish beauty to divert him from his thoughts and opened her car door. She flashed her eyes in thanks and his heart jumped. The young woman was going to be an easy convert, so long as he stayed a step ahead.

附

Paul was out when Mark returned home and he went upstairs to grab a nap before his next appointment. Tonight he was called to a young man in Athens, Georgia. He had seen the man in a vision the evening before as he opened himself up for the mission. Often, three or four evildoers were presented to him at once, their deeds black and wispy as smoke around their heads in his mind's eye. His job was to choose the worst of the pack and let that one surface to the forefront. It would become clearer as the runners-up faded completely away. Once he had the young man in his focus, he saw his sins, his dark thoughts, his bad dreams, and his guilt. Mark sensed his self-loathing along with a flickering desire for forgiveness. This repentant spirit didn't surprise him; many judging victims sought a way out, held captive by the evil in the world.

Lying quietly on his bed, Mark reviewed the man's situation. He was twenty-two, raised in a loving home, parents and sisters still living in Tennessee, but when he enrolled at the university, things changed. He fell in love with an outcast girl, a weird, hippie-like character with wild eyes and a stone-cold heart. She led the man into drugs and Satanism, and eventually into killing the neighborhood dogs for their rituals. Mark frowned as he received an image of the man strangling a newly-purchased German Shepherd puppy. When the neighborhood dogs ran out, he shelled out seven hundred dollars for the next sacrificial animal. It was a horrid sight. The pup wagged its tail when he grasped its scruff and didn't even growl as he closed its airway. Still, killing animals didn't earn the man a judging. Killing children *did*. While searching his victim's heart from ninety miles away, Mark saw at least three children die at the man's hands. After the third cold-blooded murder, Mark had seen enough. He rolled over onto his side to sever the connection. The last information he received was the time and place of the appointment: 9:30 p.m., in the kid's loft apartment. Time to go.

Nine

Wisdom will save you from the ways of wicked men...
Proverbs 2:12

"BE CAREFUL!" PAUL SHOUTED AT REUBEN WHO PRETENDED not to notice that because of his carelessness one of the bags of weed killer burst.

Reuben shot Paul a sideways glance. "I'm not your chauffeur. I'm not afraid of you, either."

"You should be. You think Mark doesn't see your behavior towards me? You'd better mind your manners."

"Mind this, fairy," Reuben said, giving him the finger. He pushed the broken bag with his toe until it stood upright.

Paul hissed and left the shed at a jog, his hands shaking. Sure, he prodded Reuben plenty, but he knew where to draw the line. The only protection he had was a threat of punishment when Mark got involved. For now, he wished the kid would go to his home. Unlike Paul, Reuben didn't live at the house. Years ago, Mark set him up in an expensive condominium thirty minutes away in Atlanta. The arrangement worked because, also unlike Paul, Reuben had a life on the outside. He socialized, albeit in a limited fashion, he drank and partied more than he should. Still, the freedom he enjoyed did little for Reuben's disposition.

Once in the house, Paul shook off the angst brought on by Reuben and climbed the stairs to Mark's room. He knocked twice and entered to find him lying down, head propped on folded arms looking well-rested and jovial.

"The prodigal son returns." Mark motioned for Paul to have a seat and he did on the foot of the bed.

"If we were to be your sons, Reuben would be the prodigal. After all, I would never have left in the first place." Paul leaned against the

36

bedpost and awaited Mark's reply. Reuben stayed with them out of fear of the master; a foreign concept to Paul who'd always loved him.

"Touché."

"Touché," Paul repeated smiling. He had been in awe of Mark from the moment they met. The only blemish on an otherwise perfect existence was the constant bickering Reuben caused. If only Reuben had never been added to the family. Mark sighed and Paul knew he'd overheard his thoughts.

"Even Adam had a good son and a bad. Who am I to ask for more?"

"Didn't Cain kill Abel?" There was no doubt in his mind if given the chance, Reuben *would* kill him. While Paul chewed on his thoughts, Mark nudged him playfully with his foot.

"No one can kill you, silly. I've made you immortal." Mark prodded him again harder and Paul righted himself, trying not to laugh. "You're stronger than I am! I can't even push you off the bed."

Paul smiled; he was taking Reuben much too seriously.

"Besides, you *raised* Reuben. You're his superior. Do not fear him. He'd never lay a finger on you." Mark sat up and scooted to Paul's side, his movements almost too fast to see with the natural eye. "I would pop his head off if he even tried."

"I know," Paul said quietly.

Mark put his arm across his shoulders and pulled him close. "I *had* to bring him home. I know you understand."

"Of course," he answered. "I just wish we got along. He has never liked me, even when he was a kid."

Mark laughed. "I know. He hates me, too." Shrugging out of their embrace, he waited for Paul to meet his gaze. "I want to talk about Hope Brannen. I saw her again today. You're going to like her."

"I know I will. I —"

"And," Mark interrupted, hand upraised, "Reuben will be civil or suffer the consequences."

"I know," he said and rose to his feet. "Are you bringing her here?"

Mark ruffled Paul's hair. "Give me a few days."

"Perfect." Paul didn't trust himself to say anything else. He had very little experience with women and since he'd joined Mark, he had no need for outside friends. Even before then, he hadn't dated. He'd been young—barely eighteen—and ambitious, intending to marry when his career was well-established.

"I find it amazing you never had a woman before I found you,"

37

Mark said, overhearing his thoughts. "I watched you with your peers, the girls loved you."

"I had my work and women were expensive," Paul added, still trying to picture life with an additional person in the house, in *Mark's life*. He wanted to like her—no—he'd *make* himself like her for Mark's sake. But he'd have to share the only thing in the world he treasured.

"Don't look so terrified." Mark put a hand to his shoulder, holding an earnest gaze. "You'll adore her. She even looks like you. I guarantee you'll hit it off."

"I know we will." Paul smiled, but still he worried. No matter what the wise men said, change was always bad.

∞

Reuben dropped his keys onto the small foyer table and fell in a heap onto the sofa. The room smelled of Pine Sol and bleach; the maids had been at it again. Every Friday, his mess was invariably picked up and the hardwood floors were spotless. It was a good thing because he certainly was no housekeeper. Wasn't it the least the boss could do to have a maid service pick up after him? After all, he should have a servant for himself, right? The housekeeper—another service provided by Dr. Mark Corescu. Reuben was a kept man; kept and carefully quarantined. The doctor knew every move he made and every thought that entered his weary mind. After all these years, Reuben only wanted what he had always wanted: freedom.

How could anyone escape him?

Reuben couldn't hide from the man; he'd tried more than once. Corescu kept close tabs on him physically and telepathically. Reuben couldn't kill him. He was fairly certain a gun wouldn't do it, and he'd never get close enough to try anything else.

Maybe a fire!

Reuben shrugged off the thought. A fire might destroy property, but he could never be accurate enough with it to ensure the monster's death. Moreover, how could he know the man's schedule to plan such a thing? Sometimes, days would pass without him ever laying eyes on the fiend that held him hostage. Besides, who was the boss trying to fool with all that judging crap? He was a monster, a vampire, not a doctor or preacher or anything other than a demon from hell.

Reuben sat up and smiled. Corescu falsified his medical *bona fides* decades ago and Reuben toyed with the idea of exposing the fraud. Sure, the man was a physician, but he acquired his most recent

38

legitimate medical license nearly eighty years ago. Since then, he merely kept up his boards and forged any documents necessary to maintain his position in the world as "Dr. Fantastic." Who could he tell that would wreak the most havoc on his boss and his ridiculous partner.

Of course, I'd be signing my death warrant.

He knew this without question, but sometimes death seemed more welcome than his current existence. Death would give him the release he so badly wanted and should have endured many years back while in his mother's dangerously neglectful care.

Reuben scoffed and shook his head. He would never turn the doctor in. Brave talk from a terrified kid was all it was. Sighing, Reuben closed his eyes.

Pizza.

Yeah.

Papa John's—the bachelor slave's ambrosia. Reuben picked up the phone and dialed the number from memory without even opening his eyes.

Ten

...the LORD searches every heart
And understands every motive behind the thoughts.
1 Chronicles 28:9

ANTHONY AGRICOLA SAT IN HIS SEAT WATCHING THE other churchgoers leave, his mind reeling with what he had just experienced. Reflecting on the miracles he witnessed at the one-day evangelism conference, Tony shook his head. He'd attended with apprehension, but now that it was over, he was ever so glad he'd come.

As Green Oaks' Administrator, he felt it his duty to reach out to local churches by attending their functions. Smiling, he trained his eye to the stage where the preachers shook offered hands and prayed for stragglers. The visiting evangelists were a man-and-wife team, Reverends Ira and Sarah Tracey, from North Carolina. Tony wasn't familiar with them, but they were well known in the Charismatic circles Tony had always avoided.

A gentle tap on his shoulder shook him out of his thoughts and an elderly African-American gentleman smiled down on him.

"You okay, young man? You look like you've seen a ghost." He shook Tony's offered hand. "I'm Reverend Elijah Prince, nice to meet you, Mr. Agricola."

Tony looked down at his nametag and smiled back. "Nice to meet you too, Reverend. This was an amazing service. My eyes have been opened."

"Amen!" Reverend Prince said and pulled Tony to a standing position with gnarled but strong hands.

"Is this your home church?" Tony asked following the gentleman to the exit and admiring the pep in his step. He looked to be over eighty, but his intellect was sharp and his soft brown eyes crystal clear.

"No, I pastor Damascus Bible Center in Columbus, Georgia." Reverend Prince saw the question in Tony's eyes and he added, "We're a Spirit-filled non-denominational church. Please visit if you're ever our

40

way."

Tony thanked him and motioned to the stage. "This sort of thing happen at your church?"

"No, not like this," the older man chuckled as they reached the exit doors. Reverend Prince lowered his glasses and winked. "But I don't mind if it did!" He laughed a little more then paused to catch his breath.

Tony smiled and waited as he collected his thoughts, certain he had more to say on the matter. After another short moment, he looked hard at Tony.

"Mr. Agricola, I just got a word from the Spirit. Would you like to receive it?"

Tony inhaled. *Like a prophetic word? From God?* He offered a cautious nod.

"I am to tell you that a trial will come that is not a punishment. God says you are to follow Him and know He's always at your side." Reverend Prince nodded. "That's it. Go and do, young man. Go and do."

The elderly clergyman shook Tony's hand once more and disappeared into the throng. Tony walked toward his truck and his mind raced with questions. *A trial? What kind of trial?* Then he took a deep breath and a long exhale. If it was set, there was nothing he could do but persevere. Go and do. It was all he could do.

⊂3εつ

Connie stormed into Grouper's office without giving the guy a chance to answer his knock. The large man clambered out of his chair, his face pink with anger and exertion.

"You'll want to be sitting down for this." Connie dropped his photo collection onto the boss's cluttered desk with a paper whisper. His editor picked up the packet with a chubby paw and tossed it back into Connie's chest.

"Get outta here, Nixon! I don't want to see you on this property again! You're fired!" Sweat popped on his brow and Connie wondered if the man's ticker could take the stress.

"Oh, I don't think so…" Calmly gathering his photos, Connie put them back on the desk. This time, he put them out of reach so the man's disproportionate arms couldn't grasp them without bending over the desktop. "I have a new one. One even you don't know about. Before you throw away your career, take a peek at that photo on top." Connie

41

crossed his arms and waited; morbid curiosity would get the better of the fat-headed bureaucrat.

Grouper took a pencil and lifted the edge of the brown folder as if it were contaminated and bent at the waist a fraction, trying not to show too much interest. He must have seen something intriguing for he then grabbed them with his porky hand and dumped them out onto the desk. A gasp emitted from his lips as Connie smiled and took a seat.

"Now about my story..." Connie pulled a photocopy of the original article out of his briefcase along with a thumb drive. "Here it is again."

Grouper gawked at the pictures and his rubbery lips quivered; the new one had him stroking. Connie smiled, immensely pleased with himself. His boss slumped back into his chair and wiped his face with a yellowed handkerchief.

"Did you make copies of these photos?" The man choked the words, as if he was about to have a coronary. Connie felt no sympathy.

"Of course. Now, can we talk business? This story is hot and needs to run before the weekend."

The new story involved Feather, Kentucky's Mayor, Steve Smithson. He was headed out of town for the weekend and Connie heard he was sneaking off to Las Vegas to gamble with his lovely new bride. Not much wrong with that, because people gamble all the time. But Smithson was a self-proclaimed, loudly-and-publicly professed born-again Christian and Connie was pretty sure gambling was a no-no in his Bible. Smithson was elected for Pete's sake on his All-American fundamentalist platform. Surely the townsfolk of Feather should know what their mayor-slash-pastor was up to, and it was Connie's duty to let them know.

"Nixon, help me out. You have no proof!" Grouper regained his composure and secreted the photos out of sight. "All you have here is guesswork and conjecture! I can't let you ruin a man's life just because you're feeling vindictive! Look, let me trash this mess. I'll pay you double for your next story." The big guy daubed his brow with his hankie and lowered his voice in a conspiratorial tone. "Smithson will have my job if I run that."

Connie could care less if Grouper was fired, but double pay for a feature was a good deal. He leaned back and pretended to consider the offer. Grouper shuffled the papers on his desk and found what he needed.

"Here, have a look at this. This is Senator Buckley's dossier. You know he hates being the small fish up there in DC and he's making a bid for the governorship in two years, hankering to be King of Kentucky. Take a gander at his past employment history." Connie's boss was still shaking. "This might be right up your alley."

Connie was suspicious; Grouper had never offered him a lead before. A casual glance at the top page and his interest piqued. Unsolved murder cases? Buckley had been a police detective? Former Feather, Kentucky, mayor, and current sitting senator, John Q. Buckley, was a notorious hot-head with the press, but the Kentuckians of all races and creeds loved him. When he ran for Senate, many of his fellow Bluegrass buds cried their eyes out to see him go to DC. But now, he was thinking about coming back to the fold. He shouted loud and hard about "doing the right thing for the poor and minorities," and hokey crap like that. Liberals loved him and Conservatives didn't hate him, so of course, Connie despised the man. Why would Grouper hand the story over when Connie was sure to crucify Buckley?

"How can some unsolved cases be more interesting than what I have on Smithson? You're going to have to do better than that, fatso." Connie deliberately baited the older man to attack, but he didn't. Instead of getting angry, Grouper shrugged his shoulders and sat back in his chair.

"This little jewel has never seen the light of day. I just thought you'd like it. I'll bet you could look up some of these people and solve his cases for him. Humiliating, eh?" Grouper grinned, his square teeth shimmering behind swollen lips.

Connie read over the paperwork more closely. Buckley had been a detective in Atlanta, Georgia, back in the '70s, and he held the record for the highest number of unsolved homicides. Connie played out the story in his mind.

Can you trust your state with a Governor who never caught his man?

It didn't have the ring Connie usually went for, but he was still intrigued. He could poke around and solve one or two of them. That'd look pretty bad for the old guy.

Feather, Kentucky, Journalist Craig O'Neal Nixon Cracks Forty-Year-Old Buckley Cold Cases

That had more of a ring to it. Connie stood and headed for the door. "I'll need travel expenses. This guy lost all of his killers in the Atlanta area so I'll have to start there." Grouper nodded

43

enthusiastically. "And a corporate Amex."

"Go down and see Taffy. She'll get you whatever you need." Grouper's hand was on his phone, presumably to prepare his secretary for Connie's arrival. "Good luck."

Connie let the man off the hook, and headed down the hall. A free trip to Atlanta, he would be there by Saturday night. It was going to be a good week after all.

☙❧

Hope let the phone ring five times, but hung up when Fran's voicemail clicked on. It was practically nine and she thought Fran went in at six. Sighing, Hope dropped her cell into the console as she pulled into Foxhollow Equestrian Center.

Her horses needed regular human contact, but lately, she hadn't given them much thought. Since her lunch date with Mark, just about every ten minutes she would walk through every word, every glance, over and over, until she was completely distracted from whatever she was doing. All weekend, she resisted calling Fran at home and now that it was Monday, she couldn't get anyone at the office. She needed the scoop. Was he married? Did he smoke? Hope's ideal would be a man as dark and sexy as Mark who loved animals and despised cigarettes. The late Kevin Brannen had met the criteria, but he was dead. *He's probably in heaven.* Hope was pretty sure the churches weren't pulling her leg about that.

She parked her car and grabbed the bag of carrots, a peace offering for her neglected equine pals. As she wandered into the tack room, she brought Mark back into focus. She imagined him as she first laid eyes on him, an ordinary physician, sitting behind his ordinary desk, dictating notes into an average voice recorder. But then, there had been nothing ordinary about him.

His eyes...

Hope grabbed a navy blue halter and lead rope from her tack trunk and paused. Mark had held her prisoner in his gaze. It had been, well, supernatural. Hope bumped into another boarder leaving the tack room, lost in her daydreams.

"Hey, Hope!" It was Amber Gwynn, a sweet teen from her lesson group. "Missed you on Friday. We had a great lesson!"

"Did you guys jump the new line along the fence?" she asked, most of her mind still on Mark.

44

Shaking her head, Amber Gwynn grabbed her Stübben off the saddle rack and hoisted it onto one arm. "Susan let us use the new water complex. You should have seen Lazarus. He jumped right in and started pawing and splashing. It was hilarious! I had to pop him three times to get him to leave the water!"

"That sounds like Lucas. He loves the water." Hope followed the young woman into the barn's main aisle. A few other boarders had arrived for various reasons and she absently watched them get their horses out and tie them in place for grooming. "I'm sorry I missed it. I just got tied up in other stuff. You know how it is."

Amber Gwynn might not know how it was since she was in high school and practically lived at the stable. There had been a time when Hope's focus was similarly directed, but eventually everyone must make priorities that don't have four legs.

"Yeah," the teen sympathized. "Hey, I'm going to hack out by the creek. You want to come along?" The younger girl put her saddle next to her stall door, eyes wide.

Hope considered her proposal. What was she going to do this morning anyway? Groom the horses, turn them out, then go home and stew over Mark Corescu the rest of the day? She might as well get a ride in before a day of wishing and pining.

"Sure, that'd be great. Give me twenty minutes to tack up. Lucas is usually covered in mud."

Amber Gwynn agreed and turned her attention to her horse, Lazarus.

Lucas was in his stall, munching happily on hay. His shimmering white coat reflected the light from the ceiling halogens with very little mud evident. Hope stared at him only a moment and found herself daydreaming again about Mark.

He likes horses... Hope imagined the two of them riding together across an Irish moor—her horse a white Andalusian, his a black Friesian stallion with a silky tail that dragged the ground. They kicked into a gallop and both laughed at the joy of it all. Hope grinned at her fantasy. Men had been chasing her since she hit puberty and she had always maintained the upper hand. With Mark, for the first time, she was ready to release control if it meant she could see him again and again. *And if we become romantic...*

A laugh in the barn aisle snapped her awake and she checked the location of the other boarders, still pondering the doctor in the back of her mind. Hope had only had one lover and she married him. *What would it be like with Mark? What kind of lover would he be?*

When the blood rushed to her face, she cleared her mind and turned to the task of scraping loose hair from her horse's silky coat.

"Come on, Lucas," she purred to her indifferent equine. "You can help me take my mind off of what's-his-name."

She promised herself she'd concentrate on riding and not on the most amazing man she'd ever met.

It wasn't going to be easy.

ᘓᘐ

Tonight's judging victim posed a different set of challenges and Mark sucked his teeth pondering the best way to pry him loose of the woman he'd bedded. He had indeed magically appeared in the man's bedroom, but the timing—the couple was in full coitus and Mark never killed someone not being judged. He dampened his image and leaned in the far corner, eyes on his prize.

Moaning, a sharp yelp, a slap, and then a throaty promise of *I love you, I love you so much.* Mark's brow raised as he waited. He had no use for sex, no blood rushed through his veins, so never would he feel the arousal of the two in the bed before him. Somewhere in his past, he recalled the stiffening that accompanied lovemaking, but he forced the recollection back. It was God's will that he remain in the present; of this, he was certain.

"Peter!" the woman said in a yelp and jumped sideways, righting herself to put both feet to the carpet. "I said don't do that!" Stark naked, she stood to cross to the attached bath and she slammed the door with a decided noise. Mark's head tilted right, watching the man in the bed and the thumb lock clicked where the woman closed herself in.

The man, Peter, chuckled and settled onto his back, grinning, happy, satisfied. Mark considered his next step. The judging required conversation; how long would the female remain in the bath? He couldn't know. *But I also don't want to remain here much longer...* Mark slow-blinked and made a decision.

In 1910, he purchased an estate in *Schwarzwald,*[1] Germany, and although he hadn't visited in several years, the property would forever be deeded to him and posted with No Trespassing signs. The forty-five

---

[1] The Black Forest

46

acres behind the ancient house would make a nice private meeting place. After one last listen for the woman, using the toilet as far as he could tell, Mark zoomed forward, yanked the man bodily from the bed covering his mouth at the same time, and wrapped both arms about him. In a blink. He transported them both to the wooded area behind the property structures.

Peter's gasps morphed into hyperventilating as Mark loosened his hold and forced the man to face him. A the pre-dawn drizzle dampened them both as Mark waited for the man to meet his eye. When he did so, his crimes streamed to Mark's mind and he narrowed his eyes. Two, three, four… five times, the man in his grasp had stalked, tortured, and murdered men slight in stature, handsome, gentle; men he had attracted with subterfuge, because they were lonely and he promised tenderness, affection, love and sex…

The facts continued to roll in and Mark had seen enough. He moved his cruel grip to the man's throat, thumbs compressing his larynx enough to allow shallow breaths, yet prevent speaking.

"Peter Obanion, you are being judged!" he said in a low hiss. "Your murderous deeds have reached the heavens. Choose now which way you will go!"

The script rarely changed, the victims would choose death or life. Mark wanted his blood and when he finally repented and ask God to forgive him, Mark's fangs sent him to his Maker.

A job well done.

Eleven

…pity the man who falls and has no one to help him up!
Ecclesiastes 4:10

GENERALLY, MONDAYS WENT SMOOTHLY, BUT TODAY Paul's head pounded mercilessly and no medicine of mortal man touched the throb wracking his skull. Paul crossed the hallway in a clumsy jog and headed for the large staircase to the second floor. What did it mean? And that sound—was it a voice?

He reached his bedroom as his knees buckled from the knife-like pain at his temples. Holding the doorknob for support, Paul struggled with the impulse to contact Mark. He would be with his first patient at this hour, and what could he say? Help me, I have a headache? Paul reached the bed and collapsed in a fog.

The first headache had been mild, surprising because pain was no longer part of his life; Mark had made sure of that. But this... it was excruciating. And there was the voice, a sound much like the groan of wet boards on the deck of a ship. Only because the odd rumbles were separated with a staccato tempo did he suspect it was a voice at all, yet he knew not the language it spoke.

A fresh wave of pain pulsed directly behind Paul's left ear and he pressed his hand against it. Without even realizing he'd done so, he cried out to Mark telepathically. Instantly he received a reply, but this voice was gentle and soothing.

"What is it?"

Paul wasn't given to histrionics and Mark's telepathic voice reflected he realized if Paul ever interrupted his day, it was likely important. Before Paul could reply, the same knife that pierced his mind leapt across their connection and attacked Mark. The inner voice dropped and the landline rang on the table near his hand. Paul answered on the first ring, the white-hot spear receding.

"How long have you had that pain?" Mark asked.

"This is the third time. I didn't mean to disturb you."

Mark sighed. "I'll be home soon. Take it easy and we'll find out

48

what this is together."

"Thank you, Mark. What can I say? My reflex is to call on you."

"That makes me your hero, eh? Get some rest."

Paul hung up and smiled, relieved the throbbing had dissipated. Had Reuben experienced anything similar? He long ago received the same gift of immortality for an eternity of service. Perhaps Reuben heard the voice as well. Paul decided to ask him and maybe the guy would have a better idea of what it was and what was being said.

಄಄

Hope lowered her cell and drummed softly on the steering wheel as she waited outside her friend's apartment. Anthony said he was close by and she wanted him to help piece through her weird attraction to Dr. Corescu. Humming to herself, she watched for Anthony's truck to turn in to the complex.

The trail ride with Amber Gwynn had been exhilarating and she smelled like a horse, but it never bothered Anthony. She met him at a party a year ago and had heard he was a preacher's son. Deep down, Hope suspected that if she married a preacher, she would have it made on Judgment Day. The guy made a good first impression. He loved the Lord, and although her own religious notions were in their infancy, she found his faith irresistible. He was cute, in a nerdy way, with a neatly-trimmed goatee, dark wavy hair just long enough to gather into a ponytail, and wire spectacles obscuring kindly brown eyes. For about five minutes, she thought he might be the man to fill the holes in her life, but unfortunately, Hope didn't feel anything for him. Their relationship fell into the friend-zone, and now he was her pal and confidant, and nothing more.

Mark Corescu, on the other hand...

Earlier, when she finally got a hold of Fran, she learned he was single and although he was on call 24/7, because of the specialty of his work, he only came in twenty hours a week. What kind of doctor would go through a decade of medical school to work just a few hours a week? Hope was thinking of going down to his office again to find out. She toyed with the idea of inviting Mark to the Block's annual high-society gala. When she mentioned it to Fran, her girlfriend laughed, but what if... Having the doctor on her arm would certainly be a thrill.

Anthony's green pickup appeared and she jumped out to meet him at the driver's side door.

ɔ୫ఌ

"Hello, darlin'," Tony said in a put-on Southern drawl, knowing his bang-on Elvis impersonation would make her laugh. "Have you had lunch?"

"Nah, but I'm not hungry. Whatcha got in the bag?" She followed him up the stairs to his second-floor unit.

"Some books from Lifeway." He opened the door. Hope entered ahead of him and plopped down on the couch. "Can I get you something to drink?"

"No, thanks, I'm fine," Hope said and looked over his shoulder. "When did you get that?"

Tony turned and looked at the painting. "*The Crucifixion.* I got it yesterday. Cool, huh?"

"Uh, it's depressing." Hope furrowed her brow. "I'd much rather look at a painting of Jesus praying or holding a lamb."

Tony chuckled softly. "So would I. So would everyone." Tony joined her in the living room and sat down. "But we're commanded to participate in His suffering, not water it down to make it more palatable." Hope made a noise of agreement, but nothing more. Tony grinned and sighed comically for her to hear. "Okay, sorry. You came here for a reason." Taking on an accent she would recognize from one of their favorite movies, he asked her, "To what do I owe this dubious pleasure?"

"Evil Ed!"

"Correct," Tony said and waited for her to continue. They had watched many cheesy movies together and this was one they had practically memorized.

"I've come for some advice," Hope faltered, her eyes flashing.

"I'm all ears." Tony leaned back, ready to help in any way he could. He mentally put on his clergy hat, his former-boyfriend-hat tucked away in the closet. Still, even with the correct hat, he noticed how cute Hope looked in her riding tights. He looked away just as she caught his eye.

"A few days ago, I met a man and I can't get him out of my mind." Tony nodded and she continued with a growing smile. "I think he might be the one, you know what I mean?"

Tony allowed an audible, *hm-mm.* Not too long ago, he thought Hope might be his true love.

"And I really don't know anything about him yet except that he's a doctor and has food allergies."

"Doctor Allergy, got it," Tony joked and reached for the bowl of M&M's on the coffee table. Hope snagged a few before replying. She respected his opinion and insights so he remembered his role. "How did you two meet?"

"At Fran's office. He's her boss." Hope crossed her legs and studied the stains on her Timberland boots. "I feel weird when I'm around him. It's spooky—but in a good way. Is that normal? I guess I want to know what I should do next."

"Oh," Tony laughed gently, "you want my advice on whether or not you should pursue Doctor Allergy?" Then he added, to clarify, "I mean, as a man-of-God wannabe?"

"Yeah, I guess. You've never steered me wrong." Hope laughed.

Tony sighed, she would see him no matter what he said so he chose a response that would keep him in the loop. "Okay, then. Let's break it down. Did he seem like a nice guy? A good guy?"

"Sure. He's polite. He listens. We have tremendous chemistry…" She trailed off, her focus going soft.

"Chemistry's important," Tony agreed and cleared his throat to bring her back. "And you want to call him before he calls you?"

"Right," she said and sat up, her spine erect, tiny fists atop her thighs. Tony noticed it all. "I'm invited to a party on Friday and I want him to come as my date. If he doesn't call by Wednesday, what do you think about me going to his office and asking him out?"

Tony huffed a friendly laugh. "Speaking as a man, that should be a refreshing surprise for him." Tony's candor amazed even himself. "I'd say, go for it. If he's a good guy, what have you got to lose?"

"Yes!" Hope said in a high voice and clapped her hands once. "Thank you. What a relief. Now it seems like it might happen; now that we talked it through."

Hope sighed audibly and leaned into the sofa. Tony averted his gaze as her T-shirt rode up to reveal her tanned midriff.

"If he doesn't call by Wednesday, I'll go to plan B."

"What's that?" he asked regaining her eye.

Hope laughed. "I don't know. Plan A always works."

Tony chuckled and handed her the bowl of M&M's. When the topic of conversation turned to other matters, he tried not to notice the things about Hope that drove men wild. It wasn't easy, but he managed.

51

 Twelve

The prospect of the righteous is joy,
But the hopes of the wicked come to nothing.
Proverbs 10:28

"*DR. CORESCU, LINE 5.*"

Mark picked up the receiver, pressed the line, and sent the call to his resident. Thursday crawled by much too slowly and he was ready to head out for the weekend. Like most physicians in the Tower, he rarely came in on Fridays. Mark was tired, physically, spiritually, and especially, emotionally. He hadn't found the cause of Paul's ferocious headaches and he'd been brooding a full week about Hope Brannen. Why? Wasn't she chosen for him by God?

Mark walked to his lavatory and splashed cold water onto his face. Why did mortal men fear women? Was it a fear of rejection? A fear of appearing foolish? Mark had never experienced this fear before. *I never desired a woman before.* Or had he? There it was again—a vague memory of a sexual Mark Corescu. *Or Markus Crump. Or...* Mark shut down his recollections before they crystallized. The Mark Corescu that worked for the All Mighty judging and killing the doomed had no sexual desires.

But my mouth on her throat, my teeth pressing into her body, would be mighty close... Mark chuckled. He would have Hope Brannen, end of story. He had never needed permission to take what he desired.

With a quick toweling of his face, he straightened and stared at his reflection. She found him attractive, most of them did; with no effort, his appearance and natural allure drew men and women to him, each soul compelled by the lust common to all mortals. He peered into his own eyes, irises nearly black, his ethnicity pegging him a Eastern European. *Maybe Balkan...*

With a huff Mark exited the bathroom at a fast walk. One day, he'd look into the psychology of why he despised the distant past. He was a genius; some sort of trauma caused him to block it out. But for now, he wanted to be home and call on Ms. Brannen.

Mark pulled open the door to the hall and stopped short; the aroma of Hope Brannen's soft floral cologne alerted him she was very near. Instead of the exit, Mark headed for Ms. Booker's office. A moment's concentration revealed she was not with his employee so he paused in the hall without disturbing the door.

Then where?

Behind him, Fran buzzed his office phone, looking perhaps to tell him he had a visitor.

But where was she?

Mark grumbled with impatience and whirled to the adjacent rooms. He heard a quiet shuffle and swept open the nearest door. Hope sat on an examining table, swinging her lower legs in the empty space below. She wore jeans with a T-shirt emblazoned with the words DRESSAGE QUEEN and had pulled her thick blonde hair into loose ponytails that tumbled over either shoulder. Struck by the picture of child-like innocence, Mark gave her a wide grin.

"So, that's where you've been hiding!" he said putting his hands to his hips in mock exasperation. "I've been looking for you."

"I've been right here," Hope joked, her smile as wide as his. "You're not a very good finder." Mark raised his eyebrows with humor and she added, "I wanted to ask you a favor."

"Oh?" Mark sought her thoughts and received an image of a grand Southern mansion among the trees.

"Will you go to a fancy party with me? It's at the Block's and I need a distinguished date. What do you say?"

"The Blocks. Impressive," Mark said and closed the door behind him. Now they were alone in the cramped space and Hope blushed.

"Dr. Corescu, *my word.*" Hope fell into an exaggerated drawl and batted her eyelashes but couldn't hide her alarm. Taking advantage of the upper hand, Mark stepped close and hopped onto the examining table, his thigh mere centimeters from hers. Hope's pulse increased in his ears and she looked straight ahead.

"I'm flattered you find me distinguished enough for the elite's biggest party of the year," Mark teased.

Hope took a deep breath and peeked to see his face. "You know you're handsome," she said very low and looked forward again. "You preen a bit."

Mark laughed out loud, nodding his head. "Yes, yes, I do. And so do you." This time, she giggled and dared to look at him to the side.

53

"How did you know the Blocks?" Mark asked relishing the electricity between them. If either of them relaxed their thigh muscle, they'd make contact. He wanted to feel her heat, the static charge every human emitted. But he remained tense, determined to allow her to move into him, as long as it took. About her invitation, he'd accommodate. It would take an act of God to keep him from her side.

"I was lucky, I think. I was painting Ninja Turtles for Third's son and Mrs. Block walked past the room, started chatting, and then invited me to the event." Hope looked away half-way through, the corners of her mouth curled into a smile. She loved the game, resisting the pull of Mark's gaze.

He leaned back on his hands and watched her profile, waiting for her to lose the battle of wills. "That is lucky, indeed."

"It's semi-formal, you'll wear a suit and I bought a gown." One quick glance, then she set her eyes back on the opposite wall.

"When shall I pick you up?" Mark asked, watching her profile and wanting to touch her back. She remained leaning over her lap and his eyes traced her spine delineated through her thin shirt.

"Tomorrow at seven o'clock," Hope said in an exhale and slipped off the table. She leaned against the wall to give them each more personal space.

"Perfect." Triumphant when she met his eye, Mark smiled as she relinquished her will in his gaze.

Hope groaned with drama. "You'll have to leave those eyes at home or we'll never get anywhere!"

"Or everywhere," Mark added playfully and she blushed. "Come. Walk me downstairs." He offered his arm and she took it watching his profile when he turned away. She was smitten; easy as pie.

⊂⊰℞⊱⊃

Tony whistled as he dropped his keys onto the dresser and headed for bed, happy with his evening. The Elder's meeting went smoothly, the church's books added up, and he was looking forward to a good night's sleep. Before long, he had shrugged into his sleeping shorts and assumed a prayerful stance next to the headboard. It was time to speak to God and all he had to do was forget about Hope and her newest infatuation.

"God, have mercy," he mumbled, as her face came to mind, her petite frame, her lion's mane of blonde hair… He laughed and looked

54

to the ceiling. "I said have mercy," he chuckled. "I'm over her, Father, but I'm a man and she's very cute."

Tony didn't want her that way. Not really. But could he watch someone else woo her? Resolute and growing quiet in spirit, Tony brought these things and more before God, ending his supplications with heartfelt thanks and a request for sweet dreams. Afterward, sleep came quickly; Tony's last thought was of Hope sitting in his living room laughing, her blue eyes sparkling. He strolled into slumber-land with a smile on his face.

"Where is everybody?"

Tony found himself in a dreamscape: white ground, white sky, no horizon, and no floor. A few yards ahead, a huge horse pawed the nothingness beneath sharp hooves. Tony approached; he was dreaming so, why not? His curiosity grew seeing a familiar form behind the horse.

"You're just in time, Tony!"

It was Hope's voice, chirping like a happy bird.

"Hurry! Help me get this muck off. It's all up to us! Come on!"

Wholly obscured by the heavy, wet mess, Hope appeared to have been scrubbing mud off the animal for a while. The horse, on the other hand, was becoming clean right before his eyes.

"What's the hold up? Come on, hurry!"

Tony startled to action and joined her, pulling frantically at the slippery clumps plastered to the beast's mane. The grime slid off easily, but as he worked, it enveloped his fingers and hands, with purposeful sentience crawling up his arms.

"Will this stuff come off?" he asked, lifting an arm to examine the slime. Hope's head had become an indistinguishable lump atop a body of mud.

"I'm afraid not, but what does it matter?" His friend's voice had grown muffled as her palate clogged. "Ith really not tho bad. It feelth good. You won't want it off thoon enough. Juth keep thcrubbing."

Tony did so, and she was right; the goo soothed him. The new muddy skin was more comfortable than the old, despite the fact that he was losing his vision, his hearing, and ability to speak.

Tony scrubbed and scrubbed until he disappeared altogether. The last thing he saw before the black goo covered his eyes was the now-white horse's eye, accusing, unblinking, and expressionless.

Thirteen

He reveals deep and hidden things;
He knows what lies in darkness…
Daniel 2:22

AS FRIDAY AFTERNOON ROLLED IN, MARK'S HUNGER gnawed at his peace. He had heard no call in his spirit for his usual nightly judging and the evening was too important to be distracted by an empty stomach. Resisting the urge to pace the floor, he waited for Paul to return. Finally, after what seemed an eternity, Paul walked in the side door near the kitchen. Mark listened as he put away the groceries, but then the movement stopped and Paul appeared in the doorway where Mark sat waiting.

☙❧

Paul sensed Mark's call and his blood ran cold. This particular situation had arisen only once before and Paul had put it out of his mind. The details of that distant time swam back to him as at the door, he awaited Mark's request.

The year was 1969, and he and Mark had moved south from New England. The time was particularly good because it was shortly before Reuben was acquired and the carefree days passed quickly. One night, though, Mark returned from an appointment, distressed and upset.

"Upstairs, now," the master had said and Paul followed. Was there trouble with the law? A danger? In all of their years together, Paul had never experienced such disarray in his companion's mind as he shadowed Mark into the back room.

"What is it?" Paul had asked as he settled on the bed corner.

"It has to be you tonight, my friend."

Not comprehending, Paul nodded in agreement watching Mark with wide eyes.

56

"Sit in this chair."

Paul rose from the mattress and sat in the soft-cushioned oak chair. His spine straight as a board, he followed his partner with his eyes. The doctor stepped behind him and placed cool hands heavily to his shoulders. Finally, Paul recognized his meaning and he steeled himself for the shock.

"Be still. Trust me."

"I trust you," Paul whispered as he allowed Mark to tug his loose cotton shirt out of his trousers and pull it over his head. "What happened tonight?"

"Shhh. Close your eyes." Mark's hands ran along the back of his neck looking for a spot from which to draw his blood. It had happened that first night, fifty years earlier. Paul tried to bolster his courage recalling he had survived that attack without issue. It hadn't hurt and it made him feel needed and appreciated. But as the seconds passed, Paul's stomach filled with dread, anticipating the sensation of his master's sharp fangs against his skin. Squeezing his eyes closed, a tiny whimper escaped his lips.

Snapping out of his memories, Paul remained where he stood in the entrance to the library, hoping he didn't look as dreadful as he felt.

ᏣᎻᏑ

Mark absorbed Paul's frantic recollections without expression. That particular night had been quite singular and its circumstances had never repeated. The judging victim had been diminutive in stature and there hadn't been enough blood. Mark returned to the present, his eyes on the slender form in the doorway.

"Upstairs," he said and stood to follow Paul's lead. The kid was frightened, but it didn't matter; he had one need and he would get to it as quickly and as painlessly as possible.

Once inside the bedroom, he listened for Reuben and found him in the garage, singing along with the radio. Satisfied they would have privacy, Mark closed the door. He had no other option. He steered Paul to a chair. Shortly, he'd be heading to pick up Hope Brannen and begin what could be the most important night of his life.

Paul followed instruction and allowed Mark to move him into place. By careful design, Mark had made Paul immortal, but mentally, he was still more human than not. As such, he had deep-rooted superstitions that shaped his view of the creature Mark appeared to be. Somewhere deep in Paul's subconscious, he saw his master as a vampire, pure and simple. Not an instrument of God, not a righter-of-wrongs, but a mystical and mythical being that supped regularly and viciously on the blood of the living. Mark positioned himself before Paul, unmoving, savoring the anticipation.

"The blood of a brother is sweeter than any other..."

Mark blinked at the thought and worked to place it. It sounded familiar, yet it hadn't originated with him. Mark shook his head and in his best doctor's voice, eased his friend down to a seated position. "Paulie, *shhhh...*"

Paul's boyish face softened and he turned to Mark. Once he leaned forward the man's pulse quickened. Undaunted, Mark moved behind the chair and examined his neck. Focusing on the skin of Paul's throat, Mark pressed it with his thumb. He wouldn't puncture his jugular; even with his immortal gift, bleeding out would prove disabling.

How do I know this? I haven't experimented with that before.

"The blood of a brother—"

Mark blinked, irritated at the errant statement arriving unbidden. Still, he had been alive for centuries; had he really not experimented on these issues? Perhaps he had and forgotten. That made sense. Then he wondered, what did it matter? He returned to the immediacy of the task at hand. By now, Paul was non-responsive, mouth slack, with his eyes wide open, fixed like a doll's on an unseen distant point.

"Okay, my friend," Mark said softly as he leaned forward, "this won't hurt a bit."

58

Fourteen

Be silent before the Sovereign LORD,
for the Day of the LORD is near.
Zephaniah 1:7

REUBEN PARKED THE ROLLS AT THE FRONT DOOR AT precisely 6:30 p.m. and waited for the boss to emerge. Stepping to the smooth cement, he settled onto the hood, his headache finally subsiding. He had heard the voice twice today and he massaged his temple. The pain wasn't as severe and he denied it completely when questioned earlier by Paul as he had no desire to compare notes with the jerk. Reuben looked at his watch and then up to the house. The lights were on in Paul's bedroom, but what they were doing was anybody's guess. Were they having sex? No, as far as Reuben could tell Paul was a virgin, and the master had no such inclinations.

Yet, we're picking up a woman…

Reuben cleared his mind as Dr. Corescu emerged, smiling and bursting with good will. He clapped Reuben's shoulder.

"The car looks great, old friend."

Even the boss's eyes were friendly and a glimmer of hope teased Reuben's heart. Maybe this night would be pleasant, no stress, no anger, no bloodshed, just a man driving his boss on a date.

Reuben escorted the doctor to the backseat and took his place behind the wheel. The drive to Ms. Brannen's would take twenty minutes and Reuben headed east.

He found the address with ease, having completely memorized the Whitford City Map six years ago, a good practice since Corescu changed cities every decade. Reuben understood why he didn't stay in one place for too long. Mortals that spent any significant amount of time around the man eventually grew suspicious. Why he never seemed to age, for one, the doctor's existence hinging on anonymity. Pressure behind his

59

eyeballs caused him to grunt, familiar with the sensation of Corescu prying into his head.

"Drive the car, Reuben. The job is not difficult." The boss's voice had turned firm, lacking the earlier jovial edge.

Reuben grunted an agreement and eased the Rolls alongside the woman's curb. What made her so special? He put the car in park and glanced into the rearview mirror. The boss met his eye, a warning in his gaze.

"Got a question, Rube?" the boss asked, informal as always. Reuben did not return in kind, never at ease with the monster that owned him.

"Yes," Reuben replied with respect, "who is this woman? We've never picked up a lady before."

The boss smiled. "You'll see. And be nice."

Reuben pressed his lips together and exited to open the rear door. The boss climbed out and slapped him playfully on the back.

"Have faith," he laugh-talked and headed for the door.

Reuben returned a smile and grumbled.

ଔୄ

Two knocks and the door opened.

"Hi! Come in! I'm almost ready."

Mark caught a glimpse of a twinkling emerald green dress before Hope disappeared into the back of the house. The door closed behind him and he stood in the foyer as a huge black cat meandered near, purred, and rubbed against his legs. Mark acknowledged the cat with a kissing noise and called to the back of the house, "Take your time."

"NEVER say that to a woman!" Hope replied in a giggle.

Mark smiled and turned his attention to the foyer wall peppered with framed photographs. The first few revealed Hope had an identical twin. Five photos grouped in a circle showed the sisters at different ages, matching in dress and hairstyle. Then, to the right hung a photo of her twin, obviously pregnant, hair cropped into a crew cut, smoking a cigarette. A chill whispered past and Mark shivered. Was it a response from the photograph? Reluctant to ponder the possibility, he moved down the wall to examine more familial history.

There was a Hope-as-bride photo, a bride-and-groom photo, a dad-and-mom photo, some Hope-and-cat pics, and toward the end, three Hope-and-horse shots. Mark considered the dilapidated barn on his property; he would have to fix it up if Hope had horses to move.

His date rounded the corner and reached behind him for her wrap on the hook. She was stunning with her hair swept into a loose jumble off her neck, small curls falling free all around. Her slim tube dress glittered and the modest scooped bodice sparkled with faux jewels. Mark was momentarily speechless. As Reuben had noted quite astutely, there had never been any other women. No matter their race, age, or sex, Mark saw the mortals he dealt with in his daily life as innocent or guilty, the appreciation of aesthetic beauty beyond him. But now? As Hope spoke of their upcoming evening, his eyes scanned her face, her chin, and her throat. The bare skin of her upper chest and neck mesmerized him. For a brief instant, he pictured his teeth there. Thankfully, her musical voice broke his unpleasant reverie.

"I like you much better in this suit than in your lab coat!" Hope put her hand on his shoulder and made a sweeping motion, flicking away imaginary dust. "Swanky!"

Mark's suit had been custom tailored and inside he thanked Paul for convincing him to have it made. He helped Hope wrap her lacy shawl over her shoulders as they turned for the door. "You look beautiful," he remarked to her back.

"Thank you. I do what I can," Hope joked and Mark managed a small smile. He followed her to the car and watched as Reuben got her seated. She slid across and looked to his face. Mark dawdled and Reuben nudged him with a quiet hum.

"Thank you, son," he murmured, aware the kid had never been called son before tonight. Mark met Hope's eye and sent her a wink. It was going to be an interesting evening.

∞

Hope leaned into the soft leather and exhaled. She looked at her date sideways and raised her eyebrows at his expression. He had grown quiet; either her appearance stunned him—which she didn't think likely, or he was woefully out of practice in regards to dating etiquette. She sent him a gentle grin. "You okay?"

With a lopsided smile, Mark didn't reply, but took her hand.

Hope licked her lips and softened her gaze. "It's me, isn't it? I make guys nervous. I can't help it." Hope slumped forward. "One guy actually *threw up* on me a year ago. Can you believe that?"

"I believe it. You are *mean*," Mark scolded.

"I'm not mean," Hope disagreed with a playful frown. "Oh... I'm *supposed* to be quiet and demure. I forgot. My bad." She turned her shoulder to face him more directly in the dim back seat. "I like to act as natural as possible. What if I do this—" Hope leaned in, vaguely aware of the driver's raised eyebrow in the rearview mirror. Why did Mark look so terrified—they were both adults. All Mark would have to do is to tilt forward the tiniest bit and their lips would meet.

Mark watched her, the corners of his mouth going down.

"Look," Hope whispered and inched in until her lips gently pressed against his smooth cheek. "See, how easy? Now we're old friends."

Triumphant, Hope leaned back. She'd done this before to ease first-date tensions and expected Mark to smile or nod or somehow show he agreed. Yet he continued to face her, a mere twelve inches away in the dim light. Another car's headlight momentarily flashed past them and for an instant Mark's face was illuminated. Hope yanked her eyes from his to her window. Her date's paralyzing gaze nearly stole her composure and her mind whirled at how to avoid falling for it when they left the dark car.

"Hope," Mark whispered and she turned, happy it was too dark to see him clearly. "You are a monster," he chided, now with a small smile. "Beautiful and mysterious, but powerful in your way. Please keep this in mind as you learn more about me."

With a small grin, Hope averted her eyes, only a tiny bit interested in to what he might have been referring. His cologne and the lilting hypnotic tenor of his voice threatened her resolve to remain stoic. If she allowed herself to relax a fraction in Mark's presence, she was certain she would give herself completely away.

The car slowed and entered the Block's neighborhood. Mark lifted her hand to his mouth. He then kissed the underside of her wrist. Hope turned as he finished the lingering contact and suppressed a squeal of delight, his face illuminated by the parking lot halogens. Dizzy and blushing, she took her hand back and laid it at her throat.

"Are you making love to me, Dr. Corescu?" Hope whispered in her put-on southern drawl, a failing attempt at flippancy.

"Hope Brannen," Mark leaned closer then and spoke into her ear; his breath on her skin only increased her lightheadedness. "I've given my service to God, but you have stolen my heart."

Hope laughed softly, wondering at his words. When she dared to look into his eyes again, she realized she no longer wanted to keep the upper hand. She would let herself go. What the hell. It would be worth it.

Fifteen

Do not turn to mediums or seek out spiritists,
for you will be defiled by them.
Leviticus 19:31

GLORIE PRESSED "SEND" ON HER LAPTOP AND AWAITED confirmation; the new Visa card had come in handy. Her round-trip plane ticket to Atlanta were in the bag, and thanks to Jim's mother for offering to keep the kids for a week. Although she had no biological connection to Jim's three stepchildren, the old woman loved them as if they were her own. Glorie needed a vacation and a break from the nightmares. The muddy horse in the toilet wasn't the only one she endured. There had been others, each worse than the one before.

Her plane didn't leave until Sunday morning, so she had some time alone. Jim's dad picked up the kids after school and took them off her hands leaving Glorie free and clear for ten days. The relief poured through her and she vowed to chill as much as possible.

She tried Hope's number and got her voicemail, which meant her sister was most likely out with Mr. Wonderful. Punching out a text message, she hit send and sighed. What made her sister fall so fast for this smooth-talking shyster? She needed to get down there and keep Hope from getting in deeper than she should. Her twin was awful stupid when it came to relationships. *She married her high school sweetheart, for goodness sake,* Glorie smirked and shook her head. Her sister probably had three real boyfriends her whole life, and only slept with one of those. Glorie grimaced and cleared her mind. Hope was her only sister, but in many ways, she was also a waste of space. Lighting another cigarette, she relaxed on top of her covers as memories of her sister refused to bed down.

What made Hope so different? They attended the same schools, shared their friends. Well, at least until high school when her gullible sister briefly became infatuated with religious guys. Glorie attended church right alongside her a few times to look at boys, but she was

63

never sucked in. The choirboys had nothing on the hard-rocking metal heads Glorie preferred.

Glorie took a pull of her smoke. It didn't matter. They were all going to wind up dead one day. Like Glorie's first husband. A sad, sad sight—cut his wrists in the bathtub. It hadn't been easy to set up, and Glorie thanked *Forensic Files* for the idea. Now where was he? Dead in the grave. Maybe one day, when Glorie kicked the bucket, he would find her and pay her back. Who knows? Maybe the dead seek revenge. If they did, Glorie had made plenty of enemies.

She crushed out her Camel and tried to get to sleep. Saturday, she would shop. The new credit card had a ten-thousand-dollar balance and with Jim out of the country, she intended to do her best to spend it all.

CৎৎৎS

Nancy Block greeted each guest personally as Hope and Mark entered the main hall. The massive marble pillars extended to the ceiling and dripped with garland and golden ribbons. They crossed the rug-covered hardwood floor to shake hands with their elderly hostess.

"Mrs. Block, this is my friend, Mark Corescu," Hope said and the woman's eyes shone with recognition at the name.

"*Doctor* Mark Corescu?" She stressed his professional title and dramatically rolled her eyes. "Oh, how wonderful! And so handsome, my, oh, my! I have heard so many wonderful things about your work at the hospital."

Hope smiled. Did everyone think Mark was Doctor Wonderful? Her date graciously took both of the matron's papery hands in his and bowed to kiss her cheek. Hope entwined her left arm around his right and they stepped into the crowd.

"Let me know if you see anyone famous. I would love to meet some celebrities. I heard that last year, Steve Buscemi and Harvey Keitel were here. I love actors, don't you?" Hope babbled on about Hollywood as they made their way through the main salon to the opposite end of the room. Guests packed the first floor and she smiled cheerily at the strangers they passed. They were almost to the back wall and the huge glass doors that exited to the yard when their host, Mr. Block, Sr., stopped them.

"Ms. Brannen," he tapped Hope's shoulder and she turned. "I love the mural you painted in Billy's room last week. The wife and I have refurbished the barn in the back. Do you think you could paint us a

64

hunt scene on the right-hand wall?" Mr. Block pointed vaguely out the glass doors. Hope peered through the thick panes to the yard. She could make out the shape of a building, but nothing else.

"It would be my pleasure. Is the barn through here?" She pulled Mark with her to the door and Mr. Block opened the door for them as they stepped into the night.

"Yes. Just follow that center path."

"How about that?" Hope said as they stepped away from the throng. "The Blocks are giving me another job. Once the word gets out that I'm the Block's personal muralist, I won't be able to close my door without hitting a new customer in the face." Hope snuggled close to her escort as the cool breeze whipped off the pond. "You know what, Mark? Ever since I met you, my life has only gotten better."

"I like the sound of that," Mark replied and led her into the barn.

◦ R ◦

Standing in the wide aisle, Hope remarked on everything she saw and spoke rapidly about the foxhunting image she'd paint on the wall. Mark grinned at her enthusiasm, feeling like himself again, powerful, content, and eager. Soon, he would segue into the business at hand: explaining Hope's upcoming role in his life. He had to be delicate. Just because he knew God's will didn't mean Hope was as intuitive. He would take care to introduce her to the idea at just the right time.

"I told you I used to own horses..." Mark said, his voice echoing off the rafters. He counted four heads peeking from the stalls and he had an idea. "Let me show you a neat trick."

Hope agreed and stepped with him to the first stall. The stall plate read JENNIFER DOES IT. Mark stroked down the horse's long face and closed his eyes.

In a soft monotone, he began, "Jennifer is a retired race horse and she carries the mistress foxhunting." Mark looked to Hope for her reaction. Her round eyes and slack jaw proved her amazement.

"What? That horse said that?" Hope watched his face. "You can talk to animals?"

"In a fashion," he said with a half shrug. He led Hope to the next stall and an old equine poked out its head.

"Do this one!" Hope said with wonder, revealing she had no problem believing what Mark said was true.

Pleased she trusted him so easily and so soon, Mark concentrated on the next animal and a stream of images rolled in to be sorted. After a moment, he gave one nod and turned to see Hope's face. "Pumpkin is *also* a retired race horse and suffers arthritis in his hocks." Mark patted the chestnut's neck and smiled. "He's happy here."

"This is amazing!" Hope hugged herself and looked eagerly into Mark's face. "What's it like? Talking to animals?"

"I can show you if you're game."

Hope nodded like a child. Mark grinned and continued.

"When I concentrate on an animal, I receive mental images that reveal things about their lives."

"Okay," Hope agreed and stepped closer. "Show me."

With a chuckle, he continued. "In this way, Jennifer *told* me she was a racehorse by sending me images of her old life. I surmised from the environment that she was racing. Get it?"

"I think so." Hope looked expectantly at the third horse in the barn. "So, you think I can do it?"

"Perhaps, let's try." With Mark's hand on top, they placed their palms on the horse in the third stall. Mark closed his eyes and Hope followed suit, her face a picture of exaggerated concentration. "What do you see?"

With a sharp inhale, Hope said, "I see children! Lots and lots of children! They're all around. Wait! They're riding me. I'm the horse. This is amazing!" Hope broke contact with the pony and clutched onto Mark for support. He took her more fully into his arms and held her until she stopped trembling. He'd hoped his extrasensory abilities would throw her into a spin. In fact, he counted on it.

"My God! I'll never be the same. That's so wonderful!" Hope still held him tight, her cheek pressed against his chest. Several long moments passed before she exhaled with purpose, melting deeper into his front. She said into his coat, "Mark... I feel like I *know* you. I'm *at home* with you. Is that crazy?"

"What does your heart tell you?" Mark asked and gently pushed her away to lead her out the back of the barn. "Walk with me."

They wove their way along the path onto the vast property beyond. As they left the halo of electric light surrounding the barn, they strolled in the glow provided by the full moon.

"This is the best date ever," Hope mused, looking at the far horizon where the purple sky belied the city lights.

Mark made a noise of agreement and stopped his forward movement. Hope turned, her eyes misty. The time had arrived and Mark tempered his tone to be as gentle as possible.

"Hope, there's a reason you feel this way. We are destined for each other. There's no denying this. And there is no turning back."

Hope didn't disagree. She said with a single nod, "It's unsettling but my heart is *aching* for you. Right now." Hope laughed. "And I'm terrified."

"But not of me," Mark responded.

She shook her head. "No, no, definitely not. It's me I'm afraid of. I want to let go. I want to trust you." She huffed in frustration. "I know I'm supposed to be cautious and paranoid—I only just met you, for God's sake! But I'm not. I'm just not."

"This is good, right?" Mark touched her cheek and she smiled.

"It *has* to be. Why else would I feel so peaceful? I mean, if I think real hard, lots of stupid questions pop into my head. But Mark..." Hope paused and licked her lips. "It's obvious that you're different, you're not like any man—or person—I've ever met, but I *like* that about you. And you seem religious; you can't be a bad person and talk so much about God, right?"

"I take my faith very seriously," Mark commented, reading a lot of what she wasn't saying in her eyes. She recognized his supernatural nature, but couldn't pin it down. Momentarily, he hoped to help her do just that.

Hope nodded. "I'm ashamed to admit I don't know much about God." Hope paused, then continued with sincerity. "I want to be with you. I want to learn everything there is to know about you."

"And I have prayed for you for years." Mark took both of her hands in his. "I need you to join me, to aid me in my work." He waited for her to show she understood. "You must hear me out. I'm going to tell you something very important and very strange, okay?"

"Okay," Hope whispered, still meeting his gaze.

"I am not an ordinary man."

"I know," she said without hesitation.

"Listen closely. I am not a man at all." He paused to see a reaction, but she only nodded, as if she expected him to say something to that effect. Mark pushed a loose curl behind her ear and continued. "I have walked the earth in this form for almost four hundred years. I am an agent of God with a sacred duty to help endangered souls pass from this world to the next. Daily, I judge and execute men and women who are so full of hate and malice that their evil nature calls to me, compelling me to act." Mark paused to read Hope's expression, but her gaze remained unfathomable. He continued as he searched her eyes for understanding or the first glimpses of fear. "It isn't pleasant for them." Mark lowered his voice. "When I arrive on their last day, I demand repentance, I offer forgiveness, and then release them into the Light."

Hope still showed no inkling to what she might be thinking, her gaze faraway. Mark took her chin gently between his thumb and forefinger.

"I am certain I'm doing the will of God." He waited for Hope's reaction. If God sent her, she would have the empathy necessary to appreciate his unbelievable story.

Finally, Hope answered with hesitation, "Then you are a miracle."

"There's more. The judging method is gruesome and violent. If you can trust me, I will teach you. I prayed for you for so long that I was beginning to lose hope you would come."

"Hmmm?" Hope murmured dreamily, Mark had hypnotized her without intention. He touched her cheek and she came around.

"Ironic your name is Hope, isn't it?" he said and she trained her eyes to the full moon. Mark led them to the car, watching her the whole way.

ᏅᎯᏚᏋᎧ

Arm in arm with the most amazing man she'd ever met, Hope gathered her wits. Everything about him set her on fire, even his strange story and invitation for her to join him in his "work." When in his arms, she sensed brute strength hidden behind his genteel manner, yet she was safe there. When he looked in her eyes, adoration and unadulterated fascination reflected back. How could she say no? Whatever he wanted, she would consent. She snuggled up closer, aware they were only a few minutes from reaching the Rolls.

"I want to learn more about you. It's got to be for a reason," Hope said, sorry for her dreamy tone.

"Then you will join me?"

Mark sounded uncertain and Hope wanted to reassure him, not cause him consternation.

"I don't think I have a choice. I'm with you—it feels like destiny, or something. But you sound in a hurry. I'm not going anywhere," she said in a soft voice watching Mark's driver pull the Rolls closer to the fence line a dozen yards ahead. "What's the rush?"

Mark pulled her to a stop. "The rush is, I've waited centuries."

"Centuries," Hope repeated nearly inaudible. Every word he said was true, she had no doubt, but how could it be? "I need time to process. You want me to understand, right?"

Mark kissed her forehead. "You're right. Come to my house tomorrow for dinner. We can discuss this until you're comfortable." He cupped her cheek in his palm and Hope's butterflies rumbled. "I'll send Reuben to pick you up at seven."

Hope nodded and squeezed Mark's arm tighter, willing her reddened cheeks to return to normal. As they resumed their trek to the car, she thought of Anthony. He would have plenty of advice about her current situation. How much, if anything, should she tell him? Hope didn't yet know; she had plenty to ponder.

Sixteen

You have made my days a mere handbreadth;
The span of my years is as nothing before you.
Psalm 39:5

REUBEN DROPPED THE WOMAN OFF AND THEY RODE without speaking. The boss's silence probably had to do with the girl. As if on cue, his passenger announced the dinner date and pick-up the following evening. Reuben nodded and hummed a tune. He had his answer; he'd be picking her up all the time now.

Until he kills her, that is.

Reuben's eyes jerked to the rearview mirror. He didn't call that last thought up, and if Corescu got wind of it, he'd be angry. But the boss was lost in his own thoughts. Sighing, he returned his attention to the black road.

Maybe to kill the silence and calm his nerves, Reuben asked, "How was the party, Boss?"

"The Lord smiled on me, Rube," the doctor said, catching his eye in the mirror a moment before returning his gaze to the dark scenery.

"Praise God," Reuben offered and fell silent. The religion bit was ludicrous; Corescu wasn't sent by God. Reuben had first-hand experience with the judging process. His earliest childhood memories were of his mother's run-in with the monster in the backseat. The images were foggy and vague, but he remembered the sounds of tortured screaming and a lot of blood. *Everywhere.*

 number

"Praise God, indeed," Mark sighed and closed his eyes. Reuben's traitorous thoughts were not new and Mark valued his perspective. It helped him remember what the general public would think if they ever found him out.

70

The scene played in his mind as clearly as if watched on a big screen television. Clara Stuckey, Reuben's mother, high on whatever she could steal or buy with her body. Five-year old Reuben, in a corner, chained to the bedpost with a tattered nylon dog leash. The water in the cat dish kept him alive, but barely.

In his memory of that night, Clara lay unconscious on a filthy mattress, surrounded by wispy spirits that fluttered around her head like flies. Such apparitions appeared regularly at judgings, but he paid them no mind. He had a job to do and he always got right to it. Clara had starved eleven of her infant children over the years, had undergone numerous non-medical abortions, sold one daughter, and had murdered two johns in their sleep for money. Her evil deeds grieved Mark's soul to the breaking point. When her time came, Mark hadn't realized Reuben was in the room. The child cowered in the shadows as Mark took Clara by the throat and lifted her off the ground. He demanded she repent for the lives she had wasted, but her mind hazed from years of drugs and alcohol. Mark reached deep into her murky past in the hopes of pulling at least one happy thought from her childhood, but she was too far gone. Then, her time was up.

Mark held her emaciated body close, fixed his mouth against her dirty throat and drank heavily. The tainted fluid that pumped her heart didn't satisfy, but he discharged his duty nonetheless. Clara's lips flapped on rotten teeth as she spoke gibberish to the air. Pinned as she was to Mark's chest, she clawed spastically, as if to grasp the spirits that fluttered in excited energy. A few moments later, with one incredible muscle spasm, Clara pushed herself from Mark's grip. Her blood spurted wastefully onto the grimy tiled floor as Mark staggered after her. He caught her before she hit the ground and pulled her gushing wound to his mouth.

Arterial spray soiled the walls, the bed litter, and Mark's black coat and still, Clara moaned and cried many minutes past her time. By the time Mark withdrew, the woman was dead weight in his arms. At that precise moment Mark felt a tug on his pants leg; Reuben, five-years-old, eyes round as dinner plates, had seen everything.

Mark stood stunned and squelched a brief moment of self-loathing as he considered pounding the child's head into the floor. Thankfully, a peaceful realization occurred to him; this terrified child was the reason he'd been called there. Mark scooped Reuben into his arms trusting his second impulse was the correct one.

ᴄᴈᔆᴆ

Hope tossed and turned in her king-sized bed and then glanced at the clock: 1:15 a.m. *Uggghhh. I'll never get to sleep at this rate!*

Pulling the comforter to her chin, she rolled onto her back and stared at the dark ceiling. Her foot struck an immoveable weight and she lifted her head just enough to see Spider's silhouette, sawing kitty logs without a care in the world. Thinking it must be nice to be a cat, Hope lay back and stared at the ceiling fan. Before going to bed, for thirty minutes, she had meditated on her conversation with Mark and wasn't any closer to comprehending her part in his strange admissions.

"Maybe that's an answer in itself," Hope said to no one in the quiet room. "Maybe I'm supposed to keep at it. Until I understand." Hope sat up to click on her bedside lamp. Spider squinted his eyes and tucked his face into his flank.

What was Mark saying he was? An Agent of God?

Hope scoffed at problem number one. She was no expert, but how could God approve of a man, by himself, condemning people to death? And how could Mark be four hundred years old, judge the wicked, kill them, read animal's minds, and hold a job at the hospital without having to run from the police? It was crazy. Yet, she knew in her gut he was telling the truth.

So... if he's some kind of supernatural angel of death character, how do I fit in?

Hope sighed, clicked off the lamp, and lay back. She needed more answers and at dinner, she'd ask more questions. Encouraged and finally sleepy, Hope resolved to enjoy her date at Mark's. Without even realizing it, she dozed off.

The cat Spider woke up and began to purr.

eventeen

Do not speak in the hearing of a fool
For he will despise the wisdom of your words.
Proverbs 23:9

THE FLIGHT TO ATLANTA HAD BEEN UNEVENTFUL AND Connie slept against the concave interior, his cheek to a miserable airline pillow. As the wheels hit the tarmac, he was jostled awake and he sat upright to look around. The sun had set and he checked his watch; he was right on time.

The previous week, Connie had connected with the police departments of Atlanta and her surrounding boroughs. One of his many contacts in the Atlanta Police Department promised him the keys to the city if he'd only take her out for a steak. Her name was Maggie King and the APD had the good sense to put her in the Information Services Section. She had a powerful computer packed with useful data and she was very lonely. Connie took her out two years ago when she visited his city for a Law Enforcement convention and she'd been a good lay. He smiled at the memory and wondered if she still liked the same wine. He made a mental note to pick some up in the airport before he grabbed a taxi to the hotel.

Hartsfield-Jackson was the busiest airport he could recall flying into, and he'd flown into plenty. The hustle and bustle of the crowd moved him along despite his attempts to steer. Luckily, they were headed the same way and he flowed with the sea of disembarked passengers. By the time he purchased the wine and used the facilities, he allowed the herd to push him to the cabstand.

Connie directed the cabby to the Sheraton on Courtland where they kept the bar open until the wee hours, which was of particular use to Connie since he used the occasional whiskey to settle his stomach. Once tucked into his hotel suite, Connie set up his laptop. There were

73

a few loose ends to tie up before he called his informant at the APD. First, though, he pulled up the APD website and picked through the options. Back home in Feather, he'd narrowed his list of possible cases down to four. All four unsolved cases had a missing person report as well as a homicide. That meant kidnapping. Not only did the future Senator Buckley allow murderers to go free, he apparently did the same for kidnappers. And they gave this guy a promotion after five years on the force? They wanted him off the streets and at a desk where the only killers he encountered were on paper. Connie laughed at the irony.

The web page offered a list of missing persons, all too recent for his needs. Clicking through the archives, he found the oldest filing was dated 1980. Connie *humphed* and shut the computer; his squeeze at HQ would fill in the blanks.

Next, he pulled out the growing file folder labeled *Buckley Cold Case Story*. The Senator had over twenty-two cold cases on the books, but even more strange, twenty of the twenty-two cases had elements of apparent suicide. In each event, the officers on the scene swore the suicides were staged, but couldn't prove it. This tidbit of information buzzed in Connie's head. If it was an M.O., he saw no evidence indicating the police thought so. If the forty-year-old trail led to a possible serial killer, why was he the only one to see it? Things were looking up. Not only was he about to bring down a United States Senator, but also tarnish the reputation of one of the most hailed police forces in the country.

Connie jotted himself a note to ask the ISS gal about the serial killer angle when he got to the station. What if the killer was still in Atlanta? Connie's pulse quickened. He was in his element and doing what he was meant for; digging, digging and more digging.

Skimming the four missing persons files he'd settled on a few days ago, Connie decided to look them up in the local phone directory. All four homicides had occurred in the city of Atlanta in 1970 and '71, and of the four, two names were hits in the white pages; Nancy P. Colder and Reuben Stuckey. These names had been pulled from unsolved murder cases, each with a missing person report filed afterwards by the deceased's relatives, but no kidnapping charges were ever formally filed.

The Colder woman was the wife of a murdered man. Her college-bound daughter reported her missing shortly after the case opened. Connie glanced at his watch and picked up the phone. It rang once, giving Connie a surge of adrenaline, but then a recorded voice let him know the number had been changed, *yada, yada, yada.*

That left the kid.

Stuckey was the five-year-old son of a drug-addict named Clara Stuckey. The dead woman's mother had filed a missing person's report the day after her body was discovered. Connie did a little mental math and calculated that Mr. Stuckey, if he was indeed alive and living at 3344 Sherwood Drive, Atlanta, would be forty-five now and might even remember the murder. He made himself another note to hit the library and get the microfiche news from that murder since an internet search came up empty before he left Feather.

Connie grabbed the receiver and this time dialed Reuben Stuckey's number. It rang twice and on the third ring, an answering machine picked up. The voice was a mechanical one, "Please leave a message at the tone…" Connie hung up. Maybe he would drive by after he finished at the library.

One more call to his ISS sweetie at the APD. She told him how to get to her new office upstairs and Connie freshened for his date. Then he scooped up his briefcase and the wine and headed to the lobby to grab a taxi. Hopefully, Maggie King was still as cute as she'd been two years ago. Connie loved attractive women, but had no tolerance for even the mildly ugly. He crossed his fingers and headed to the police station.

ೕ৵ৎ

At precisely 7 p.m., Hope pulled the door open and said hello to Mark's driver. She'd barely noticed him the night before because of her preoccupation with Mark, but tonight, as he was alone, there was no missing him. He wore an elegant black suit, mustard yellow shirt, and color-coordinated tie that complimented his smooth even complexion and piercing brown eyes. When he put out his arm in the old-fashioned manner, Hope took it and pulled her door closed on her way out. Just as she was about to make small talk, he stopped with a jerk, squeezed closed his eyes, and pressed his fingers to his temple.

"Are you okay?" she asked, but Reuben recovered and waved off her concern.

"I'm fine," Reuben chuckled. "Did the boss tell you he was, well, different?"

"Yes…" Hope said as Reuben opened the rear door. "Why?"

"Well…" Reuben stalled as he slid into the driver's seat. He caught her eye in the rearview mirror. "Think twice about giving the boss this number." He tapped the side of his head.

75

Was he referring to telepathy? Queasy at the thought, Hope looked out the window. Mark read the horses at the barn; did it work on humans? She crossed her arms and tried to clear her mind. What if Mark was listening right now? In the mirror, Reuben's mouth was frozen in an impish grin. Maybe he was teasing. Hope broke the silence to disguise her unease.

"How long have you been driving for Mark?"

"I've been drivin' Dr. Corescu for twenty-seven years, give or take."

"Huh," Hope said and fell silent. To drive Mark almost thirty years, Reuben would have to be in his forties, but the kid didn't look a day over eighteen. Would he lie? And if he was lying, why? Puzzling, Hope allowed the silence to reign the rest of the way. Thankfully, Reuben did as well.

⊂₰⊃

Mark dragged the corpse to the bedroom window. They were only seven stories up and although the fall may not break any major bones, it would have to do. So what if they knew it wasn't suicide. Let them investigate.

I wasn't even here, technically, forensically... Mark mused, peering through the slatted blinds to the road below. Ninety minutes past rush hour, and the street was practically deserted.

Six-thirty already? Hope will be waiting.

Mark realized the judging had run long, but it had been particularly satisfying. The unmistakable pull of evil reached Mark's consciousness from a long way off, almost a hundred miles from his cozy neighborhood in the outskirts of town. *Child abuser,* the call had said. A heinous crime against God. More a transgression against God than against the children themselves. These were Mark's favorite victims; people who abused children. And this judging had gone well from beginning to end.

At 5:45, Mark stood against the wall in the dark room and listened as his victim entered the apartment and engaged someone else in conversation. A door closed in the hall and the man's footsteps padded toward the bedroom where Mark stood obscured by shadow. The evildoer was a middle-aged man, unassuming features, with a soft, medium build and he entered the bedroom without flipping on the light. Mark was ready either way; he stood immobile against the wall directly beside the bathroom door, ready to pounce, not caring how the

76

attack initiated. It would end like all the others, with his belly full and a dead sinner in his grip.

"Zip-edee-doo-dah," the man sang. He came toward Mark, still unaware of his presence, and stopped at the bedside table to play the answering machine. As the contraption beeped, the man removed his tie and unbuttoned his shirt. A woman's voice on the machine, probably the wife, said she'd be home by nine.

"My, oh my, what a wonderful day…"

The man was giddy. Mark searched his thoughts and saw his evil intentions. Through this psychic link, he knew a frightened form in the next room shivered in wait. Although it was this man's daughter, the thoughts seeping from his mind weren't fatherly in the least. Mark's grin disappeared.

See me.

Mark pulled at the man and willed him to acknowledge his visitor. Engrossed with his evil constructs, the guilty man remained oblivious.

"Carl J. Odom," Mark called telepathically, *"you are being judged."* He then opened his hands to take the man by the throat.

ೞഓ

"Wha—?" Carl didn't have time to go for the light. There was someone—no some*thing*—in the room and it wasn't human. He lunged for the bedside lamp, but couldn't move. Steel-like arms wrapped around him from behind and a voice in his head commanded him to be still. Carl quieted, his mind racing with terror.

"Carl J. Odom, you have sinned against God. You have spit in the face of your Creator time and time again with your sins of the flesh. Your time is up."

Carl wilted, the fight draining from him like water.

"You are about to die."

Carl believed the voice; God had sent the Angel of Death to kill him. Guilt and sorrow welled in his chest and he found it hard to breathe, more from the emotional pain than from the firm embrace of his attacker. Abruptly, he was spun in the devil's grip and forced to face his judge. Like a spoiled child, Carl squeezed his eyes shut. When telepathically commanded to open them, he did so and looked into the face of hell.

"Oh, God…" His voice trailed off and his attacker grinned.

"No, but close."

Speaking aloud for the first time, his Judge held his gaze, speaking

77

just loud enough for him to hear.

"God loves you, Carl. You are His son. He is willing to have you come home, if you will repent. You have made a mess of the life He has given you."

"Oh, God!" Released by his attacker, Carl fell to his knees. Twenty-two years of his youth were spent in church and his ritualistic training returned in a rush. Praying as he'd never prayed before, Carl beseeched the Virgin, Christ, the Saints and the Father, begging to be forgiven. He was about to breathe his last, but not before he set things straight with God. When he had said all he could think of in his fevered state, Carl began to cry.

⊂⊃

Mark took Carl J. Odom into his arms as a father might a small boy. This was the best part; the penitent man begging for his salvation.

Okay, maybe it isn't the best part, Mark corrected, *but it is way up there.*

Odom's fervent supplications faded to a low moan and he buried his face in Mark's coat. He continued to cry as Mark found his way to his throat. Brushing the man's shirt collar aside, Mark's eyeteeth extended as he prepared to take his portion.

Like a B-Movie Dracula.

Not amused he had compared himself to a Hollywood fable, Mark plunged his fangs deep into the neck. Then, unbidden, he heard a reply in his head not his own.

"Or a four hundred-year-old vampire…"

Grunting, Mark shut out that voice. Once in a while, he would hear from "The Other," an insidious opinionated utterer who spoke to him when he fed on human blood. The Other constantly belittled Mark's work, belittled *God's* work, and Mark had long ago decided this counter voice was Satan, himself.

"Oh, that is rich. That would give you permission, wouldn't it?"

Again, Mark ignored The Other's remarks and focused on the task at hand. Once the fountain flowed, Mark drew Carl's prone body closer and drank deeply. His victim did not fight, rather, his sobs slowed and stopped, until he hung limp in Mark's arms.

Eighteen

He has given us his very great and precious promises,
so that…you may participate in the divine nature
and escape the corruption…caused by evil desires.
2 Peter 1:4

"HI, YOU MUST BE HOPE BRANNEN." A TALL, SANDY-HAIRED young man met Hope at the door and led her into the foyer. "I'm Paul Black, Mark's assistant. I'm glad to finally meet you."

Paul's enthusiasm caused Hope to return a warm grin as the uncomfortable memory of Reuben's evil glare faded from her mind. On the drive over, he remained quiet until the car reached the iron gate at the head of the drive. In very few words, he frightened her with rude remarks and veiled threats regarding Mark and his intentions. Now, as Paul showed her to the next room, she released the negative emotions in the face of Mark's friendly assistant. Standing over six feet, Paul was markedly slender, his hair a shade lighter than her own with bright blue eyes shining in a boyish face. Like Reuben, he didn't appear to have yet reached his twentieth birthday. Hope followed down a short hallway taking in the décor.

"This house is beautiful," Hope offered and Paul grinned.

"Thank you. We'll wait for Mark in the library." Paul motioned for her to sit in a sprawling brown leather loveseat and he didn't sit until she did. "His appointment ran late."

"That's fine." Hope smiled. "I think I'd wait for him forever," she said in a laugh which drew a genuine smile from Paul.

"How about something to drink," he asked, twirling his ankle at the end of crossed legs. "Iced tea, cola, or maybe wine or brandy?" He looked as if he would rise if necessary, but Hope shook her head.

Her eyes roamed the cavernous room. "There must be a thousand books up there." Impressed by the packed shelving, she tried to read some of the spines from where she sat. Paul cleared his throat and she

79

returned her attention.

"This is our favorite room," he said. "We spend a lot of time here."

"I believe it. Tell me how you came to be Mark's assistant. Is he such a mess that he needs attending twenty-four-seven?" Hope meant it to be a joke, but Paul didn't laugh.

"Well, I should ask you first, what has Mark told you? I wouldn't want to speak out of turn."

Hope rolled in her lips before a halting reply. "Mark started to tell me about his, uh, calling, and that he's been at it for centuries." Paul's expression didn't change at her outlandish statements, which gave them even more credence.

"Okay," Paul said, rubbing his neck. "I know where to pick up."

Hope waited for him to begin, but his focus had gone soft. Like her, he seemed easy to distract. Hope changed her leg position and the movement jostled him awake.

"Where was I?" he asked through his infectious smile.

"How you ended up with Mark," Hope laughed.

Paul smiled and lifted an imaginary book. "How I ended up with Mark Corescu, by Paul Black. Has a nice ring to it, eh?" He pretended to set the book down and clasped his hands behind his head. Then he winked and took a deep breath. "I used to be a blacksmith and I met Mark through his horses."

"Oh, he told me he used to keep horses!" Hope said and instantly regretted the outburst. She sounded all of twelve-years-old. She attempted to cover up her idiocy with another question. "You don't have horses anymore?"

"No, nowadays, Mark collects cars. You should see the garage." Paul trailed off as he changed subjects and Hope redirected.

"So, you were shoeing Mark's horse one day and he asked you to work for him?"

"It's a bit more complicated. I met Mark in Maine in 1915."

"1915?" Hope recalled Mark's claim to be centuries old, but to have another person confirm it so nonchalantly surprised her into a remark. "So, you must be a hundred years old."

"That's about right. I don't keep track." Paul looked up to the ceiling in thought. "I'd been shoeing Mark's horses for a few weeks, and one night, he invited me to dine with him. He was the town doctor and a respected member of the community. I think he spread the word for me, because my business picked up like crazy when I started his account."

"Huh, sounds familiar," Hope said with a new smile. "I'm getting more business, now, too." When Paul inhaled, she had the feeling he would tell it as a story if she'd only be quiet. "Go ahead, tell me what happened. He is so interesting." Mark's assistant blushed, an adorable look for him, and began the tale.

๛

"He has always been that," Paul responded and sighed as the memories flooded in. They were happy for the most part, and he didn't mind reliving them. It was nice to have an attentive audience; no one had ever asked him *his* story. He leaned over his knees and remembered.

Business was booming and an endless line of horses stood at the end of Paul's hammer that fall. Even though the automobile had become more affordable and many city people bought into the horseless carriage, Paul had plenty of work.

Mark was known as Dr. Crump, the only physician in their small New England town. He kept seven horses that required a blacksmith; an eclectic assortment of top-of-the-line thoroughbreds and imported carriage warmbloods, highly trained and easy to handle. Paul had recently completed his apprenticeship with a senior smithy and after adding Crump to his schedule, dozens of wealthy townsfolk began dropping their blacksmiths to favor his services. Paul soon became the envy of the farrier community with his elite clientele, and so far, he hadn't even met the man in person.

It was more than anyone could ask for. Paul was raking in money so fast, he wondered if he might be able to build his own blacksmith shop in town before the year was out. If the people came to his shop, he wouldn't have to make barn calls. And if he set up his business early, he might be able to find a wife, settle down, and raise a family. Not that Paul had any romantic prospects. He had a few boyhood crushes on some of the local maidens, but since he'd become a man and focused on his trade, he hadn't sought female companionship. Before his Quaker father passed in '09, he had instilled Paul with the sincere desire to build a career and not become too soon entangled with the opposite sex. Like a good son, Paul honored his father's memory and worked hard.

81

Crump had a reputation as a kind man, but when he met the doctor face-to-face, he found him to be so much more. The day Paul shod the doctor's three cart horses, he had packed away his tools when the doctor's buggy came around the main house toward the barn. Crump jumped down from the driver's seat with an agile leap and sent Paul a nod as he neared. Stepping up to greet him, Paul noted first the man's bronzed skin and dark eyes. What mysterious country had he come from? Was he Arab? Greek? European? Paul didn't know enough about the world yet to guess the man's ethnicity, but certainly no one else in town had such striking features. Blushing and wondering why, Paul smiled and stuck out his hand.

"You must be the blacksmith I hired. Paul Black, right?" Despite his foreign appearance, the man had no accent. The doctor took Paul's right hand and pumped it twice.

"That I am, Dr. Crump. It has been a pleasure shoeing your horses. They are well-behaved and easy to manage. I would love some insight into your training methods." Paul hoped his compliments didn't patronize; he meant what he said, but he felt deficient in the doctor's company.

"It is not complicated; I simply whisper in their ears the morning before you come. And they have whispered back that you're the best smithy in town." The doctor laughed as he spoke and came towards Paul to lead him back into the barn. Crump untied the tether on the nearest horse and led him to its stall. "Are you all done, then?"

"Yes, sir. Your gray mare needed only resetting and the matched geldings received new shoes all around. Those gravel roads do a number on these steel shoes."

"When do you next come around? Farriery interests me very much; I would like to see you at work."

Crump had returned to the barn's entryway and leaned against the whitewashed wall. Most of his clients watched him work and he wasn't surprised this imminent citizen might want to do the same. Paul closed his eyes to consider his mental calendar.

"Yes, sir, your cob needs resetting in two weeks. The matched grays will be trimmed then, too. How about September third at three-thirty?" Paul opened his eyes and awaited a reply.

Crump shook his head. "Can you come a tad later, say five? I will have you for supper afterwards."

As he spoke, Paul became aware the doctor's words never reached his gaze. His dark eyes shone like glints of coal making eye contact difficult for more than a few seconds. Yet, the offer to feed a hungry laborer worked and Paul smiled with a bow. "I don't usually shoe horses by lamplight, but if this is the only way, so be it. And as for supper, I accept. Thank you."

Paul wrenched his eyes from Crump's and walked his tools to the cart, preparing to leave. The doctor followed, carrying the one-hundred-pound anvil as if it were made of air. At the buggy, Paul reached for it and Crump passed it over with nonchalance, afterward, swishing the dirt from his palms.

"Watch your toes," he said with humor and clapped Paul on the back. "I look forward to seeing you on the third. Until then." And he disappeared into the house.

The next two weeks, Paul had more clients than he could handle, and he didn't have the dinner invitation on his mind when he returned to Crump's farm. Only when he saw the doctor's buggy beside the barn did he recall their arrangement. Remembering how easily Crump carried the anvil, Paul removed it first and headed for the indoor wash-rack where he shod the horses. He placed the anvil and when he turned to retrieve his hammers, the doctor stood in the door, tools in hand, grinning in the dim entryway. He placed the wooden box at Paul's feet and crossed his arms at chest level.

"I will now see the master at work," Crump announced, moving aside so Paul could begin.

Paul fixed the first mare to the posts. Crump watched, questioned, and made small talk as he worked. Even though the doctor possessed an eccentric manner, Paul liked him. He spoke as if they were equals and gazing upon his dashing features was pleasant. Paul's pals were rough-and-ready sorts, farmers and cattlemen, all still in their teens, where Dr. Crump appeared mid-thirties, European, debonair, and exotic. To converse on topics with an older man brought him comfort. Not that Dr. Crump reminded him of his deceased father, but having his more mature perspective made their conversations novel and thought-provoking. In addition, Crump had a great passion for horses and their discussions on training led Paul to believe the man was a lot more than a simple country doctor.

Halfway through, Paul's hammer came down upon his thumb and he jumped back, cursing. Even though the pain abated in seconds, the horse sensed his moment of fear and danced on its lead. In the manner of all highbred, hot-blooded horses, the mare's agitation grew each passing second.

"Whoa, girl. Whoa, easy girl," Paul said as he grabbed the taut rope and spoke gently to the bundle of nerves tied there.

Blushing with embarrassment, he glanced at the doctor. Paul was mortified to appear inadequate but Crump's eyes sparkled with humor.

"My apologies, Dr. Crump—" Interrupted, Paul was violently jerked to the side by the horse's movement. Beside itself with terror, the mare's cotton lead frayed threatening to snap. Paul opened his stance and held fast. "Hush now, whoa girl!" he barked, fearful she was too far gone to be calmed. Then, the horse sank onto her haunches tensing to break free from the rope. Paul prepared for the worst, but the doctor stepped close alongside him and placed his hands on the creature's withers. Paul's shoulder touching the doctor's, he watched helpless as the animal strained, the metal ring threatening to slip out of the wall.

"Hush now. Shhhh…" Softly, the doctor spoke over the scrabble of hooves. Within seconds, the mare grew calm. Her nostrils still flared, but her eyes were no longer white with fear. Her hooves ceased raking the floor and her cropped tail came to rest.

Paul turned to the doctor against him. Eyes closed with a peaceful expression, Crump had both hands on the horse's back, as if administering an invisible tranquilizer through his touch. Before a full minute passed, the mare quieted, blowing soft puffs of air from her velvety nose. With a sigh of relief, Paul wiped his sweaty brow.

"That was amazing. Can it be learned?" Paul asked, and the doctor stared into his face inches away without replying. Feeling odd under the scrutiny, Paul lowered his voice. "Will you show me how you did that?"

After another lengthy moment, Crump smiled, stepped back, and resumed a spectator's stance against the wall. "Young man," he said, his voice somewhat softer than earlier, "I will show you many wonderful things now that we are acquainted."

Paul nodded his thanks and turned to finish trimming the mare's hooves. The doctor remained quiet as Paul trimmed the queue, and when the last horse was done, the clock chimed the hour.

The outside world had grown dark, quiet, and cool, and Paul's stomach grumbled with hunger. Crump stepped toward him, seemed about to clap his shoulder, but changed his mind. Instead, he clasped his hands behind his back with a broad new smile.

"Come up to the house, Mr. Black. Let us see what there is for supper." Crump moved aside offering Paul a slight bow.

"Don't put yourself out. I can run home if you prefer." It would be a first to break bread with such a distinguished client and it was sure to be a hot topic among his friends later at the pub.

He gestured toward the house. "No trouble; I'm looking forward to it. Come." The doctor reached the back door and opened it wide for Paul to enter.

Inside, the doctor flicked a switch to fill the kitchen with electric light. Although clean and tidy, the various modern appliances appeared new and unused. Add to that, the house sported a quiet, empty feel, and there was no hint of a prepared dinner. Paul walked the length of the kitchen and stopped, unsure if he should continue into the next room.

"Your home is very nice," Paul said in an attempt to hide his growing unease. Crump didn't respond, but strode past, flipped a second switch and led him into a bright dining room.

"Have a seat and I'll see what is in the ice box."

Crump disappeared into the stark white kitchen and despite his misgivings, Paul chuckled. He smelled no supper because none had been cooked. Either the doctor was ill-prepared or his serving staff had quit. Paul pondered the absurdity of the events, and by the time he had settled into one of the twelve tall-backed chairs, Crump returned and placed before him a platter.

"Now, I had some wine…" His host rummaged through a wooden chest along the wall. "Ah-hah," he whispered, carrying a vintage Merlot to the table. With flourish, he filled a wineglass and stepped well back.

Paul thanked him trusting his disappointment didn't show on his face. On the hammered pewter platter, Crump had placed a thick slice of bread, a wedge of hoop cheese, and an apple. It was almost funny. Did Crump treat all of his guests so well? Paul sought to catch the doctor's eye to see if he played a prank, but his host only smiled back.

"Will this do? I don't keep much food about." He paused, then added with a grin, "Just enough to lure in my prey."

His last remark rattled Paul into a gasp and he dropped the apple.

He laughed. "Joking, my good man! Where is your sense of humor?"

Paul stumbled over his reply and retrieved the dropped fruit from the tray. He refrained from taking a bite; could the food be poisoned? Inside, alarms sounded and he placed his hands into his lap to quiet the shaking. More talk was needed and he cleared his throat.

"Do you live alone? Is there a Mrs. Crump?"

"No more meaningless chatter," the doctor said, waving his hand before his face. "I cannot bear it. I am interested in you, Paul Black.

Tell me about you." The doctor pulled out the chair adjacent to Paul and sat. He leaned in to rest his head on his hands and his bewitching gaze sought a connection. "I am very interested in *you.*"

Paul exhaled, wanting to please although he did not know why such a thing was so important. Instead of wracking his mind any longer, Paul began the tale, his entire life story—as short as it was to that point—and Crump listened, intent on every word. When Paul finished, he realized he had also finished his meal. Swallowing the rest of the wine, he looked expectantly to his host. Dr. Crump had not eaten at all.

"Come, Paul Black, the blacksmith. Join me in the study."

With a sideways grin, Paul rose to follow, his spirit calm and his ears enjoying the sound of his name on the doctor's lips. Had the wine done this? Perhaps the food *was* poisoned and that was why his head swam. Paul's vision blurred and he stumbled once halfway to the next room. Crump grasped his elbow, preventing him from falling, and walked against him the rest of the way. In the doctor's opposite hand he carried Paul's wine glass and Paul eyed it as they entered the study.

The wide doorway had emptied them into a dark wood-stained room with the walls, desk, and shelves all the deepest brown. A massive upholstered chair rest in the far corner and Paul headed for it. The doctor released his arm and he swiveled to drop his weight and smile up at his host. Crump's brow lifted in amusement and he crossed to the desk to pour a new dark liquid into the empty glass.

"I have a proposal for you, young man," the doctor said and Paul watched his movement, so lithe, athletic—watching in a way he hadn't noticed before. "This is my special vintage, a red merlot combined with the richest and rarest grape."

"Grape," Paul said under his breath and the doctor chuckled and lit an oil lamp on the desk. Facing Paul in the huge chair, Crump leaned his backside on the desk edge and regarded Paul with black eyes, the wine dangling in his elegant fingers.

"Paul, I want you," he began and allowed a decided pause that brought a question to Paul's face. He completed his sentence with, "to work for me." The older man spoke with no condescension, nor humor in his dark gaze.

Paul huffed. He already had a job; a lucrative career with no end in sight. What could he do for a country doctor? "I don't understand," Paul stammered. "Work for you as what? In what capacity?"

"You will be my manservant. I have been looking for many years. I will pay your way for the rest of your life. You will never know want or need; anything you ask will be provided. All I require is your devoted service."

Flabbergasted, Paul licked his lips, his fuzzy head clearing. He enjoyed his work, his fame among the community, his independence. He had no desire to perform menial tasks and enjoy servitude.

With his jaw taut and his mind racing he narrowed his eyes. He wanted Crump to like him, to want him around, but… Was that it? There were men who preferred the company of gentlemen to women; was this the doctor's agenda? Paul gathered his nerve, he needed to leave. Then, without intention, his mouth smiled and he nodded, yes…

Paul's inner focus snapped to the present and he sought Hope's face, searching for understanding and empathy. He found both and she had listened at rapt attention.

"From that night," Paul said with a shrug, "I have been Mark's right-hand-man." He lifted a decorative ashtray, fondling it as he finished the story in his mind. The details remained vague, but there had been unpleasantness that night. Hindsight told him what he knew in his heart; that evening, he voluntarily gave Mark his blood. Paul also didn't tell Hope after that dinner date, he stopped aging. She would find out soon enough. She asked a new question about the library and his smile returned. She was pleasant. Maybe this would be easier than he had thought.

Nineteen

Contend, O LORD, with those who contend with me;
Fight against those who fight against me.
Psalm 35:1

IN CARL J. ODOM'S BEDROOM, MARK PARTED THE BLINDS
and opened the well-greased apartment window. Turning his head to
the opposite wall, he sent a telepathic suggestion to the frightened girl.
"Daddy's hurt; call 911." Then, as an afterthought, he added, *"Do not go
into daddy's room."*

Mark listened as the child tiptoed to the front of the house and
dialed three familiar tones on a landline. *Good.* It was time for him to
go. Carl's body dropped to the asphalt below, witnessed by no one.
Mark backed into the shadows and mentally visualized his bedroom in
Foxwood Estates. When he reopened his eyes, he was home. Police?
Just let them track that escape route... Mark chuckled and headed to the
master bath for a quick shower before he joined his date.

"Paul Black, the blacksmith..." Mark overheard Paul say downstairs
and he grinned with the memory. It had certainly been an evening to
remember. As he showered and dressed, Mark re-lived the event Paul
described, his mind filling in what Paul rightly left out.

Mark had to have Paul close from the moment he first saw him. In
the pub, he watched the lad from a corner table and studied his every
move. The boy laughed, drank, played cards, and danced in the glow of
the fire roaring from the stone hearth. Mark had come to vicariously
enjoy the robust humanity of the place when he spotted the fair-haired
youth. Within moments, he sensed the young blacksmith was meant for
him and Mark mustered his willpower, biding his time until he could
privately make his approach.

Days later, he arranged through a mutual acquaintance for Paul to
tend to his horses' care. He would have liked to have converted Paul

88

the night they met at his barn and it pained him to wait. But at that time, there had been an evildoer in the next town Mark needed to judge, and there had been the bother of a local man who had become too entranced with Mark's doings. So biding his time, Mark judged the murderous sinner, and over the course of a few days, rid himself of the pestering busybody tailing him. The next two weeks were as an eternity, but he forced himself to wait.

When the evening finally arrived, Mark waited for the young blacksmith to come around the corner into the barn. Up close, the young man looked even more just a boy, his wide eyes as blue as the sky with an innocence Mark wished he himself possessed. The man had been startled to see him waiting, but was polite and got to work, making intelligent conversation amid his efforts with the horses' hooves. The skill with which he handled the horses, the deft way he swung the hammer, even the sweat that fell from his brow mesmerized Mark fully. He had never paid so much attention to any one mortal. This one was different; this one was *chosen*.

There had been a close call when they stood shoulder to shoulder and Mark calmed the beast under their hands. When Paul thanked him and met his eye mere inches away, it took every iota of Mark's self-control to not attack the man that moment. He wanted his blood, and not gently. The uncharacteristic desire to injure a person not being judged surprised him into controlling himself and the tense moment passed.

When Paul was in the house, Mark was ecstatic to have him alone. He didn't care that Paul was afraid for this was expected; his life would be forever changed. The Other said it could be done, and instructed Mark on how to accomplish the task. And Mark *wanted* to believe it; he'd lived his strange and lonely existence for two hundred years and found himself desperate for companionship. When he brought Paul into the study, his entire body hummed with joy. Since he'd never tried such an experiment, Mark didn't know exactly what to expect. When Paul consented, Mark clapped him on the back.

"There is one more thing..."

In a single motion, Mark sliced his own palm cross-wise with his thumbnail and a dark line of blood welled. He caught the first drop in the wineglass and let it run to the count of five.

Ignoring Paul's horrified expression, he handed over the glass saying, "Drink my blood and you will live to serve me forever."

The wine and blood mixed perfectly, and as Mark's gentle hypnosis took hold, Paul did as he was ordered. Mark watched him drink and held his emotions in check. His thirst was terrible, but he resisted. In all his years, he'd restricted bloodletting to the guilty. Still, Mark rationalized as the seconds passed, a little blood loss wouldn't hurt him. While his patient was submissive, Mark loosened Paul's collar to reveal his sun-burnished throat. Then, as if commanded to do so, Paul removed his shirt.

Well, that was easy, Mark mused and moved to stand beside his new partner seated on the chair. He touched Paul's skin with his fingers and before he realized what had happened, he was there, fastened like a beast on the youth's thin shoulder. Paul cried out and after three vicious and delectable pulls, Mark withdrew. The boy's pulse was strong, no worse for wear. Mark's blood had already begun its work in the blacksmith's gut and the hasty throat wound healed before his eyes. As The Other indicated, Paul Black would have none of Mark's bloodlust, but would live forever to serve his needs. The experiment was a success.

Lifting Paul into his arms, Mark took him to a spare room to recover. When the smithy awoke, twenty-four hours had passed and he was a new man.

Literally.

wenty

"...Let us eat and drink," you say, "for tomorrow, we die!"
Isaiah 22:13

FRESHLY SHOWERED, MARK STRODE INTO THE LIBRARY and sent his date an enigmatic smile. Paul and Hope both stood, and he motioned for them to sit. The sight of Hope made his old heart young again. Dressed in a denim and rose ensemble, she appeared vulnerable and feminine. And although her clothes were modest, the scooped collar on her lacy top revealed her beautiful neck. Mark marveled at how so much interest could be piqued by so little flesh. Breaking up his thoughts, Paul stepped close and grasped his fingers to shake.

"You were right about Ms. Brannen; she's the loveliest woman I have ever seen."

"I never lie." Mark crossed to Hope's position and sat down beside her. The generous back cushion enveloped him as he exhaled. "I could get used to coming home to these beautiful faces." Mark relished the moment for a few seconds before turning his attention to Hope. "I have so much to share, but first, the both of you are hungry. Let's see what Paul has made for supper."

"Let's hope it's more than you served him that first night," Hope joked.

Paul shot Mark a worried glance, but he wasn't offended. "You're safe there. Paul is a much better cook than I have ever been."

"Right this way," Paul said and motioned for the exit.

ୠ

Hope took Mark's arm and he escorted her down a wide hallway to the dining room. Mark absolutely glowed this evening; quite different from the brooding and serious lover she had seen the night before. His cheeks were rosy and his eyes sparkled with humor. She subconsciously

91

admired the way his turquoise turtleneck arched across his chest and down his muscular arms. When she caught herself thinking of him that way, she blushed, certain he could read her mind, or at least her expression by the way his mouth turned up at one end. Hope took her seat at the elegant table and Mark took her hand in his.

"I think Paul is in love with you," he whispered and prepared to toast with his water glass. "To us."

Hope clinked her glass, but said nothing. The little doubter in her mind tapping, and no matter how she tried to ignore them, her reservations remained. Her subconscious said, *stay alert, something's amiss*, but Hope wanted to trust Mark more than ever. She was tired of taking the predictable path and oh, how she wished something new would come her way. And here was something new, in the flesh.

And what glorious flesh, at that.

Hope smiled sheepishly at Mark, because once more, a knowing smile touched his lips. If he read her thoughts, how cool was that?

Paul clambered in through the swinging doors carrying a large tray. "Your entrée, madam."

He placed before her a large platter of vegetables and a similar one on his embroidered placemat. Hope inhaled with surprise. Paul prepared for her an elaborate salad with several varieties of lettuce, baby spinach, carrots, mushrooms, olives, nuts, and mandarin oranges. Her eyes filled with moisture and she scolded herself. How was she going to hold a serious tone with Mark later if she couldn't accept a salad without crying? Hope swallowed her tears and waited for Mark to be served. It took her a few seconds to realize he wouldn't be. Paul salted his salad and Hope put her fork in to have a bite, but what about Mark? She remembered his excuse at the park regarding his food allergies, but did he not eat at all?

ભ્ઠ

"As I have mentioned, my diet is highly specialized." Mark caught her eye and responded to her unasked question choosing his words. The dinner table was no place to discuss the important business at hand. "Don't worry for me, Hope. I've already dined." Paul shot him a knowing glance he ignored. "I hope it doesn't make you uncomfortable. Think of it as one of my many eccentricities."

"Oh, I'm just sorry for you. The world is full of such wonderful foods; the pleasure of eating is a terrible thing to go without."

"To the contrary, my dear, I am allowed the pleasure." Mark didn't want to read any educated glances from Paul or explain his eating habits. He sighed and lifted his eyes. "I just can't eat this."

Hope ceased her line of questioning and nibbled at her meal. The conversation turned to horses and the subject of Mark's diet was effectively closed.

When dinner concluded and the trio rose from the table, Mark turned to Paul and asked him to take Hope to the library. Once she was settled, he pulled Paul aside and spoke into his ear.

"I'll return shortly. Reuben's in the garage awaiting my presence. Remind me to talk to you about him later." Paul sent him a grave nod, aware Mark took to heart his favorite's issue with the increasingly recalcitrant driver. With one more glance at Hope in the library appearing more a teenager on the oversized couch, Mark turned away and left Paul to hold his place.

⊰⊱

Mark entered the garage and found Reuben in the office. His driver stewed over his situation and contemplated revenge. How could Mark keep him around?

What do I do with him?

"You must destroy him," The Other offered then, deep in Mark's mind. Pretending he'd heard nothing, Mark opened the office door.

Inside, Reuben reclined in a chair, feet on the tidy desktop. He did not look up when his boss entered, but continued to stare at his hands and mumble curses. The boy willed an altercation and Mark refused to be pulled in. He leaned against the doorframe and waited to be acknowledged. After a minute, Reuben did so with one word.

"Boss."

Mark clinched his fists at his side. Why was the kid so insolent? Was it the liquor? Reuben purposefully drank himself into a stupor nearly every night. Mark took a breath and kept his tone even.

"It isn't appropriate for you to misbehave around your new mistress." His disregard for Paul was bad enough, but since Hope had been injured by Reuben's behavior, Mark found himself doubly incensed. "Is this going to be a problem?"

Reuben shrugged and Mark tightened his jaw. Reuben barely survived his last correction. When the boy was seventeen, months before his conversion, he grew impossible to control. Mark came down on him hard in an attempt to terrify him into obedience. Beginning with starvation and isolation, Mark was eventually compelled to beat him

93

within an inch of his life before he would bow to his master. When even that didn't work to his satisfaction, Mark had grabbed him off the floor—bloody and swearing—and taken his blood directly from his throat. It had been a cruel and messy night, but finally young Reuben cried uncle. When the dust settled, the boy needed a cast, several stitches, and a week in bed to recover. It was a lesson he never forgot. Until now, that is.

"Look, Boss," Reuben slurred, his eyes at half-mast and staring off. "Your world is crashing down. You and Pretty Boy can't see it, but I can. These are the last days of your reign."

"Look at me." Mark's voice was stable, his fury barely bottled. *"Look at me."* The younger man blinked and met Mark's gaze. "Go home and sleep this off. I want you to think on this: I can't fire you. If this job doesn't work out, I have to *retire* you."

Mark was certain Reuben got his meaning. His driver pulled his feet off the desk with some effort and stood up.

"Maybe it's time for that," Reuben mumbled and turned away, headed for the garage exit.

Mark wanted so badly to lunge across the room, wrap his hands around Reuben's throat, and silence him forever. It would take absolutely no effort to twist off his head. Why did he hold back? Was it because of Hope?

"Go. Now!" Mark snarled. "Paul will call you when you're needed."

"You're the boss." Reuben's sarcastic tone dripped with acid and he skulked out the door.

Mark exhaled. He would let the kid go for now; he knew where to find him. Reuben had fulfilled his purpose. For now, Hope was inside, and she would be a much better companion. As calm as he was going to get, Mark headed for the library.

ॐ

Hope felt sublime. Her stomach was full and even though they waited a half-hour for Mark, Paul was excellent company. Now and then, she would catch herself studying him. He looked out of place in the old-fashioned room. With his long legs crossed, angular and adolescent, he appeared more a kid than ever. She tried to imagine him a hundred years ago, completely oblivious to the fact his favorite client was about to turn his world upside down.

How exciting that must have been!

She shivered as she realized she was in the same exact position. What did it mean? What did Mark expect of her? To *serve* him? Her questions waited on the tip of her tongue and when Mark entered moments later, her pulse quickened.

"Okay," Mark said, taking a seat directly across from Hope. "Let's get this party started." He slapped his knees and leaned forward. "You ready?"

"Yes," Hope replied, nearly done gathering her thoughts. "I'm ready. I have some questions for you."

To her right, Paul raised an eyebrow and watched Mark for a reaction. Mark didn't seem to have heard; he still leaned over his knees, making no response. Silence filled the library. Was Paul holding his breath? Hope looked back and forth between the two men for a second and pressed on, strangely exhilarated.

"I didn't sleep a wink last night, going over and over what you told me at the Block's party. Now, understand, I believe you, but these are modern times, and I'm a modern girl. Just because I believe, may mean that I believe that *you* believe. Does that make sense?"

"I'm listening," Mark said in an odd voice. His smile disappeared and he leaned back as Paul made a noise in his throat with lowered eyes. Hope barreled on.

"I think of all the weird things that brought us together... My friend Anthony says there are no coincidences. Everything happens for a purpose, every situation has a higher meaning. Little things and big things alike. That's why I know we're *supposed* to be here tonight discussing this. Fran just happened to work for you? I just happened to meet you at this point in my life when I'm pondering why my husband died so young and wondering if I'd ever have any feelings for another man again?" Hope could name a thousand such facts, but maybe Mark got the idea. "I grew up with an open mind. My generation believes in aliens, ESP, magic, miracles. Just about anything is possible; monsters, werewolves, vampires..."

With her last word, Paul looked to Mark and paled. When she noticed, Hope wondered at his reaction. Was he afraid?

"Well?" Hope pressed him to respond. Mark looked ready to answer so Hope pressed her lips together and waited.

Twenty-One

Let us discern for ourselves what is right;
Let us learn together what is good.
Job 34:4

"YOU WANT TO KNOW IF I'M A VAMPIRE?" MARK ASKED, indignant. "Of all the idiotic…" He stopped himself. "You have questions. What if I don't have the answers?"

"She's handling this pretty well," Paul offered telepathically, but Mark sent him a glare. His friend was right, but the truth brought no comfort.

"I can handle it from here." Mark made a shooing gesture to Paul who nodded and stood to leave.

"Like that," Hope interjected. "What was that?"

Mark dismissed her query. "Paul has things to do. Proceed with your questions."

Paul excused himself to the kitchen and Mark watched Hope follow him out with her eyes. Her mind was a jumble, but she was calm and she didn't fear him. Still, how far would they go with their current experiment? Was he going to tell her things he'd never spoken of before? Mark loathed admitting it, but he was at her mercy. Maybe she would be kind.

"What won't you tell me?" she asked in another moment, her expression of a virgin studying a unicorn.

"Paul and I share a telepathic link," Mark said at last. "What else would you like to know?"

"Well, for one, can you read all minds or just some of them?"

"I do not read minds. I hear thoughts and see images; there's a difference." Mark sagged into his chair not yet particularly threatened.

"Oh, okay," Hope sighed. "I have so many questions. Let's start with Paul. He told me you met in 1915. I mean, look at him. He doesn't look a hundred years old. What did he leave out?"

"You want the gory details?" Mark was prepared to speak plainly and he relished the thought of her response. Would she recoil in horror

96

or be fascinated? If God sent her, she'd understand.

"Just be straightforward. I can handle it."

"If you continue down this path, you will be at her mercy. Destroy her now!"

Mark placed a finger to his temple and considered the words of The Other. He had abandoned his first plan early on, which was to subdue her first and explain himself later.

"Why is this so important?" he asked. "These minute details?"

"Because you want to get close to me, and I assume you'd like me to get close to you. Isn't that what you mean by getting me to join you?" Hope's face softened. "I'm not a wide-eyed innocent like Paul was, so you should be open with me. I mean, you said you're doing this for God. Maybe He wants you to be more introspective."

"Introspective?" Mark asked and a nagging worry tugged his mind.

"Well, sure, I mean, four hundred years is a long time to be doing things the way you think they should be done."

Hope's tone was neutral, but Mark bristled at her assertion.

"This is not the way I *think* things should be done," Mark said through clenched teeth, an odd claustrophobia clouding his psyche. "I've been called to this, I didn't choose it."

At least, I don't think I did…

For a moment, Mark thought back, before Reuben, before Paul, before he came to America. How did he begin his quest? Hope was right. He had never retraced his steps; in fact, he'd never wanted to.

"Look, Mark, I'm not your enemy. You think I'm the one you prayed for. If I am, then talk to me. You act like I'm supposed to go along with whatever you're talking about without reservation. Well…" Hope folded her arms resolute, but with compassion in her gaze. "I have reservations."

"Hope Brannen, you think I have to ask?" Mark spoke the hateful words in an undertone and instantly regretted it. He would never force Hope to do anything against her will. Unlike the rest of the mortals that peopled the planet, she was unique and precious. But the damage was done.

Hope glared and leaned back, ready with a reply. "No, I had hoped…" Her voice cracked and Mark watched her suppress her tears. "I *hoped* you wanted me to know you better."

She looked away and stood. Mark thought she was about to leave the room, but she didn't. With her back to him, she continued her thought.

"Mark, all I want in the world is to be with you. It's weird and it's scary, but I can't change the way I'm feeling. I have opened myself up to this despite how badly part of me screams to run away as fast as I can. Why won't you trust me half as much and lower your guard?" Hope waited a beat and then tried one more tactic in a near whisper. "All I asked you was to tell me about how you met Paul. Are you too afraid of your past to even try?"

Mark considered her words. Was he *afraid* of his past? He avoided traveling memory lane, but he wasn't *afraid*.

"You are terrified because you are a monster in priest's clothing."

The unmistakable voice of The Other. That voice was a major part of his past. If he traveled down this road, he would have to let that voice speak. The Other had his own answers and Mark delighted in none of them. But... Hope was a prize worthy of the struggle. Decided, Mark would play it her way and see where it led.

"You're right about a lot of this and I have never spoken of the past with anyone. Not even Paul. There is much pain there and a lot of death. Steel yourself."

Hope's eyes were moist, but she returned to her position across from him on the couch. "I'm ready."

"So, your question is, when I invited Paul over for dinner that night, what were my intentions?"

"Yes," she whispered.

"Okay." Mark relaxed back, put both hands behind his head and laced his fingers in his short black hair. "I wanted Paul from the moment I laid eyes on him, and I had to have him, body and soul." Her eyebrows went up, and he added with a tight smile, "I don't mean sexually, my dear. I am not a man; my nature doesn't permit that expression."

When he paused to gather the next thought, Hope leaned closer and clasped her hands in her lap. Her eyes were huge, but she still wasn't afraid. Mark continued.

"I wanted him emotionally, spiritually—*totally*. I had prayed incessantly for him for years and then one day, there he was." Mark grinned as he noticed Paul tuning in. "I thought of nothing else day and night for the two weeks I waited. I blew off patients and avoided taking house calls. I fantasized about what I would do when he finally came to me. I'd been alone for over two hundred years." Mark stretched out his legs, becoming more comfortable with the telling, as if setting down a heavy weight he had carried for decades. "The task was simple; I had to get Paul to drink my blood. This was the alchemy required to keep him with me forever without affecting his, how do you say, humanity."

"Drink your blood? Your blood is what has kept him alive so long?"

Mark nodded.

"Like a vampire?"

"No," Mark cleared his throat, hating her choice of words even though he was aware of his kinship with the famous fable. "I mixed my blood with the wine and he drank it. Very neat. Very clean."

"Did you just cut your finger?" Hope obviously wanted more detail and Mark sat up to lean closer.

"No, my hand…" Taking his left thumbnail, Mark drew it down the lifeline of his opposite palm. A line of dark red fluid welled and seeped from his partially closed fist. The blood dripped onto the carpet between his feet for several seconds. "Then, I closed my fist."

Mark regarded her as he reopened his hand, the laceration knitting before her eyes. In a smooth movement, he licked his hand clean and she gasped. She had spoken of monsters and vampires; now that she had seen an actual demonstration, Mark would see what she was made of.

❧

Hope's throat constricted at the sight of Mark's blood, and when his palm healed, and he ran his tongue to the blood, her head swam. Across from her, Mark softened his voice.

"This is what you wanted, no? You wanted to know everything."

Hope swallowed and searched for the right words. Her new flame was a real-life vampire. She could no longer pretend he was a handsome but deluded megalomaniac.

Light-headed, Hope pointed to the carpet. "That stain will never come out," she mumbled, not intending to be funny, but Mark tossed back his head and laughed. A sense of relief washed over her and she assumed a half-smile. Then, they quieted and stared at the stain.

Mark placed his foot over the discoloration and said continuing, "Thus, Paul drank my blood mixed in the Merlot. He has never regretted it."

"I can see that Paul's happy. He worships you."

Mark inclined his head toward the door. "Paul is my ever-dependable rock. I know you will be the same."

Hope swallowed, again wondering what Mark expected. *The details.* She steeled her nerve and tried to appear relaxed.

"What were your intentions regarding me tonight? Did you expect me to come along as easily as Paul?"

"Frankly, yes," he answered with a nod. "I assumed it would go very much the same."

Hope studied her fingernails. How should she respond to that? She didn't want to drink Mark's blood. It was inconceivable that he could imagine her accepting his plan. Still, she *was* intrigued. Who in the world wouldn't want to get inside the mind of the most unique creature on the planet? Out of simple curiosity, Hope had to ask the next logical question.

"What if I hadn't been so inquisitive? What if I had jumped on board, no questions asked?" She lowered her voice. "How would you get me to drink your blood?"

Mark rose from his chair and fell into the sofa inches from her side. Resisting the urge to pull back, Hope watched as he turned to face her and placed two fingers on her knee.

"Hope," he whispered, matching her tone, "the procedure that worked for Paul wouldn't do for you. See, you are to be *transformed*. You are to be my equal. Do you understand?"

He wants to turn me into a vampire! Hope's hand flew to her throat. In her wildest dreams, she never would have thought the man she would fall so hard for wouldn't even be human.

"If...if..." Hope said, her breathing rapid, but her voice calm. "...if you're a vampire, that explains a lot." Hope let the realization of the truth sink in a little more before continuing. "I never imagined vampires were real."

Mark shook his head. "I consume the blood of evildoers, yet I am *not* a vampire. 'Vampire' is a word created by men to explain something they feared. A *fictional* something at that. I have a higher purpose. I don't hide in the shadows and kill the innocent. I fear God and perform His will. I am not a monster."

Hope fell quiet, going over his last admission. She was about as far away from knowing God as she could be, but there was something backward about Mark's claim. Could a person drink blood *and* serve God? Even to her ignorant ears, the two had to be on opposite ends of the spectrum. What would Anthony think of all this hocus-pocus?

Hope took a deep breath. "Tell me what you have to do to transform me into your equal?" Semantics and theological arguments aside, she desperately wanted this final bit of information.

"Let me show you." Mark took her hand in his and turned it palm-side-up. With his forefinger, he traced her veins from wrist to the inside of her elbow. Hope's pulse quickened at his touch and she wondered if it was fear or exhilaration.

"Transfusion."

One word? There had to be more to it than that. Hope waited for the rest as his hand left her elbow and moved to rest on the back of her shoulder.

"I will drain your blood here, then I will transfuse you with my blood, here." He let his hand caress her skin on the way back to the inside of her elbow. "It will only take moments for the transformation to be complete. Paul ingested my blood. To be transformed, you would have to absorb it directly into your bloodstream."

No matter how electric his touch, Hope could not picture what he was describing. *"Are you saying,"* she was barely audible, but she knew Mark could hear her, *"that you have to drink my blood?"*

Mark was still close with his hands holding hers gently. His reply was just as quiet and it made Hope shiver.

"I don't have to, but I would want to." Mark's eyes were on her and she didn't look up. After a moment, he briefly stroked her cheek and Hope's heart raced. "Are you going to be okay, Hope, dear? Did I answer your questions well enough?"

Hope held her tongue. The image of Mark latched onto her throat like Bela Legosi or Frank Langella made her queasy. *Funny, it's not so sexy now that MY neck is on the line,* she thought and Mark huffed, as if he'd overheard her thoughts. Hope's mind numbed and finally she answered in a small voice. "I'm freaking out." Sitting up straighter in her seat, Hope freed one of her hands and rubbed her neck. "Back to the vampire thing. You're not a vampire, but you drink blood."

Mark nodded.

"What makes you *not* a vampire?"

"You've read stories, right? Seen the enchanting films?"

"Sure."

Mark held his hands up in front of him, palms out, and Hope understood. He wanted her to try out the old legends on him.

"Okay. Vampire laws. Sunlight. Obviously not a problem."

"My eyes are sensitive, but I am in no way handicapped by the sun."

"And crosses, also not a problem."

Mark nodded. "Correct."

"Garlic? Are you repelled by garlic?"

"No, another silly superstition. And I don't sleep in a coffin or turn into a bat." He chuckled as he brought up the last two examples.

Hope smiled, trying to remember more vampire attributes. Hope didn't mean to be disappointed, but the longer they went on, the less supernatural Mark appeared to be. She sighed. "You sleep in a bed like everyone else?"

"I sleep in a bed when possible, but not like everyone else. I sleep very little. About every thirty days, I will settle down for a really deep rest. That's all I require."

"So, you're awake all that time? Don't you get bored?"

Mark smiled at her as if she were a small child. "You have not yet grasped my true nature. You can't put yourself in my shoes because they don't fit you. *I am never bored.* I delight in many things and I am always occupied."

"You're right. I can't even imagine what it's like to be you." Hope couldn't think of any other response and silence filled the room. Finally, she had an idea of where to take the conversation. "I know this is morbid, but can you die? I mean, how about a stake through the heart? Would that do you in?"

"No, a mere distraction is all that would be." Mark shook his head and kissed the top of Hope's fingers. "I've taken a stake to the heart. It's messy, but not deadly."

Staring at her own hand, Hope asked the next thing that came to mind. "Who staked you? A vampire hunter?"

"No," Mark chuckled more forcefully as if the thought of being hunted amused him. "I've never been chased by vampire killers. I was caught in a tornado and was impaled by debris. I pulled it out and dove for cover. No drama."

Hope sighed. "You're right. You don't seem to be much of a vampire."

"I never consider myself as such," Mark replied, with a sideways smile. Hope took her hand from Mark and fussed with her hair. When she continued, she clasped her hands in her lap.

"How're you *like* a vampire, aside from the...blood?" Hope gulped the last word, the conversation souring her stomach.

"Yes, that might be easier. Let's see," Mark said with ease, "Stoker's Dracula had the strength of twenty men. I haven't measured my strength, but it is many times that."

Hope huffed. The way he replied... *He's telling the truth.*

"And don't forget immortality. I haven't aged since I began my

102

calling in the 1600s."

"Geesh!" Hope hadn't done the math, but hearing it that way dazed her all over again. "I can't imagine living all those years, watching history unfold. It's mind boggling!"

"I imagine it is," he said with a small nod.

Paul appeared in the door and they both looked over.

"Can I get you anything, Hope? More Coke?"

She shook her head.

"I'll call you when Hope is ready to go home." Mark returned his attention to Hope and dismissed Paul with a backward wave of his hand.

Hope pitied the guy, but he retreated with a neutral expression. She caught Mark's eye. "What about Paul? What is he to you? You call him your assistant, but you treat him like a servant."

"He *is* my servant," Mark replied without emotion,

"Just like that?" Hope's skin prickled. "He worships you. How can you treat him so coldly?"

"Coldly? I adore him. He's the son I never had, my closest friend and confidant. Still, I must maintain my status." Mark lowered his voice. "I'm his master. It's incomprehensible to your generation, but it's all he knows. I created him and he serves me. As does Reuben."

Hope had two questions, one about his servants and also herself. Did Mark expect her to call him master?

"Okay, here's my next question," she said once she'd worked up the courage. "Do you think it's appropriate for Paul to worship you? What does God think about that?"

Hope waited several seconds and realized for the first time in the conversation, the great Mark Corescu had finally been stumped.

ᑕᗷᔕᗝ

It was Mark's turn to ponder.

No man can serve two masters.

The phrase struck a chord of familiarity deep in his memory. He'd heard it in a distant life, who or what or when was veiled by the shadow of time, but it made him uncomfortable. He cleared his throat.

"This is how it has always been and it's not a bad life for either of them. Through me, they have eternal life, all the material things they need, and my constant protection." Mark stopped short. There was no avoiding it. Hope was about to accuse him of a messianic delusion. No matter when spoken aloud, that was exactly how it sounded.

103

Twenty-Two

*Let all who live in the land tremble, for the Day of the Lord is
coming. It is close at hand—*
Joel 2:1

HOPE APPRECIATED THE PRONOUNCED HUSH IN THE
library as she rehashed everything she had heard so far. Her eyes dim
with fatigue and her head dizzy with the strangest information she had
ever heard, she couldn't help but wonder at the bigger meaning. Why
was she here? Could God possibly approve of all of the vampire stuff?
Mark sighed just then and Hope avoided his searching gaze. Was she
supposed to ask him to make her a—a—call it whatever he wanted.
Was he going to make her into a vampire?

"It's late. Let Paul run you home," Mark said, his voice sad.

"I wish I wasn't so exhausted, I need to know about the rest. I
need to know about the Judging and how this all fits together." Hope
met his gaze and her resolve melted. She would stay with him no matter
what he turned out to be. She was hooked. "You're right about one
thing; you're not a movie vampire. You're real and what you're doing is
real. I'm amazed, but I'm also kind of afraid." Hope shrugged. "That's
the truth."

Mark stood and helped her to her feet. "You have nothing to fear
from me and we have all the time in the world. Eternity, if you want it.
Come, Paul has brought the car around."

Hope allowed him to lead her by the elbow to the door. Once
there, she turned to face him. "You didn't say if there were more, uh,
like you out there in the world."

Mark paused, one hand on her arm, the other on the doorknob.
Hope watched his gaze soften as he regarded her question. She had the
distinct impression he might not know the answer, but then, he smiled,
winked her way and pulled open the front door.

"No, I'm one of a kind. That makes you a lucky girl, doesn't it?"

104

Hope gave him a demure smile, grateful the planet wasn't crawling with vampires, at least as far as Mark was admitting. When she met his eyes again, they were moist and his vulnerability surprised her. Without thinking, she tiptoed up to kiss his cheek. A melancholy smile reached his lips.

"You will come back tomorrow?"

"No, I'll have my plate full on Sunday." Hope had already decided before the night began that she would distance herself from him for one full day to work things out in her mind. Now that she knew more of the truth, she was very thankful she had rehearsed such a response. "Call me Monday."

"I will. Be careful and I will see you then. Hope, you could stay..." Mark whispered as he tried once more to sway his date.

Hope pretended she didn't hear and stepped into the crisp night air. On the driveway, Paul stood waiting to help her into the back. Before she could turn, Mark pulled her head to his mouth and kissed her hair. Hope turned in his arms and escaped to the car. Paul had the back door open, but Hope motioned for the front. He let her in the passenger side and waved to Mark on the porch.

ଓଥେ

Driving from the neighborhood Paul frowned. He had experienced an odd pain in his heart when Mark kissed Hope goodbye. Why did it matter if he added her in? *Is there not love enough in his heart for the both of us?*

Even as the internal question arose, a twinge of the now-familiar headache returned with stealth. Paul wished Hope would tell him something about her discussion with Mark, but he wasn't going to be the first to bring it up. Telepathically, he heard very little, which made him wonder if Mark was blocking him out for their deepest conversations. He also didn't want Hope to think he was meddling, so tried a simpler tact.

"Are you coming over tomorrow? I'll make dinner."

"No, I can't." She stared at the colored dash lights, lost in her thoughts. "Dinner tonight was wonderful. Thank you, again."

"So you had a nice evening?" Paul pried, convinced Mark held nothing back tonight. Finally, as her street appeared in the distance, she spoke again on the subject, albeit subdued.

"Mark told me he was on a mission from God," Hope chuckled

105

without humor. "He also told me he drinks blood—but he's not a vampire." She met his eye when he glanced her way. "It's going to be okay, right? I mean, you're okay. You seem normal. You seem fine..."

"Of course."

"Good," Hope said with finality. She picked her small handbag off the floorboard as they turned into her driveway. "All that matters to me right now is that I'm crazy about Mark. We were meant to be together. I don't mind taking some time to sort this stuff out."

Paul nodded. The woman had pluck. Now he only hoped she did everything Mark required. It was not wise to disrupt his world.

⚭

"Yellow and blue make green! Leave a message and I'll call you back!"

Glorie hung up, determining her two previous messages should be sufficient. Wherever her sister was, she would hear them soon enough. Besides, if she had to listen to that ridiculous message one more time she was going to puke. It originated with Hope's late husband. Every time Glorie would call, the silly dolt would answer the phone with the same idiotic line. Glorie was glad he was gone.

Her plane would arrive in Atlanta at noon and Hope would pick her up at the airport. Briefly, she wondered if it would interfere with her date with Mr. Wonderful. Glorie chuckled and hoped it would. What's more important? Your twin sister or guy who would most likely dump you as soon as he got what he wanted? Hope would come get her. It was in her twin's nature to serve, just as it was Glorie's nature to delegate work to others.

Glorie headed to her bedroom to finish packing. It was going to be an awesome week.

Twenty-Three

If you do what is right, will you not be accepted?
Genesis 4:7

IN THE SHERATON LOUNGE, CONNIE PROPPED HIS feet on the seat of the chair across from him and took a swig of his Bud. He felt magnificent; it had been a successful and satisfying evening. With very little coaxing, Maggie turned the keys of her PC power over and he dug up everything he needed. The floor was practically deserted at that late hour, and not a soul molested them as he plucked away on her keyboard. He jotted down three pages of notes before the love connection began, and those turned out to be more than enough.

Reuben Stuckey, at 3344 Sherwood Drive, Atlanta; employed by Dr. Mark Corescu of Whitford City Memorial Hospital. Race, Black; height, 6'0'; weight, 165lbs; eyes, brown; hair, black; D.O.B., December 25, 1966.

The guy had no priors, and his driver's license picture was very old, causing him to look like a kid in the low quality photocopy. But it had to be the missing child. Now all Connie had to do was run him down and expose the Senator as an imbecile.

At the same time, Connie would keep looking for the killer. He dug around in the other cases for similarities the officials of the time may have passed over. The twenty homicide victims with staged suicide attempts were from all walks of life, occupations, and social status. No common denominator on location, either, the crime scenes as random as the choice of victim. He did find a curious similarity in the cases within the coroner reports: unexplained blood loss. Many of the ME reports were incomplete, but seven made brief mentions of an unusual amount of blood unaccounted for at the crime scene or in the bodies. A rush of adrenaline buzzed Connie's mind. What was going on in 1970 that had the APD so distracted? He didn't have the interest or inclination to find out, but he was happy they missed what would be his claim to fame.

Connie sipped his beer and considered Stuckey's address; he could cruise by there and see what he could see. But it was Saturday night, the kid would be out. And Connie had to drink. He'd pick up the trail in the morning. No rush. Stuckey, if he turned out to be the man, had been "missing" for over thirty years. One more night shouldn't make much difference. Connie took another swig and settled in for a long comfortable binge.

⚬⚭⚬

Paul found Mark in the library on the same loveseat where Hope had been an hour earlier. When he entered, Mark didn't look up, but continued to stare across the room. Paul took a seat and leaned forward, resting his elbows on his knees.

"That was some evening, wasn't it?"

Mark didn't respond and Paul let the silence settle between them as he studied his master's profile. Mark's brow was furrowed, deep in thought, and Paul hated that he couldn't soothe whatever bothered him. Several minutes clicked by and Mark had still made no acknowledgement. Growing drowsy, Paul fought the urge to yawn, not fully recovered from his earlier blood loss. Finally, he did yawn and Mark looked his way.

"I know you're tired," Mark said, his voice even and soft. "You take good care of me, Paul."

Mark met his eye only the briefest second and then cast his gaze to the floor. Paul was instantly ashamed he had been thinking of sleep when Mark needed him most. It was no use to apologize, so he did the next best thing: offer help.

"My life for you, as you know." His sincere comment brought Mark's eyes up and Paul's heart broke to help him. "What can I do for you right now?"

A sad smile reached Mark's lips and he patted the seat next to him. Paul moved close and turned to look him in the face.

"Is there anything you need?" he asked, but Mark shook his head.

"Hope is entrancing, isn't she?"

Paul nodded; Mark was pining for the woman. It was okay, there was enough of him to go around. What Mark needed most at the moment was reassurance, and Paul said what he thought would help most. "She's crazy in love with you."

Mark grinned, looked away, and closed his eyes. He leaned his head back, chin up, and rested it on the back of the couch. "We're in for a big change."

Paul watched Mark's Adam's apple waver and he wondered at the extent of the emotion coursing through his partner. He turned a little more to his left and sat upon his leg. Cautiously he draped his arm across the back of the sofa behind Mark's head and shoulders. Mark made no response, only continued to think behind closed eyelids. The image of Mark's last embrace of the woman rose in Paul's memory and he was ashamed that it made him anxious. As usual, Mark was on top of his subconscious thoughts, and he languidly rolled his head to the side to meet Paul's gaze. Picking up Paul's right hand, Mark allowed his lips to brush against his skin for several long moments.

"No one will ever take your place, Paulie. Know this above all things." That said, he released Paul's hand and leaned back on the cushion, closing his eyes once more. "My sensitive son, I treasure you. When you add a new family member, you don't forget the ones you have already loved."

Paul nodded and resumed breathing. At the touch of Mark's kiss he hadn't let his breath escape. He deserved a rebuke for his doubt, but his master did not admonish him.

"It's going to be great." Paul wasn't entirely sure what changes to expect, besides the obvious, but he instinctively knew it had something to do with what the couple had discussed tonight when they were alone.

Mark lifted his head then and turned to Paul. "She's going to force me to discover my past." Before Paul could ask him to clarify, he added, "The beginning. *My beginning.*"

Paul nodded. He never questioned Mark about the past. In fact, he never questioned Mark about anything and his master never invited the intrusion. Now, a newcomer was going to dig up everything that had remained hidden over the years. Just then, he had a flash in his mind of Reuben in the garage. "You wanted me to remind you about Reuben?"

Mark's expression intensified. "Reuben's service has come to a close. I must terminate his services," Mark said in a low growl.

Paul had an intuitive account of what transpired between them earlier. He shook his head as Mark continued.

"He has become a risk to me, and therefore to you and Hope."

"Where is he now?" Paul asked quietly. It would be tricky to terminate the man. No corpse could ever be found else Mark would be implicated. There was paperwork all over town that stated Reuben

Stuckey was Dr. Corescu's driver. Plus, the man would be difficult to kill. Paul wasn't even sure how it could be done. The problem had never come up.

"Reuben must be decapitated and," Mark said, interrupting Paul's thoughts, "as for his location, right now he's trying to become intoxicated at his favorite bar." Mark closed his eyes again.

With his master so forlorn, a pang of grief touched Paul's heart. *If I could ease your suffering even the slightest bit, I would.*

Mark would sense his thoughts and Paul didn't hide them. He had no secrets from this man. They sat in a comfortable silence for a long time. Mark's thoughts were invariably on the woman, but Paul was now too worried about Reuben to be jealous. If Reuben was in the habit of getting drunk, surely he had spilled the beans to someone. Paul cleared his throat and touched Mark's sleeve.

"Has Reuben betrayed us?" Paul imagined Reuben stumbling into the police station to tout a wild tale of murder, mayhem, and blood. The cops would likely throw him in the drunk-tank, but there was always that one cop, that one young and eager detective that goes to investigate. Mark couldn't weather an investigation. They hadn't covered their tracks well enough to withstand scrutiny by the authorities. They never had to before now.

"No, not yet, but he knows I can't reach him when he's under the influence. He could spill it all and I wouldn't know until the police come knocking at my door."

The exasperation in Mark's voice was more than Paul could bear. He withdrew his arm from Mark's shoulders and cradled it in front of him, a crazy idea blossoming.

"We may need to skip town…" Mark's voice trailed off.

"Nonsense." Meant to encourage his friend, Paul chuckled. "We'll take care of Reuben tomorrow." Paul pulled his knife from his pocket as he spoke. His head was dizzy with exhaustion and his insane notion wasn't helping. He continued, "We'll hole him up in the basement while we figure it out."

Paul flipped open the knife, and with a gulp of air to steady his nerves, he punctured the inside of his arm. As he expected, there was no pain, only an irritating throb that instantly abated. Dark red blood welled and threatened to fall into his lap. He palmed the knife and cupped his left hand behind Mark's head bringing the gruesome offering to his master's parted lips. With his eyes still closed and with no hesitation, Mark fixed his mouth over the wound. Not a drop hit the sofa.

"Everything will be fine," Paul said as his master drank with huge pulls. He rested his head on Mark's shoulder and his eyes fell closed like shutters. He was finally going to get some sleep.

"My life for you, Mark."

Paul thought he heard horses galloping in the distance, but then it was only the pounding of his heart as it worked on a shortage of fuel. Yet he wasn't alarmed. Mark had always told him he was immortal. Why worry? His consciousness slipped away as if he hadn't a care in the world.

☙❧

After his third beer, Connie moseyed up to the bar to be closer to the source. The bartender acknowledged him with a nod and asked his order.

"Scotch. On the rocks." Two stools down, a fellow drinker drowned his sorrow in a whiskey glass. By the way he tossed them back, the kid was old hat at it, too. He looked much too young to be hitting the hard stuff, but Connie didn't care. It was a free country and folks could drink, smoke, and cheat themselves to death. It was their right as Americans. Connie propped his elbows on the bar and listened to the young man's conversation with the barman. His journalistic drive was strong and he had always been nosy.

"That'll do tonight, sir." The bartender removed the youngster's empty glass. Connie's brow lifted with surprise. The kid didn't look drunk; he sat straight on his stool, fully aware of his surroundings.

The young man tapped his empty coaster. "Set me up, Tommy. You know I can drink a whole lot more than that."

Connie got the distinct impression these two had a history and this scene played out often.

"You're over your tab and I'm not going to cross the line with your boss." Tommy twirled a hand towel and left the youngster to serve another customer.

"Hey, I got cash." With that, the younger man reached into his back pocket and accidentally flipped the contents onto the floor. A wallet fell beside Connie's stool and he instinctively retrieved it for the boy. It was an inside-out wallet, where the photo-ID sat in plain view on the cover and Connie almost lost it when he read the man's name: Reuben Stuckey, Sherwood Drive.

Well, of all the crazy coincidences!

111

Connie resumed a passable poker face and handed the wallet to the young man. Grabbing his whiskey, he moved toward him, leaving one stool between. He then flagged the bartender still ignoring Stuckey.

"Barkeep, we need another round. Me *and* the kid." Connie put a fifty-dollar bill on the counter. The youth tapped his coaster and mimicked Connie's gesture. Connie smiled warmly and considered his opening line. He wasn't prepared to meet his missing child at present and he didn't want to scare him away. The kid, Reuben, didn't seem to mind that a stranger bought him a round. He nodded his thanks and awaited his drink.

"And keep 'em coming until that money is spent!" Reuben instructed the bartender, who put the money in the register and set them up with identical drinks. Connie watched with interest as the man then turned and hit the bar phone.

"Looks like he's about to call your daddy, Reuben," Connie said, and hoped he didn't offend the kid before being introduced.

"Wuss," Reuben mumbled under his breath and turned to his benefactor. "Thanks for the drink, man. Do I know you?"

"Maybe," Connie said in a mysterious tone. Stuckey didn't take the bait, but rolled his eyes and took a long drink of his whiskey. After filling his cheeks and sloshing a few seconds, Reuben swallowed and shook his head. He caught Connie's eye, and lifted his glass.

"Let's drink 'em fast, mister. I have anywhere from zero to twenty minutes before a big, scary-looking dude waltzes in here and yanks me off my stool."

"Oh?" Connie waited to see if he was joking, but the kid was dead serious. "Bottoms up, then."

The boy finished his drink, a secretive smile on his face.

Connie loved the guy already; secrets were his best friend.

Twenty-Four

O Lord, You have searched me and You know me.
You know when I sit down and when I rise;
You perceive my thoughts from afar…
Psalm 139:1-2

TONY ROLLED OVER AND READ HIS CLOCK: 12:15 A.M. He had lain in bed for the better part of an hour and still wasn't drowsy. Sleep had a way of eluding him when under stress, and all week, he'd had a lot on his mind. As ideas and abstract thoughts paraded past his subconscious, Tony lost the battle and sat up to turn on the lamp.

"Okay, Lord, what can we talk about?"

Tony was in the habit of praying casually with God, and tonight maybe it was no accident he couldn't sleep. Maybe God kept him awake for a reason.

"I give my life to You. Do with me as You will…"

His own words to the Lord came back to him as he sat in the dim light. This week, he had promised his life to God all over again, and he had meant it. Was he going to be used for something new? Something important? Tony spoke into the still room in a low voice.

"Send me, Father. I will go for You," Tony said as peace filled his heart. Before too long, he heard these words in his subconscious.

"I have laid the foundations of the earth; all things are the works of My hands. You, My son, have loved righteousness and shunned evil all of your days. Your enemies will perish, they will be rolled up like a garment and tossed into the fire, but you, My son, will remain. You will trust your God and lean not on your own understanding."

A vision accompanied the voice and Tony did his best to discern its meaning.

A man, dressed in linen, rode toward him on a great white horse. Tony had dreamt of horses a lot lately and he had decided they were

113

related to his unrequited love for Hope. But now, an angel of the Lord rode upon one of the majestic beasts. Had God sent the other dreams to accompany this one? To prepare him for the current vision? The glorious angel approached and stopped just before him. In his vision, Tony approached the rider's left leg and looked up, eyes wide. The shining man pulled out an enormous pair of silver sheers and deftly cut off a large portion of the white stallion's lustrous mane.

"Take this," the angel said, though his lips did not move. *"Take and eat. This is your portion. This is your armor. Eat of it and step into your purpose."*

Tony reached out his hand and grasped the feathery hairs from the brilliantly-garbed man. Obediently, he stuffed the entire handful into his mouth. As soon as the fine strands hit his tongue, they became as sweet as honey and as warm as the evening wind. The sensation soothed him and he smiled with relief.

"What does it mean?" Tony asked in his heart.

"Watch that you are not deceived. Be encouraged and know that your God will protect you. On your journey, keep the word of God in your heart at all times. My Word shall be to you as blood and bread. My Word is living and active, sharper than any double-edged sword and nothing in all creation is hidden from My sight. Trust Me. Follow Me. Remember your First Love."

The vision faded and with his body completely limp, Tony called aloud to the Lord from his prone position on the bed. "Thank You, Father! I won't let You down! I will follow You!"

Rolling out of bed, Tony reached for the notepad he kept nearby and scribbled down all that he had seen and heard. When he was done, he read over it and praised God in his heart and with his mouth. Sleep came easily soon after.

❧

Mark rose to his feet and placed a pillow cushion under his partner's head. *I suppose you're getting your sleep now...*

Mark smiled, but he wasn't happy. Paul had never given blood two days in a row and there was no telling how long it would take him to recover. Was there a limit? Mark didn't know for sure; they never had a reason to experiment. For that matter, why did he accept the offer? He wasn't hungry. What made him take more than he needed? The word "monstrous" came to his mind and Mark growled. Did he no longer control the variables in his life?

Disconcerted, he glanced at his watch and sniffed at the time: 2 a.m. He thought of Hope. *She'd be fast asleep by now.* He ached for her.

114

Paul tried to fill the void the only way he knew how, but Mark's unnamed desire was not satisfied. His compulsion was not about blood, but about Hope, herself.

Wouldn't I feel the same without Paul? Mark glanced back to his servant-son who snored peacefully on the sofa. *I will have both of them.*

With that thought, Mark closed his eyes and concentrated on Hope's entryway, where he had stood and studied her photographic family tree two nights before. With a flash of light behind closed eyes, and a soft gush of air, he'd been transported via the strange and fantastic *Mobius Continuum,* as some theorists called it. Mark rode it like a subway, he always had. Even in the beginning.

Beginning? Who showed me how? I was born this way. I don't have a beginning. Oh, how Mark loved that voice of assurance.

But The Other always said its piece. *"You were made, not born. Remember that."*

Mark narrowed his eyes. What exactly was he doing? He believed God had sent Hope to join him in his work, but now? She hadn't jumped on board. Had he misunderstood God? Was that possible? Aborting the midnight visit, Mark opened his eyes back home and allowed his mind to rest. Before long, he dozed off in his favorite chair, his mind pondering eventualities.

The telephone's bell jarred Mark awake.

"Dr. Corescu," he barked, his voice resounding through the quiet room. Whoever called his house after 2 a.m. would have a grave purpose.

"Doc? It's Tommy. Your boy is past his limit and making friends."

Mark snapped fully awake. He ran a tab for Reuben at the Sheraton Lounge and the bar manager reported back whenever he discerned a reason. Tommy's next words chilled Mark's soul.

"This guy knew his name."

Mark had heard enough. He stood up, squelching a stab of paranoia. *What if it's the police? Reuben what have you done?*

"I'll be there in twenty minutes. Watch him until I get there." Mark hung up and grabbed the car keys. He tried to reach Reuben telepathically, but drew a blank. Zooming down the interstate at breakneck speed, he prayed his driver would hold his tongue.

☙❧

A second round was set before them when the bartender got off the phone. Connie grinned at Reuben and held up his glass. "Cheers."

"Back at ya," Reuben said and downed the whiskey in one gulp. He didn't gasp afterward and Connie marveled. He'd been sucking back hard liquor for decades and it still burned his throat going down. The kid was a real drinker, in every sense of the word.

"I say if a man can drink like that, nobody has the right to stop him!" Connie tried a new tact and so far, the young man didn't mind the intrusion. "Do you believe in destiny, Reuben?"

"Nope." Reuben finished off his shot and pounded the counter for another. When the third was delivered, he nursed it and turned to his bar companion. "How did you know my name?"

"I saw it on your ID, there. Weird thing is, I came all the way from Kentucky to find a guy named Reuben Stuckey; a missing child from 1971. How about that?"

The kid didn't seem startled, an encouraging sign. He simply raised an eyebrow and made the tiniest nod. Had Connie hit the mark? It was hard to tell, the expression read so many ways.

"So," Reuben said, his mouth curled into a half smile. "That kid would be like forty-something years old. How old do I look to you, Mr. Kentucky?"

"'Bout seventeen and drinking age is twenty-one, so I suck at the guessing game, eh?"

Reuben didn't reply. He faced forward and sipped his drink, his sly smile in place.

Connie tried again. "So you could be his…son?"

Reuben snickered and shook his head. The two of them sat in silence for another minute before either spoke. The clock was ticking. The kid said someone was coming to pick him up. Before he could formulate another question, Reuben had one for him.

"You a cop?"

"Hell, no!" Connie lowered his voice. "I'm a reporter. I'm out to expose a senator who happens to be the cop that lost the killer in the Clara Stuckey case all them years ago. That's what I do. I expose corruption and vindicate the oppressed." It sounded good coming out of his mouth and Connie watched for a reply.

"Clara Stuckey and a sinful senator. That's an exciting job you have there, Kentucky." Reuben's remark was laced with derision, but Connie hoped for a spark of curiosity to ignite as the kid finished off his drink

116

and looked to the exit.

Despite his baby face, Stuckey sounded like an odious old man, mean, hateful, and full of an old man's rage. Still, in the short time they had been talking, Connie was impressed. Reuben had poise and an actor's face. What if the kid *was* the story?

"What do you think? Do you know anything about this case that could help me catch the killer?" Connie waited as the kid again glanced at the door.

"I'm afraid I can't tell you anything about that case, Kentucky. My ride's here." The kid's previously arrogant demeanor wavered and he leaned in to Connie's left ear. "But if I was you," he cocked his head toward the door. "I'd follow the trail of *my* oppressor…"

Before Connie could respond, a man's hand patted Reuben's shoulder from behind and he stood to leave. While the stranger had a word with the bartender, Connie casually leaned back to consider the kid's parole officer. He was tall, professional, and quiet. He looked kind of foreign, but he wasn't *scary*. He wore a calf-length black coat with a high collar and a pale green button-down shirt with no tie. Just an ordinary guy. The man's behavior was more parental than anything and Connie watched with interest as the two made their way to the door. Reuben walked two steps in front of the man, head down, hands clasped together, resigned, like a teen about to be grounded for a month. Connie couldn't be certain, but Reuben may have tossed him a glance as he left. It was very discreet, but it was something. He pondered the last thing Reuben said before being taken away: *"follow my oppressor."* Was he referring to the man who came to get him? Connie took out another fifty and pushed it toward the bartender also watching the two exit.

"Hey." Connie waited for the man to pick the bill off the counter before he finished his question. "Who was that guy?"

The bartender folded the fifty and placed it in his pants pocket. He rubbed the counter where Reuben's glass had been and after a moment, he looked at Connie and smirked.

"His boss," he said. He removed Connie's glass from the counter and turned his back. "And we're closed."

The kid's boss was Dr. Mark Corescu. Connie stood and headed for the door to the lobby. If the kid fingered his boss, then things were really getting interesting. As he rode the elevator to his room, his mind buzzed with story angles and ideas. He would get some sleep and start first thing in the morning.

117

Tomorrow is Sunday! Connie cursed aloud and tried to think of places he could hunt for details that didn't close up on the Christian Sabbath.

"The Bible Belt," Connie mumbled with disgust. Refusing to be deterred, he made a new plan. He'd buzz by Reuben Stuckey's house tomorrow and request a more complete interview.

His new objective? Dr. Mark Corescu.

Twenty-Five

To the pure, all things are pure,
But to those who are corrupted and do not believe, nothing is pure.
In fact, both their minds and consciences are corrupted.
Titus 1:15

REUBEN HAD COME VOLUNTARILY, THANK GOD. OUTSIDE in the cool morning air, Mark took the kid by the arm stopping at the curb. The street was deserted and the sidewalk lit by a dozen street lamps. "Are you going to come quietly?"

Reuben nodded and looked out into the night. Mark pulled him gently to the Lexus and settled him in the passenger front. Once he was himself seated behind the wheel, Reuben broke the silence.

"I guess this is it." His words were barely audible. "What're you going to do?"

"I don't know." Mark didn't sense fear in the boy and he was no longer intoxicated. His body cleansed itself a hundred times faster than a normal man's and he'd been cut off by the bartender before he had a chance to get really wasted. Still, was any of it the kid's fault? *Did not I bring this upon him?*

Mark was not accustomed to second-guessing himself, and he'd been doing that a lot lately. What if Reuben was not destined to have come with him that night? He would've been taken into the hands of his family or the State.

But not into the claws of an unholy monster.

Again, Mark worked to shake his negative thoughts. *I'm doing the Lord's work. I only do what I am told.*

"Told by whom?" The voice of The Other had gained power in his embattled mind. *"You can no longer ignore the fact that you are the monster and you corrupt everything you touch."*

"No!" Mark said aloud and Reuben jumped. He glanced at him to gauge his reaction, but Reuben wasn't wondering about the outburst. His mind was on other matters. He hadn't given up entirely. He

119

desperately wanted to escape. Mark sped towards home and kept himself aware the kid's thoughts, hopefully to stay one step ahead.

ଓଝୋ

Reuben's heart raced as fast as his mind plotted and the silence in the car only increased his anxiety. They had always despised each other and Reuben was comfortable with that, but the boss's unpredictable behavior left him morbidly afraid.

At the shout, Reuben recalled his earliest days with the doctor; there had been plenty of shouting in the beginning. From age six, Reuben attended an out-of-state boarding school, but no matter his excellent grades, nothing pleased the master. Holiday school closings were most dreadful. Paul treated him as subhuman and the doctor pretended he didn't exist. Reuben rejoiced each time classes resumed and he was chauffeured to the dorm.

He was almost sixteen when Paul revealed his true purpose in the household. It was the summer before tenth grade and Paul took him for a drive to lay it all out. The doctor's assistant informed him that he was to be a servant of Doctor Corescu, and that the next time he saw him, he was to refer to him as "Boss" or "Master," and nothing else. The thought of serving the man as a slave repulsed him, but he couldn't refuse lest he risk severe punishment. When fall arrived, and Reuben was packed for school, it was the doctor who drove him to the airport. Even though these events took place years earlier, Reuben remembered every detail.

Dressed in a gray business suit, the doctor wore dark sunglasses that hid his eyes. He didn't speak directly to Reuben as they prepared to go, and once in the car, Reuben remained silent, deathly afraid of the quiet and mysterious man who piloted the vehicle. Sick to his stomach the entire ride, Reuben wasn't acknowledged even once, and his head spun with terror. When they reached the departure gate, the doctor stopped the car for him to get out. Once on the curb, Reuben reached back in to grab his travel bag and his master put a hand on his arm.

"I'll see you at Christmas," he said, swishing off his sunglasses.

Frightened, but not knowing why, Reuben vomited in his mouth, and then just as quickly swallowed the bile down. Back-pedaling away from the car, he stumbled through the sliding glass doors of the terminal. The doctor's words said one thing, but his gaze spoke of unmentionable dread. Reuben had seen his mother's death in those eyes and he vowed to run away and never return to Corescu and his freaky friend. By the time his plane was in the air, he had hatched an entire escape plan.

Naturally, when Christmas came around, Reuben returned, crawling back to face his master. He was sixteen with a driver's license, and to his horror, he was withdrawn from school and put to work. Reuben became the master's full-time driver and discovered that Corescu was a hard boss that did not tolerate mistakes. He punished Reuben for the slightest error, and after two years of harsh corrections, Reuben ran away. Within the space of an hour, Reuben was located. Corescu confronted him with a mad and dangerous eye, but with the bravado of a teenage rebel, Reuben stood his ground. The price was high; Reuben was left crushed and broken, and when he returned to consciousness, he finally understood what power his overseer possessed. It was the very power of hell, and like the devil, the doctor had no mercy.

☾☽

"You were a difficult child, Rube," Mark said to shake Reuben from his thoughts. "I gave you the gift of eternal life. Wasn't that enough?" The car pulled into the driveway as he spoke and he didn't expect the kid to answer.

"Eternal slavery."

Reuben sent the focused thought to Mark who smirked. The boy was entitled to his perspective. Mark parked the car around the back to access the cellar. He'd incarcerate the kid for now, but why not kill him? A month ago, he would've eliminated him without a thought. Now, he couldn't bring himself to do it.

Shrugging off his unease, Mark led Reuben down the cellar steps into the basement. The room was empty save a thick straight-backed wooden chair with a small box beneath it. Mark motioned for Reuben to sit and withdrew a roll of heavy-duty duct tape from the box. First, several layers were wrapped around his chest and upper arms, then a similar treatment went around his thighs, lower legs and forearms. When finished, Reuben was securely fastened, and Mark stood to admire his work.

"Oh." Mark tore off a six-inch piece and placed it over Reuben's mouth. The kid submitted, glaring. Mark smiled and patted him on the head. "I'll be back for you soon enough."

"I hate you," Reuben accused telepathically.

Expecting nothing less, Mark turned and left him alone in the dark.

Twenty-Six

I belong to my lover and his desire is for me.
Song of Solomon 7:10

HOPE AWOKE SUNDAY MORNING AND YAWNED AT THE time. It was still early, at least by her count. She had to pick up Glorie by noon; what else did she forget? Rubbing her eyes, she thought it over, not surprised when Mark's face came to mind. Now, with the morning sun streaming into her bedroom, she doubted the strange things she witnessed were real. Could Mark truly be some kind of vampire? No matter what he called it, sucking blood and living forever was Dracula to a "T."

The doorbell chimed and she sat up, remembering what she forgot.

Anthony! Her friend was taking her to church. Hope threw off the covers and grabbed her fuzzy pink robe. Tripping over the cat, she shouted through the house, "Just a minute!" With her robe fastened, Hope flung the door open wide. "Hey!"

Anthony stood on her stoop looking at his watch. Then he glanced at her attire and tossed her a look she recognized. "*Why does it always have to be about you?*" He didn't have to say it; Hope knew she exasperated him to no end.

Hope turned on the charm and smiled. "Good morning."

"Did you forget something?" Anthony gestured to her bathrobe and smiled back.

"I overslept. I'm sorry." Hope pulled his arm until he stepped inside.

"It's okay," Anthony sighed and allowed himself to be tugged into the room. "They have the last service at eleven, so just get dressed."

Hope motioned for him to sit down. "I can't, I have to pick up my sister at the airport at noon. I should have called."

"It's okay," Anthony repeated, his shoulders slumping.

"Since you're here, I need some advice." Hope paused as

122

unwarranted concern crossed her friend's face, suspicious that she was in trouble. How did he get so intuitive?

"What's wrong?" Anthony asked as his fingers grasped the arms of the chair. Hope laughed to allay his concerns.

"Nothing's *wrong*. Just hold that thought. I need to throw on some clothes." She spun around and went to her bedroom and returned moments later in baggy sweats and a big T-shirt. Anthony still looked pensive.

"Did you want to talk about your date? Was there a problem?"

"Yes and no. If you have a minute, I have some questions." She couldn't ask him about vampires, but he might not get too curious if she asked about the other stuff, *The Judging*.

"Shoot," Anthony said in a serious tone.

"Okay, we've had three dates so far." Hope quickly formulated a coherent question. "Nothing bad happened, I had a great time. It's just that he has some mixed up ideas about God."

"Oh, all right." Anthony sounded relieved. "Go on."

"I don't want you to think anything bad about him because he's a great guy, but he and I were discussing a hypothetical situation and I wonder about his conclusions."

"And?" Anthony prodded.

"Okay, what does God think of a man who kills only evil people? If a vigilante were to seek out and murder hundreds of really evil people, is he guilty?"

Anthony leaned back a fraction. "How does the vigilante know the person is evil?"

"Well, he can read their thoughts." Hope trailed off, afraid of sounding ridiculous. Leave it to Anthony to ask such an intelligent question.

"I see. There's problem number one. God despises mind reading. If a person feels they have telepathic powers, then they might be getting help from the devil."

"But," Hope paused and reformulated her question. "I want to know is it okay to kill evil people? For God I mean."

"All right, this vigilante with telepathic powers, he finds these people guilty by *whose* judgment?" Anthony removed his glasses and cleaned them as he spoke.

"First of all, I see your wheels turning. Stop thinking that Mark is this vigilante. We're speaking hypothetically." Hope's shoulders dropped and she regretted opening the conversation.

"Hypothetically, how does the vigilante know what men deserve? Only God can judge mankind. A killer who kills an evildoer is committing the same sin as if he had killed an innocent baby. He has made himself out to be God. There is only one Judge."

Hope processed his words and swallowed. "You're saying that the vigilante is deluding himself?"

"To justify his crimes, I'm afraid so." Anthony straightened his tie and scratched absently at a stain, but Hope wasn't done.

"But think of all the people who live because the murderers are killed. I mean, a baby killer brought to justice by this vigilante, doesn't God want those children to live?" Unable to squelch the desperation in her voice, Hope knew the answers in her heart already.

"No 'buts' Hope. God is God. You can't make your theology fit Him. He has never changed; it isn't our place to question His authority on sin. It's written plain as day in the Bible. Does your doctor friend believe otherwise?"

"Yeah," Hope responded in a soft voice, "I knew it was wrong, but I've fallen so hard for him. I wanted everything to be perfect."

"Does he believe in God? Lots of people have similar ethical dilemmas."

"Oh, yes. In fact, he talks about God a lot."

"Interesting," Anthony said, eyebrows raised. "So, he's perverting the Scriptures to suit his ideology?"

Hope lowered her eyes.

"What're you going to do? Are you going to see him again?"

"Of course." Hope leaned back and closed her eyes. "Remember that *huge* purpose you said God had for me? I think Mark is it."

"Huh," Anthony was silent a few clicks, then sighed. "Hope, is Dr. Corescu doing something illegal?"

Hope's eyes snapped open and her face went white. Fumbling with the couch pillow in her lap, she stammered her reply. "What? Of course, not. Are you crazy?"

"You have to trust me. Haven't I always been there for you?" Anthony smoothed back his hair and waited for a reply.

"Anthony," Hope struggled with her response and took a deep breath. "I will tell you the truth, but not yet. You have to believe that I will tell you in my own time."

Anthony nodded, but he wasn't satisfied with her answer. "So, he *is* up to something. And you're telling me I don't need to worry?"

"Right. Let me find out more and then I'll get back to you. I'm seeing him again soon and I'll get to the bottom of it."

Anthony stood and straightened his tie. "I don't like it, but I'll give you some room. Call me as soon as you get home tomorrow, or else I'll come looking for you."

It was no empty threat and Hope didn't take it as one. She pecked him on the cheek and walked him to the door. "Thank you. You're the best friend a girl could ever ask for."

"Call me." Anthony waved and got into his truck.

Hope closed the door and faced the morning. Things were definitely going to get worse before they got better.

Twenty-Seven

See, he is puffed up; his desires are not upright—
But the righteous will live by his faith—
Habakkuk 2:4

MARK LEFT HIS ROOM DRESSED FOR WORK AT THE ER. The drama and adrenaline they endured every shift should be enough to distract him for the day. Crossing the hall, he spied Paul still asleep on the library sofa. He glanced at his watch. So what if he was late? Volunteer work was not one of his strong points.

Mark put his briefcase near the door and entered the library to check on Paul's condition. His friend had always been anxious to please, but did he never consider the consequences? Sighing, Mark gathered him into his arms and carried him to his room. Paul didn't look good, Reuben was on death row, and Hope was unavailable. When did he lose control of his life? Mark shook his head, more resolute than ever to get the situation back into his hands, to find a way to placate Hope *and* retain his superiority. Once in the bedroom he tucked Paul in for a long rest.

He remembered Reuben's anger. The thought of the furious kid he locked in the cellar sent a pang of alarm down Mark's spine. He jotted a short note and left it beside Paul's inert form on the bed.

P- Don't leave this room until I return for you. – M

In his debilitated state, Reuben could do Paul serious damage. Mark hated the helpless feeling associated with his worry, but what could he do but lock the door and head out? Checking the locks on the rest of the house, Mark no longer felt like a powerful, unstoppable force. He felt weak, vulnerable, and impotent. Doing his best to shake his nagging concerns, he thundered away in one of his favorite cars and hoped for the best.

ଔଷ

Connie slept until well past nine and woke with a killer hangover. After a brisk shower and an extravagant $19.95 breakfast buffet in the hotel restaurant, he was ready to hit the streets.

126

It was a bright and deathly quiet Sunday morning. Connie spent his youth in Brooklyn and begrudged any city that closed shop on the weekend. Atlanta was the Deep South; would anything of any use be open? Connie waved at the doorman on the way out and handed him a folded five dollar bill.

"Where's the closest public library?"

The baby in a man's uniform stuttered a moment, nodded and then shook his head. "Uh…"

"Are the libraries open on Sunday?" Connie tried again. The doorman nodded and shook his head simultaneously.

"Is that a yes?" Connie snapped. Was everyone in the city an imbecile?

"Yessir, some are open, some ain't. Which one you headin' to?"

"The closest open library," Connie mumbled scrutinizing the guy's acne.

"Uh," the kid stammered and looked at his watch, "the closest one is closed for renovations. Ummm, the Peachtree Branch is open 2 to 6. My mom works there…"

Connie cursed. The kid looked like he'd toss his breakfast if he asked anything more. Done with the guy, Connie turned on his heel and headed to the parking garage. He had rented an emerald green Ford Taurus, much like the one he drove back home in Feather. Before he pulled out, he shuffled through his notes for the Reuben kid's address. After a quick glance at the city map, he headed off.

Stuckey was going to make him rich. He had something on his boss and Connie decided the best course of action would be to ask the kid a few more questions before he checked out Corescu. Physicians lived large and he would have many powerful friends, not to mention top-of-the-line security at his residence. If Connie could get the boy to tell him what he knew, he could stake out the man's house and really get an investigation going. Then the doctor wouldn't know what hit him. Connie fantasized about his coming achievements all the way to Stuckey's condominium. It was going to be glorious.

He found Sherwood Drive and picked his way through the narrow street. The landscaping and the proliferation of luxury automobiles belied the wealth of the residents. Connie parked in front of the house and turned off his car. Was the kid independently wealthy, or did the doctor pay his rent? Connie mulled it over as he walked to the door.

The clean porch sported one cheap plastic potted plant and a worn Welcome mat. With a sardonic smile, Connie punched the doorbell.

127

After an appropriate pause, he rang a second time. When no one answered the third attempt, Connie peered into the cut glass set in the top of the door. A small table sat in the foyer decorated with a plant—possibly another plastic one—and nothing else. No feet came to meet him. No music or TV noise filtered from inside. Connie stepped from the recessed doorway and looked to the left and the right; no one in sight. He moved into the yard to a big front window. Slatted blinds partially hid a tidy living room with a leather couch, a love seat, and a television stand. No Stuckey.

Disappointed, Connie walked back to his car and leaned on the hood to adjust his plans. He'd been certain the kid would be home and now he was at a loss how to proceed. A noise next door distracted him and Connie watched the neighbor open her garage. With a purposeful stride, he paced up the woman's driveway and pasted on his sweetest smile.

"Excuse me, ma'am. Sorry to bother you."

Attractive in a matronly fashion, the neighbor lady instinctively clutched her purse to her chest, but smiled nonetheless. "Can I help you, suh?"

She spoke with a very distinct southern accent, straight from the set of *Gone with the Wind,* and Connie put on his best Sunday demeanor.

"I hope so. I was supposed to meet up with your neighbor, Reuben Stuckey, yesterday for an interview. I'm a reporter. Anyway, my plane was delayed and I missed him. Do you know where he might be if he isn't home?" Connie's mouth hurt from his ridiculous grin, but the Georgia Peach bought it. She tossed her Louis Vuitton bag into her Beemer and joined him in the driveway.

"Mistuh Stuckey ain't home? Well, that *is* a little odd." She peered at Reuben's quiet doorway and smiled demurely at Connie. "Why in the *world* would you want a story on that boy? He never did strike me as Mistuh Excitement."

"He entered a writing contest and won first prize. You didn't know he was a writer?" Connie gambled the southern belle wouldn't know any better.

"Well, goodie for him!" She laughed with a single *hah* and gestured to Stuckey's driveway. "Well, if his Jag ain't there, he ain't there, you can bet on that. Let's see…"

She sucked her teeth, looked up to the sky and hummed, while Connie resisted the urge to tap his foot. She finally continued in her lilting drawl.

128

"I've *never* known Mistuh Stuckey to be gone Sunday mornin'. See, I usually come out to leave for church at the same time he gets his paper out of the yah'd. He's a very polite young man. Always says good mornin' and how are ya. And he's a good lookin' fella, for a Negro that is."

Connie dismissed the woman's condescension and continued with a toothy smile. "Do you know where he might be? I have to get back to Kentucky tonight."

"Well, I really don't know him well enough to tell ya. He's courteous enough, but beyond that, I don't think I've ever really talked with him." The neighbor shrugged her shoulders and smiled her apology.

"Do you know his boss, Dr. Corescu?" Connie pulled the last rabbit he had out of his hat.

"Not personally, but my girlfriend went to see him about some test results. She said he was absolutely *dreamy*. He's at Whitford City Memorial. Do you know where that is?"

"Yes, ma'am. Do you think Reuben could be working for the doctor today?"

"He could be. My husband told me that that kid works seven days a week, so I guess on Sundays, he leaves after I go to church." She checked her watch and inclined her head toward her car. "I'm so sorry, Mistuh, but I gotta be goin'. I'm runnin' a bit late and I don't want to miss roll call in the Bible Belles."

"Sure, sure. Thanks for your help." Connie waved and headed back to his rental car, ruminating over what he had learned. The kid was nice, but kept to himself, and the doctor was a philanthropist who worked Reuben every day.

Connie dropped into his car, allowing the air conditioning to freeze his face. What did Stuckey do for the doctor? Some sort of serving capacity, Connie surmised. He fumbled around for his map and looked for the best route to Whitford City. He had an address on the doctor thanks to the lovely ISS gal and he pinpointed it on the map. It was nearly eleven and he figured he could be sitting at Corescu's house within the hour.

Connie put the car in drive going over a list of questions for the kid. Just for kicks, he memorized a few for the doctor if he should cross paths with him there as well. You never know. It paid to be prepared.

Twenty-Eight

Blessed is the man whom God corrects;
So do not despise the discipline of the Almighty.
Job 5:17

CONNIE PULLED OFF THE INTERSTATE THREE MILES from Whitford City; the three coffees he consumed yearned to get out. Pulling into the first gas station on the right, he stumbled inside, happy to find the restrooms unlocked. He chose a stall with a door and just as he finished, he glimpsed a leather strap wedged tightly under the wooden frame that surrounded the tank. With one forceful yank, a hunting knife in an ornately-tooled leather holster popped free. Wondering at how it got there, Connie went on alert and listened to the bathroom. After determining he was alone, he held the item to the light. The quality of the craftsmanship on the leather was extraordinary. Sliding the knife out of the scabbard, he marveled at the blade's beauty. Eight inches long and three inches wide at the thickest point, the knife had a cruel serrated edge half way to the tip. The artfully detailed bone handle swarmed with hand-carved serpents. If it had value, his cousin Opal in Columbus, Georgia, could look it up for him. Connie examined it a minute longer, nodding with approval. He unbuckled his belt to thread the holster and once done, he enjoyed the comfortable weight of the knife in the small of his back. Shrugging on his blazer, he opened the stall door and stood in front of the mirror.

"What was that, punk? Make my day!" he growled at his reflection and whipped the knife out of the holster with a flourish. He looked cool and a little dangerous. Smiling, he tucked it away and practiced whipping it out a few more times. So what if it was stashed there by a burglar, or worse, a murderer. It was Connie's now and he definitely wasn't turning it over to the police. What terrific luck. A knife might come in handy if the doctor should try anything funny when he confronted him. A gun would be better, but a knife was okay too. Connie wasn't picky.

130

ოჳ৪ი

Mark slowed his Lexus at the gate and spotted a green sedan parked on the opposite side of the street. As the electronic gate responded to his presence, he peered into the car's windshield. It was empty and he put it out of his mind. He could no longer allow the tiniest thing to draw his attention away from the desperate present.

Minutes later, he was in the house and he climbed the steps to Paul's bedroom. Inside, Paul lay in the same position as if comatose. Mark's heart fell; ten hours had passed and if anything, the kid looked worse. After shaking his patient's shoulder and getting no response, Mark followed up with more force until Paul roused. Groaning, the kid's eyes fluttered open to meet his gaze.

"Hi," Paul said in a hoarse whisper.

Mark lifted him upright, leaning him against the thick scrolled headboard. Paul sipped the water that was offered, but coughed and sputtered with the effort.

"You've done yourself in good this time, young man," Mark scolded with mock admonishment. "What am I going to do with you?"

Paul offered a weak smile and tried to apologize; no words would come. He could barely breathe, much less speak.

"Shh. You sleep." Mark cupped Paul's pale cheek in his hand and waited to garner his full attention. When Paul's tired eyes focused upon his finally, Mark smiled and removed his hand. "I'll take care of you, Paul. Very soon, you'll be feeling better than ever. You believe me, don't you?"

Paul mustered the strength to nod and one corner of his mouth turned up into a grateful smile.

"Good. I have an appointment, but when I return, I'll be right here by your side." Mark carefully repositioned Paul so that he lay on his back. "This door will be locked. You're not to leave this room until I return, understand?"

This time, Paul didn't nod in overt agreement, but he understood. Mark exited the room and locked the door behind him. He headed for the study to begin the appointment.

Atlanta's own Terri 'B' Joiner, Hip-Hop king of Georgia, unknowingly awaited him at a concert downtown. Mark concentrated on the physical location of his next judging and before he knew it, he was there, fulfilling his Calling. At least, that's what he told himself as he began the task.

"How do you feel about blaming God for this evil?"

The Other piped in unexpectedly and Mark forced him away with difficulty, the ethereal nuisance growing in strength. With no other recourse but to proceed, Mark set his jaw.

ೞೞ

Terri Joiner couldn't find his hat.

Through his fuzzy memory, he retraced his steps. An hour ago, it sat on his head where it belonged. He definitely had it on when they hustled the old woman in the alley. Didn't she stare at his hat? Maybe she was a witch.

I'll bet she cursed me and that's why I lost my hat.

Well, she was all beat up now, so her curse should have faded, shouldn't it?

Wait a minute...

Terri scrunched his pock-marked face and concentrated. Something else happened after that. Oh, yeah, his bossy agent called to nag about a gig he skipped. Then he slipped into a cab with 'Quinus and Steve to make a bee-line for the auditorium.

Was I wearing my hat in the cab?

He thought so. Didn't the cabbie stare at it, too?

It was an awesome sight, glittery and soft at the same time. Made of the most luxurious mink money could buy, the hat was studded with eleven thousand dollars' worth of diamonds, a gift from the recording studio when his album went platinum.

Who exactly gave it to me?

He couldn't remember names, but that didn't really matter. All that mattered was the hat. He had four people looking for it; 'Quinas, Steve, and two fine groupies that hung around when they toured Atlanta. So far, no one appeared with the glorious announcement, "Here's your hat, B!"

Terri crossed his dressing room and turned over the chest of drawers with an oath.

Did they look behind all this crappy furniture?

Probably not. He pulled out the couch and turned it onto its back. The dirty cushions were tossed into the small bathroom on his right. *Maybe it's trapped under this stool...*

Terri lifted a heavy swivel chair from the ground and heaved it into his full-length mirror. The glass shattered into a million pieces on the

132

stained carpet. Nope, the hat wasn't there either.

They probably hidin' it. Yeah, playin' a trick on me. Well, I gotta surprise for the sucka who tries to suck me...

Terri put his hand under his leather jacket to fondle his pistol, warm and cozy against his stomach. He used it a half-a-dozen times already and had so far evaded prosecution. Fate had a way of protecting him. It was good to be the king of hip-hop.

Through the increasingly loud noise emanating from the opening stage band, Terri heard a faint knock at the door and he told them to buzz off. He was due on stage in a few minutes, but no one in heaven or hell was going to make him go on without his hat. *Just let 'em try to make me.*

The knock came again more adamant, and further expletives flew from his mouth before he crossed the room. He patted the gun through his jacket once more and jerked opened the door.

"What do you want?" Terri spat, his head buzzing pleasantly from the tequila he consumed earlier. *Oh, maybe this jerk-wad found my diamond hat...* He looked the tall stranger up and down and frowned. "You got my hat?"

The stranger didn't answer, but instead pushed past and entered the small room. Terri stood in place, dumbfounded at the man's audacity. *Who the...*

Before he could finish his thought, the man closed the door, locked it, and took him by the throat. At the same moment Terri had a crazily detached notion—the band on stage was playing a cover of an old Beastie Boys tune. And it sounded awful.

"Terri Joiner, you are being judged."

The voice resounded in his head and the stranger's lips hadn't moved. Terri's eyes bulged from the pressure at his throat, the killer allowing him just enough air to answer, but not enough to scream.

"What?" Weakly, Terri responded. *This must be the guy that stole my hat!*

"You have sinned against God and have shown no repentance. Your sins cry out ahead of you and the misery you are reaping on the earth is too vast to tolerate."

Terri flailed his arms and legs, but no amount of struggling reduced the strength with which he was held. He sucked in a tiny breath and pounded his attacker's chest with his hands. He couldn't reach the man's head, so he struck everywhere else.

"This is your last chance to repent of your sins, Terri Joiner. This is your chance to beg forgiveness. What do you say?"

The blows didn't affect the tall stranger in the least.

Where're my bodyguards? Where's 'Quinas? Who's gonna get this scary dude off me? Maybe this guy took the hat so that while everyone was looking for it, he could kill me.

Terri remembered his gun.

I'm not helpless, you freak!

Grabbing his gun with his right hand, Terri flicked off the safety. So far, his attacker hadn't noticed. Without a second thought, Terri fired off a round into the man's gut. The only response he got from his attacker was that he stopped his insane silent preaching. The stranger's eyes closed momentarily then reopened, red and angry. Terri was able to fire again, but aimed wild as his gun hand was seized and squeezed in the vise-like grip of his attacker.

"Agghhhh!" he screamed before his airway was completely shut off, the stranger pinching closed his trachea. Terri's wrist bones shattered like glass in the killer's left hand. Pain exploded up his arm and he struggled for air. The killer dragged him into the bathroom and just before the door closed, they both heard banging on the outer door.

"B? B? Was that a gunshot?" Then louder, "Terri? ARE YOU OKAY?"

My...peeps...now you're gonna get it. Terri tried to respond, but he hadn't been able to breathe for over a minute. He was about to black out. His attacker pulled him close and shut the bathroom door.

In the tiny space, the man held Terri's windpipe closed until his heart stopped beating. By the time the Hip-Hop prodigy hit the dingy bathroom floor, his attacker had magically vanished and Terri "B" Joiner was most assuredly dead.

'Quinas burst into the room and the door flew off the hinges as a result of his powerful kick. The room was a mess, wholly turned upside down. The bathroom door was closed and 'Quinas moved aside to let Steve have a whack at it. When the flimsy door was pushed open, Terri was on the floor, dead.

"Give me that hat."

The plucky groupie on his right, Lasheeta, pulled it out from under her T-shirt and handed it over without question. The prank might have been a bad idea. 'Quinas shoved the hat down on his bald head and touched the dead musician with his boot. Terri would have wanted him to have it. He pulled the door closed and pulled out his cell to dial 911.

134

As he waited for the police to pick up on their end, he nodded to Steve.

"Nobody say nuthin' about this hat. Terri ain't gonna need it in hell." The friends agreed and waited for the excitement to begin for real.

ᏣᎡᏪ

The round went clean through his abdomen and Mark stared at the wound in his bedroom mirror. It wasn't the first time he'd taken a bullet, but it was the first time he'd been shot by a judging victim. Sadly, he hadn't even seen it coming.

Was he losing his concentration? Now his blood would be at the scene. So much for a clean getaway. Mark sighed. He had no DNA on file and the fingerprints required by his employers were faked. But still, he left a piece of himself behind. His blood was assuredly different from their normal fare and the lab would certainly discover some abnormalities. His blood may even carry DNA from any number of his past victims.

"*...And the pieces begin to crumble down around you. Your servants hate you and your victims do not fear you. You are a very poor vampire.*"

"*No.*" A one-word response to The Other was all he would allow. It wasn't as bleak as all that. It was inconceivable that a criminal investigator would even suspect him; he was miles away and not even slightly connected to the victim. He was in the clear.

"*The mortals have your blood. You better leave town.*"

What would the blood show? The Other was paranoid. Mark washed his face and cleared his mind. Finding the first aid kit under the sink, he taped his wounds, front and back, so they wouldn't leak onto his shirt. They'd close within the hour, and even though they pinched, there was no pain. Mostly he was hungry.

Not only had he lost the musician's soul, he had failed to feed. Now he was starving and that poor wretched kid was going to hell. Mark frowned at the realization of his first total failure. What did he do wrong? Going over the event, he picked it apart. Maybe there was something he could've done differently. When he remembered Paul suffering in the next room, he shook his head. He could contemplate his failures later, for now he wanted to check on his partner.

Mark steeled himself before he put his key in the door to Paul's room, hoping to hide the recent events from his old friend. Paul was especially sensitive to Mark's emotional state so it wouldn't be easy to hide. Inside the dark room, he clicked on the bedside lamp and Paul covered his eyes.

"It lives!" Mark playfully mussed his hair, inwardly ecstatic to see him conscious.

"How'd it go?" Paul asked, sounding better, but still weak. Mark shushed him and took his wrist to check his pulse, listening with his ears as well.

"Don't worry about me. How do you feel?" Mark sat on the edge of the bed and straightened the hair that curled over Paul's forehead. He was pale as the sheets he lay on, and only his lips showed any hint of pink in his ashen face.

Bad timing, little buddy. I could use your special gift right now...

Mark shielded his gruesome thought to focus on Paul's condition instead of his own. It was difficult; he wasn't accustomed to enduring hunger.

"I'm okay." Paul held his right hand over his eyes, his smile more a frown. Mark waited for the truth and Paul sighed. "My head's pounding and," he pulled in a lung-full of air, "it's hard to breathe."

"Sit up." Mark gently lifted him into an upright position and leaned him against the pillows. "Do we have any wine?"

Paul nodded and answered in a whisper. "Liquor cabinet. Kitchen."

"I'll be right back." Mark headed downstairs to the kitchen, easily finding Paul's stash. He shuffled through the bottles until he found a red wine.

A Merlot. How fitting.

Finding a glass in the cupboard, he filled it halfway, then found a large silver platter and placed it on the counter.

"Let's see," he mumbled to himself. "I wonder..."

In the well-stocked refrigerator, he found a zip-lock bag of cheddar cheese cubes and pulled them out, remembering his first night with Paul. Two slices of bread and an apple from the hanging basket beside the sink and he was ready to return upstairs. Once inside Paul's room, he set down the tray.

"'Tis a humbling thing when the master serves the servant." Mark sat on the edge of the bed with a wistful smile.

"That looks familiar." Paul's voice was soft but audible. He forced his hand to reach for the apple. He grasped it with difficulty and held it in his closed hand.

"This is my specialty, you know." Mark stood over the bed, lifted the glass of wine, and held it to the light. Paul's pulse quickened.

"Another Corescu Cocktail?" Paul's words were halting, but clear, barely hiding his sudden unease.

"Another one?" Mark smirked and brought his hand over the wineglass. "Nearly a century has passed and it was a Crump Cocktail in those days." Just as before, Mark drew his own blood effortlessly into the glass. "Drink this down."

Paul grasped the glass as Mark steadied it for him. With some effort, he was able to swallow without gagging. As unsavory as it was, the light returned to Paul's eyes as soon as the liquid hit his stomach.

"You'll feel much better now." Returning to physician mode, Mark helped Paul lie recumbent. "I want you to rest, and when you can, eat."

Paul glanced over to the tray and nodded. Suddenly, his countenance darkened and he took Mark by the arm.

"You've been shot." In his weakened condition, his words carried little drama, but his expression was one of terror. "Mark, how?"

Mark put a finger to his dry lips. "Hush, now. It's none of your affair." He stood and sent Paul a stern glare. "Stay in this room until morning. Reuben is in the cellar. Do not go in, no matter what." The alarm returned to Paul's eyes, and he hushed him. "When you're yourself again, we'll go down there together and do what needs to be done."

"Did he shoot you?" Paul's voice was barely a whisper in the quiet room. "It's too dangerous for you to face him alone." Again there was real fear behind Paul's eyes and Mark looked away.

"You insult me. Do you think I'm helpless?" What Mark wanted to ask was *have you lost all confidence in your master?*, but he was afraid of the answer. Paul had telepathically witnessed some part of the shooting, which could account for his anxiety. Mark shook his head, his partner even more telepathic than he realized. If his weakened condition caused his paranoia, it wasn't affecting his mental abilities. Mark put his hand on the knob and turned for one more reiteration. "I'll be back soon. Now, rest."

He locked the door and headed to the cellar. An uncomfortable rumble returned his attention to his missed supper. *What am I thinking? Why should I starve when there is a perfectly good sacrifice downstairs?*

Mark hurried down the steps. Reuben's blood should be just as sweet as Paul's.

Ten minutes later, Mark stooped in front of Reuben thinking clearly now that his hunger had abated. In centuries, he'd never gone without a blood meal and he didn't care for the sensation. His driver gazed at him with narrowed eyes. He hadn't lost consciousness and his hate glittered at Mark in the low light. He did finally offer a quiet telepathic word.

"Monster."

"So you say," Mark replied telepathically. *"How do I deal with you? You're a danger to me, my loved ones, everything I've worked so hard to achieve here."* Mark didn't pick up any further reply. *"I should take care of you right now. Right here. Be done with you."*

But he couldn't. What had Hope done to him?

"She has awakened your conscience, and that has awakened me. Remember the priest."

A priest?

Mark bolted up the cellar stairs; he had to go see her. He was remembering the priest and he didn't want to recall his past alone.

Twenty-Nine

What has happened to us is a result of our evil deeds
And our great guilt, and yet, our God,
You have punished us less
than our sins have deserved.
Ezra 9:13

HOPE TILTED HER HEAD TO THE SIDE, REGARDING THE specter in her room. The dream was back. Mark came to her nearly every night in her dreams, but tonight, the shadow didn't leave when she blinked. Without fear, she rose and padded into her bathroom, stared in the mirror, and tried to decide if she was awake. The longer she gazed into the mirror, the more she discerned a texture to the room that was never present in her dreams. When she ran her hands under the cold water, she was convinced she was awake. Hope turned off the faucet and stood in the bathroom doorway.

The shadow now sat on her bed.

"Wha—?" She placed her left hand on the bureau to steady herself. A few feet past the figure on the edge of the bed, the bright red numerals on the digital clock read 3 a.m. The dark form hadn't moved and she forced herself to speak. "Mark?"

The shadow stood and stepped toward her. Hope steeled her nerves and held up her hand. It was definitely Mark, but he looked distressed and confused. She couldn't reach the lamp, but she desperately wished for light.

"What's wrong?"

The shadow didn't reply. Instead, it closed the gap between them and took her into a tender embrace. In a halting manner, Hope returned the gesture and her visitor stroked her hair.

"Are you all right?" she asked, a knot in her gut as she worried for him. How or why he'd come, she didn't question, she only wanted to comfort him, erase the despair on his handsome face. Maybe he needed blood. Maybe he needed *her* blood.

139

Hope glanced in the mirror and caught her reflection in the moonlight. She was barely dressed in a silk camisole with matching panties, standing in the arms of a shadowy figure that hadn't spoken a word. Hope inhaled sharply and snapped wide-awake.

౸

Mark recognized Hope's unease as instantly as she reacted. Her vulnerability hadn't even occurred to her until she'd seen their reflection in the glass. Her natural impulse was to help.

I have to tell her about the priest...

It was his own internal voice that egged him on and Mark shushed it. Hope looked into his face, her expression pained.

"I am sorry to visit so late," Mark whispered. Hope's sense of vulnerability hinged on her scanty dress and she blushed deep red. Mark didn't want her to be afraid and he searched for the right words. "I've remembered something. I need to tell you about the past."

Hope's face relaxed and she raised her eyebrows to ask for more. In the low light, Mark could see Hope clearly. His body did not function as a normal man's, but since he met Hope, something new stirred deep within. Its novelty was foreign enough that surely it was meaningful. He allowed his eyes to caress her exposed skin and her eyes darted to the dresser. Mark let her off the hook.

"Put something on and we'll talk." He didn't avert his eyes when she stepped away and lunged for the dresser. Hope pulled a satin robe over her shoulders with her back to him and suppressed a grin when she turned.

"You could at least pretend to not look."

She whispered as if they were not alone and Mark went on alert. He listened to the house; a third heartbeat entered his awareness, female, and nearby. *I walked right through the house!* His carelessness surprised him and when Hope touched his arm he stared at her fingers a moment to put his mind back in line. When she gave a tug he relented and followed her to the edge of the bed. She sat and looked up at him as if waiting for him to join her. He remained standing, looking into her face and running over what could happen if he didn't stay alert.

"It's no biggie," she said still whispering. "It's only my sister. I picked her up from the airport after lunch." Hope pointed toward the door and pulled her robe tighter to her chest. "But she's a loudmouth. It'd be better if she didn't know you dropped in at 3 a.m." Hope had smiled, but he read her seriousness.

Mark put out his hand. "Then come with me. Let's go for a drive." She hesitated and he barreled ahead before she could refuse. "It's important."

Civil proprieties aside, the young woman didn't need convincing. She wanted to be with him, believed him without question, and he watched her gather some clothes from a drawer.

"I'll leave Glorie a note. Just let me get dressed."

Hope disappeared into the bathroom and Mark was in the same place when she came out. He watched her make a short note and tape it to Glorie's door as they passed. Within five minutes, they were driving east to the country and the sky had just begun to lighten along the horizon.

☙❧

In the Lexus, Hope watched Mark's profile mesmerized. Her stomach ached when she looked at him; like being hungry, but not knowing for what. Hope exhaled to calm her nerves and broke the silence with a question.

"What did you remember?" She placed her hand on his shoulder and he lifted it to place a gentle kiss. Hope flushed and watched for his reply.

"I'm remembering a priest, and I think it's very important." His voice wavered, pained by his own words. Hope waited a moment and he continued. "All my life, I've disregarded the past and avoided any research of my origins. I follow the calling of God to judge the evil and purge them from the world. But recently…"

Hope didn't interrupt when he paused, aware that she'd awakened something in him.

"I'm not *certain* anymore. I can't seem to make the simplest decision without second-guessing myself. It's horrible and dangerous, and if I don't get my life back in control, it will destroy me." Mark sighed, exasperated.

"Tell me what happened," she said and wished she could see his beautiful eyes. "Did something happen to Paul?"

Mark shook his head and again kissed her hand. The car picked up speed. They would be at his house in fifteen minutes. *Then he'll tell me all about it,* Hope thought and believed it.

☙❧

141

Tony awoke in a sweat; he had the dream again, Hope and her ridiculous muddy horse. This one was nearly identical to the previous incarnation, but this time, as he removed the muck and grime from the horse's mane and neck, it turned to bite him. The pain from the beast's sharp teeth in the soft crook of his arm was so intense, that he snapped awake in a panic. The dream was more *real* tonight; the mud, the white, stark surroundings, the sweet, nauseating smell of death. Then there was the *bite*.

Tony lay back on his pillow and tried to recall the details, absently rubbing the inside of his arm. Was it his imagination or was that area a sore? He turned his eyes to the ceiling. Was it God warning him, or the devil trying to frighten him?

The sensations of the nightmare remained fresh, swallowing and suffocating on greenish-black muck. He actually tasted the stuff in his mouth; thick, gritty and cool on his tongue.

And it means something—it has to. We help the horse get clean, but the action destroys us. And why did it bite me? I was getting him free... Tony frowned, unable to make sense of it. *I should warn Hope.*

But warn her of what? A dream? Tony rolled over and closed his eyes. He couldn't help Hope with a stupid dream. He would only succeed in scaring her away. Thankfully, sleep came within minutes and he didn't have to face the muddy horse again.

⊗⊗⊗

"You'll be comfortable in here." Mark led Hope into the dark house, flipped on a light for her in the foyer, and motioned for her to sit on the now-familiar love seat in the middle of the library. Before they'd left the car, he forced down the memories that floated to the surface. They came fast now, Pandora's Box wide open. He remembered a fire and heart-wracking grief. Now, he regretted starting down this path and if Hope weren't already with him, he would've abandoned the exercise. He cleared his throat and looked down upon her sweet face.

"I would rather crawl into a dark hole and never return than remember my past." Finding a chair across from his guest, he regarded her with a stern gaze. Rather than pull back, she leaned closer and waited for him to continue.

"I'm with you," she whispered, touching his knee, her gaze full of

142

compassion. "Just close your eyes, and tell me what you see."

Mark did as she suggested and peeked under the lid of his psyche, trying to control the flow of memories. He was quite sure he couldn't handle it if they poured out all at once.

"Remember the priest," The Other prompted in his mind, and this time, Mark permitted his input.

"I remember a priest," Mark spat out and squeezed Hope's hand. *How do I explain this weakness to Paul?*

"Paul is locked in his room. Now, remember the priest…"

Obediently, Mark continued. "There was a fire and the priest was killed." Mark stopped short. There was terror and pain in that memory. He shuddered No more Superman, just a pitiful monster about to be betrayed by an innocent. Mark waited to see if he could avoid the memory as it washed back. *Did the priest die?*

As if on cue, Hope squeezed his hand. "I'm listening."

"Something terrible happened to him. And his boy." He paused. "Not his boy; a boy that loved him." Mark sat up a little straighter and dropped Hope's hand, his eyes still closed. "The whole town was burning, the work of the evil one. Miki is dead and the devil that killed him is smiling at me."

I am the priest?

Mark gasped and allowed the shock of the recollection to sink in before continuing. The Other insinuated already that he'd been a man of the cloth, that he had a human past before his divine calling. But, if he was the priest in his memories, who was Miki?

"He was such a good boy." Mark resisted less and the words came easier. "He loved me as a father, not a priest."

෬෪෯

Mark's voice changed and Hope sat forward to hear him. He spoke softer, with a thick accent, and recounted the past behind closed eyes. Hope's mind raced with the images his words conjured.

"Miki," Mark said his voice mournful. "The devil has tossed him aside and is coming for me, but the smoke is so thick, I can't breathe. The flock is screaming… and the sanctuary is aflame. This is no longer God's house. It has become the very depths of hell."

The clock ticked on the shelf beside them and Hope remained silent. She wondered when this all took place. Was Mark the priest? That would explain a lot and pose a ton of questions. He began again

143

and his accent grew thicker. Hope strained to discern the words.

"The devil is dragging me back into the church. Everything is going black…." Mark's voice was nearly inaudible and Hope leaned in closer. Then, in a loud voice, Mark burst out, *"Oh, God. Oh, God."* And then in his first language, he cried with even more despair, *"Bejárónö… Jézus…egyáltalán nem!"*

Hope started in her seat and gasped as Mark leapt up and crossed the room incredibly fast, holding his head in his hands. She didn't recognize him or his last few words. He bolted from the library and mounted the steps two at a time to the upstairs rooms. Hope heard a door slam and she was alone.

After waiting a nerve-wracking twenty minutes, Hope left the library. She went to the base of the stairs and listened. She was sorry for him, but it was a pain he must endure. All those years ago, something attacked him and the boy, and whatever happened after was simply too much to handle. How could he have forgotten? So many questions, but Hope would get no further answers tonight. She glanced at her watch and then to the front door. It was almost five and Glorie would be rising soon. Hope dreaded the sight of her; Mark needed her more. Deciding to leave him a short note, she went into the study down the hall from the library and found a sheet of paper and pen.

Mark, Call me. I'm here for you. -Your Hope

It wasn't Pulitzer Prize-winning stuff, but she thought it would do. Whenever Mark was ready to face her, he would call. Then she had a thought.

P.S. I will come visit you at your office today.

Hope placed the note beside the front door on the small table and retrieved the keys that lay there. The key chain said BMW and she recalled the car Paul had used to take her home. She found the arctic blue sedan in the huge garage and drove home as quickly as she could, praying Glorie would still be asleep. Of all the times for a visit from her sister. Hope sighed and set her jaw.

Thirty

See, I set before you today life and prosperity, death and destruction.
Deuteronomy 30:15

THE PRIEST WAS BLIND. HIS EYES WERE OPEN, BUT THE world had gone black. Aching from head to toe, he was weak as a baby, every bit of energy sapped from his body. He sat up with effort, his hands searching for clues in the dark. Cold wet dirt sifted through his shaking fingers. The air was damp and the only sound, his belabored breathing accompanied by the tinkling of water in the distance. The priest closed his eyes with understanding; he was in a cave.

His village sat atop miles of underground mazes. As a boy, he spent many fun-filled hours exploring them with his brothers. But this was no voluntary expedition and the priest fought the urge to scream. Cautiously coming to his feet, he was forced to stoop his six-foot-plus frame to take a few steps. He found a moist rock wall which he followed with his fingers, then froze in place when a faint noise, like the shuffle of feet in the dirt, sounded on his far left. The priest's heart skipped a beat, he wasn't alone. He was in the demon's lair. Gasping, the priest hugged the wall with his back. He opened his eyes wide in the darkness, but heard no other sound. Surely, whatever caused the first noise now watched him in the black hell.

"Sit down. It is day, yet."

Father Corescu heard the voice in his head, but it was louder than an entire choir in the quiet of the cave.

"I said SIT DOWN!"

He obediently found his seat in the place where he stood and faced the direction of the last audible noise.

Silence.

Father Corescu closed his eyes and prayed. First internally then aloud as he mumbled any words of comfort he could think of. The instant his meditations became audible, the creature that shared his

145

grave released a low growl that grew in intensity every second the priest continued. Father Corescu raised his voice in response to his evil companion's moan and as he reached the Lord's Prayer, the creature drew near and took him firmly by the throat. Father Corescu's windpipe was compressed with calculated pressure, just enough to silence him, but not enough to stop his breathing. The rough hands that held him were ice cold and smelled of burnt flesh.

The priest ceased praying and waited for the claws to open. When he was able, he whispered, "What do you want of me?" He sensed the presence of The Other kneeling beside him, although they were no longer in contact. He could hear raspy breath that smelled of decay. "Who are you?"

"Do not speak. I command you to sit still and be quiet." The Other shuffled away to its corner of the dark. Its command had been spoken without words, as before, and the priest obeyed, fearing another confrontation.

Father Corescu leaned against the dirt wall and closed his eyes. Before long, he slipped into a fitful sleep.

The priest awoke to a burning sensation in the flesh of his right arm. As before, his eyes were open, but could see nothing. He remembered to be silent but tugged at his arm and then used his left hand to feel the wound. When his fingers reached the fiery pain, he found the face of The Other fixed upon his arm. Father Corescu couldn't pull free so he used his left fist to pound the head of the beast that held him. After two short blows, his wrist was caught in mid-air by a cruel hand, invisible in the black void. He broke the silence with a shout and immediately his cry was squelched by the voice of The Other in his mind.

"SILENCE!" The unmistakable gritty voice of the beast rumbled to a growl in the priest's mental ear. Its claw-like fingers playfully pinched the priest's lips together. *"I will not hear another word from you. Nod your head if you understand."*

Father Corescu nodded, and slumped helplessly against the earthen wall of his lightless dungeon. Where was God in this prison? He wanted badly to pray, but couldn't muster the strength. How long had he been in this hole? Why was he being tortured and would it get worse? Was he in hell?

In time, the creature removed his mouth from the priest's skin with a loud smack. Dropping the limp arm into Father Corescu's lap, it spoke to him telepathically. *"Do not speak and I will not kill you. Now, open your mouth."*

The priest did as commanded and a warm liquid hit his tongue. At first, he thought it was water, but once it registered a few seconds, he knew it was blood. Disgusted, he spat and stubbornly pressed his lips together. *What is happening to me, Lord? Where are you?*

Desperate for the guidance he had always depended upon, tears welled in the priest's eyes as he realized he was alone with the monster and God was nowhere in sight

Thirty-One

Blessed is the man who does not walk in the counsel of the wicked...
Psalm 1:1

PAUL OPENED HIS EYES, NOT SURE WHAT TO EXPECT. For hours, he'd been assaulted by any number of painful episodes. Most of these were in his head and he hoped the worst was past. Peeking through half-open eyelids, he gazed about the room.

Nothing. The pain was gone.

Paul sighed with relief and sat up. The night before had been hellish. Not only had he suffered through the worst head pain yet, but he had been tormented by dreadful dreams that were real enough to frighten him awake. He had never been much of a dreamer, but these night terrors were ghastly.

Paul's life before and after meeting Mark had been pleasant and simple, thus he wasn't familiar with tragedy or trauma. As a result, when the horrible dreams hit, filled of gory and detestable images, he didn't know what to make of them. Should he share them with Mark? Or was his partner too occupied with the woman to give his nightmares any attention? Paul had decided to ignore them and put on a happy face.

The night he took Ms. Brannen home, he barely repressed the horrible images his night terrors had supplied. Even later that night, as he sat with Mark and attempted to comfort him, Paul realized the reason he had opened a vein that second time was due to the dreams. In every dream he had, Mark fed off him or he fed off someone else. Paul loathed the idea of drinking blood and couldn't wrap his mind around how anyone could make themselves do it.

So why do I drink blood in all my dreams? Is it because of that voice?

The dreams were accompanied by a disembodied voice, the same raspy grumble from his torturous headaches. But in the dreams, Paul understood the language and he listened to every word. The voice comforted him and told him he would be all right, that the future was

148

brighter than ever. And even though it never occurred to Paul that he was missing out on anything, the voice assured him regularly that he was. The voice assured him that he was missing out on a lot.

Paul put his feet to the floor and disguised his state of mind. Mark would be in to check on him soon and he wanted to at least appear refreshed and back to normal. He headed to the bath and turned on the shower.

They're just dreams. They don't mean anything.

Paul barely finished his thought when he heard a reply, deep within his subconscious. The voice teased him now in English, reminding him that he was getting the short end of the stick. That he could have much more. That life was meant to be full of pleasure and power. And then the voice told him that his master was losing his mind.

"You better help him straighten this out before he dooms us all…"

"No!" Paul grasped his head with both hands and squeezed his eyes shut as if the voice could be squelched by willpower. It looked to have worked; the only noise he heard was the running shower, his only sensation the rising steam. Paul lowered his hands and peeled off his clothes.

Yes, a long, hot shower is all I need. I lost a lot of blood. Of course I'm going to be mixed up in the head for a few days. It's only natural.

Paul stepped under the hot torrent. No matter how the headaches might affect him and no matter how frightening the dreams, and no matter how heretical the raspy, ghostlike voice in his head became, he had to hide it from Mark. It wouldn't do to bother him with such trivialities. No, it wouldn't do at all.

ৎৡৎ

Mark combed his ruffled hair in his bathroom mirror. The epiphany was good; he was now aware of his origins. So what if a demonic creature abducted him four hundred years ago? He was still a man of God. He was still called to Judge sinners. Surely he didn't fabricate his calling, create a delusion out of fear and self-loathing. Such behavior belonged to the insane, not hard-working servants of the Most High.

He rolled the previous evening's events around in his head as he showered and dressed. He planned to go into the office, wrap up loose ends, cancel his appointments, and sign off for a vacation. He had work now of a more personal nature and he wanted to get to it. The memories of the devil that attacked him in the chapel were now clear and he

149

thought it amazing he had suppressed them for so long. Although he spent only a few horrific days in the clutches of the beast, he marveled at the creature's tenacity and devotion. If the devil-beast hadn't pulled him from the fire and used him as a plaything, he wouldn't have survived. It had been in God's hands.

And what about Hope? Would she support him or attempt to convince him he was doing evil instead of good? Would she even see him? He'd run out on her rather abruptly.

She said she would never leave, no matter what I remembered.

Mark held on to that promise as he stepped to Paul's locked room. Once the door was open, Mark was relieved that Paul was not in bed.

"Paul?" Mark called just as his patient stepped out of the large walk-in closet with two empty hangers in his hand. He was freshly showered and dressed in his usual Dockers and comfortable Polo. "Welcome back to the land of the living."

Mark pulled him into his embrace. He had only recently become so demonstrative and by the way Paul stiffened without returning the contact, it was obvious he didn't understand the change. Mark ignored his unease and didn't immediately let go. He held on, emotionally moved by the sight of his old friend recovered, taking in his smell, and the feel of his slender shoulders. He closed his eyes to capture the moment in his mind, as if he might never have Paul to himself again. Finally, his long-time companion began to squirm. Mark didn't release until he had made a mental imprint; in many ways, things were about to change forever. Finally, Mark dropped his arms and stepped back, searching Paul's face.

"What happened?" Paul asked seeing something in Mark's countenance.

Ignoring Paul's query, Mark asked his own. "How long have you been up?"

"Since about seven," Paul answered, but his eyes filled with frustration.

"How do you feel?" Mark attempted to read what Paul was hiding. The man had never been disloyal, but for the moment, his mind was shut down.

"I feel like a million bucks."

"Good," Mark replied, hiding the weariness brought on by recent events. "Is there something you want to tell me?"

Paul paused a moment and shook his head. "No, really, I'm feeling great. Can I get anything for you?"

Mark regarded Paul a moment longer and decided to let it go. Maybe it was his imagination. He was exhausted and he sincerely didn't want to go into the recent events concerning Reuben right away. Paul picked the name out of his head.

"What're we going to do with him?" Insistent, Paul placed his hands on his hips. "He's still in the cellar?"

"Yes, I was just about to go check on him." Paul looked like he was about to head out the door and Mark stopped him. "No, I don't want you near him yet. He's poisonous."

Mark stepped into the hall ahead of Paul and started down the stairs, issue settled. Paul didn't give up. He followed, his step light and strong.

"I've known Reuben as long as you have. Do you think he can overpower me with mere words?"

Mark sensed Paul's willfulness stemmed from his recent medicinal treatment. It would pass, but for the moment, he found the boy's impudence irritating. Mark turned to face him and captured him with his eyes. In light of his new awareness about his wicked origins, Mark distantly wondered if he had the power or conviction to control his favored servant. He held his gaze a moment longer. Paul's blue eyes were clear and they awaited his command.

"I forbid you to go to Reuben." He waited for Paul to nod, and then he continued in a softer tone. "I'll return around two and we will handle him together."

As he spoke, Mark remembered the matter of his abandoned BMW at Hope's and he didn't want Paul to be aware of it. Paul nodded, clearly dissatisfied with his master's orders. He excused himself to the kitchen.

Mark followed. "Get something for Reuben to eat," he said, his tone stern. "Something simple. Get it now."

Paul opened the icebox and removed a stack of sandwiches on thick bread. Without a word, Mark took one off the top and turned to leave the kitchen. He sensed Paul about to remark, but chickened out.

Good thing, Mark thought. *I can't take any more insolence right now.*

He proceeded down the hall toward the cellar entrance. When he passed the foyer, he saw that Hope had left him a note. A warm feeling washed over him and he pocketed the piece of paper and continued to the cellar. He'd give Reuben some water and food and then head to the office to await her arrival.

In the basement, Reuben slept, slumped as far as his duct tape

151

prison allowed. Mark stood before him and silently regarded his driver. The kid showed signs of neglect in his hollow cheeks and the stench in the cellar was incredible since he hadn't been untied to relieve himself. He hadn't been fed and had only received a small amount of water. Mark pitied him then and hated his weakness.

"Fool! Destroy him while you can still think straight. You are losing your nerve as you lose your power. Do you not feel it?" The Other whispered cruel words in Mark's mind.

Yes, he was not feeling himself lately, but he wasn't losing his power. The Other was a deceiver and shouldn't be trusted.

Reuben's eyes fluttered open and he met his master's gaze. *"Yep, still here. What're you going to do to me? Starve me to death?"* The tape over his mouth remained secure, but Reuben focused his thoughts with precision.

"I suppose I will kill you. What do you think I should do?" Mark knew what he was going to say before he said it.

∞

"I don't care. I hate you." Reuben closed his eyes and looked away. His head swam with lack of sustenance and even though he desperately wanted something to eat, he would never ask the creature before him for help, his hate thick enough to die for. The boss stepped forward and ripped the tape from his mouth and then sliced the tape from his right arm with his pocketknife.

"Eat this. You have two minutes…"

Even as his pride screamed foul, his flesh delighted at the sight and smell of the hastily-made meal. Reuben grabbed the sandwich without a second thought and stuffed it down. The boss would tape him up in another minute but he was so very hungry. It didn't matter they were going to kill him, maybe even tonight. For now, he would eat. His traitorous belly convinced him that it'd be much better to die with food in his stomach than not. Swallowing in huge gulps, he just managed to get it down before the boss grabbed his free arm and resealed it to the chair with the tape.

I might be dead tomorrow, but for now, at least I'm full.

Reuben closed his eyes and tried to think of something nice to occupy his mind. It wasn't going to happen, so he fell asleep and dreamed of freedom however it came.

152

Thirty-Two

For God did not give us a spirit of timidity,
But a spirit of power, of love and of self-discipline.
2 Timothy 1:7

PAUL HUNG UP WITH HOPE AND FINISHED HIS COCOA. Mark wanted the woman at his office at noon, so he obediently relayed the message via telephone. Rinsing out his mug, Paul grimaced, his jealousy growing at the mere thought of her. Something would have to give and soon. He stared out the kitchen window, wondering how long he could hide his displeasure from Mark and he hated that he had to do such a thing.

And what of Reuben?

Mark's driver was in the cellar right now. Paul pictured him, strapped to a chair, sitting under the light bulb, wondering what was going to happen. What *was* going to happen? Mark was definitely not himself or he would have already finished him off. Mark said there'd be changes, but Paul didn't expect his master to lose his nerve.

A loud noise emanated from the direction of the basement. Was Reuben loose? Paul took a few steps toward the hall that led to the cellar entrance. Certainly Mark would understand Paul's need to check.

Thump!

Sure he heard it that time, Paul proceeded to the basement door and listened. No other sound issued forth. Why didn't Mark want him down there? The guy was tied up and helpless. Paul put his hand on the knob and paused; Mark had expressly forbidden him from going down there.

But there's that noise. Paul's pulse quickened. *I think Mark would want me to check it out. If Reuben gets away and runs to the police, then Mark will be cross at me for not checking on him.*

Convinced, mostly, Paul turned the knob only to be stopped by the front gate bell. Huffing in frustration, he turned back toward the front and clenched his fists.

153

ख़ॐ

Connie pressed the intercom button on the device again and was surprised to see the gate swing open to admit him. The day before, he'd been reticent to confront anyone, but today things were different. He'd waited two hours for Reuben to show, but only the doctor passed his hiding place at the top of the drive. Then he returned to the kid's condo and came up empty a second time. Connie was running out of options. After two stiff shots of whiskey from the mini-bar, he hopped into his car determined to waltz right up to Corescu's door and ask to see the kid. Just in case there was any trouble, he was pleased that he'd decided to wear his new knife.

Connie pulled the Taurus up to the front door. As he placed his finger on the doorbell, the huge door swung inward.

"Yes? What is it?"

Connie found himself face-to-face with *another* kid, eighteen if that, and by his demeanor, also in the service of the local medical philanthropist. Who was this guy that surrounded himself with young men?

"Well, hello there, Mister...?" Connie usually got an introduction with that line and the man stammered before responding.

"B-Black, Paul Black. Do you have a delivery or something?"

Connie smiled at the guy's agitation and held out his business card. "Mr. Black, I'm Connie Nixon, of the *Feather Herald*. I've come all the way from Kentucky to interview Mr. Reuben Stuckey for a Young Fiction Writer's award that he won from our publisher. Is he in?" The Paul character didn't reply. Connie added, "I checked his house and musta missed him. His neighbors told me he might be here, at work."

"You came all the way from the city?"

Connie wondered if his ruse was too transparent and he didn't answer, but instead waited to see what Mr. Black would do.

"Well, you wasted your gas and your time. Reuben's not here. He took the day off."

Paul was closing the door as he spoke, but Connie caught it with his palm before it shut in his face. "Uh, Mr. Black, may I call you Paul? Do you know where I might find him? It's very important."

Black gave him a sidelong glance before snatching the offered business card and stuffing it into his pocket. "Try the zoo. Bye, Mr. Nixon." Connie objected to a closed door.

A bizarre young man lying about Stuckey. *Check.* Connie didn't need a crystal ball to see through the guy's B.S. He drove back down the driveway and parked across the street for another stake-out. Eventually, someone had to go in or out and he'd follow. For now, he'd wait; as Connie had always been a patient sort.

కుస్తా

"Ms. Booker, cancel my appointments, today and all week." Mark flipped through his Rolodex and found the intern's pager number. "And page Doctor Wedgeworth. I want him to take my rounds. Also, I do not want to be disturbed until Ms. Brannen arrives."

Mark didn't wait for a reply, but hung up and sighed. A few loose ends to tie and he would be covered for a week. Mark leaned forward and rested his head face down in his palms. Paul was trying to contact him telepathically and he couldn't bring himself to listen. An uneasy feeling washed over him and he squeezed his eyes against it. He simply didn't want to investigate. Whatever Paul needed would have to wait. He concentrated on Hope and effectively blocked any other communication.

Maybe I can keep this up until noon.

Mark's stomach growled and he grumbled to himself. He'd sensed another Calling this morning. At 7:30 p.m., he was to judge a widow three states away. Her misdeeds were many, but he didn't know if he would heed the call or not. In the past, he knew why and who was calling him. Now he wasn't sure. Mark concentrated a little harder and tried to see the widow's face. He could not; in fact, he was completely disconnected from the unseen world he normally frequented. Had he heard the call? Maybe he dreamed it. Still, the emptiness in his stomach was real and he couldn't ignore that particular call for long.

Mark closed his eyes and turned his thoughts to Hope; her face, her smile, her radiance. She had helped him resurrect the memory of the priest, but along with the priest came The Other. Mark sighed and gave himself over to re-live another portion of his revivified past.

Thirty-Three

Look to the LORD and His strength;
seek His face always.
1 Chronicles 16:11

"OPEN YOUR MOUTH, PRIEST."

In the pitch black hell, the voice in his head was adamant and Corescu obeyed. He parted his lips and this time the liquid ran faster and with more volume into his throat so that it spilled over his lips and onto his chest. Once again, it was blood, but this time, it poured directly out of The Other's open vein; an abomination that he didn't have the strength to resist. After the third gulp, he decided that it wasn't so terrible.

Presently, The Other removed his arm and pushed Corescu against the wall to sit him upright. *"Now, one more thing..."* Father Corescu's right arm was extended and he tried in vain to pull it back. *"So close. It is almost finished, see."*

"I can't SEE anything." Corescu didn't speak, but he hoped his sentiment traveled telepathically. He longed desperately to regain his vision and his patience wore thin.

"You will. Now, be still."

Exhaling, Corescu relaxed his arm. A sharp blade raked across the soft underside, slicing it deep and sure. He gasped, but caught himself before he screamed. After a few seconds, his arm was pressed firmly, and the wound stopped aching. As he waited in the dark dirt cell, he took inventory of his condition.

His headache had cleared and his aches and pains from lying on the hard earth were gone. He turned his attention to his arm wounds and no pain lingered there either. It dawned on him that he actually felt quite glorious. When he reached out his hand, he wasn't entirely surprised to find that The Other's arm was pressed into his own. For some evil purpose, the beast spilled his blood directly into his open skin.

156

Father Corescu attempted a telepathic question. *"Why do you do this?"*

"You have been chosen. You are mine. I will make you mine for eternity."

The Other's thoughts carried a grateful tone, but he couldn't fathom what the beast meant. He ran his palm tentatively along his captor's arm and brushed the crumbling, brittle skin. Had he been burned so badly in the fire or was this the normal state of a demon's flesh?

"Hah, no," The Other responded with a laugh. *"I became trapped in the fire myself. It seems I allowed my lust to overwhelm my common sense."*

A conversational, almost friendly tone had replaced the bitter cruel voice of minutes past. The priest didn't know how to react. Should he speak? Should he resist?

The Other said then in his mind, *"I have been watching you for days. If you would have only listened, if you had only heeded my call, I would not have had to smoke you out."*

"Wha—" Father Corescu stopped himself only to continue in his mind. *"What do you mean? I would have done anything to avoid that carnage."*

"No, you did not come to me. You turned your back on me repeatedly. You thought I was the devil." The Other paused as its words sank in. *"I am not the adversary from your Old Testament storybook. I only wish I was, and then perhaps I would not have suffered like I have waiting for you."*

The priest didn't understand. *"You've been calling me?"* Father Corescu vaguely recalled an instance a week before the fire. He had been asleep in his own bed when he awoke in a sweat, his mind seething with unclean thoughts. *"Was this your way of calling me?"*

"Dreams are a window to the subconscious. If they had only worked, and you would have allowed yourself to be beckoned this way, you could have avoided the death of your sheep. But, no matter...you are here now. I forgive you. Come."

The priest allowed the creature to help him to his feet. When they were both upright, The Other took his wrist and pulled him along.

"Look at the night, priest. Look with your new eyes."

Father Corescu followed for several meters and soon began to see the faintest light. When they reached the mouth of the cave, he saw that it was night, the moon obscured by thick thunderclouds. They stepped into the brisk air, the evening alive with scents and shining with unearthly light.

"How?" The priest clamped his mouth shut to continue silently. *"This can't be real. This is a trick."*

"This is real, priest. Come, have a look at your master." The Other

157

stepped in front of the priest and placed a hand on either of his shoulders. A head shorter, The Other looked up and stared directly into Father Corescu's face.

The Other was a *he* not an *it*. His face was that of a man, but his skin was blackened and burned and the eyes were shining red orbs in dark bruised sockets. The priest recognized him as the devil that killed Miki. At the recollection, Father Corescu put his hands to his eyes to weep. He could find no tears even though his heart burned with grief. The Other pulled the priest's hands down and his red eyes softened.

"Hush that nonsense. Priests do not have sons. That child belonged to his Maker, not you." The Other turned and began toward the tree line hobbling with a side-shuffling manner. Father Corescu didn't follow, but stood and watched him go. *"Follow me. We must find food before the sunrise."*

Still, Father Corescu didn't move, still trying to bring Miki's face to his memory. Then, he couldn't remember how he knew the boy, or what his life was like before the cave. His memory was dissolving in real time and he scrambled to retain something before it erased completely. He heard the Other's second command to follow and he took a step, only to stop again.

"PRIEST!" The Other screamed in his mind and the father jumped, forced his feet to move, and he caught up with the dark form of his new master. *"Stop trying to recall yourself. The old priest is dead. You are mine, now. Reborn. A new creation for my pleasure."*

Father Corescu followed his mind numb. But what about God? How could he serve this devil *and* his God?

"What is the Scripture, priest? Quote it for me."

A few days ago, Father Corescu knew the Holy Scriptures forwards and backwards, but now he remembered nothing. His mind reeled with the realization that he had no past, that this demon had stolen it from him.

"No servant can serve two masters. You are of no use to your God. You are unclean, a beast, a monster." The Other pressed the priest's shoulder firmly enough to make his knees buckle and he squatted on the damp leaves coating the forest floor. *"Wait here."*

With sadness, the priest acknowledged his weakness compared to the brute strength of his master. With his new eyesight, he watched The Other jog ahead ten strides and dodge left into the heavy brush. *How long will I have to wait?*

"As long as it takes." The Other's raspy answer came as soon as the

158

question was thought and a chill went down Father Corescu's spine. His most private thoughts were no longer his own. The Other truly did have control over him body *and* mind.

Helpless and alone, Father Corescu examined his fingers in the cloud-filtered moonlight. Was he a monster now? Although his hands were caked with mud and dirt, he didn't have claws. He held them out from his body to see the horrible wound on his arm. It was gone. He looked down at his bedclothes. They were tattered and stained black with blood.

Bedclothes? He couldn't remember the last time he slept in a bed.

The Father settled down on the leaves and listened to the night. His new ears heard everything. He'd been reborn into a wondrous being, but was now reviled by God?

Still, he marveled at his newfound abilities. It was superhuman, yes. The work of the devil? Probably. But he believed firmly he could use Satan's power against him if he understood it further.

Father Corescu continued to look and listen and perfect his control over his senses as he waited for The Other to return. Until he could figure out how God fit into his life, he would conquer the devil in it..

Thirty-Four

Anyone who strikes a man and kills him shall surely be put to death.
Exodus 21:12

PAUL SLAMMED THE DOOR IN THE NOSY REPORTER'S FACE and an incredible sense of unease gripped his spirit. Before he could squelch his unnamed fears, he heard from The Other in his mind.

"And the walls come tumbling down, Paulie. You better set things right before we are all destroyed."

Unconsciously, Paul agreed with the now familiar inner voice. The Nixon guy knew something and probably had been talking to Reuben already. Paul hurried to the cellar, a growing panic in his heart. The basement was a big empty room with no windows and a single light bulb. In the center, Reuben sat in the chair, just as Mark had described, securely taped. The stench of urine, feces, and sweat turned Paul's stomach. He approached Mark's driver, hopefully appearing ferocious, but—completely out of character—Reuben whimpered, inclining his head toward the water bottle on the concrete floor. Paul grasped the bottle and ripped the tape from Reuben's mouth.

"I'm so thirsty," Reuben gasped and Paul put the bottle to his lips. After two huge pulls of water, Paul returned the cap and stepped back from the chair. Reuben regarded him in silence as Paul gathered his thoughts.

Finally, he nodded toward the driver and spoke in a low voice. "You okay?"

"Yeah," Reuben said, his angry, more familiar persona rolling into view. "I'm fine as wine, queer as beer, frisky as whisky. Can you cut me loose? I'm getting a rash."

Paul sent him a glare, temporarily disoriented. If he waited, maybe the voice would tell him what to do.

"What are you staring at?" Reuben taunted. "Are you wondering how I got here? The boss not keeping you in the loop?" When Paul

160

didn't reply, he continued, "Well, I'll tell you what I'm doing here. Besides sitting here like a freaking blood bank, I'm waiting for the boss to find the time to lop off my head."

"Blood bank? What does that mean?" Paul stepped closer.

"I thought that'd pique your interest, you freak," Reuben smirked and turned his head. "Why do you think I'm sitting here tied up and defenseless?"

Paul cautiously leaned to Reuben's left to see the back of his neck. He wore a loose tank undershirt and wasn't there a dark spot of blood dried on the collar? Of course, there would be no evidence of a laceration or bite. Paul clenched his jaw at the notion of Mark drinking the kid's blood and Reuben laughed.

"You are *so sad*. It pains you that you're not the only pin cushion in the family, huh?"

"Shut up!" Sputtering, Paul grabbed the roll of tape out of the box at his feet. His face burned with revulsion and he wished to silence the man before he could say anything else. Mark had said it; Reuben's words were poisonous.

"Don't be jealous. I'm sure that when I'm gone, you'll get your boyfriend back. I mean, after he gets tired of his new lady-friend."

Struggling with the tape Paul couldn't find the edge. He pulled at it frantically as Reuben continued to berate him from his chair.

"I think he might have liked it, having some of the old Reuben in his gullet. I think he might like to come back again before he does me in for good." Reuben watched Paul wrestle with the tape. "I'll bet he likes my juice better anyway."

"Shut up! Just shut up! If you don't be quiet, I'll-I'll-I'll kill you!" Paul stammered, still struggling with the tape as sweat popped up on his brow.

"You thought you were special. You get off on it, don't you? You're one sick puppy." Reuben whistled a little tune in between provocations. "How can you live with yourself? Your lover is a monster. He's a *vampire,* for crying out loud. How do you sleep at night?"

Paul growled and reached forward with his fist. As hard as he could, he struck Reuben across the face, drawing blood from his lower lip.

"That man is not a monster! He's our friend. He takes care of us. You have no right to judge him. *You* are the one who's dangerous. *You* are the one ruining everything. You're the bad seed, Reuben!" His voice

161

firm but plaintive in his own ears, Paul stopped before he struck the man again. Leveling his gaze, he scowled, "You never got it, did you? You love no one but yourself."

"The best day of my life will be the last. I hate you both."

Paul sputtered, "You may not be so lucky. I don't think Mark has made up his mind. Maybe you'll be a blood bank forever. Maybe we'll keep you down here and you can feed his hunger. You could last decades, maybe centuries, tied to a chair like this, sitting in your own filth, begging us for every morsel of food and each drop of water. That's what you deserve."

Reuben stopped whistling. "He's made up his mind, all right. I saw the look in his eye."

Paul gave up on the tape and it fell back into the box. "You have no idea what goes on in his head. He always has our best interest at heart and you have always tried to derail him." Paul hoped he sounded tough. "I'm not going to let you ruin us. Guess who just rang our doorbell looking for you."

Reuben looked away and resumed whistling.

His chest tightening, Paul slapped his cheek. "Tell me about that reporter! Why did he come here?"

"Look, man, I ain't answering. The reporter is my business, not yours." Reuben stubbornly set his jaw.

"You'll answer the question if you know what's good for you."

"Whatever information I have in my head is mine. You can't force it out of me like your sweetie-pie can. So just stuff it, *Paulie.*"

"If you want to keep your head," Paul replied, mimicking Mark's subtly powerful voice, "you'll answer my question."

Reuben laughed in his face. "Like you're going to relieve me of my head? Let's not get all in a tizzy," Reuben said, not cowed.

"What did you tell that reporter?"

Reuben shook his head.

"You led him right to our door! What did you say to him?" Paul no longer hid his panic.

"Would you chill out? The guy's snooping, that's all. What could I tell him, anyway?" Reuben paused then continued with a chuckle, "No one would believe me."

Paul cursed and sharply kicked Reuben's shin. When he got no reaction, he headed for the stairwell. A scrabble of noise behind him caused him to turn in time to see Reuben straining violently against his bonds. His cocky smile had evaporated and his eyes burned with hate.

"I wish I had told someone! I wish I told that stupid reporter more than I did!"

Paul jogged back to his side, his heart hammering. "You *did* speak to that reporter! What did you tell him?"

"Shove it," was all he would say.

Paul clenched his fists and screamed his frustration to the ceiling. Turning back to the steps, he returned to the main floor.

"Mark! Mark! Please!" Paul tried in vain to connect to his partner, but the line was dead. Slamming his fists against the wall, Paul sniffed back real tears. *Reuben's going to bring us all down!*

The wheels were in motion and Mark wouldn't be home for hours. Paul would have to get the information out of the kid on his own. What if the reporter dragged Mark's name through the mud or worse—contacted the police to fill out an arrest warrant?

Without forethought, Paul grabbed a butcher knife from the block on the kitchen counter and headed back to the cellar. One way or another, Reuben would answer his questions.

⚜

Hope's twin sister spent nearly two thousand dollars before they loaded up the Suburban and headed for Whitford City Memorial. She desperately wanted to keep Glorie and Mark apart, but couldn't think of a legitimate way to do so. Could she waltz into Mark's office and pretend that everything in the world was normal and sane?

Can I forget that my new boyfriend is a ritualistic killer with a god complex who wants to transform me into a vampire so we can suck blood together for all eternity? Hope chuckled and Glorie sent her a look.

"What's so funny?" Her voice was hard and Hope shook her head.

"Let's just go on home—"

"No way José," Glorie cut her off. "I came nine hundred miles to meet this Prince Charming." She smoothed down her lavender linen skirt and checked her make-up in the sun visor mirror. "Plus, it's not often I look better than you." Glorie applied fresh lipstick and kissed the air. "It's almost noon. We'd better hurry."

Hope nodded and pulled out of the parking space.

"I hate to break it to you, but you do *not* look better than me." She said to lighten the air between them before they reached the hospital.

"We may be twins, but I'm the hot one," her sister replied, still admiring her face in the mirror. Glorie sounded like she meant it and Hope left it alone.

163

❦

In his office, dozing fitfully with his head in his hands, Mark roused to the sound of the women entering Fran's office. He sat up and concentrated on their voices. Although he dreaded meeting her miserable twin sister, he could hardly wait to see Hope again.

He closed his eyes and eavesdropped on the women's conversation.

❦

"Hey, Fran! You remember my sister Glorie?" Hope smiled at her friend as the two women shook hands.

"Of course, how's life in the Mary Land? Last time I laid eyes on you, you were to move into a *biiiigggg* house!"

"I love it. How're you doing?" Glorie and Fran exchanged a few more pleasantries and Hope stood by, her mind racing to their meeting with Mark.

"And what is it I been hearing 'bout you and the doc?" Fran shook Hope by the shoulder. In a softer voice, she whispered, "*Ewwww.* He's me *boss* for lardssake!"

Hope smiled and shrugged. "We can't choose who we fall in love with." Spoken before she even knew what she was going to say, Hope instantly regretted her words. Fran was still whispering *ewww* to Glorie as she went over to her desk phone.

"Dr. Corescu? Hope Brannen and her sister are here." Fran stood again and returned to Glorie's side.

"Is there something wrong with this guy?" Glorie whispered as if the doctor could hear them several doors away. Hope figured he probably could.

"Oh, he's just peachy." Fran sat on the edge of her desk and waved her hand to Glorie. "He's me boss. It just doesn't seem right. Now when Hope and I have lunch, she's gonna be after telling me how good he is in the sack!"

"Fran!" Hope flushed red and shushed them. "He'll hear you!"

"He can't hear us in here, luv, his office is three doors down." Fran winked at Glorie who laughed and started for the office door.

"Well, what're we waiting for?" Her twin pulled it open and stepped into the hallway.

"Wait, Hope, do you know anything about Dr. Corescu taking a leave? Are you guys, ya know, getting married or something?"

Hope's eyebrows went up at Fran's conspiratorial tone. "No, why?" *What has Mark been telling her?*

"Well, he nixed all his appointments for the week. I just figured he's going on Holiday."

Hope shrugged and played dumb.

"Oh, well, I guess I'll be takin' the week off me-self…" Fran trailed off as she sat back down to her desk.

"Come on, Hopie, the Doctor is *in*." Impatient, Glorie tugged Hope's arm again.

Hope pasted on a smile as she knocked on Mark's door. When he beckoned they enter, he was seated at his desk, half-heartedly ruffling through a file folder. Instantly, Hope saw the weariness in his countenance and her heart broke for him. He was really suffering, and he was suffering alone.

☙

Reuben spotted the knife in Paul's hand and laughed aloud. In all their years together, the guy had never exhibited any real aggression. Now the man's thin frame shook with rage and his floppy hair hung in his eyes in wet strings.

"What're you going to do with that?" Reuben asked, still giggling at the spectacle.

"Shut up!" Paul paced the room, slicing the air with the knife. Reuben stifled his laughter, growing wary.

"You plan on cuttin' me? Why? What can you do? Unless you chop off my head, I'll just heal right up. I'm cursed—*you're* cursed. Freaking idiot, your boyfriend cursed us forever, or did you—"

"Shut up!"

Reuben laughed. "I know what happened. You were up there chopping onions and thought 'Hey, I think I will go check on 'ol Reuben'."

"How did that reporter know to come here?" Through clenched teeth, Paul drilled Reuben with his glare.

Reuben raised an eyebrow. "Does Dr. Corescu know you're down here?" With the mention of the doctor, Paul's face froze and the knife clattered to the floor. "Hah! He told you to stay away from me, eh? You've forgotten who's the master and who are the slaves." Reuben reveled in Paul's sudden anguish. "Yeah, that's right. My skin may be darker, but you're as much a slave as I am, ya jerk."

"Shut up! I'm nothing like you!" Paul stooped down and retrieved the knife. "Shut up!" He made a threatening gesture, but Reuben didn't flinch.

"Oh, you're just like me, only you been relishing your delusion—just like your master." Reuben lifted his chin inviting Paul to slit his throat. "Go ahead. I want to die, I hate this whole thing. Just don't fool yourself; you're the master's house boy, I'm his sweaty field hand, and we both answer to his appetite."

Paul growled deep in his throat and stepped behind Reuben, laying the blade of the knife against the taut skin of his throat. "You are so wrong," Paul hissed in his ear. The sharp edge nicked Reuben's skin just enough to pinch. "We're partners. I've never been a slave. You have no idea what you're talking about. Tell me what you told the reporter before I slit your throat for real."

Was he serious? Couldn't be, the guy was too squeamish to commit murder. A tiny trickle of blood oozed down Reuben's chest from the wound Paul made and he allowed a quiet chuckle.

"Look, Paul," Reuben spoke carefully, as to not brush against the blade. "He was just some guy at the bar, he's nothing. Chill out before you hurt somebody." Reuben experienced the first pang of fear when Paul didn't remove the knife. Was this boyish waif of a man capable of cold-blooded murder? Reuben realized too late that he was. "Wait, Paul, I'm sorry. Wait." Reuben humbled his tone. "The boss is going to be awful mad at you for being down here. Have you ever made the boss mad? It ain't pretty."

Reuben strained against his bonds, keeping still against the blade making its impression in his skin. For the first time since his youth, a tear escaped his eye and ran down his cheek.

ⳁ℘ℰℼ

Paul didn't say a word, but pondered Reuben's challenge. Yes, Mark would be angry at his disobedience. But something was askew with his partner the last few days. A month ago, he never would've tied Reuben up and left him in the cellar. It would have been a non-issue; Reuben would be dead. End of story.

Yes, your master needs your help. He will be happy for you to dispose of the traitor. Help him help himself.

The voice in his head whispered advice and he listened. It cared. It knew things. And it thought Paul was the man to solve their issues.

It's my duty to protect Mark from himself. Paul agreed with the

166

disembodied voice that plagued him. He would prove his love and devotion by taking care of this nasty matter alone. Mark might even thank him. Resolute, Paul increased the pressure of the knife against Reuben's throat. He'd seen it done in the movies hundreds of times, it shouldn't be hard. For dramatic effect he whispered into Reuben's ear. "Any last words?"

"Wait!" Reuben struggled against the duct tape crying for help.

Paul took a deep breath. *How hard can it be?*

"Just do it."

Paul released the air from his lungs and simultaneously drew the blade as deeply and firmly as he could across the front of Reuben's throat. It wasn't hard at all.

"Look at that, little Paulie. Look how his life flows out so easily. Haven't you ever wondered what it is like? Do you want to be like your master? What are you afraid of? It will make you stronger. Quick, before he is dead…"

What could it hurt? Paul did as The Other commanded, and it was right. He had been missing out.

Thirty-Five

Where, O Death, are your plagues?
Where, O Grave, is your destruction?
Hosea 13:14

AN UNIMAGINABLE IMAGE FLASHED ACROSS MARK'S mind as he entertained the women in his office: Paul standing over Reuben's headless body. Mark bolted from his chair and Hope and Glorie jumped with fear. Mark hardly noticed and he pulled Hope out of the office and closed the door, his mind racing with what the image could mean.

Paul! Oh, Paul, what have you done!

"What? What?" Hope asked, her eyes searching his.

Mark took her by the shoulders, his mouth a firm line. "I have to leave!" Hope grabbed at his arms, but he pulled away and headed down the hall. She didn't follow and he sensed somewhere far back in his mind that she wondered if she should stay with her sister or chase him down. He had reached the stairwell when he heard her say to the women, "Emergency, I'll be right back!"

After that her heels clattered to his position. Mark couldn't allow her to interfere, not with this, not yet. He slipped from the hospital stairwell to his cellar in a matter of moments.

Paul was in trouble. And what of Reuben? The answer lay in the floor at his feet.

C380

Scoffing into her hand, Glorie joined Fran at her desk. Hope's boyfriend was even freakier than she'd imagined. "Fran, your boss is weird." Glorie took a seat across from the desk. "He just ran out of here for no reason. Zoom, right out the door; scared me half to death."

Fran put down her remaining files and brought her finger to her temple to make a circle. "Don't be too surprised, luv. If you ask me, he's off his nut."

168

"You think?"

"Well, I'm not much to gossip, but," she leaned in to whisper, "he gives me the creeps." Fran jerked herself upright and tightly crossed her arms. "There, I've said it! This is the best job I've ever had, but if I never had to see the boss, I'd be a singing bird."

"Well, I don't like him. What does Hope see in him? She's totally gah-gah." Glorie threw her hands up in exasperation. "Gah-gah!"

"I fancy she's after his looks. Hope can have any man she wants, but, I'll tell you the truth—he makes me feel *icky*. Does that make sense or am I heading for the loonies?"

Glorie agreed. "No, it makes perfect sense. He was sizing me up. Morally. Like some sort of priest. He was *judging* me in there, and he doesn't even know me, the ass!"

"Me, too! Me, too!" Fran lowered her voice conspiratorially. "I feel like he's reading me mind all the time. And don't even try to look at him hard. Thank the good Lord he comes in but a few hours a week or I would've quit months ago."

"Why doesn't he make Hope feel that way?" Glorie was truly puzzled. Fran didn't answer, instead she shrugged. "Where does Dr. Corescu park? Maybe I can catch them in the garage."

"Ummm," Fran hummed and pulled a slip of paper from her top desk drawer. "Level two, space three. Right next to the elevator. I'll walk you, I'm closing up. That's enough shenanigans for this lass."

As they exited the outer office, Hope came around the corner from the elevator.

☙❧

"I lost him." Speaking mostly to herself, Hope took her purse from Glorie, who had the foresight to bring it. "I hope everything is okay."

Fran turned for the elevators, the other two women close behind. "Must have been personal, I didn't get a ring at my desk."

"Yeah." Hope turned to Glorie, "Sis, can you get a ride with Fran back to my house? I really need to run by Mark's and check on him."

"I'll come with you. Let's go." Glorie put on a serious face, but Hope stopped her.

"No, really. Fran, will you run Glorie home? I have to go by myself, sis. I won't be late." Hope pleaded, not wanting to be rude. There was no way she was going to let her sister tag along to Mark's house.

Glorie turned to Fran and shrugged. "Where're you headed?"

Fran grinned. "I'm taking you out to lunch!"

Glorie laughed and took Fran's arm. "Sounds good. And afterwards, we'll hit the pub. I'll bet you know the bartender by name!" Fran assured her that she did and the two ladies skipped toward the elevators. Glorie called back to Hope, "Don't wait up!"

Hope sighed, relieved, and took the elevator to the parking garage. She checked her watch: 12:45, and hesitated in her heart. Would Mark want her to come? Steeling her resolve, she got into her truck and headed for the bypass. He'd welcome her assistance, he'd just have to. Weren't they "destined for each other"? Hope wanted to believe it more than anything and she sped toward Mark's estate.

ᲚᏕᲘ

Mark stood in place and stared at the headless body of his driver, dumbfounded. How had this happened without him knowing? Without him giving the order? Mark stepped around the body, careful to avoid the pooled blood. Surveying the rest of the scene, in the end, he glared at his last remaining servant.

Paul looked miserable. He sat on his rear against the wall with his legs out straight, arms limp at his sides, and his head tilted at an odd angle, his gaze fixed and vacant. Mark took a few steps toward him and the boy shook out of his fugue enough to look up. Following Mark with his eyes, Paul showed no recognition. His hands, clothing, and face were smeared red and... did he have blood on his lips? Mark pushed the thought from his mind, thrown off by Paul's murderous actions. But it would do no good to let his imagination run rampant. Paul had an explanation and he would wait for it.

Mark stood over his old friend, his expression even, and studied the view. The heavy wooden chair was tipped onto its back with Reuben's headless body still taped in. The decapitation wound was jagged, the cervical bones separated above the skin. Shoe prints in the blood beside the neck led Mark to believe that Paul stood on the knife to separate the vertebrae.

Mark regarded Paul's slack face. *He stood on the blade?* Paul was a kind and gentle man; a boy, really. How did he wind up covered in Reuben's blood? Why had he ignored Mark's order to avoid the cellar? Mark sought Paul's gaze. *Am I such a poor master?*

Paul's lips parted, but no words came forth. Mark stooped and the boy flinched. But Mark wasn't angry. More than anything, he grieved. For Paul, for Reuben, and even for himself.

"Paulie…" Mark said low and at the sound of it, Paul exhaled. "Are you hurt?" Mark scanned Paul's shirt and looked for evidence of violence. But then, Reuben's hands were still bound. Only the boy's head was loose at this point. In sorrowful response, Paul shook his head. Mark sighed resigned and began to make things right.

"Remove your clothes and pile them here." His voice stern but gentle, Mark helped Paul to his feet. Moving in jerks, Paul shrugged off his T-shirt and jeans and dropped them onto the body.

"Your shoes..."

Paul stepped out of his loafers and with his toe, pushed them to the edge of the pooling blood. He hadn't been wearing socks. Now dressed only in his boxers, he looked more like a victim than a cold-blooded murderer. Mark took pity on him and smiled.

"Go upstairs, clean up, and redress. Then, bring down the empty trunk in the spare room." Paul backed until he was at the bottom of the stairs, his eyes trained to the bloody corpse. Mark shooed him with his hand. "Go on, hurry."

Paul climbed the steps and disappeared to the upper floor.

The situation was messy, but Mark had a plan to dispose of the body. The aroma of Reuben's coagulated blood curled his lip, but he pressed on. Mark scanned the floorspace; where was the head? It wasn't near the body. He set the chair upright with Reuben's cooling corpse strapped tightly in, and then arranged the clothing into the lap. He lastly peeked into the cardboard box that sat undisturbed on the floor. The head was there, face up, eyes open and accusing. Mark's heart ached with regret.

Oh, Reuben, I wouldn't have let you go like that.

Yes, he intended to kill him, but he also intended to send him off with a proper judging. Paul had effectively sent him to hell.

I am so very sorry.

Mark used his pocketknife to slice through the duct tape that bound his driver's corpse. He watched where he put his feet, but the arterial spray had not expressed much further than the chair. Judging by the forensic evidence, Paul removed the head after the heart stopped pumping. The telepathic horror that Paul had been trying to hide from his master must have broken through on its own when Reuben's head fell free.

Paul must have been terrified to find Reuben's head at his feet.

Mark grinned despite the seriousness of the situation. Paul *was* too kind and gentle to commit such an act. But somehow, he did. All by

171

himself.

You have to watch the quiet ones.

Mark smiled again. Maybe this was graduation night for his pal. As Mark collected his thoughts and waited for Paul to return, his mind wandered back to the cave.

The cave where the Other ruled the dark.

Thirty-Six

Bloodshed pollutes the land
And atonement cannot be made
For the land on which blood has been shed...
Numbers 35:33

MOST OF AN HOUR HAD PASSED BEFORE HE SENSED HIS master's return. The priest sat up, almost glad to know he'd have The Other's company once again. Why did he fear him so? Was it his appearance? His ravaged visage was alarming, but The Other had for the most part been kind. Was it his telepathic acuity? Surely not. The universe was too vast and complicated for any one man to understand everything in it. Was it the attack in the cave?

Yes, what about the attack? The only evidence I see is a bloody shirt.

Maybe he imagined it. Maybe he dreamed it. How could he know when he was awake and when he was dreaming in that darkness? Had he misjudged his companion? The creature rescued him from death. Didn't that make The Other his savior?

A faint rustle reached his ears and his master was beside him in an instant. Standing to meet him, he bowed in deference. He waited patiently for The Other to address him, but he did not. Instead, he motioned that the priest follow him back to the cave. Once there, they stood inside the entrance facing each other.

"Open your mouth."

This time Father Corescu obeyed without question. The Other's rough fingers peeled back his lips as he examined his teeth.

"Good. Good." He allowed the priest to close his mouth and he stepped back, seemingly to look him over. Through thin, cracked lips, Father Corescu watched a smile of pleasure cross The Other's charred face. *"You make me proud, my priest. Are you hungry?"*

Father Corescu regarded his stomach and then shook his head.

"You will be soon. Come, sit, we will watch the sun come up." The Other

173

sat down slowly, like an old man, but it wasn't a sign of weakness. Perhaps he was a very old creature. Perhaps he wasn't a devil at all.

Finding a flat spot next to his master, the priest looked at the night sky. It was getting lighter and he looked forward to the day.

"You will no longer enjoy the day, my priest. My children never do." The Other turned his head to see the priest's profile.

"There are others? Others like me?"

"Alas, no longer. They do not all survive." The Other shrugged, a small smile playing with the corners of his lips. *"They do not all please me. But you are different. You have something my other children did not."*

The priest did not ask the question that hung in the air before him. The difference was his profession. He was chosen because he was holy, a child of God.

"Hah, that is correct. So do not look to the day. It will no longer give you the satisfaction. The sun is cruel to new eyes and burns new skin. The night is our domain. Oh, we will rule the night."

Father Corescu met The Other's gaze. *"I don't understand."*

"Watch and learn." The Other nodded toward the sky and they both turned their attention to the purple horizon to wait for the sun. Before long, the dawning light crept up to the cave entrance and The Other withdrew to the shadows.

"Retreat is best, my priest. You will no longer find your mortal blindness in the cavern."

Father Corescu remained seated and allowed his companion to melt quietly into the blackness. The sunlight was warm on his skin and he didn't pull back.

I am not a creature of darkness. I will not withdraw.

Whether he commanded himself or the spirit world, he sat in place and allowed the white light to slowly envelop his stoop. For twenty minutes he sat with his eyes closed absorbing the rays of the sun with pleasure. The Other's prophecy had proven false.

"How is this possible? How are you not writhing in pain?"

Father Corescu heard his master's voice in his head from the safety of the earthen tomb.

"Come inside before it is too late!"

There was urgency in his companion's voice that he hadn't heard before. Father Corescu opened his eyes and shielded them with his palm. The day was brighter than he remembered and a garish glare illuminated everything in sight. The luminescence caused him to squint and he backed into the darkness. His master was directly behind him, safe in the shadows.

"Well?" The Other shuffled beside him as they retreated into the blackness. *"You were not consumed by pain?"*

Father Corescu shrugged and squatted on the dirt. *"No, I did not notice any pain."*

In awe, The Other sent the sentiment, *"Nothing, then?"*

"The sun was bright, but bearable. And you? You cannot allow the light to touch you?" The priest noticed with real pleasure that he could now see in the dark as the Other had promised.

"No. But then…" The Other turned his face and closed his eyes.

"You were never a child of God, were you?" Father Corescu grinned as the idea blossomed in his mind. If God's face is like the sun, then symbolically it would burn a demon's skin. *But I belong to God. That is the difference.*

"Hah. Do not deceive yourself. You will only cause yourself heartache. I am a very old creature. That is the difference." His tone was meant to end the discussion, but the Father wanted more answers.

"How old are you?" He imagined that The Other was as old as time; utterly wise and powerful, an earthbound god, trudging through the ages. He sensed images from The Other's mind, living pictures of pyramids under construction, ancient lands, and rough open seas. But his master's reply made his blood run cold.

"I saw them hang that poor Jewish Carpenter on a tree. And I was old then."

Father Corescu recoiled in horror and looked away. *He is exaggerating. That is impossible. He is toying with my loyalties.* Almost convinced, he cleared his mind. It would be more pleasant to ponder the night's events than the history of his demonic new companion. *What will tomorrow bring?* His stomach growled. *How will we find food?* He regretted not eating when asked earlier. *I'll sleep now and eat tomorrow.*

Eventually he did sleep.

And once again, he didn't dream.

The following evening, The Other elbowed him awake, excitedly prodding his shoulder. Father Corescu rubbed his face and sat up. As his eyes focused, he found that, as before, he could see fairly well in the absence of light.

"You sleep heavily for a vámpír. Come." The Other scrambled toward the entrance and left the priest behind.

Did he just say 'vámpír'? Puzzled, Father Corescu stood carefully so as to not bump his head and followed in the direction of his master.

175

The *vámpír* were vile creatures of the night; the stuff of myths and legends. God would not permit such vermin on the earth.

"You know everything do you, my priest? You can't remember what day it is, yet you know all the secrets of the underworld?" The Other said, already outside the cave and standing in the moonlight. *"You will find that you know nothing."*

Father Corescu stepped into the clearing and turned his gaze to the full moon. No clouds tonight and a symphony of creatures filled the forest with song. Now he realized why The Other didn't permit him to speak, because of super-sensitive hearing. Father Corescu hadn't spoken aloud in three days and he decided to brave a quiet word.

"There," he said, clearing his throat and garnering a sideways glance from his master. They locked eyes for a moment and The Other sent a crooked smile.

"Did you think you would lose your voice?"

Father Corescu was surprised to hear his master's voice aloud. It was very much like the sound in his head, but raspy and menacing.

"Am I permitted to speak?"

The Other grabbed his wrist. "I'd rather you did not." His voice, again spoken aloud, gave the priest chills and he finished telepathically. *"Are you hungry?"*

"Your voice does not sound human to them, does it? That is why you do not speak."

"Precisely. And I hear so perfectly, that it is a chore to listen at all. Give it time, and you will hear the world as I do. You will be able to hear the thoughts of men a hundred miles away." The Other wiped his mouth with the back of his hand and repeated his original question. *"Are you hungry?"*

Father Corescu tried to imagine what he would eat. He hadn't eaten in at least two days, maybe longer. The only thing he'd ingested was the blood that his master administered the night before. *I drank his blood. Does that make me a monster?*

"Look, dear priest, you have been transformed. Are you so dense? Can you not feel the difference in your flesh?" Impatiently, The Other approached and took him by his chin. *"Open your mouth and feel here."*

The Father did as he was told and the rough fingers pressed against his canine teeth. Father Corescu brought his own fingers up to the same teeth and pressed them, not expecting anything to be amiss. He was mistaken. His eyeteeth were sharp as steel and centimeters longer than before.

"What does—?"

The Other winced and closed his eyes. Father Corescu continued his questions in his mind.

"What does this prove? I do not drink blood."

"Hah!" The Other cackled a few moments still holding the priest's chin. *"Yes, you do drink blood and you will do so forever. I have seen to that. Come, we will find your first meal."*

He took his wrist and resumed his shuffling walk, pulling the priest along with him deeper into the dark forest. Father Corescu followed, but he had no intention of drinking blood. What about free will? Could the creature force him to do this vile thing?

"I won't have to. Now, stop." The Other hunkered down and the priest did likewise. Ahead of them a hundred yards sat a tiny cabin with a trail of smoke wafting from the chimney. *"Wait here."*

Father Corescu watched him jog up to the house and around the back. Within minutes, he slinked back with a bundle under his wiry arm. It was a child, a toddler by the looks of her, asleep or unconscious. The Other lifted the child up, displaying his catch in the moonlight.

Father Corescu stared at the babe in disbelief. What could he possibly want with such a tiny waif? He watched in horror as his master pulled the child close to his face and nuzzled the tiny throat. Father Corescu gasped and stumbled back in the leaves behind him. When he saw the monster's sharp teeth through parting lips, Father Corescu had no illusions as to what was about to occur.

He turned back to the direction of the cavern and ran. He didn't know if The Other followed or not, but he ran as hard and as fast as he could. When he reached the cave entrance, he paused, and then ran past. He ran until he could no longer feel the presence of The Other in his mind or spirit. Finally, he stopped at a trickling stream glistening in his new vision and he collapsed onto the bank.

I am not a vampire. That creature may be, but I am not!

Father Corescu realized he wasn't out of breath. Surely, he should at least be breathing more heavily after his sprint, but he wasn't, and neither was he sweating.

I may be transformed into something else, but I do not have to drink blood.

He lay back on the cold ground and stared up at the clear sky. The moon sat full in a heaven of stars. Father Corescu wished he could be joyful at the sight, but he only despaired. Closing his eyes, he prayed for forgiveness and received no reply. A quiet rustle from behind revealed he had been found.

"I had no idea you would be so difficult," The Other sent, more

exasperated than angry. He fell onto the grass beside Father Corescu and propped himself upon one elbow to stare at his companion. *"Are you still trying to get God to help you? I told you. He is done with you. You are with me now."*

"I don't want to be without God."

"God does not know you anymore." The Other placed his hand on Father Corescu's chest. *"You are my magnificent creation, transformed from what was pure and holy into what is unclean and detestable. Do you know how long I searched for you? How many inferior specimens passed through my hands?"*

"But I still know Him. You are wrong." Surprised at his own impertinence, Father Corescu expected his new master to fly into a rage, but he did not. The Other stroked his chest and pulled himself closer until his breath fell upon Corescu's skin through the tattered clothing.

"You will learn to love me instead." The Other changed position and lay sideways across Corescu's upper body. *"I have something for you."*

They faced each other now, the priest below and The Other above. Father Corescu gasped and tried to sit up, but was pinned by his master's brute strength.

"Open your mouth."

Father Corescu squeezed his eyes closed and faced away. The Other scoffed and jerked his head around with his rough grip. Jaws clenched tight, Father Corescu tried once more to break free.

"My dear priest, you disappoint me." The Other's terrible audible voice caused Father Corescu to open his eyes and stare into the face of the demon. "Open your mouth, I will not tell you again."

The Other's once friendly gaze had turned red and Father Corescu did as he commanded. He watched in horror as The Other opened a vein in his own arm and pressed it to his lips. This time, though, the Father didn't resist. After the first drop hit his tongue, he took the creature's arm in his grip and drew out the blood as fast as it would flow. The Other closed his eyes and smiled with triumph.

Defiled and detached, the priest watched the scene from far away, as if he had no control over his actions. His body was not doing the will of God, but had fallen into the clutches of the devil himself. He was helpless to resist. So he drank. And he didn't stop until the creature violently pulled away his arm, laughing out loud.

Back in the gloomy unlit interior of their cave home, Father Corescu and The Other sat together against the wall as the sun rose outside. They had been silent a long time and it was the priest that finally broke the quiet.

"This is my new life? Days holed up underground and nights sneaking around in the dark?" Unsatisfied, he frowned. He was a priest, and he still thought like one in his heart. He only wished that he sensed the presence of the Holy One as well. *I will find a way to win back God's favor.*

"You must crawl before you can walk, my priest. Look." The Other held up his hand in the father's vision. Even though there was no light, Father Corescu determined the outline of a hand before his eyes. *"Already I heal. These bodies we alone have regenerate miraculously. When the Creator made man in His image, He made them perfect. They were made to live forever. We are Adam incarnate. In another day, I will be completely whole and we will leave this sanctuary and make a life on the outside."*

Father Corescu took The Other's hand in his and turned it over to examine the palm. It was indeed healing, as he said, and the burned flesh sloughed off to reveal shiny pink skin. The priest looked to The Other's face and saw evidence of new flesh replacing the fire-crisped epidermis. A man would eventually appear from underneath; large black eyes with the bronzed skin of an Egyptian pharaoh.

"Oh. I had assumed..."

"Hah. No, I am not as comely as you, but my visage will repair itself soon enough."

The priest closed his eyes and mentally constructed a wall against the Other's intrusions. To be slave to a demon was bad enough, but to have no mental privacy was worse.

"Why do you veil your thoughts? We can have no secrets between us." The Other's gravelly voice spoken aloud sliced through the silence of their tomb. Father Corescu put his hands to his ears.

"Please, please." When The Other spoke aloud, he was filled with dread. *"I have no secrets master. I'm confused. I can see no future and I cannot recall my past."*

"You are a new being. You have no past and I will lead you into your future. We will rule the world of man. We will conquer kingdoms. We will overcome nations."

"At what cost? Even if we could accomplish those things, what of eternity? What about God?"

"We are god now, my priest. We cannot die. And this is our church." He made a sweeping motion with his right arm. *"You will go insane trying to understand the Creator's motives. You feel alone and separated from Him because you are no longer in the fold. You are with the legion now. We will plunder creation and make it ours."*

The Other reached out and took the priest's wrist. He tugged twice and Father Corescu scooted closer in response.

"What is it now?" He watched in the eerie dim glow as the monster brought the arm to his face and inhaled deeply.

"And the other use I have for you, my priest..."

Father Corescu remained immobile as his master nuzzled his outstretched arm. Even before the creature initiated his next deed, the priest knew what he was going to do, seeing it in his mind. The Other opened his gory mouth wide and clamped down on his priest's thick wrist. Father Corescu inhaled sharply, but didn't pull back.

"But you have already fed tonight. Am I to be a perpetual open vein to your bloodlust?"

The Other sighed with contentment. *"This is what I have longed for. This is what I need. You will want to know that the blood of a brother will sustain like none other. The blood of a brother can erase all weaknesses in the flesh and spirit. Hmmmm...my brother...you can feed me forever."*

Father Corescu cringed at the words, feeling more despicable than ever. Was his blood to be prostituted forever to this demon? Did he really have no say in the matter? Would he taste the blood of a brother himself one day?

"Yes, my priest, I will feed you as well. We will grow stronger every night. We will fear no one and the world will be our playground." With a satisfied groan, The Other ceased his feast, and returned the priest his arm. *"But for now, say goodbye to your past. Tomorrow, you will earn your keep."*

The Other then got up and crossed to the other wall.

Father Corescu turned away from his master and put his head in his hands. He didn't truly believe that he could be forced to kill anyone and drink their blood. Yes, The Other was stronger physically, but certainly he could resist him on this very important issue.

Tomorrow we will see who wins this battle of wills. Holding onto that last vow, Corescu fell into a fitful sleep.

Thirty-Seven

"What good is it for a man to gain the whole world,
yet forfeit his soul?"
Mark 8:36

LUNCH-HOUR TRAFFIC CLOGGED THE INTERSTATE AND more than once, Hope honked at the slowpokes blocking her frantic progress.

"Come ON!" she breathed as yet another tiny car shot in front of her and caused her to decelerate. From out of nowhere, a red Jeep swerved into her lane, and Hope slammed on the brakes.

Geesh, people!

The Jeep corrected and returned to the right lane. Hope sped past at eighty, wondering if she should turn on her radar detector. She never used it, but today—

Pop! Whap, whap, whap, whap.

Hope applied the brake and signaled to get over, familiar with the unmistakable sound and feel of a blowout. Because of her tendency for procrastination, she had them at least once a year and had never replaced the spare from last time. Pulling to the shoulder, the Suburban rolled to a stop in the gravel. Tapping the steering wheel in frustration, Hope considered her options. Who would come pick her up? The only name that ever came to her head in times of trouble was Anthony. She picked up her cell phone and prayed he'd be home.

ᗉᔓ

Tony answered the second ring. "Hello, darlin'."

"Anthony! I'm broke down! Can you come get me?"

Traffic noise filled his ear and he asked above the din, "Where are you?"

Hope reeled off the nearest mile marker, there was a pause, and then, "I'm in the truck! You can't miss me!"

Tony checked his watch, already heading to the door. Sure, he was supposed to be in a meeting at the church in a half-hour, but when a

181

lady is in distress…

"I'm coming! Put on your flashers and lock yourself inside."

The static crackle of the cell made her reply unclear, but he was certain she would do as he suggested. He jumped in the truck and headed to the interstate like the knight in shining armor Hope expected.

ଓଞ୍ଚ

"Back the truck to the door," Mark said, not attending Paul's fragile state of mind. He kept him busy to keep him functioning. The boy still had not said anything about Reuben, but he would when the shock wore off.

The mention of the truck reminded Mark of his Lexus left in the hospital parking garage. Would anyone notice? Then, Reuben's Jaguar. It was still parked at the Sheraton. He made a mental note to pick it up as soon as he and Paul could manage it. Hopefully, it would draw little or no attention until they could retrieve it. Then, of course, he had to recover his BMW from Hope's place. Things were getting out of hand.

"Yes, my priest, listen to me and I will help you put your life back in order."

Mark refused to acknowledge The Other and returned his focus to the job at hand. He was pleased at how easy it had been to fit the corpse into the trunk. A tarp down first, then the body folded up with its head in its lap, then Paul's soiled clothing and the knife, then all of the cleaning sponges and towels. The last thing to do was to tuck it all in with the remainder of the tarp. Tidy, drip-proof and simple to transport.

The sound of the Tahoe's engine at the top of the stairs brought a nod as Mark lifted the oversized trunk without effort. From the top of the stairs, he took one last look around the room. The killer himself had tended the worst of the mess. Three gallons of bleach, a bucket, a mop, and a few kitchen sponges had the smooth concrete floor spotless and clean-smelling. The chair had been disassembled and burned to ash in the huge house furnace along with the mop and the cardboard box. No evidence of the murder remained. With a last approving nod, Mark joined Paul waiting in the truck.

ଓଞ୍ଚ

Hope's diagnosis of a flat tire in reality turned out to be a blown tread that, at seventy miles an hour, shredded much of the wheel-well, leaving the SUV undriveable. She'd need a ride and Tony mentally cleared his day to see her through to the end. For the moment, she sat in the passenger side of his S10 as they awaited the tow, rambling in partial sentences about her new friend.

"Take a deep breath..." Tony said to encourage her to slow down. "Now, what's the emergency?"

Hope cut her eyes his way. "Don't dare tell me to calm down."

Their repartee had never been confrontational and he hadn't expected her to bite back. Tony showed his palms. "You want me to take you over there? To his house?"

She lifted her hair, fanning her neck with her hand. "Yes. No. Maybe... I want to check on him, but I might be overreacting." She blew a huff and again sought his eye. "Yes, please do. I appreciate it."

Tony switched off the engine to prevent overheating. He rolled down his window to let some air in the hot vehicle, but the roar of the passing tractor trailers forced him to roll it up. "Tell me what happened. Why were you rushing after him?"

Hope released her hair and put her face in her hands. "I don't know where to start. So much has happened..."

"You mean, since I saw you Sunday morning?"

She nodded. "And I need your help. Help me sort it out."

"You saw him again? Sunday?"

Hope turned a sorrowful gaze to Tony. "I think he needs your help, too. He has some weird ideas about God that don't line up with what I learned in church."

"Oh. Want me to talk to him?"

Hope's eyes widened. "Oh, would you? I never thought of that. I think he would go for it if I asked him."

"I'll do anything to help." The knot that formed in his stomach as he agreed confirmed what he feared all along; he was *destined* to help Hope and her weird new friend. God's trial may have arrived in the form of a cute friend and an apostate physician.

"Anthony, he's amazing. I don't want to lose him." Hope held back her tears. "He's so smart and interesting. He showed me how he can talk to animals." She said the last while looking aside and Tony hopped on it.

"He talks to animals? Do they talk back?"

Hope nodded and hid her face in her hands.

"Um, you're aware that animals don't have language," Tony said in his gentlest tone. "What makes you think he can hear animals talking?"

"It's for real. I know you don't believe it, but it's real. Just like the animal psychic on TV." Hope peeked out to meet Tony's eye.

"Hope," Tony began with a frustrated tone and remembered to remain calm, "a real psychic receives information from demons, immortal spirits that whisper in their eager, listening ears." Tony placed his hand on Hope's shoulder. "What animal did your doctor friend talk to?"

"You don't know everything, Anthony. Mark laid his hands on these horses and knew all about them. And then, I did it too. I laid my hand on its head and I saw things. I saw children!" Hope's voice raised an octave. "Not everything is explained in the Bible. Open your mind, geesh!" Hope finished in a shrill tone; he was losing her trust.

He said in a new, softer voice, "I don't know everything, but there is nothing new under the sun. I'm sure Corescu *believes* the animals are communicating with him. It's an innocent enough conclusion to draw before you understand how demons work. But we don't live in darkness that the wiles of the devil should fool us." Tony saw the all-too-familiar veil drop, but he pressed on. "Hope, there are no such things as animal psychics."

"You're so single-minded about God! Don't you know that there are other opinions?" Angry, Hope turned to stare out the window. "You don't know what you're talking about. You don't know what I've seen."

Tony sealed his lips and a frustrated silence filled the cab. Soon enough, the tow-truck arrived. What could he do? Hope had shut him out. Tony resolved to be as patient as possible and see what God had in mind.

CR&O

Fran and Glorie walked the mall and rubbed their bellies, still full from a gluttonous lunch. They stuffed their mouths for over an hour at the seafood buffet, drinking beer and laughing. Finally, when Glorie belched loud and caused Fran to laugh so hard she spilled her drink, they pushed back from the table and paid their tab. Now, an hour later, they were uncomfortable but happy as they window-shopped in the aging mall. It wasn't as fancy as the mall that she visited earlier in the day with Hope, but as it was air-conditioned and indoors, it served its purpose. Fran picked up a few sale items at Belk's for her nieces and asked Glorie how her kids were doing. Glorie shrugged and leaned against the display as Fran shopped.

184

"They're fine. I wonder how people who have four kids fare. I really have my hands full with three. It gets pretty old."

Fran nodded, sympathizing. "Sure, and three boys. Boys are much tougher. I had me girls and they were hard enough."

"They complain all the time. They need so much attention that I can hardly get thirty minutes to myself on any given day. I wish—" Glorie stopped in mid-sentence, realizing that the edge in her voice might alarm her friend.

"Sure. Me girls never gave me a moment's peace 'til the day they flew the nest!" Fran laughed and then added with a passionate tone. "They're such darling angels though, aren't they?"

"Hmmm, I don't know. The devil was an angel once too, I understand."

Fran laughed and clapped Glorie on the shoulder, admonishing her choice of words. "Stop it, you nut!"

Glorie smiled in response, but the expression never reached her eyes. They were ice cold and as hard as glass.

Thirty-Eight

I saw the Lord always before me.
Because He is at my right hand, I will not be shaken.
Acts 2:25

HOPE DIRECTED ANTHONY TO MARK'S HOUSE AND AS soon as she spotted the fence-line, she second-guessed her decision to have him along.

"Let's come back later. I mean, I should have called ahead," Hope stammered as they slowed at the gate.

Anthony sent her a playful glare. "Don't be silly. If there's trouble, maybe we can help. Look, someone's heading out."

Hope followed his line of sight and her heart leapt in her chest.

"Is that him?" Anthony backed his truck to the shoulder as the heavy gate swung open.

"He's the one in the passenger side," Hope replied on autopilot. "Paul is driving." Hope stared hard into the truck wishing to ascertain Mark's state of mind. She opened her door and motioned for Anthony to stay put.

"You never mentioned Paul," he said, but Hope ignored him.

The Tahoe halted before Anthony's green Chevy. Hope ran to meet Mark as he exited his vehicle, but he held her at arm's length. Through dark lenses, he questioned her with his eyes.

"Oh, Mark!" Hope said, tears springing to her eyes. "I thought... I thought something terrible had happened. I thought..." She ignored his piercing gaze and fell into his arms. At first, he didn't return her embrace, but then softened enough to kiss the top of her head. She spoke into his shirt, "I'm so glad you're okay."

"Shhhh." Mark pushed her away to see her face and brushed her hair from her wet cheek. "I shouldn't have alarmed you. I apologize. We had a little housekeeping problem. Everything is fine."

"Was it *Reuben?*" Hope whispered.

Mark bristled and changed the subject. "Who have brought with

186

you? I'm surprised that you would bring a stranger into our midst."

Hope's countenance slipped at his hardened tone. "Oh, Anthony? That's my friend I told you about. My car broke down on the way here and he gave me a lift." Hope looked over to Anthony who waved. "He's harmless." She touched Mark's lapel hoping he'd meet her eye but he had his eyes on the green truck. "Anthony is my most trusted friend. He could be *your* friend, too."

Mark slipped out of her grasp to approach the S10. Hope trotted behind him glancing at Paul as she passed. He sat behind the wheel, expressionless, his eyes glassy and vacant. She snapped her gaze to the front in time to avoid a collision with Mark.

"Anthony, I presume?" Mark extended his hand through Tony's open window and the two men shook. Hope squeezed in and put her hands on the sill.

"Anthony Agricola, Dr. Corescu. Nice to meet you. Hope has said many nice things about you."

Anthony's words were sincere and his manner relaxed. Hope's heart raced, fearful she had angered Mark and endangered Anthony with her carelessness.

"That is nice to hear," Mark replied, his tone icy.

Hope bit her lip and remained silent worried about what Anthony might say. Blocked by Mark's back, she couldn't see her friend's face. Had Mark already assumed the worst concerning the nature of their private conversations?

"She thought you were having an emergency, so I ran her by…"

Hope peeked around Mark to see her friend open his door. Mark backed to make room and soon the men faced each other in the driveway. In her eyes, Mark's impressive stature dwarfed her friend; the way Anthony raised his chin to meet Mark's eye, he may as well have been a teen admonished by a parent.

Mark crossed his arms and lowered his chin, and to Hope's surprise, with a friendly grin, Anthony squared his shoulders and tucked both hands into his pockets. Mark's expression remained hard and Hope placed a hand on his arm. She wanted to say something to break the ice, to shut down the battle of wills.

"Mark, did I tell you? Anthony's a preacher."

Mark smiled. "Oh, so you're a man of God." He uncrossed his arms and placed his hand over Hope's on his left arm.

Anthony nodded. "Hope tells me that you're also a man of faith."

"Absolutely." Mark swiveled to see Paul in the SUV. Hope and

187

Anthony followed his gaze.

"Is he okay?" Anthony craned his neck to see over Hope's head.

"He's fine," Mark replied as he turned. "Forgive me, we have an errand. It was nice meeting you Mr. Agricola. Please come for supper some evening. I think you would prove to be delightful company."

"Thank you, Dr. Corescu. I'll do that." Anthony nodded and climbed into his truck. He eyed Hope to follow, but she turned to trail behind Mark on the way to his SUV.

At his door, he gave her a private smile and took her into his arms. "I'll call for you when we return."

Hope squelched frustrated tears. "Let me go with you."

"No. Wait for me." Mark pulled out of her grasp and slipped into his truck.

Hope watched them leave. She'd be strong for Mark, strong for Anthony, and dammit, she needed most of all to be strong for herself. Mark was her future and as weird as her world had become, that single fact compelled her to succeed.

ꩰ

In his reliable rental, partially obscured by a stand of decorative shrubs and brickwork, Connie watched the white Tahoe pull off. Two people remained. Were these friends of the doc's? Accomplices? Curious, he hastily drove across the street to interview the young couple in the green truck. The way the doctor embraced the blonde, they would definitely be hooking up again soon. He parked in front of the pickup and trotted up to the driver's door.

"Can I help you sir?"

"Maybe. Do you know Reuben Stuckey? I've been missing him all over town. I'm a journalist and I'm doing a story on the kid's writing award."

"Reuben won an award?" the blonde knock-out asked.

"Yes, ma'am. I had an appointment with him yesterday and my plane was late. Now I've been all over the place trying to find him before I miss my plane home."

"I didn't know he could write," Blondie said, leaning over the driver and Connie peeked down her red scoop-necked Tee. He resumed his prepared chatter, openly smiling at her cleavage.

"Yes, ma'am, he's a natural. Have you seen him today?" Were these two going to jerk him around? If they did, he'd just tail them for a while.

188

The woman and the doctor were close, maybe even lovers. Any man attached to this lady would not let her out of his sight for long.

"He's visiting his grandmother in Alpharetta. She had a fall at the nursing home."

Connie smiled, Blondie was a terrible liar. But why would she steer him away? He said, "Well, that's a shame. I guess they'll have to give the award to someone else."

"I'm sorry. I guess we better go."

Connie watched the woman tap her friend's leg and return to her seat, interview concluded. He grinned at the couple again and returned to his car, cursing. What was she covering up? How deeply was she involved? He decided a few rounds in the lounge should straighten up his attitude. Heading back to the interstate to Atlanta, he planned his speech to Grouper. He was going to need more money and more time. End of story.

○§○

Tony didn't know what to make of Hope's outlandish tale, but it had to be a fabrication. The gawky stranger with the hooked nose and the legal pad hadn't bought it either and Tony told Hope as much.

"Well, he was lying, too." Hope turned back to watch the stranger drive off in the other direction.

"What are you mixed up in? This feels like a Mystery Theater episode. Lurking, lying, strangers with notepads…"

"Don't be ridiculous." Hope faced front and leaned her head against the window. "Thanks for helping me out. I'm really tired. Will you just take me home?"

"Sure." Tony let it go for now. He was ready for a nap. What else was new? Time with Hope always wore him out.

Thirty-Nine

"Remind the people to be subject to rulers and authorities,
To be obedient, to be ready to do whatever is good."
Titus 3:1

"I'LL HAVE YOUR EXPLANATION NOW, PAUL." MARK KEPT his voice even, not wanting to intimidate him further. They were ten minutes into the drive and Mark discerned Paul was ready to speak.

He cleared his throat. "Master, I—"

He cut off in mid-sentence and Mark wondered about his choice of words. Paul had not addressed him as master in decades.

"Mark," Paul choked, his voice a combination of regret and fear, "I did it for you." When Mark didn't reply for several long moments, Paul spoke again. "Please say something."

Mark looked back to the road and crossed his arms. *What does he want me to say? How do I feel about all this?* Surprisingly, Mark realized that he had no feelings about the incident one way or the other. But shouldn't he? A gentle, quiet, unassuming boy that he had held close to his heart for almost a century had a psychotic break. Now, Mark's only other servant was dead. He searched his soul a moment longer then replied. "What can I say? You defied my absolute orders."

Mark's words opened a floodgate and Paul's story poured forth. "You were right about him; he was planning to spill it all. He told a reporter about us." Paul's voice grew stronger as he unraveled his side of the tale. He repeated Reuben's accusations and sent play-by-play mental pictures as well.

Reuben's acid remark, *"Are you forgetting who's the master and who are the slaves?"* Then Paul's defiant reply, *"We are partners... I have never been a slave."*

When Paul finished his narrative, he fell silent and awaited Mark's response. Mark thought over the master/slave position, the jab that pierced Paul's armor. It rang true; Mark had always considered Reuben a servant, and Paul a companion. Still, was it right? A month ago, if

190

Reuben had disobeyed him, severe and absolute punishment would have been in order. Was Mark losing his power as he regained his past?

"You are becoming as helpless as those poor fools you judge. You are destroying us. I can tell you how to solve this whole mess."

This time, out of morbid curiosity, Mark allowed The Other to offer his suggestion.

"Kill the girl, her sister, and the reporter and start over elsewhere…"

Just for fun, Mark replied. *"And where would you have me take us, Master?"*

"Home."

Home meant Hungary. Mark scoffed and Paul looked over.

"Things are going to be different from now on. As you know, Hope Brannen is the catalyst bringing me to a new awareness. We will find this reporter tomorrow and deal with him. Then, we will start anew, the three of us." He lowered his voice to continue. "Do you think it's likely that you're going to kill again?"

Paul didn't answer.

"If you experience the urge to murder someone, will you come to me first?" Mark gave Paul a moment to respond, but the man was having difficulty putting his thoughts into words. Mark waited but The Other broke in with his own insights.

"Maybe he wants to go off on his own. Maybe he doesn't want a disappointing weakling such as you for a master."

Mark shook his head. If Paul wanted to leave, he would let him.

"Paul," he said, his gentle tone causing the guy to look over. Emotion passed between them and Mark continued. "You'll notice changes in me, you may think me a foolish and unworthy master. If you want to leave, I will allow it. You have my blessing."

Paul gasped and gripped the steering wheel tightly. "No! Please, don't send me away! I couldn't bear to live without you. My whole existence is for you. I—"

"Shhhh." Mark interrupted his panicked rant. "I want you by my side. Forever. That's why I chose you. But you might find the new Mark Corescu less appealing."

"Never." Paul's chin went out in defiance.

"Good. Then I'll continue on this track and you will refrain from homicidal rages. Deal?"

"Deal," Paul responded with an obvious sigh. "So, we're okay?"

Mark nodded.

"And I won't kill again. I just—*I was so angry.* Reuben wouldn't stop

191

mocking me." They were off the freeway now on County Road 254 to the lake house. Mark chuckled at Paul's remarks.

"Makes it hard to stop when they won't take you seriously, eh?"

Paul nodded with emphasis. "And there was a great power inside of me when I got angry. I was invincible. I've never felt like that before." Paul stopped his narrative as he turned down Lady Lane, the bumpy dirt strip that served as the driveway to the cabin.

Mark thought about that a moment. The Corescu Cocktail might have sent Paul over the edge. Essentially, Mark was a vampire; his past was as clear as his present. Didn't he feel quite different all those years ago when he tasted his master's blood? Of course, he had been given the entire gift, not just a deposit. Paul only consumed the smallest diluted amount. Was his blood that powerful?

"I don't hold you accountable, Paul. I love you dearly, but I am also your master. Ultimately, your deeds are my responsibility. Don't get me wrong, I was surprised to find you the way I did. And it's unfortunate that Reuben went without a proper judging, but in the end..." Mark paused. They had arrived and Paul turned off the truck. "I was impressed."

"Impressed?" He palmed the keys and looked over, "I was afraid I lost you. I expected...." *termination*. Paul couldn't bring himself to finish the thought, but Mark heard it just the same.

"No," Mark reassured him with a smile. "I can't think of anything that you could ever do that would make me furious enough to destroy you." Mark followed Paul up to the side door and waited for him to find the right key. "But please don't push your luck."

"Don't worry," Paul said finally looking more himself. "I still can't believe it. That wasn't me in there. I want to forget this ever happened. I want us to be like we were before."

"As do I. Come. When night falls, we'll bury the evidence and the memory at the same time." Mark followed Paul into the dark cabin and they settled in to wait for sundown.

Mark and Paul buried the trunk without incident. Not a soul witnessed their silent departure from the cabin or their equally quiet return an hour later. The house was situated on the lake, two hundred yards from the road, and Mark owned the fourteen acres that surrounded it. He didn't sense anyone within a mile of the place and he breathed a sigh of relief as they closed the cabin door and sat in the rustic den. Paul cleared his throat.

"Yes?" Mark asked, and met his eye.

"I was wondering who that man was with Hope."

Paul referred to Agricola and Mark raised an eyebrow at his question. "No one of consequence. Do you no longer trust me to handle my affairs?" Not intending to scold, Mark realized he already had. "He's a friend of Hope's. Leave it at that."

"I found him interesting..." Wounded by Mark's callous retort, Paul asked another just-as-bizarre question. "Don't you have an appointment? It's nine o'clock."

Mark looked at his watch. He *had* an appointment, but the time had come and gone with the business at hand. Searching his memory, he couldn't recall a single time that he'd missed a judging. Could they be rescheduled? He glanced to his partner. Since when did Paul become so interested in his schedule? In the past, he waited in obedient silence. *Paul is evolving before my eyes, but into what?*

His friend got the gist of his thoughts and sat up, clearing his throat. "I just worry about you. I know it's been a while since you—"

Mark cut him off. "You worry too much." He leaned forward to rest his elbows on his knees. He then offered with a gentle smile to Paul's unspoken innuendo, "If memory serves, you offered yourself that second time. Don't pin your extended bedrest on me."

Paul lowered his gaze. "I won't let it happen again."

Mark slapped his knee. "Don't say that. There's no other being on this planet that I would rather accept that gift from. I would tell you the truth, if you want to hear it…" Mark watched Paul nod his head in reply, eyes wide. "I much prefer you over them any day."

Paul's mouth turned up into a tight smile and he relaxed a bit more in his chair.

Paul is developing quite a personality.

Mark watched his long-time companion daydream, tousled hair framing his cherubic face, rumpled Polo shirt bunching at his thin waistline. A remnant of the dirt they had used on the grave tinted his cheeks and hands giving him the look of a child on the playground.

Still my precious Paulie. Still my innocent creation.

But hadn't his innocence disappeared when Reuben's head hit the concrete floor? Mark's silent, obedient, happy-go-lucky Paul had faded away and been replaced with a suspicious, second-guessing hired hand. "Paul, look at me," Mark pressed. "You don't seem yourself."

"What do you mean?"

Mark tried again. "What're you hiding?"

Paul opened his hands. "What're you talking about?"

Mark studied him in silence. *Yes, what am I talking about?*

"Your creation has tasted the fruit. Are you blind, my priest? I had such high hopes for you. You disappoint me to no end..."

Mark paused and considered The Other's remarks.

"What do you mean? What fruit?" Mark replied, aware that he was validating the presence now, bringing him strength and power.

"Ask."

Mark looked hard at Paul and discerned his discomfort. Within seconds, he destroyed the man's flimsy telepathic wall and dug around. Paul flinched, moaning deep in his throat. It was completely unlike him to be deceitful and in less than a heartbeat, Mark found what he sought. When his driver was attacked, Paul feasted on his blood. Worse, Reuben was alive for the first few minutes.

Paul groaned louder and got to his feet. He backed all the way to the door and mouthed a single word under his breath. *"Master..."*

Mark followed with his eyes, unable to comprehend what it might mean as Paul exited and slammed the door. Seconds later, the Tahoe pulled away and Mark's mind raced. What did it mean for their future? What would happen now? Getting a hold of his slippery emotions, Mark sighed and rose to his feet, a new plan forming. Mark focused on Paul, who had reached the main road.

"Bring Hope home. Bring her now. I'll meet you there."

Through their connection, he viewed a vignette of what Paul saw through the windshield. On top of that, Mark sensed his servant-son's fear and panic, and he tried to soothe him.

"Paulie, Paulie, it'll be okay. You are and will always be my precious son."

"I'm unworthy! I've ruined everything."

"You haven't ruined anything," Mark returned aware that Paul had been shouting his sentiments in the cab of the truck. *"Bring Hope right away, and when you return, I will bring you even closer. It's time you became my partner, for real."*

The idea only occurred to Mark as he said it, and he wondered if he meant what he promised. Would he really bring the curse completely upon the man? *Why not?* He answered himself. His companion was half-mad from consuming the blood of two immortal creatures back to back.

Presently, Paul slowed the truck to the speed limit sending, *"If I can help in any way, I will. I live for you, master."*

194

Mark tsked. *"I don't want you to refer to me as master. Why do you do this?"*

"The Voice. It torments me day and night. The Voice told me to drink Reuben's blood. It said it's a vampire and Mark…he said he's your master…"

Mark inhaled. The insipid subconscious demon haunting his own mind haunted Paul's as well? What about Reuben? Had he caused the driver's bad behavior? Mark swallowed, his eyes narrowing.

Is The Other responsible for all of the recent unpleasantness?

Mark had to acknowledge the truth—the moment he recalled The Other, the evil creature's power over him increased. He may have influenced Reuben to turn traitor and then pick a fight with Paul.

The Other choreographed my servants like puppets…

Mark returned his attention to Paul. *"I will tell you about him; it is time you knew. For now, don't trust him. Bring Hope to me and I will bring you into the circle. I will tell you everything I know."*

"I'd like that. It will help me to serve you better," Paul returned and with a final sentiment of assurance, Mark release him.

Within the hour, he should have Hope at Mark's estate, so Mark would take a moment to sort his thoughts. He leaned against the back of the over-stuffed sofa and closed his eyes doing his best to ignore the hunger that burned his gut like acid. Had he disappointed God by ignoring tonight's calling? Now the murderous widow he'd been called to judge would continue her evil deeds until her natural death.

I'm not the same Mark Corescu that I was a month ago. I can't concentrate on the evil-doers. I cannot locate them as easily. I can't subdue them as I did before. Mark recalled the musician, the entire scene a fiasco. He thought of Hope's twin; she needed badly to be judged, but he ignored that call as well.

This is because I'm no longer convinced of my purpose.

As usual, Mark heard no response from the heavens, as isolated this evening as he was that first night in The Other's lair. Perhaps God *had* abandoned him.

…Hope will help you find God.

Where that thought originated, he wasn't sure, but Mark longed to believe it. He concentrated on his study and with the familiar rush of air, he opened his eyes at home. Then, keeping the house dark, Mark paced the familiar room, his mind on the coming events. Hope's scent hung in the air from her earlier visit and he imagined her face, her eyes as blue as the sky.

I should have made her mine that first night…

If he'd only taken her as his partner then, force-fed her this new mission, he could have persevered as she came to understand his calling. If he hadn't been so distracted by the novelty of such a challenge—wooing a Twenty-First-Century woman—he would have sensed Reuben's subterfuge. He would have recognized Paul's discouragement and fear of the unknown. The Other wouldn't have been so forcefully resurrected and thus, enabled to corrupt Mark's servants.

"They are mine. As I am your master, I am theirs. You forget too easily."

The Other, his mental voice hoarse with age, thundered into Mark's psyche. *"I am in you. Thus, I am in all those you create. I know you remember that much, my priest."*

Mark sighed. The Other spoke the truth; because of his awakening, he recalled how he literally and voluntarily assumed the beast into his body. Awaiting Paul and their guest, Mark endured his growing hunger, coupled with exhaustion of spirit, and slipped into his memories.

Forty

The path of the righteous is like the first gleam of dawn…
But the way of the wicked is like deep darkness…
Proverbs 4:18-19

FIRST, HE HEARD THE CRY IN HIS HEAD, LOUD AND FULL of fear, but then in his ears, loud enough to wake the dead.

"PRIEST! COME QUICKLY!"

Father Corescu snapped awake and scrambled to his feet, knocking his head on the low rock ceiling, instinctively aware something was terribly amiss. He sought the dim outline of his master, but he was alone. The cry for help came from outside the cavern and it was day. Without hesitation, Father Corescu rushed to the entrance.

In the clearing, twelve men encircled a smoking mass twisting in pain on the hard ground. In the bright sunlight, Father Corescu shielded his eyes and approached the mob, not sure what he would find, or what he would do when they noticed him. Three strides closer, he recognized The Other, writhing in agony as the light struck his once-healing flesh like a whip. The men shouted and beat him as he cried out. Corescu had not yet been noticed and he stared in disbelief at the ugly scene.

"What can I do?" he asked, his muscles taut and ready to act.

"Quickly! Come close! Ignore these men and come close!" the desperate voice in his head pleaded.

Corescu took a step and hesitated, recognizing the closest man: Emil Broga. The name came in a flash and he wondered, *how do I know these men?* And, *will they try to kill me, too?*

The Other's voice pleaded again, deafening and terrified. *"You must come close! Let me see you. COME!"*

Father Corescu shoved Emil aside and stooped to the head of the burning creature. *"I am here."*

He ignored the men's curses as they suspended their murderous attack. Father Corescu met his master's gaze and was transported.

It was a vision. In a blink, Father Corescu and The Other stood

197

together, peaceful, quiet, and unharmed. And his master was not burned, but glowed with health, his face that of a young Arab in the prime of his life. His crisp white tunic sashed with a silken yellow belt shimmered with a pleasing glow and his tightly-wrapped turban gave his shortish frame more height. He turned to the priest with full affection in his dark brown eyes.

"What is this? What is happening?" the priest asked, amazed at the sight. The Other smiled and clapped his shoulder.

"You have seen me. But alas, this shell is ruined. No worry, my beloved. It is accomplished. You have saved me. I will be with you always. Now, RUN!"

A heavy thud between his shoulder blades snapped Father Corescu to the present. Registering no pain, he whirled to face Broga before the man struck him again.

"He is one of them!" the man shouted in Hungarian. "Kill him!"

"But he does not burn! He is human!" yelled another man.

"It is Father Corescu!" said a third, and all three men froze in place to study the priest's face. Father Corescu spun out of their grasp and headed into the woods.

"That is not our priest! He is one with Lucifer! Get him!"

Emil and the others chased him into the forest. Father Corescu outdistanced the mob in a matter of minutes, but he did not pause when he no longer heard their pursuit. He ran for nearly an hour through heavy underbrush beneath a canopy of lush trees. He eventually ran out of forest and reached a clearing. Even though he didn't sense any response from the heavens, he automatically gave thanks for his successful escape. The chase had not exerted him in the least, and he marveled at his endurance. Hidden in the tree line, he peered out to the overgrown pasture peppered with grazing livestock. In another minute, he closed his eyes and considered The Other. Was he dead? He considered returning to see, but put the idea out of his mind. If he had been asleep alongside his master when the mob came to drag him out into the sun, they would have killed him, too. Father Corescu shuddered. He was not prepared to die again.

"Find us shelter."

Startled at The Other's voice again in his head, Father Corescu turned a circle. *Wait...* He considered the possibility that he had lost his mind, and shook his head. Somehow, the demon survived, or at least some part of him had.

"Master?" the Father sent as he had before. *"What is this?"*

"They will be coming for you. Find shelter now!"

"I will do it," Father Corescu returned and approached the clearing's edge. Across the wide field sat a tiny farm house. Fifty meters behind that slumped a sinking, thatch-roofed barn. Staying as low to the ground as possible, Father Corescu covered the distance. He then slipped inside to find the space cool and dark, the windows well-shuttered against the coming winter. Moldy hay filled the aisle and the stalls stood empty. Finding the rickety ladder access, he crammed his tall frame into the loft's farthest corner. Hugging his knees to his chin, he waited for nightfall, and hoped for the best.

∞

"So when are you coming home? You want me to wait up?" Hope sat at her dining room table in the dark with her eyes closed against the world. Her sister called to report that she and Fran had gone into Atlanta to hit the nightclubs. Her sister's slurred voice belied her intoxicated state and Hope frowned. "Glorie, be careful."

After a loud peal of laughter at her location, Glorie said, "Don't wait up, Mom. Do I still have that key you gave me at Christmas?"

Hope looked toward the door. "I don't know. I'm putting one under the mat anyway, okay?" Glorie grunted a reply and hung up. Hope took her spare key from her purse and opened the front door. As she knelt to the fuzzy brown doormat, an approaching voice gave her a start.

"Are you sure that's a good idea?"

Hope looked up to see Paul Black on her stone path.

"There are plenty of psychos in this town, you know." Paul's grave expression did not match his humorous words.

"Hey," Hope said and gave him a smile. "Everything okay?"

Paul glanced backward to his truck and then returned to give her a shy smile. "Will you let me take you to the house? Mark asked me to come get you. He's waiting for us right now."

Hope's eyes widened; the kid knew precisely what to say to get her moving. "Yeah, sure," she said ready to go inside and leave Glorie a note. "So everything's okay?" she asked, considering his smudged face and wrinkled shirt. He could have been a runaway teen for the level of innocence his appearance portrayed.

"Sure, and I apologize for earlier." Paul met her eyes, and then looked away. "I had an accident in the house, that's all. We took care of it." He took a step to the side, expecting her to join him.

Hope moved the door open only an inch, and Paul closed the distance between them and touched her arm, his eye-lock more compelling than she remembered from before.

"Right now. Let's go."

Hope watched his lips as he spoke what sounded like commands and pulled the door fully closed where it locked on its own. She had no purse, no keys, the lights were on inside, and her cat would go unfed, but something about Paul's eyes...

"You'll be home soon enough," he added and she allowed him to pull her gently by the wrist. Spider pawed the front window glass as they walked away and with a strange, sideways smile, Hope accompanied Paul to his truck.

∝≈∞

Once Hope had settled in the passenger side front, Paul noticed the BMW on the curb, glimmering in the streetlamp's glow.

"What tha—?" he mumbled approaching the car. After peering inside, he checked the license plate just to be sure. When did this happen? What was Mark up to while he was recovering?

Reuben said it; Mark isn't keeping me in the loop.

"Oh, geez, he didn't tell you? I had no choice. Sunday night, I had to drive it home myself. I'm sorry about that." Hope slipped out of the truck as she spoke. "The keys are in my purse."

She gestured toward the house but Paul's mind sought more answers about Sunday night. Why hadn't Mark brought her home himself? *Why hasn't he confided in me?*

"He doesn't trust you," The Other said returning with power. *"You still have to prove yourself to him. You should take care of the girl just as you took care of Reuben. You are an excellent killer, Paul. You make me proud..."*

"No! I won't do that!" Paul pushed the voice away and reached for his keyring. As he spun it to the BMW key he kept there, another vehicle approached and then stopped only feet away, blocking in the Tahoe. It was Anthony Agricola. Standing at the Beemer's trunk, Paul placed his hands on the cool surface and closed his eyes.

"Mark! The preacher is at Hope's house!"

Paul only had to wait a second before Mark replied.

"Bring them both."

200

೦ଃ৪៦

"Mr. Agricola? Paul Black. I'm glad to meet you."

Tony shook hands with Paul and turned to Hope. "You okay? Why didn't you answer the phone? I must have called six times."

"Oh? Sorry. I guess I was taking a nap." Hope leaned against the Tahoe, sullen and frowning.

Tony clenched his jaw and tipped his head to Paul. "Okay, then, what's going on here?" Paul Black watched with interest listening with an odd sideways grin. Not distracted enough to care, Tony gave Hope a new glare. "Are you leaving with him this late?"

"As a matter of fact, Paul is taking me to see Mark. No big deal. Did you need something?" Hope replied regarding Tony with a blank expression.

Tony's frustration grew. Had she lost her mind? "Excuse us," he said to Paul taking Hope's elbow. He led her to his driver's side door and scolded in a low voice, "You can't let this guy drive you to Dr. Corescu's house this late at night. What're you thinking?"

Hope tugged her elbow from his grasp. "Look," she hissed, "I don't know what your deal is, but I am not a child. Thank you for caring, but I'm going."

Paul stepped between them interrupting their argument. "Mr. Agricola, See that BMW?"

His lips parted, Tony took a moment to change gears. "Um, yeah. It's nice," he said and Hope slipped away to climb into the Tahoe. Paul inched closer and Tony backed up to regain his personal space.

"Can you do me a solid? I need to get that car back to my garage. If you'd drive it back for me, I'd bring you home after."

Tony shot a glance to Hope who refused to meet his eye. Something was up and his entire spirit shouted for him to stay close. He gave Paul a nod. "Yeah, no problem."

"Excellent!" Paul replied and draped an arm across his shoulders. "Mark said you should come over some time. Let's do it tonight. How convenient." The kid smiled and Tony's flesh crawled at the close proximity. Paul walked him to the Beemer where Tony wiggled free of the contact.

With a chirp and a flash of the parking lights, the doors unlocked and Paul handed Tony the key fob. In another minute, Tony had parked his truck and they were on the road, his heart sending up prayers of protection and he didn't know why.

201

ോ

Mark paced the library stewing, the negative variables snowballing out of control. The reporter and now a preacher? Mark had never shed innocent blood, but feared he may have to tonight.

"What do you call those lambs you took as servants? Humans do not come any more pure than those." No longer easy to silence, The Other spoke with disdain.

"I'm fed up with you," he sent over. *"Depart, if you can."*

He had suffered under the demon's advice more strongly since its resurrection. Maybe he didn't have to. *Maybe now that I understand it's a demon and not an agent of God, I can simply send it away...* With a sense of finality, Mark imagined slamming a door on the demon's communication line. Then he sank his weight into a chair and waited. Several long seconds passed and The Other returned no reply. Was he gone? Didn't he feel lighter? Mark grinned and opened his eyes. *Now, if I may, I have some things to work out.*

The reporter. Most likely, the guy was staying at the hotel he drank in. What was to stop Mark from slipping to his room tonight and dealing up a little death? What would that be like, killing someone who hadn't been singled out for a judging? *Can I take a life without God's permission?*

Mark scoffed. According to his new revelation, God had not sanctioned any of the deaths he had perpetrated over the centuries.

If that's the case, Mark reasoned, *one or two more dead bodies won't make much of a difference.*

Then, there was Hope's friend. He would also have to go. How could he be left alive now that Hope brought him into Mark's secret world? The easiest route would be to dispose of the reporter and the preacher in one night, and then escape to Europe. It could be done. Hope would be put off by the cold-blooded murder of her friend, but what choice did he have? The man was involved, and Mark could leave no witnesses lest he endanger everything his life entailed, including Paul.

Mark peeked in to check Paul's progress and found them almost home. He sent a new command: *"Send Hope to the library. I will meet you and the preacher in the garage."*

When he was certain Paul understood, Mark left the library to open the front door for Hope. *Let's get this show on the road.*

202

CRED

"Here we are," Paul chirped. Hope hadn't spoken, probably unhappy Tony had been invited.

"She wants your master for herself. Get rid of her. There is still time."

With effort, Paul ignored The Other's suggestions and exited the truck. Then he challenged the voice with, *"Mark has enough love for us both."*

"You fool only yourself," The Other replied and Paul frowned.

He walked Hope to the door and motioned for Tony to wait in the BMW. To Hope he said, "Mark asks if you will go to the library and we'll join you shortly."

She nodded. "I'm sorry for pouting. It just seems that between my sister and my friends, I'll never get to be alone with Mark."

Paul gave her a nod, but glared at her back as she turned for the house. He then called out across the cobblestone drive. "Tony, it'd be a big help if you just park that car right in the garage for us."

To his pleasure, Tony tipped his head and waited for Paul to get his truck moving. The driveway wrapped to the back, and Paul gestured for Tony to pass. With care, the preacher tucked the BMW between the wall and a late-model Cadillac. Paul pulled the Tahoe behind Tony and entered the garage.

Got him boxed in, Paul thought. Sensing Mark hiding out of sight, he pasted on a grin for their guest. Whatever Mark had in store was going to be interesting and Paul could hardly wait to see what would happen next.

Forty-One

Take to heart…all the words of this law.
They are not just idle words for you—they are your life.
Deuteronomy 32:46-47

SECLUDED IN A CORNER OF THE GARAGE, MARK LEANED against the wall awaiting his moment. Paul played his part, grinning, making small talk, and leading the preacher deeper into the space. It didn't feel natural—working prey with his long-time servant, but… *Isn't this my future? I promised to bring him close. He understood what I meant and he embraced the notion.* Mark's eyes narrowed as he watched Paul's dance. He looked much too comfortable; giving him the curse The Other bestowed upon that priest three centuries ago could be an enormous error of judgment. Mark nearly smiled at the irony, but an angry voice in his head stole his attention.

"Stop crying and take your medicine! I'll give you something to cry about!"

Mark winced and waited; they always came in pairs. The evil-doer's hateful deeds treated Mark as a cosmic sin magnet seeking a connection. He shrank further into the shadows, purposing to exorcise the black thoughts before dealing with the problem at hand.

"You, too. I'll slap you into next week!"

Mark visualized the human monster matching the vehement words. It was Hope's sister Glorie, cursing as she forced onto her children cough syrup laced with ammonia. This poison, when administered a little at a time, proved particularly cruel, causing slow perforation of the soft tissues in the palate, esophagus, and stomach, which then led to leaking ulcers and toxic shock.

Damn that woman! Mark's brow creased with effort as he dissolved the sickening images from his mind. It took almost thirty seconds for the episode to pass and he sighed, disgusted with his shortcomings.

This evil woman will succeed in murdering her three children if I do not

204

intervene. Mark saw the woman at that moment, deep in his mind he witnessed her laughing with Fran Booker in a dark and boisterous tavern. But he couldn't go…

"Oh, he's been collecting cars since I met him…" Paul was saying, killing time and awaiting Mark's entrance. Mark pressed his lips together and made a choice. He would tend to the moment at hand: Paul, Hope, and Agricola, here and now. Glorie Hershey and her children would take a backseat. The end. Mark grumbled as he shelved her for good.

"Hit that button for me," Paul said to Agricola who leaned in the open BMW's window to do as he asked. *"I sure appreciate it."*

The garage door lowered and Mark watched Agricola scan the room with his bespectacled gaze. What had Hope told him? What were his intentions? There was only one sure way to find out and Mark watched for his cue.

രുട്ടോ

Paul walked clear to the interior wall, his attention on an oversized map filling the panel. Tony inhaled and quieted his spirit, his instincts on high alert. He checked the dark corners before moving past the luxury automobiles filling the showroom.

"Tony, look at this, I mean…" the kid said pointing to the map, his back to Tony. Black's behavior did not ring normal, but Hope had come voluntarily; Tony would stay and make sure she was safe. He reached Paul's position and cleared his throat.

"Oh, there you are," he said and turned, facing Tony, and as he had done multiple times already, he stood too close. Tony backed one step and inhaled to speak. Paul beat him to it. "Here's Mark."

The guy's eyes flit over Tony's right shoulder and Tony whirled about. That corner had been empty, he was certain of that. Approaching in a smooth step and holding Tony's gaze, his host reached them and stood square.

"Mr. Agricola, nice of you to come on such short notice." Mark extended his right hand and instead of take it, Tony dropped his eyes, his mind racing.

Don't touch him. Don't do it. He's going to grab your hand and … Tony stopped his mind and remembered he was on a job for God. In a jerky movement, he shook the doctor's hand two quick pumps and released.

"I'm happy to be here. Mr. Black said you wouldn't mind."

"Mr. Black?" On his left, Paul laughed and put a hand to Tony's

205

shoulder. "I'm Paul. We're friends, right? Call me Paul."

Tony forced a smile. Paul's hand, the doctor's proximity, and a car behind him, Tony had nowhere to run. *But so what? Why am I panicking? It's just a guy! A man confused about God. He's not crazy. He's not a murderer!* All that Hope related about the man ran past his memory. *What else had she said? That he talks to animals? Why am I so terrified?*

Neither man had moved, but stared into his face, waiting. Waiting. For what? Tony paced his breathing, but beyond his control, his heartbeat quickened. He clapped his hands. "So, are we going in?"

The doctor tilted his head to the side. "Yes, shortly, but first, I need to ask you something."

Tony tucked his hands into his jeans pockets to disguise any shaking. "Shoot."

Mark chuckled and Tony's blood turned to ice. Something in the man's eyes. He was in grave danger and his heart asked God to pile on the courage.

◯౩౮◯

"You and Hope are close?" Mark asked, skewering the shorter man with his gaze. In his ear, Agricola's pulse raced like a man running a marathon, yet he held his expression well.

"Platonic, but yes," he replied with a humorless chuckle.

Mark continued. "She puts her trust in you. Comes to you for guidance and counseling?"

"That's what friends are for..."

The wanna-be preacher held it together as Mark stepped closer. It was time to act; what would he do? He had asked an internal question and The Other returned with an answer.

"Just do it, you simpleton. You are pitiful. Earn back your servant's respect in the process. Look at him. He doubts you even now. Just do it."

Mark met Paul's eye. He did indeed eagerly await Mark's retaliation, expecting a show, desiring to see his wonderful master overcome a man in cold blood. Mark returned his eye to the preacher. Agricola was innocent, without a shred of malice or ill will in him. Then as if on cue, Mark's hunger cramped his middle. He revealed nothing, but imagined Agricola's blood on his tongue. Oh, it would be ambrosia like none other. *I will take his blood,* Mark said inside, maybe to himself, maybe to the demon. *But I might leave him alive...*

It made sense. If the preacher made a nonfatal donation and

learned Mark's true nature in the process, wouldn't that facilitate their conversation inside? *I can kill him any time I choose…*

Mark nodded to Paul who moved behind Tony and viciously grasped him by both arms, pulling him into his body.

"What're you doing?" Tony hissed. He managed to keep his voice low, but he was obviously terrified. "Let me go."

"Are you afraid to die?" Mark asked and searched Tony's eyes.

"No, I'm not." The defiant glare the preacher returned said it all. This man was a hero and he would not leave tonight without his friend. "Now, let me go."

"Hold on…" Mark took one more peek of Paul's eye which now glinted with evil intent. He enjoyed the preacher's squirming, his mounting fear, and Mark sent Paul a message to keep them on the same page. *I'm not going to kill him just now. I want to scare him a bit. Hold him tight."*

The side of Paul's mouth curved and he further braced the man against his chest, planting his feet.

"Are you going to kill me, Dr. Corescu?" Tony's voice was strong, but his eyes were frightened.

"I'm going to show you what Hope was trying to make you understand. I know she came to you, I see it in your eyes. I also know she told you things she should have kept to herself." Mark reached for and grasped Agricola's wrist and tugged him close. Paul's contact followed and he looked down upon the preacher giving him a shhhh gesture. "Be still. It will be over soon."

ભ৪৯

Tony resisted, but couldn't break Dr. Corescu's grip on his arm.

"All she said was that you might be a vigilante!" Tony said with urgency as the doctor reeled him closer. What was he planning? Was he about to break his arm? "Let me go!" he said in the same voice and struggled in Paul's grip.

The young man held him with bonds of iron, his cheek to the back of Tony's head. The doctor didn't answer, but came toe-to-toe with him in the brightly-lit garage.

"What're you going to do?" Tony whispered now that there were mere inches apart. He hadn't envisioned this scenario. If someone was going to kill you, they usually didn't get close enough to bite.

Bite? The horse in my dream!

207

Tony watched with detached horror as the doctor stretched out his arm and positioned his face to the crook of Tony's elbow. "Are you going to bite me, Dr. Cores—"

Tony didn't finish, gasping in the sudden pain. The doctor *did* bite him; unbelievably sharp teeth punctured the tender flesh inside his elbow. Tony blinked back tears and tried to twist away. Paul held him fast and his own voice in his ears seemed to emanate from another dimension when he whispered, *"Jesus! Help me!"*

"Shhhhh. It's not so bad. Be still," Paul whispered at his ear, his lips brushing the lobe.

Tony's abused appendage grew numb as the monster pulled blood from the wound, his grip violent and strong as steel. In another second, his mind hazed and Tony's knees buckled. He had no interest in resisting and allowed the men to support his weight. Whatever God was doing, Tony's heart screamed for it to end soon.

᎒᎒᎒

"Shhhh…" Paul again spoke tenderly in Tony's ear. "See…it's almost over. All that fussing for nothing." He supported the preacher under the armpits, and watched in awe as Mark fed. In his belly a yearning grew and a desire for power increased every passing moment. Mesmerized, he watched Mark feed. He'd never seen this, Mark taking blood from an outsider, so animalistic, feral, primal… Surely no man in the world could possibly be more magnificent than his master at this moment. Paul's heart quickened.

The Other said it, I have been missing out.

But not for much longer; Mark promised.

After another long moment, Mark withdrew from the preacher and pressed a handkerchief to the puckering wound. He straightened with a flourish and flashed Paul a victorious grin. Paul returned the expression, his eyes hungry for the next step. In his peripheral vision, Tony clutched his wounded arm to his breast. With an amused wink to Mark, Paul pecked the top of the preacher's head and opened his arms. In slow motion, the man slumped to the polished concrete floor.

"Is this what you expected to find, Mr. Agricola?" Holding the preacher's eye, Mark wiped his mouth with his forefinger and thumb. Then he lifted his eyes to Paul, who inadvertently sent a questioning sentiment of, *and me?* His master's response involved a miniscule eyeroll and Paul sent apologies. He would wait. Mark was good for his word.

He raised his brow and Mark said as he turned away, "When he's up to it, bring him into the library." And then he entered the house, leaving Paul alone with his new acquaintance.

"He bit me."

Paul lowered his eyes to the man on the floor, sitting now and leaning on his palms.

"Monsters," Tony added, his tone flat and emotionless.

Paul gave him a grin. "And when we go inside, keep that to yourself, eh?" He put out his hand. "Come on, get up."

The preacher looked at Paul's fingers and sucked his teeth. He then met Paul's eye, his gaze hard. "Is he insane? Does he think he's a vampire or something?"

Paul wiggled his fingers and with a resigned huff, their guest grabbed them. Paul pulled him to his feet recognizing greater muscle strength.

It's the blood. Mark's and then Reuben's... just think how powerful I'll be when Mark finishes the job!

He watched Tony dust his slacks one-handed, his wounded arm folded to his chest.

"What are you going to do? Why have you brought us here?" the man asked grimacing after a peek at his punctures.

"First, we're going to bandage your arm," Paul said in a happy tone. He watched the preacher's face; the man wasn't irrational or terrified. If anything, he appeared annoyed. Paul smiled. He was an odd one— one to watch.

Forty-Two

Have we not all one Father? Did not one God create us?
Malachi 2:10

MARK FOUND HOPE IN THE LIBRARY, BY HER POSTURE and expression, *sulking*. She had leaned against a bookcase, a hardcover volume in her hand, flipping pages without reading the passages. The woman did not yet comprehend her place in his future or even the being he embodied. Now that the door to his past had been opened, what sort of creature he was would need to be reexamined. Then he considered, Hope. *She is impulsive and self-centered...* but didn't he have the same personality traits within himself? Didn't he long to be alone with her, sharing his world with the only female that had ever turned his head? Hope sniffled to herself and he recognized a more altruistic emotion: *worry*. She'd inadvertently brought her friend into their drama and considered herself responsible—not only for whatever trouble he caused Mark, but also, for his safety. For although she did not yet fully know what Mark *was*, she understood on some level that he was a killer.

Enough of this, he scolded inside, ready to move the evening along. He cleared his throat and she looked up, her blue eyes huge.

"Mark!" she breathed and rushed close. He opened his arms, happy to see such a fearless response. "I'm sorry for messing things up. Anthony's a good man. He—"

Mark put a finger to her lips. "Quiet now," he said smiling and walked her further into the room. The preacher's blood settled warmly inside, providing a pleasant buzz. He sat Hope on a two-seater couch and then stood before her, looking upon her anxious face.

"Your friend should be joining us shortly. How much does he suspect of me?"

"Nothing, honest," she answered in a rush. "I asked him for advice, but I never let on anything important. I was careful." She

210

clasped her hands in her lap and held his eye, her face turned up. "He's so smart and knows the Bible forwards and backwards. I think ya'll could be friends. I really do."

Mark regarded her assertion. After his earlier display, Tony would rightly be wary; would he maintain peace of mind to help Mark divine God's will in the current predicament? And if the preacher failed in this, would he be the first innocent Mark murdered?

With an invisible sigh, he sank into a soft chair across from Hope, but still near. "Do you trust him with my secret? If we talked openly to gain his biblical insight, how will he respond?"

Gathering Hope's opinion should help him deal with Agricola once he joined them. Whatever the preacher thought right now, alone with Paul with fang marks in his arm, when he heard the balance of Mark's situation, he would need to be made of incredible stuff.

"Anthony is the wisest man I know," Hope replied with serious eyes. "You can trust him."

"You have to kill him, my priest," The Other piped in, always lying in wait to add his opinion. *"He knows you now. He despises you. He belongs to his God and cannot let you live. If you do not kill him, your mistakes will kill us all."*

Mark rolled in his lips, but couldn't disagree. "Good," was all he said and for a moment, they sat, gazes locked, but their minds on entirely different matters. In the garage, Paul had nearly finished. Mark attended their conversation anticipating an interesting evening.

⊙₰⊙

Paul had settled Tony in a small office containing a tidy steel desk bordered by labeled wall-files. Whoever ran the garage did so with precision and care. He watched the slender oddball character rummage through the narrow draws. Without looking up, the guy asked, "What are you thinking?"

Tony maintained a blank expression. "That you are insane and so is your partner in there."

Paul looked up, first aid items in his hand. "Oh, you're wrong there, preacher man." The man stepped close and reached for Tony's injured arm. He allowed it and Paul leaned his rump against the desk, his eyes on the work of cleaning the wound.

Tony watched not seeing, his mind asking questions of himself and of God. *What is going on here? Is this Hope's huge purpose?* Reverend Elijah

211

Prince's prophetic word returned; a trial was coming that was not a punishment. How could he ever guess the trial would be a vampire attack? *Is this it? De-fanging a modern-day vampire?*

As the thoughts tumbled around in his head, Paul disinfected and bandaged Tony's laceration as well as any medic.

Maybe he has a lot of practice with bite victims.

That thought brought a groan of dread from deep within and Paul grinned at him, fastening a clip to the wrap.

"You're all fixed up," he said and released Tony's arm. "Shall we?" He motioned for the door to the main house.

Tony did not get up, but studied his hands with a vacant downcast stare. "In a moment. Just be still a minute," he mumbled. Paul nodded and leaned against the doorframe watching him with a curious expression.

Assured a moment of quiet, Tony bowed his head into his right hand and held the left one close to his chest. For the first few moments, nothing happened; his brain cloudy and his memory sluggish. With a bit more effort, he finally formed a coherent prayer to his God.

"Be not far from me, O Lord, I need you," Tony said under his breath and ignored Paul who leaned in to hear. When Tony rebuked the devil, Paul huffed.

"Does that really work?" Paul asked in a snicker. "I mean, are there evil spirits in here or did you just scare them away?"

Disapproving Paul's mocking tone Tony sent him a glare. "You'll find out soon enough."

Paul again smiled, his expression of amusement. "You're a fascinating little guy. And so spunky. Not afraid of anything." Paul stood off the wall as if prepared to move on to the house. "Are you finished or is there more?"

"No, that's all." Tony rose to his feet, unsteady at first and then balanced as his head cleared. "You'll see the power of God before this night is out. He has big plans for you and your partner, whether you know it or not."

Paul chuckled. "I sure hope so. So far, I like what He's doing."

Ignoring the remark, Tony moved forward only to trip over his own shoe as he passed Paul's position. The guy caught him by the bicep before he hit the floor.

"You're okay," he said waiting for Tony to regain full control. "Give it another minute."

Tony agreed and leaned against the wall. Paul continued to analyze his every move.

"You're a tough cookie. I'm impressed."

Tony glanced toward the door the doctor had disappeared through and then looked back to Paul. "What's it to you? You're toying with me, playing. Aren't you going to kill me later anyway?"

"Hah, such talk!" Paul laughed. "I don't think so. I like you. You have a good shot of getting out of this alive. Just behave yourself and do whatever he brought you here to do."

"I can't believe this is happening." Tony pointed to his bandage. "He bit my arm. That is insane."

Paul tossed back his head and laughed louder. "Yeah, drank your blood, too. Pretty awesome, eh?"

Tony only shook his head, even more convinced of the young man's unstable mental state. He started moving again and made it to the house door, Paul two steps behind. When he stopped at the mat to catch his breath and steady his nerves, Paul touched his shoulder.

"Be sure you're ready. No sense in going in there only to pass out again."

Tony braced on the lintel and met Paul's eye. "What is this? Is he for real? I mean, is he a real vampire?" The question needed an answer. Yes, the man had sucked Tony's blood. Yes, it certainly felt as if his teeth had sharpened into fangs. But, no, none of this was possible. Was it?

"Add it up," Paul shrugged, still smiling. "You have a hole in your arm and he has a belly full of your blood. What does that spell?"

Tony thought on his reply a long moment and settled with, "I think it spells trouble."

"Wrong answer." Paul reached past him and opened the door. "But let's go see."

"What's the right answer?" Tony asked, his strength returned.

"The one that will most please Dr. Corescu, of course," Paul said and nudged him inside the house. "I'll be rooting for you."

"Well, great. Just great," he deadpanned.

Paul laughed aloud and showed him the way to meet the others.

213

Forty-Three

Trust in the LORD with all your heart
and lean not on your own understanding.
Proverbs 3:5

THE PREACHER ENTERED THE LIBRARY AND PAUL MET
Mark's eye. Time to start the show.

"Ah! Mr. Agricola, please, come in. Have a seat." Mark stood as the men entered, suggesting with a gesture that Tony take a seat also across from Hope. He looked to Paul who clasped his hands behind his back.

"Can I get you anything to drink? Hope? Mr. Agricola?" Both guests shook their heads and Paul asked silently, *"Shall I stay?"*

Mark shook his head and sent him out. Paul exited the library biting his tongue. As much as he loved and respected Mark, an unfamiliar anger scoured his spirit. Opening up to the outsiders—first the woman and now this preacher—his master brought them sure peril. *Can he not see it? Do I need to set it right myself? Can I?*

"You will have to," The Other piped in, his mental voice a raspy whisper. *"He will thank you when the deeds are accomplished. See, I was right about the traitor, Reuben. Your master is pleased with you."*

Paul listened, the pain previously associated with such a visitation no longer evident.

"Alas, the discomfort was necessary to break through. You and I are soulmates. I will help you. Your master is going to try to leave us. If the woman and the preacher succeed in turning him away, he will abandon you...abandon us."

Paul paced to the study and sat at the large oak desk in the center of the room. The light of the writing lamp barely illuminated the four corners. Not that much different from the study in which Paul had been transformed so many years ago.

Where is the master I knew then? Would he leave me for this woman?

Such a thing would have never crossed his mind without the help

214

of The Other, but it rang true. All of Paul's sacrifices, his obedient and loving servitude, his unquestioning devotion, might be tossed to the wind for a woman.

"He will choose this woman over you," The Other whispered.

Paul cringed, eyes moist. *"No! Mark would never do that. He loves me."*

"He loves her more."

"He does?" Paul lay his head on folded arms and wept.

ൟ

Taking a seat across from Hope, Tony disguised his unease. *Act normal. It's all good. That unhinged maniac will kill us if I'm not careful.* He pressed the bandage that covered his new wound and prayed Hope wouldn't notice.

"Geesh, Anthony, you took forever. What happened to your arm?"

Tony widened his eyes but his host answered in his stead.

"I'm afraid he cut himself in the garage." The doctor turned Tony's way, his face the picture of concern. "Doing better?"

"Yes, thank you," Tony replied through gritted teeth.

"You should be more careful," Hope said in a huff. She may have been concerned, but mostly she seemed annoyed at his presence. Tony dodged her irritated glare and focused on the doctor.

"Mr. Agricola, from the top." Mark assumed a chair adjacent to Tony completing the triangle. "Hope has great faith in your, well, *faith…"* Tony swallowed and awaited more, the madman (or monster) beside him playing his role to perfection. "She considers you an excellent theologian and feels you may have insight on a handful of philosophical issues that have come up of late."

"I will do the best I can," Tony said through a forced smile. He reached out his left hand to Hope and his right to the doctor. *Courage, man!* "Let's open with prayer."

Still pouting, Hope took his hand. Tony cleared his throat as the doctor followed suit with an amused expression.

Tony bowed his head and prayed aloud for God's guidance over their meeting.

"Amen," Hope agreed when he concluded.

"Well done, Mr. Agricola. We will certainly need the wisdom of God here tonight."

Silence assumed the air for a time as the three regarded one another. After what seemed an eternity, Tony pulled a compact New

215

Testament from his back pocket. The movement brought Mark to attention and he leaned in.

"Tony—may I call you Tony?" The doctor asked the epitome of a generous and polite fellow citizen. Tony met his eye and gave him a nod. "Tony," he began again, his voice smooth, "whatever Hope may have told you, I am not a monster." He shot a glance to Hope who frowned. "Whatever you may think of me right now, I am not the devil."

Tony paced his reply. "To be honest, Dr. Corescu, Hope didn't tell me that you were a vam—" Tony corrected in a flash for Hope's sake— how much did she know? Certainly, she didn't know her boyfriend had fangs. "Hope only asked me a few theology questions, like what did I think about a vigilante killing for God." Tony blinked and looked away, Corescu's gaze too severe.

"And what was your advice?"

"Well, I'll tell you," Tony said, his courage growing the longer he avoided the doctor's eye. "What she described is not biblically sound."

There, it was out. With his head tilted down, Tony lifted his gaze enough to catch the doctor's reaction. The man wasn't angry or enraged; but rather thoughtful. A good sign.

"Tell him why," Hope said then, her voice urgent.

"Yes, if you have given it some thought, I would appreciate your insight." Leaning over his knees, Mark waited for Tony to brave a new eye-meet.

Tony's mind raced and he finally did take tiny glances at the doctor's face. "Where do I begin?" *Where did this man get the insane notion God wanted him to judge people to death?*

Corescu gave him a jumping off point. "Before I met Hope, I lived my life as best as I knew how, upholding God's will and performing my calling with purpose and dignity. I was born Markus Corescu in Hungary, 1600…"

Tony's eyes found a resting place now in Hope's gaze. *1600? Hope?* he accused with his expression and she looked away. Corescu continued.

"I lived an average and uneventful life. I joined the priesthood when I came of age and through a meeting ordained by God, I was later transformed into a vampire."

Tony re-met Mark's eye and remained, steeling himself against the nausea growing deep within.

"Because of the trauma I suffered at the hands of this demon, I forgot my past. I have been under the impression for the last three centuries that I was called by God to pass judgment on the evil in mankind."

Acknowledging his confession with a grunt, Tony turned to Hope. His words had not fazed her. *She knows. God help me, she knows he's a vampire.* Tony did not hide a miniscule headshake. *Unbelievable.*

Corescu had reached the end of his opener and awaited something from Tony. With a dry swallow and a wish he had accepted that drink Paul Black offered, he nodded to the others and worked it through.

Did God allow such a monster to exist?

Obviously, He had; Tony had the proof in his flesh.

Did the devil have the power to transform a God-loving man into such a monster?

Obviously, he did. Now, the creature wanted to be justified. Did he expect Tony to absolve him of his transgressions? There was no way.

Tony exhaled and the doctor resumed his attention. "Tell me this. Why now? Almost four hundred years have passed." The doctor turned his gaze to Hope.

"Hope has been the catalyst. She is my gift from God, the one I have been waiting for. Before she arrived, I was convinced that I was doing the will of God. Now, I'm not so certain. I cannot move forward until I sort out this confusion. I can do it without you, but it feels right that you would arrive and toss your ideas into the mix."

Tony tucked in his cheek in thought. It was feasible that God would use her this way. Then he trained his gaze on the vampire.

"It sounds as if you admit you may have misinterpreted God." The doctor sucked his teeth holding Tony's eye. He pressed on. "Doctor, I need to know if we're going to proceed with a discussion."

Expressionless, Doctor Corescu said, "Speak freely."

"Okay. Dr. Corescu, when was the last time you read the Bible?"

His host pursed his lips and then smiled bursting with confidence. "It has been centuries since I last picked up a Bible, but I'm a theologian and I have everything I need to know stored in my heart and mind."

This was easier, a claim many mortals might pose. Tony leaned forward mimicking the doctor's posture. "Forgive me, but you don't. If you'd been consistently reading the Bible, the Lord would have been speaking to you about these things." Tony's words now flowed without hindrance. "God's word is your foundation. If you don't read it, your foundation crumbles. You've been operating on a centuries-old revelation of Satan that God could not correct. Why? Because you stopped listening to Him. You closed the door when you sided with the devil. You have no foundation. Your house has sunk into the pit."

That said, Tony exhaled. The wound in his arm periodically relayed painful reminders of his host's supernatural ferocity and he watched the doctor's eyes.

☙❧

The preacher's accusations intrigued him. Plus, Mark reveled in the excitement of revealing himself to yet another mortal. He'd been complacent a long time and the look in the preacher's eyes egged him on. Before he responded, Hope hopped in.

"Wait, Anthony, aren't you exaggerating? Mark was a priest. He knows the Bible, too."

Mark tempered his tone but needed a moment alone with her friend. "Hope, let Tony ask the questions." With a gentle mental suggestion, Mark added while holding her eye, "The powder room is down the hall to the right. You were about to ask me where it was, correct?"

Hope rose to her feet. "Uh, yeah, thanks." She walked away and Mark turned to Tony happy she was so easily manipulated. Agricola possessed useful insight and he would get to it. "Please proceed, Tony."

"Was that a Jedi mind trick?" Tony asked without humor. Mark did not want to divert the conversation so he offered a tiny shrug. The preacher slow-blinked and continued. "Doctor, tell me about the first time you judged someone. Maybe I can shed a third-party perspective. Maybe, just *maybe*, this vigilante idea was yours, not God's."

"Explain." Mark remained mum and waited for the preacher to expound on his outrageous comment. As before, the man's candor didn't bother him. Tony was terrified, and that was enough.

"It's like this. If this thing happened to me…" Tony cleared his throat to continue. "…and I woke up one day as a *vampire*," Tony whispered the word, "I would do all that I could to rationalize my situation. I would try to make peace with God, and if I couldn't do that, I'd try to make peace with myself to get what I needed. Understand?"

Mark arched his brow and waited for more.

"I would try to figure out how to make it work for me as well as for God. If you tell me how it started, I might be able to help." When Mark still did not comment, Tony added, "Dr. Corescu, if we work together, maybe I can help you find God."

Mark blinked, the phrase striking a nerve and giving him courage to continue. "Yes, Tony, I would like to relate it to you."

Mark leaned forward and waited for the clock to finish chiming the half-hour. After the last bell, Mark began his tale with a simple fact.

"The monster that transformed me into this creature was killed by men from my parish before my very eyes. I ran for my life and spent the night in an abandoned barn. I was still innocent; I had not killed of my own volition. I was a babe turned loose in a monster's body…"

…As the rooster announces the day by the pull of the sun, a caustic hunger awoke the priest from a fitful sleep. His hunger, more invasive and torturous than ever, he clutched his middle and peered through the barn wall slats to the moon above. The song of crickets clanged like cymbals in his hyper-sensitive hearing and the light of the stars caused him to squint against the discomfort. If he didn't find food and soon, he would go insane. The next thing he acknowledged—it was a novel fuel he required now—the same sustenance his master had required before his demise. Mark hopped down from the loft and listened out for fresh blood.

The livestock ambling within reach did not pique his interest, but the line of smoke trailing from the chimney of the tiny farmhouse consumed his attention. He approached the structure with stealth and waited by the door.

Am I actually going to kill for blood?

"Of course, my priest. This is the only way you will survive. It is you or them." The Other, dead in the flesh, but alive in Mark's spirit, urged him to comply.

Mark stepped to the side of the dark entrance and flattened himself against the wall. Could he resist? What if he returned to the barn, begged God for forgiveness, and let death find him?

"Death touched you and left you alive. You will never see death again, my priest. Wait too long and you will kill without even knowing it."

As Mark contemplated his options, the door opened and a man called out into the dark, speaking the local dialect.

"Who's out there? Show yourself!"

Secluded by shadow, Mark studied the man, missing nothing. Short and stocky with a frizzy beard and dirty flop of black hair, the gruff character barked a few threats to the dark. Mark watched him from his position on the wall, inches away. If the man turned back, he would see him. Mark held his breath and waited to see what would happen.

Then, the man huffed, cursed, and reentered the house with a slam. Mark exhaled and his stomach grumbled anew. Waiting for the man to bed down for the night, Mark listened to his heartbeat. Within ten minutes, the lamp giving off the glow in the house was extinguished. Mark listened as the single occupant grew still.

I won't do it. I don't have to…

A terrible emptiness wracked his entire frame and Mark doubled over in pain. Without waiting for his conscience (or The Other) to pipe in, Mark approached the door. It opened soundlessly on well-oiled hinges giving him access to the one-room home. In the light provided by the embers glowing on the fire, Mark spied the man lying on his back on a soft bed. A fluttering noise to his right caught his attention. Mark scanned the opposite side of the room and peered into the dark. Whether he used his new eyes, or his new mind, Mark thought he saw spirits in the room, wispy, brownish-gray puffs that swirled and maneuvered around the table and chair in the corner. Mark rubbed his eyes and stepped closer. The ghostly ribbons continued to waver in and out of the small area.

In his spirit, Mark asked, *"What is this?"*

Immediately, the apparitions ceased their lazy movements and settled before Mark's amazed face. They were sentient and he searched his mind for an explanation.

"Who are you?"

"Guilty! Guilty!" A telepathic reply from several ethereal sources resounded in his head. Surely, they didn't accuse him. So far he'd done nothing wrong.

"I don't understand." As Mark watched, the spirits floated to the dark form on the bed.

"Murderer!"

A barrage of horrible images flooded Mark's mind. An entire family had been butchered; a woman, a man, and two curly-haired toddlers. This sleeping devil didn't belong in this house. He had only just killed the entire family of four.

Mark gasped. *I am seeing the murders from the killer's perspective!*

He looked to the snoring man, a human monster. When Mark concentrated more fully on the evil images, more crimes appeared, each more heinous than the first, committed in all imaginable places. The man sleeping before him was a bane to humanity, the sort of man one should kill before he murdered again.

"Ahhh, yesss… Take him, my priest! Protect the living. Release the dead who

wander the earth, cursed by their murderer."

"Yes, yes," the fluttering ghosts chanted in his mind.

Without further hesitation, Mark rushed to the man and yanked him out of bed. Holding him fast, he stared into the face of the killer, his mouth an indignant snarl. When the man's eyes opened, a look of shock crossed his dirty face.

"You have shed innocent blood! What do you have to say for yourself?" Mark's voice, ravaged from his unintentional self-starvation, rumbled through the small room, piercing and unbearable to his own ears. His victim shouted with surprise and strained against his captor.

"Speak, for tonight you will surely die." This was much better. Using focused thoughts instead of words saved his sensitive ears.

"Who are you? Let me go!" the man screamed.

The man's name popped into Mark's mind and he used it.

"Carnul Frescol, you are being judged for your sins. Tonight, you will pay the ultimate penalty for the crimes you have committed against God. Repent! Repent!"

Mark desperately wanted the man to beg God's forgiveness before the hunger overtook his senses. Without realizing it, his now-fierce hands tore at the man's collar shredding the cloth like paper. With the killer's throat exposed, it would be only seconds before he dove in, his starvation so acute.

Frescol screamed like a woman, and looked into his attacker's face. Mark recognized his expression of cold dread in Frescol's eyes, and then something else—*incredulity*. Frescol had no knowledge of God. He was destined to hell.

He was also out of time.

Without orchestration, Mark yanked the man's throat to his fiery lips, gnawing the skin like a rabid dog. After a few false starts, he clamped down where the muscle bulged out and Mark's newly sharpened teeth ripped into his flesh. An explosion of ecstasy flooded Mark's mind as the man's blood filled his mouth faster than he could swallow. The unused portion dribbled to the floor as Mark drank as much as he could hold. Somewhere along the way, the killer grew limp in his grasp, though his heart continued to thump a slow irregular beat. Before the pump stopped entirely, Mark pulled back to consider the face of the murderer in his arms. Frescol's eyes were half-open and his mouth moved with inaudible sentiment. In his elation, Mark relaxed his focus as the familiar breeze of spirits he had seen earlier swirled close-by. He closed his eyes and continued to watch them in his mind's eye. With a triumphant cheer, the specters gathered and headed through the ceiling and disappeared.

The killer's corpse met the floor and Mark collapsed onto the sloppy bed. The satisfaction in his soul overwhelmed him. *I can do the Lord's work here!* Mark laughed aloud. *This* was the way he would get back at the devil that transformed him and took his mortal life. He would spend his eternity, if indeed he was immortal as the creature had said, righting the wrongs of the mortal world. He would avenge the innocent and serve God's wrath on the wicked. *I will win back God's favor by judging the evil in mankind!*

Mark turned to the limp form on the wooden floor. The man's eyes were closed and his lips slack. To Mark, he looked like a man-eating tiger finally destroyed by a heroic hunter. A predator that had been served his own medicine.

An eye for an eye.

A life for a life.

It was good.

Forty-Four

Give ear O LORD and hear;
open Your eyes O LORD and see…"
Isaiah 37:17

AT THE CONCLUSION OF MARK'S GRUESOME TALE, TONY sat speechless. He rehashed the vampire's predicament, impossibly attempting to put himself in the doctor's shoes. In a way, he empathized. Why did God let this happen to a simple village priest? He didn't ask to become a vampire. *What would I have thought in a similar predicament?* With considerable effort, Tony set his emotions aside and attempted a response.

"That first victim… it doesn't sound as if he repented." Tony waited as the doctor nodded in agreement. "I assume you had better results on future attempts?"

"Nearly all of them accept my offer. This is why I know it's God's will. Without my help, these souls would be doomed to eternal damnation. Can you see that?"

Tony was on a short leash, but he had to speak his mind. "Doctor Corescu, you misunderstood those spirits in the murderer's room. Do you realize that?"

Mark's shook his head. "Explain."

Again, Tony formulated his question carefully. "The interpretation of what you saw isn't biblical. What you saw were spirits, all right, but they were not from God. Demons often imitate ghosts to get you to believe what they want you to believe."

"Continue…"

"Did those spirits have anything to do with your decision to make that first kill?"

"Perhaps," Mark answered, epiphany dawning in his dark gaze.

"From what you told me, your first impression was to return to the barn and pray. That was God speaking. But then you began to think about your hunger and how you might go insane if you didn't kill. That was The Other, and he's definitely not of God." Tony paused, reading derision in the vampire's face. Tony commiserated, for who wants to

223

be told that they listened to the wrong voices?

"What of the spirits?" Corescu grumbled.

"I think those were designed to trick you into attacking that man. I think they were there to be sure you did what the devil wanted you to do. I think they were there to make sure you became everything your vampire master wanted you to be."

The doctor sighed after a few thoughtful moments and leaned back in his chair. "You are very bright. What else?"

Before Tony could reply, Hope wandered back into the room.

"What?" Hope asked. "Did I miss something?"

Mark looked at Tony who shrugged, neither man willing to repeat the heavy truths coming to light.

ℭ℥ℬ

Paul endured a five-minute lecture from Mark's woman before she left him in peace. She had passed by his door and popped in to tell him how to run his life. She told him that Mark should "dump the servant routine". Who did she think she was? Paul was livid, but also exceedingly sad. When left alone once more, he rested his head on folded arms and brooded over the evening's events. He overheard their muffled voices in the next room. Was Mark telling the preacher his life history now? Jealousy pricked Paul's heart. A hundred years had passed since he dedicated himself to Mark, and he had never shared his past. *Why should I be left out, but two strangers completely taken into his confidence?*

"You must set things straight, little Paulie."

"But how?" Paul listened to the only one willing to speak to him.

"Look in your left pocket."

Paul sat up and reached into his pants pocket. He pulled out a handful of coins followed by a business card.

The reporter! Of course!

The loathsome journalist had handed it over at the front door. On the back, he had scribbled his hotel phone number. *"In case you have anything to tell me,"* the note said.

Paul smiled, a perfect plan forming. The reporter—he glanced at the front of the card and read the name again—Connie Nixon, could be eliminated right away. Paul could take care of him while his master played with the two in the house. It was perfect.

Without disguising the sound of his exit, Paul walked past the library to the kitchen and out the garage. If Mark noticed, he didn't comment. It shouldn't be too hard to get the reporter to meet him at a desolate location, kill him and dispose of the body.

I could be home within the hour. Mark would appreciate the effort.

"Yes, Paulie. Remember how impressed he was with the work you did with Reuben. Show him that you are ready for the gift he promised."

Paul nodded and opened the garage door. The Other's suggestion made perfect sense. Mark had been proud of him for his bravery when he dispatched Reuben. He needed a partner who would carry out these grisly errands while he got in touch with his past.

I can be that partner. It was not that difficult.

The worst thing about killing Reuben was the fear of the punishment he would face, and there had been none. He would kill the reporter and bring in any evidence he collected against Mark at the same time. They could actually escape this whole mess unscathed.

Paul pulled the BMW out of the garage and headed down the driveway. As he waited for the electronic front gate to open, he pulled out his cell and dialed the Sheraton.

"Room 402, please." The phone was picked up on the second ring.

"What? Who is it?" an intoxicated voice growled.

"Mr. Nixon? It's Paul Black. I need to see you right away," Paul said with urgency, smiling at his histrionics.

"Oh, oh, oh. Hang on." There was a shuffle and bang on Nixon's end. "Okay, where are you?"

"First, listen up. You're not safe. He knows where you are and he's going to break in there tonight, kill you, and steal all of your evidence. Any paperwork you have on him, take with you in your car, now." Paul headed toward the interstate, enjoying the ruse he performed for the reporter. It was going to be *so easy.*

☙❧

"My hotel room? That's a stretch. This place is pretty secure." Connie considered the locks on the door and shrugged, but the urgency in Mr. Black's voice unnerved him nonetheless. If this doctor was anything as bad as he was looking, he could really be a threat.

"He has people with keys, people with guns. You're not safe. Get ready for a great story. I'm going to tell you everything. First thing is that you'll never believe what really happened to Reuben Stuckey."

Connie reached for his briefcase and stuffed the early drafts of his headline story into the pocket. It sounded very juicy; like the Stuckey kid may have met his end. If this Black character was about to flip on

225

his boss, Connie was about to be very rich indeed. Forget Grouper and his cheesy scandal rag. He could sell this story nationwide. Maybe even negotiate a book contract and a sweet movie deal.

"Where are you?" he asked.

"Bring all of your stuff with you, so after we talk, you can check into a different hotel. And don't tell me which one so you will be safe."

"Okay, I'm leaving now. Just name the place." Connie set about folding his laptop and sliding it into its leather cover. He would return for his clothes in the light of day.

"Head up I-85 and take exit 12. There's an abandoned BP station on the left and I'll be parked behind it. I'm driving an arctic blue BMW sedan."

Connie jotted down the information and fled. He used the stairs to avoid the elevators and exited the rear doors of the lobby in case Corescu was after him at that moment. The tone in Mr. Black's voice put gas in his tank and he thanked his lucky stars that he had returned to his room tonight. Earlier that evening, he had been tossing back beers and was just about to hit the hard stuff when a serious (*private*) nature call forced him upstairs. As Connie jogged across the parking lot with his belongings, he considered the perfect timing.

What are the odds that I would go up to my room, take care of business, and then get the phone call that saves my life and advances the story of my career?

Connie loved happy coincidences and this one was turning out to be very joyous indeed. He piled into his rented Taurus and headed toward the interstate. The skinny little Paul fellow was about to make him very rich.

ᘓᘔ

Readjusting to Hope's presence, a wry smile crossed Mark's face as he caught her eye. She raised her brow.

"What did I miss?" Hope hovered near her seat awaiting an answer. "It must have been good because Anthony's as pale as a sheet!"

Mark regarded her, completely oblivious to the fact that she'd crossed the line by lecturing Paul. Did she not realize Mark heard every word of their discussion? Mark shook his head. Hope brought a special element to the situation, but his heart swelled at the sight of her.

He decided to test her. "Did you and Paul have a nice chat?"

"Oh, you… was that bad?" Hope asked crestfallen.

"It was unwise," Mark said, allowing a half-smile and then turned to Tony. "Hold that thought. I must have a word with Hope in the

226

hallway." He stood and walked to the door with Hope following behind. Tony stood only to have Mark gesture for him to remain seated. "We'll only be a moment." Mark led Hope into the hall and out of Tony's earshot.

"Hope, Paul is sensitive. He wears his heart on his sleeve. Everything I say to him is magnified because of his gentle nature." Mark pulled her close, his mouth above her ear. Her heart-rate increased and Mark smiled. "You can't psychoanalyze him. He's not like any man you've ever met."

Her face against his lapel, Hope disagreed. "But—"

Mark hushed her with, "For a century, he has served me. It's all he knows. If I cut him loose, he's liable to hurt himself or someone else. Understand?"

She huffed, unhappy at what she took as a chastisement. "But you'll change this master-slave arrangement around, right? Now that you know?"

Mark didn't like the question and he didn't have an answer. He decided a placation might serve the moment. "Perhaps, but even now, because of your conversation, he has left the house in an emotional fugue." Mark gestured for the door. "If I wasn't so interested in what your friend Tony is sharing, I'd tear out of here looking for him."

"I'm sorry." Hope said, near tears. "Is he going to be okay?"

"He'll be fine. Rest assured, if he runs into trouble…" Mark took her back to the library as he spoke. "…I will know."

Tony was at his feet when they returned and settled down as they did, again in the triangle, only this time, Mark tugged his chair closer to Hope. Tony visibly bristled when he did so, but Mark ignored the man's hyped respirations. Two seconds later, Hope had another question.

"Mark," she said and looked backward toward the hallway, "Where's Reuben?"

Mark smiled at her boldness but never did enjoy being interrogated. Tony's questions were about all he was willing to tolerate for the evening. Plus, it wasn't the first time she'd asked about Reuben. *Maybe I should tell her, otherwise, what is all this sharing about?*

With a calming exhale, he placed three fingers to her knee and said in a kind voice, "Hope, listen close…" Mid-sentence, Mark grinned as Tony inhaled and leaned forward, his heroic intentions cascading across the charged atmosphere. Mark ignored him, the man was no threat. Holding Hope's eye, he finished with, "Reuben is dead. Do not ask about him again."

Neither guest replied audibly, and Mark allowed the silence, his mind searching Paul. He would complete his discussion with Agricola but keep a simultaneous eye on his errant son.

❧

At the doctor's confession, Tony looked between the two of them; whoever Reuben was, the doctor or Paul (or both?) took his life.

And we're up to our necks in his filthy lair! How did we get into this mess? He considered Hope; when the doctor admonished her with his last words, she had simply huffed and crossed her arms, turning her face to the opposite wall. *Who is this woman?* He realized with marked sadness that his friend Hope was not the heroine he wished she was. Her selfish leanings had caused a lot of distress and although he didn't blame her for tonight, he couldn't help being sorry she wasn't more awake to the wiles of the enemy. The hairs on the back of Tony's neck came erect with sudden trepidation and he closed his eyes.

"Father? What now? I am completely lost! This is nuts! Please, let me hear you!" His companions remained silent as he prayed, lost in their own thoughts. When he reopened his eyes, Corescu and Hope were regarding each other, Hope with an expression of disappointment on her pretty face, and on the vampire, a look of what? Apathy? Maybe. Teaching the vampire to love would be an almost impossible task. Still, the nudge in his spirit reminded him he'd been brought there to at least try. Tony swallowed hard and trusted God would give him the words.

"Dr. Corescu…"

At the sound of his voice, they looked his way as if awakened from a trance. *That's too formal,* Tony said inside. Then, *What the hell…*

"Mark…" he waited for the vampire to acknowledge the use of his first name which he did with a nod. "Have you kept God's law? Have you kept the Ten Commandments?"

The doctor's blank expression remained as he replied, "What are you getting at?"

"God judges mankind by His standards. So, have you kept the Commandments of God all this time?"

"This is irrelevant," the doctor replied with a slight waver.

"On the contrary, it is 100% relevant. You said that you were once a man and a supernatural being turned you into this creature. Therefore, you *are* a man, and so this law applies to you. Because, what did Jesus say? If you love Me, you will keep My commandments."

The vampire looked away, as if in thought and Tony watched his

228

profile, strength returning to his spirit.

Then Hope touched his knee as he had earlier hers. "Just answer him," she said in a tiny voice.

The doctor considered the contact she initiated and frowned. He answered, still looking downward. "How can I answer? You are incorrect. I am not a man. Not anymore. I am above."

"You can't be both," Tony urged reading the vampire's uncertainty. His entire countenance had softened since the start of their talk and Tony wanted to take him all the way there. He trusted God to fill his mouth and continued. "You are a man trapped by the wiles of the enemy. Of course, you would tell yourself you're doing God's will. Of course, you'd pride yourself on your piety. If I was in your shoes, I'd do exactly the same thing." Tony's empathy grew every second and the doctor's expression said he noticed.

Corescu rose to his feet and strode to the bookshelves, showing them his back. He pulled out a book and returned it, dusting off his hands before turning to meet Tony's eye.

"If I am indeed a man, to be judged like a man, I have broken God's law many times. I have killed over a hundred thousand people since my transformation." He crossed his arms and leaned against the bookcase. A hush filled the library as the weight of thousands hung in the air.

The first one to touch the topic, Hope asked in a whisper, "Is that an exaggeration? That's like an entire city."

Corescu swiveled his gaze to hers. "Multiply my years times one judging a night. I do not go hungry."

Tony's nausea pinged. When a vampire eats, he's swallowing blood. *"This is too real,"* he sent upward. *"Please, let us be finished!"*

To Corescu, he said in an even tone, "Okay, that *is* a lot of people..." He gave a serious nod. "Here's the bottom line. From God's perspective, you are a sinner. You are not a magical, supernatural creature roaming the earth devouring the flesh of the unholy."

Tony's words stung, evident as the doctor stood off the furniture and dropped his arms. He might have been about to speak but Tony forged on.

"You must repent. Forsake your evil ways and turn from them. You must allow God to deliver you of this affliction. And you must walk in His ways."

Tony stopped, breathless, a sense of *it is finished* deep inside. Now, they'd see what the vampire would do. Now they would see if God broke through his defenses or he lashed out with violence and fury. Tony caught Corescu's eye, reading unease and something else. For the first time of the evening, the vampire's gaze expressed *self-doubt,* and in his heart, Tony prayed for them all.

Forty-Five

"As you go, preach this message, 'The Kingdom of heaven is near.'
Heal the sick, raise the dead, cleanse [the diseased],
And drive out demons."
Matthew 10:7-8

SPEECHLESS, MARK HELD THE PREACHER'S EYE AS THE teaching seeped acid-like to his conscience. He *knew* this truth. He had *lived* this doctrine in his human life. Why and how did it get so very far from him? For the first time since that first few days in The Other's lair, Mark's soul wracked with pain. He turned his back on his audience and sensed Hope come up behind. She put her hand to his shoulder and whispered soothing words that Mark did not attend. With ferocity he composed himself, horrified of manifesting weakness.

And where was The Other? Had he finally departed? Still with his back to the room, Mark quieted his mind and sought the demon's presence. Surely, he had an opinion on Mark's revelations. After a few long moments, he heard a voice, but it wasn't The Other. It was Paul and the boy was in terrible distress. Mark focused on the tenuous connection, Paul calling for help from a shadowy place.

His guests questioned his movement and he held up his hand.

"Silence!" he said with authority and squeezed his eyes closed, willing Paul to call him again, a dagger of dread piercing Mark's weary heart. Finally, the call repeated, distinct and dreadful.

"Master...Mark... please... I'm dying." And with that, Paul's telepathic voice went silent.

Without another thought and with a vicious hold on the last coherent transmission from his partner, Mark pushed himself physically to Paul's side.

☙❧

231

On the forest floor, Paul lay on his back, sifting the damp soil and leaves between his fingers. The knife still wedged in his chest had turned his shirt black with blood. The reporter had managed to plunge the steel between two ribs and the tip had pierced his heart. Paul knew this to his bones and the unmistakable sensation of slipping into the void seemed final. *This is how you kill me,* he thought as if speaking to Mark. Mark, his master, his friend, who loved him, who promised him the world, but now? *And it had been going so well...*

The reporter lay ten yards away gurgling, helpless, and choking to death on his own blood. Paul attempted to call Mark again but heard no reply. Only emptiness returned. Has his master abandoned him? Maybe, but The Other was silent as well. Paul closed his eyes in the dark, bleeding out, alone, and very afraid.

But Mark said I was immortal.

Then again, he also said he'd protect him. Paul wept silent tears.

What went wrong?

The reporter had arrived as planned. They met behind the BP Station where Paul instructed he follow on foot into the woods behind the structure.

"Did you bring a camera?" he had asked Nixon. "We buried one of the bodies back here. Come on. I'll show you." Without a concern, the reporter had followed Paul deep into the woods and when they reached a small clearing, Paul had the reporter dig in the wet earth, as if to disinter a hastily-hidden corpse. Then as Nixon knelt to scrape the leaves off the forest floor, Paul pounced onto his back and sliced his pocketknife against the man's throat. The weapon had been hastily chosen, but the three-inch blade did its damage to the reporter's carotid. Yet, even with a fatal wound spurting his lifeblood at volume, the journalist had slung Paul off his back with surprising strength. Then, in the same moment, Nixon removed a hunting knife from a hidden sheath in his back and lunged. Paul read wild animal urgency in the reporter's eyes as he did not dodge the blow well enough. Nixon's torso slapped into Paul's causing them to both tumble to the earth. When Paul rolled the gasping journalist away, the man's knife had been buried in his own chest to the hilt.

He turned his face to watch the reporter take his last breaths and Paul found he could no longer feel his legs.

So here he was.

Paul looked through the trees into the clear night sky.

232

Is this the end?

No one was coming. Paul closed his eyes and concentrated on his wound. He had no pain, yet he could not rise.

What if I'm discovered by the authorities? What will they do to me? The mortals will find Mark. I will have brought ruin upon us all. What if…

"Paulie."

A gentle voice whispered in his ear and he climbed back to consciousness.

"Paulie, Paulie, I'm here. I'm here."

The sweetest sound in the world. Paul opened his eyes and looked into the face of his savior.

☙❧

Mark held Paul close, one arm under his body lifting him into his lap as he sat on the earth beside him. The other hand grasped the knife buried in the boy's chest.

"I did it," he sputtered. "Everything that guy had on you is in his car. You're safe." Paul didn't take his eyes from Mark's dark gaze. "Master, I did it *for you...*"

Mark nodded and shushed him. "You need to *stop* doing this for me," he said with a chuckle fueled by his affection. In a deliberate movement, Mark excised the knife. Pressing his hand against the wound, he glanced at the dead reporter and considered his options. Yes, it would be light in a few hours. Yes, the cops might see the cars parked behind the station once the sun was up. And yes, the police would search for and find the reporter's corpse in the woods and recover his effects in his car.

Mark made a decision and got to it. In his arms, Paul whispered, blood on his lips, "I think I'm dying…"

"No, you're not," Mark soothed. " Didn't I tell you you're superman? You can't die. I won't allow it." Mark removed his hand from the knife wound. He put his own wrist to his mouth and bit down hard. In moments, his tainted blood rushed from his palm, spilling onto Paul's already soaked Polo. Paul watched with glassy eyes as Mark pressed his bleeding wrist into the ragged chest wound.

"Let my life mingle with yours," he whispered holding the boy's gaze, "You will not die so long as I can do something about it."

It would take mere seconds for Paul to feel the effects of the transfusion. A memory filled Mark's mind as he waited for his gift to

233

take root in Paul's circulatory system. He envisioned his own master mixing their blood so many years ago. The very source of his present problem manifested itself in him just this way.

And now I place this evil inside my beloved Paul.

Paul squirmed to pull himself more upright in his master's arms. Then he remained there, eyes glazed, head resting against Mark's chest, receiving the gift. With his free hand, Mark stroked Paul's damp locks.

"You naughty boy, look at the mess we have here," Mark chuckled, shaking his head. "Hope and that preacher are waiting for me at the house. I was moments away from..." Mark didn't need to say it and Paul nodded, rolling his eyes closed.

"Now there will be two *vámpír* in the house," he whispered, not ready to contemplate anything beyond that fact.

Paul lifted his head to look Mark in the eye. He had lost a lot of blood, and Mark read the need in his unnaturally pale complexion. He sighed at the unasked favor in Paul's bloodshot eyes.

This is all too familiar. Did not my master open a vein for me that first night?

Mark removed his hand from Paul's chest and brought his wounded palm to his lips. The blood had stopped its flow and the laceration had healed. But his son would need to be fed. Mark raised his eyes to the starry sky peeking between the trees and sighed.

⊂ℬ℘⊃

Tony gave a cry of alarm. Hope stood at the bookcase, her hand in mid-air where Mark's back had been. They had both seen their host magically disappear. Tony stood and crossed to the door of the library. *This is our chance! We can make a run for it!* Yet, he went nowhere. He peered down the hall, checking both ways for any sign of Mark or Paul, but the house sat dead quiet.

"What now?" he said to the air.

Hope shrugged. "I don't know."

Without turning, he asked, "How long have you known he was a vampire?"

Hope sighed and returned to her sofa. "I think I knew from the beginning."

Incredulous, Tony turned to catch her eye.

"I didn't think he was a bloodsucking real-life vampire, but I knew from when I first saw him that he wasn't normal. I can't explain it."

"Unbelievable," Tony replied, unsure of how he felt.

"Please don't give me that look," she said, her tone edgy. Tony

234

raised his brow and she pointed to his face. "Like you're disappointed in me. Stop. I'm not doing anything wrong. I'm in the right, here, and you know it. I can't help it if this is hard." She stressed the word and Tony wondered where her anger originated. Was she mad at him? Or the situation?

"Hope, wait," he began and she shook her head.

"Look, I'm sorry I'm not more churchy, but I am a ga-zillion percent sure I'm right on this. We did the right thing coming to help Mark figure this out!"

"Hey, I know, I'm sorry for my face," he said. He wiggled his eyebrows and waited for a grin. She deflated enough for him to finish. "I agree, God wants this. None of this is your fault. You had nothing to do with arranging this meeting tonight." Tony nodded at her wide eyes. "Yeah, and Dr. Corescu was about to have a breakthrough before he disappeared. Did you know he could do that?"

"No way—"

"Where do you think he went?"

"I think he went to help Paul. They're connected." Hope tapped her temple. "Mark had a similar reaction today when Glorie and I were in his office. I think Paul is in serious trouble."

"Are we done?" Tony had meant to ask the question inside and Hope sent him a new glare.

"But we haven't *done* anything. He's still confused!" Hope cleared her throat. "God! I'm thirsty. I'm going to get something to drink."

Tony followed her down the dark hall and into the kitchen. Out of a huge side-by-side refrigerator, she grabbed a can of orange juice for herself and handed Tony a Coke. It was time he told her about the incident in the garage. Tony opened his arm and Hope trained her eyes to his bandage. The bright kitchen light gave him courage and he said, "I need to tell you about this."

She gave him a *duh* look. "Okay. What did you do?"

"This is a bite." Tony took a swig of his Coke and leveled his gaze. "A vampire bite."

"What?" Hope was incredulous. "Anthony! Not funny."

"Dr. Corescu has fangs. Paul Black held me still and his boss— your boyfriend," Tony added accusing on purpose, "sucked the blood from my arm."

"Oh, God, that's stupid. Paul couldn't hurt a fly." Hope shook her head. "You're so dramatic. He was crying in that other room earlier. *Crying.*"

235

"That doesn't surprise me." Tony peeled the bandage corner to display the wound. Clearly delineated, two punctures puckered purple with bruising. Hope leaned close and her fingers flew to cover her mouth.

"Oh, God."

Tony re-sealed the tape with a sad nod. "You underestimate these people. They're not moral or ethical. These guys are serious psychopaths. If I wasn't compelled to stay here, I'd be gone in a flash. But God is doing something—"

"Stop exaggerating!" she said breaking in. "Yes, that bite is horrible, but he wants help. He asked you to help. They're not psychopaths, Anthony. Everything with you is so histrionic!"

Tony narrowed his eyes. "Wake up, Hope. No matter what God is doing here, you have to wake up. You can play naïve for only so long." Hope lowered her eyes, but she wasn't contrite. She was angry. "You're not safe here anymore than I am. They serve their own self-interest. They'll probably kill us tonight."

She shook her head and walked from the kitchen. "You have them all wrong…" she said, Tony looking at her back. He trailed her wondering what to say or do. Could they walk out? Leave? Escape while the monsters were gone?

"Mark will come back and we'll continue. He's not killing anyone."

Tony's temper flared at her obstinance. "Hello? Hello?" He raised his voice. "Dr. Corescu *attacked* me in the garage. I almost *died*." Tony paused for effect and she still didn't get it. Tony sighed, "He sucked my blood! He will kill us!" They had reentered the library and Hope turned to face him, her hands to her hips.

"Just go, okay? You're done. Good job. Thank you." She thrust out her bottom lip. "You act like there's no hope. I mean, geesh, Anthony, that's my *name*. Ever think of that?"

Tony sighed, his shoulders drooping. "How about this. You go. I promise to see this through to the end. But at least you'll be safe. He threatened me in the garage. He told me not to mention this wound. Paul threatened me, said I might get out of this alive. You know what that means, right? If things don't go his way, they are prepared to kill at least me. I wish you'd go. We don't both have to be in danger."

Hope's hard gaze softened a smidge and she shook her head. "No way. I'm staying. He's not killing us. I know him and you don't. Trust me."

Tony listened to his spirit, awaiting anything from God. Nothing new flowed through so he sighed. "Look. When he gets back, I'm going to finish it. I'm going to tell him to repent. If he kills me, he kills me. I know I'm not supposed to leave you alone, so there's my decision." He crossed his arms and leaned against the back of the closest sofa.

Hope walked close and touched his upper arm. "Don't be mad. I think God brought me here to *marry* him. I really thought I was supposed to join him. You know, get on board. Help him with this calling." Embarrassed now, she didn't meet his eye. "I realize now the vampire part is wrong, but I still think he needs me. I don't want to leave…"

Tony ran his fingers through his sweaty hair and sighed. "Let's see what happens. This is God's show. Just be ready for anything. I am ready to die… are you? If it comes to that?"

Hope shook her head.

"Hold my hand. I'll pray with you. When Corescu returns, I won't waste any time. He'll have to choose sides right away."

"Choose sides?"

"He's on the fence. He'll have to choose light or darkness. I think God wants him back. Who knows the heart of God?"

Hope had no answer.

ཚ

Paul watched his movements, mesmerized, the lust in his soul obvious to Mark at the work of making a wound for the new vampire to suckle. He'd already opened his shirt and he pulled his collar aside. When he turned his face away Paul knew what to do and surged close, pressing his face to Mark's neck and stabbing his flesh with newly sharp teeth.

"Just this once," Mark sent telepathically. *"We may both be destroyed tomorrow. Just this once."*

The sure sensation of Paul's fangs seemed bittersweet. Finally, Mark understood the complexities of The Other, the passion he directed at his priest, his creation, his son. Why he had been so patient; why he had been so gentle; why he had brought him so carefully into his dark world in the first place. *He was weary of being alone.*

As Paul pulled reverently now, quiet as a babe on a bottle, Mark thought of The Other. The sensation of his own blood draining from his body had him feeling philosophical and far away. The Other had no one with which to share the world, no one with which to discuss the

237

infinite nature of things. Yes, Mark had enjoyed companionship these last hundred years, but not the kind he needed. His mistake dawned in his consciousness and he whispered in Paul's ear, "I should have done this in the beginning. Forgive me, Paul, forgive me."

Paul ceased feeding and closed his mouth, embracing him as a child might his long lost parent.

Mark gave him a gentle nudge. "Let's go home."

Mark waited for Paul to rise first and the two of them stood together in the dark clearing. Completely restored, Paul stretched his arms high above his head and looked about the woods with wonder and awe.

"This is how you see the world? It's beautiful." Paul studied the trees above him. "I never knew."

Mark followed Paul's line of sight and nodded in agreement. "Yes, it's breathtaking. Come, experiment with your new eyes later. Let's get home before we're discovered."

"I'll bring the reporter." Paul turned to grab Nixon's corpse, but Mark stopped him with a hand to his arm.

"Leave him. He won't be discovered for days." Mark kicked leaves across the body and Paul matched his efforts. "We will be long gone before anyone finds him." Mark turned for the cars. Paul rifled the reporter's pockets and removed his wallet before jogging up behind.

"We're leaving Georgia? You and me?" Paul asked and Mark enjoyed the hope shining in his blue eyes. The future had brightened and those eyes had everything to do with it.

Mark gave him a sideways grin and clapped his arm. "And Hope."

Although he hadn't decided now what he'd do when they arrived home, he would take Hope. His earlier folly arose from fighting his nature, trying to be something he wasn't. Now he knew what he was, and he would embrace his immortality. The search for God's approval no longer held merit. Life could really be good.

Why didn't I see this before?

Paul lowered his chin, eyes up. "And the preacher?"

Mark huffed a smile. Paul liked him, what that meant, he wasn't sure, but something about Agricola drew Paul's keen interest. "What do you think we should do with him?"

Mark allowed the question to hang in the air. He had never asked Paul's opinion before and enjoyed watching him ponder an answer. *But, it's moot, right? Agricola must die. He cannot be allowed to live knowing what he knows...*

"I like him," Paul said then. "I'd like to keep him."

Mark laughed. "Keep him? Whatever do you mean?"

They had arrived at the cars and Paul reached into the reporter's rental to remove a briefcase and a laptop computer.

"You know, keep him around. Subdue him, take him, too," Paul said raising his brow before tossing Nixon's belongings into the BMW. He opened the passenger side door for Mark and then took his place behind the wheel.

"Oh, you'll be needing a pet now, will you?" Mark chuckled. Paul did not understand the power behind the preacher's faith. He could not be subdued, ever, but Paul needed more time to learn such things.

"He fascinates me," his new partner added. "He's so determined. So plucky. And this high." Paul held his hand at chest level and Mark chortled. Agricola stood 5'8" if that, but his strength came from within. *Paul doesn't know the power of God...*

"Do not seek trouble. You never appreciated my infatuation with God, but He's real, and He lives inside that little man. Never underestimate Him or the power of His saints."

Paul gave a thoughtful nod. "I just don't believe the two things are related. I've never seen God and I don't want to. But I want Tony. I want to watch him squirm as I take his blood."

Mark held his expression, his mind looping Paul's last sentence. *What did I do? This Paul is brand new...*He thought of his guests waiting at the house. Had they stayed or run? And if they had waited, what would he do when they reached them? *I can't possibly continue the current conversation... look what I have now. I have a partner in Paul and will have Hope soon—maybe tonight.*

"Is salvation no longer your concern?"

Ah, there it was, the Voice in his heart, the One who spoke to him in the chapel nearly four centuries ago. It was too late, for what use was a soul to an immortal being? No use at all.

Mark set his sights on the future and not on Tony Agricola's theology.

Forty-Six

"Away from me Satan! For it is written:
'worship the LORD your God and serve Him only.'"
Matthew 4:10

"WE COULD LEAVE NOW, FLY OUT BEFORE DAWN," PAUL said, as they waited for the electronic garage door to lower.

"Slow down, my friend," Mark said with a laugh. "Wisdom dictates we close this chapter first."

Paul turned to him, eyes wide. "They didn't leave? That's odd."

"No, it's as I told you; Agricola has a mission from God and he's deadly serious about carrying it out."

"Deadly is right," Paul snickered and covered his mouth.

"You should take this seriously. Tony Agricola has the power of God inside of him and that power is bigger than both of us combined."

Paul exited the car and grinned back. "Okay, I'll watch out. If his head starts spinning or flames shoot from his eyes, I'll run for cover." Mark didn't respond and Paul's smile remained. "I could get used to this."

Mark ignored his last retort. Paul's long years of servitude were over and he wasted no time asserting his new position. As they headed down the hall to the library, Mark considered Tony's zealousness. Would that be the reason they killed him? Would Hope's preacher friend be Paul's first mortal victim? A lot had changed in so little time, but overall Paul impressed him. If he had to accustom himself to Paul's new personality, he would. Simple as that.

Before they reached the library, Mark pulled Paul to a stop in the hallway. "That blood-soaked shirt should pique their interest, eh?"

"Should I change?" Paul put his finger in the rip the knife created.

"No, they wanted truth. Let us show them this side of us."

~*~

240

Tony's eyes jerked to the doorway as their host returned. Mark's white dress shirt was open and Paul's clothing ripped and saturated with blood. The doctor strode in with flair, catching Tony's eye.

"Thank you for waiting."

What now? Hope sent Tony with her eyes.

"Be still," he whispered and locked his gaze with Dr. Corescu. "We've had an adventure, have we?"

The doctor opened his hands in apology. "I'm afraid I have wasted your time." As he spoke, Paul crossed the room to stand a few feet from Tony, who, in response, backpedaled to the bookcase. Paul smiled, but his expression wasn't one of kindness.

"I've had a change of heart," the doctor said and his eyes followed Hope who crossed to where Tony leaned on the bookshelf. Before she reached him, the vampire blocked her access, his back to Tony. "Hope, do you still love me?"

Hope put her hand to the doctor's chest as if to prevent him from advancing. "What's going on? What's Paul doing to Anthony?"

"I'm not doing anything. I just wanted to get a better look at him." Paul reached for Tony's injured arm and grasped it before Tony could react. "Let me see how this is looking."

Once Paul had his wrist, resistance was as futile as before. Paul pulled his arm out straight and ripped off the tape exposing the wound.

"Stop it! Just stop!" Hope yelped and bypassed Corescu to reach Tony's side. When she wrapped her fingers around Tony's injured arm and tugged, Paul released him and held his hands up.

"I wasn't hurting him. I was being very gentle."

"Get behind me," Tony instructed pulling his wounded arm to his chest.

"Why are you trying to scare us?" Hope asked her voice shrill, and she did not move to allow Tony to guard her with his body.

The doctor chided then, "Yes, Paul, give them some room. Tony is scared out of his wits."

But Paul remained and leveled his gaze to Hope. "Are you finally scared, Ms. Brannen?" he growled. "Weren't you alone with me earlier giving me advice on how to become better friends with my master? Well, look. It happened. So what frightens you now? Do you think we're going to hurt you?"

"I. I. I don't know!" Hope stuttered and Tony's eyes covered both men, back and forth, wishing to be ready to jump if they did. Hope's indignant tone held. "Stop bullying Anthony. He didn't do anything to either of you." She turned to face Corescu, pleading, "Send Anthony home. He doesn't have anything to do with this. He won't say anything, will you, Anthony?"

It looked as if the doctor would agree, but when he reached for her, he pulled her out of Paul's way. The young bully moved in and grabbed Tony about the chest from behind. Tony had already surged when the vampire touched Hope, but now he struggled in Paul's iron grip.

"Mark, what're you doing? Paul! Stop!" Hope yelped fighting Corescu's embrace. "Let me go! We're leaving!"

Paul's immoveable arms held and Paul touched his lips to Tony's ear. "Preacher man," he said in a throaty giggle. "What *is your problem?*"

Tony shouted to be released and fought with all his might, unwilling to submit as he had in the garage. Hope was in danger and he would fight to the death to protect her.

"Dr. Corescu!" he shouted in a clear voice, his heart screaming for Jesus to help them. "What about your salvation? What happened to making amends with God? "

◯�◯

Mark swiveled Hope in his grasp so she faced outward, both facing Paul. The new vampire's actions had been unexpected, but so far, Mark had no intention of stopping him. Agricola shouted his question again, his voice that of a man who feared for his life.

"What about God?" Mark frowned. Hadn't he given up on God back in the woods? Didn't he allow the devil to reclaim him? Paul met his eye and Mark read the expression: Paul held the man's life in his hands with a taste for death Mark never possessed. *My God! I did it again. Without even knowing it, I fell for The Other's tricks!* With a gasp of private shame, Mark abruptly opened his hands and Hope stumbled out of reach. He rumbled to Paul deep in his chest, "Let him go."

Paul made no sign he heard the command. He stood against Tony, his lips at the preacher's ear, whispering threats and frightening invitations.

"Paul," Mark said, his tone grave, fully expecting his partner to obey, "release him."

"I'd rather not," Paul said low and bodily shuffled Tony toward the door. Then he whispered in his ear, "You can tell *me* about your God if you want. Come with me. Back to the garage. I have something

242

to show you." Hope shouted for Mark to do something and Tony writhed in Paul's iron grip.

Mark had had enough. He narrowed his eyes and reached the door before the duo, blocking passage. "Paul, do as I said," he hissed and Paul lifted his gaze to meet Mark's eye.

"Remember what you said," his former servant sent to his mind, his telepathic voice clearer than ever. *"Remember your promise. The preacher is mine."* He did not attempt to push past, expecting Mark's acquiescence. The room fell silent as the two faced off in the doorway.

"Release him. I'm not finished with him." Mark did not relish the idea of having to subdue Paul, but he had run out of patience with his disobedience. *"I am still your master."*

Paul frowned and increased the pressure of his forearm against Agricola's throat.

"Our Father who art in heaven," the preacher prayed, gasping for air.

Mark's frustration grew until his wrath would not be subdued. He laid his left hand upon Paul's shoulder and gave one more command. "RELEASE HIM!"

Mark hadn't applied physical pressure but allowed the full force of his will to cascade upon his partner's mind. As a result, Paul crumpled to the floor and Tony scrambled away on all fours to Hope's feet, sucking desperately for air.

"What're you going to do to me?" Paul pleaded silently from the floor at Mark's feet. Mark blocked his mind and his partner's eyes revealed a new respect for his master's power. He said then with a tremor, "What're you going to do to me?"

Mark looked away, disregarding Paul and leaving him paralyzed and defenseless on the library floor. He crossed to Hope who clung to Tony, tears on her cheeks, the disappointment in her eyes the most obvious emotion. Agricola's expression read frustration, relief, and the remainder of the fear Paul had instilled. Mark sympathized with him, the duality in his spirit causing him to wonder, *Tony must think I am a lunatic.* And Hope's gaze… *Am I? How am I so easily swayed, like a ship on the open sea?*

"Tony," Mark said, his voice steady, "are you okay? I apologize. I… This…"

"Dr. Corescu," Tony replied on top of his apology, coughing past a bruised trachea, "it's not too late. You were once a man and a child of God. He loves you and calls you to repent. There is nothing He cannot heal. He can cure this lust for blood as easily as you dominate

243

that poor soul at your feet." Tony gestured to Paul on the floor. "What do you say?"

Mark sighed and swept his arm in a semi-circle. "I don't want this…" He glided past his dumbfounded partner to sit where he had been earlier. Hope and Tony remained standing but closed into their previous triangle formation. "I'm black inside. I can't recall my first love, my love for Jesus and His word." He lowered his gaze to the floor, so close to relinquishing his will to the issue at hand. Close to giving away his power. He drew a palm across his mouth and said in a whisper, "I have been deluding myself, I see that now. And forgive Paul." He flicked his gaze to the kid still paralyzed and twitching near the door. "This is not his doing. I did that. I did." He returned his gaze to Tony. "Remind me, Tony. Remind me about our Creator."

Agricola's face softened, the earlier pain filtering from his eyes. "I will. And you'll remember, I promise." Tony regained his chair catty-corner to Mark and Hope also found her seat, her eyes wide. "Before this demon possessed you, you were so in love with God. He was your comforter, your best friend. He offers you His grace and mercy even now. Pray with me. We can send this demon out right now. Tonight."

"NO!" From his spot on the floor, Paul shouted, his voice shrill and panicked. "Mark! Don't! Please stop! They'll ruin you! You don't need to do this! We can live! You don't need them. I will be everything to you! Let me help you, let me…"

"Quiet." Mark's soft-spoken command had a noticeable effect on Paul who fell silent at once. To Tony, he said just as quietly, "Continue. I forgot myself a moment." Mark gestured to Paul. "I have transformed Paul into my likeness, and as you can see, he isn't in control of his impulses. I was so elated to have Paul restored, that I was tempted to return to my old ways."

"We understand," Hope said and reached for his hand.

He took her small fingers in his. Would she still love him if he were mortal? Then there was the question no one knew—*could* he be mortal again? His flesh was four centuries old. Would he turn to dust if the demon left him? Mark was miserable that he didn't know. And worse, he was afraid to die.

"Markus Corescu." Tony took his near hand and waited for Hope to complete the circle. "Do you repent and forsake your sin, your bloodlust, and promise to seek after the things of God?"

Mark offered a nod and the preacher closed his eyes. He spoke prayers to the air and Mark watched his lips, allowing the comforting words to calm his spirit. When his guest had uttered every prayer against the devil he could imagine, Tony squeezed Mark's hand meeting his eye. "Now," he said in a voice filled with compassion and empathy, "confess to the Lord, ask Him to save you."

Mark gave a small nod and did so, his voice breaking with emotion early on. Would God deliver him from the vampire inside? Or would he cease to live? When he had prayed as earnestly as he could, he held his breath, taking stock of his body. Nothing. The same lust for blood lingered deep within. The same confusion about God's will stumped his heart. *What did I expect? Lightning?* Still, he had expected something.

As he pondered God's apparent lack of action, a faint electric buzz pestered his mind. Still grasping hands with his guests, Mark listened, the white noise magnifying by degrees. In another moment, it grew so loud that he was certain Hope or Tony would notice it as well. He squeezed his eyes shut and thought he felt hands to his shoulders from behind. And did he hear Paul? The boy was up, shouting for him to run. But Mark couldn't move, and the buzz steadily threatened to unhinge his mind.

 Forty-Seven

"Go…teaching them to obey everything I have commanded you.
And surely, I am with you always, even to the end of the age."
Matthew 28:20

FRAN STUMBLED TO THE CAR AND GLORIE GIGGLED.

"You are *so* drunk!" Glorie's voice wavered with intoxication and she barely made it to the car without falling over.

"I'm Irish! We don' get drunk!" Fran laughed and leaned on the hood. "I can't drive, luv. You better be after callin' us a cab."

Glorie pulled down the hem of her cropped shirt and considered Fran with bleary eyes. It was after two in the morning and the last open bar they could find had pushed them out the door.

"I'm not even buzzing. Here, get in. I'll drive." Glorie grabbed the keys and unlocked the doors. "Go on. Get in. I'm not drunk."

Fran swaggered to the other side of the car and both women fell into their seats, still giggling like children. "Did you get a look at that bouncer? Big as a mountain, he was! I think he was a giant!"

"The Jolly Black Giant?" This revelation caused Glorie to belt out an entirely new round of laughing and she could barely breathe with the effort of it. Then she noticed someone approaching from the direction of the club. "Frannie! The Jolly Black Giant is coming to get you!"

The man walked briskly with huge strides. A modern-day Goliath, the bouncer stood nearly seven feet with a bald head that reflected the light of the parking lot lamps.

Fran gave him a smile when he leaned into her window on the passenger side. "You rightly have the face of a'cherub, don' you? Would you be one of them angels then, Jolly Black Giant?"

When Glorie heard Fran's question, she paused her cackling, considered the man's appearance, and then resumed her hilarity with, "Angels aren't black, stupid!"

"Sure they are!" Fran laughed. "Hey, you're a looker, too. You married, Jolly Black Giant?"

"Gimme your keys." The gentle bouncer held out a huge hand. "Why don't you ladies let me call you a cab?"

Glorie closed her fist around her keyfob. "No way, José. I'm not junk. Go on back to heaven and kill some devils for us."

☙❧

The big man backed away and lifted his cell phone to dial 911. The driver started her car and pulled off. Sure, they'd be angry when the sheriff pulled them over in about five minutes, but at least they'd be alive. The bouncer hung his head and prayed they'd be safe.

☙❧

Paul had expected Mark to be pleased with the way he had handled Agricola and the power his master displayed to supplicate him had been frightening. Thankfully, Paul was free, the weight removed in the last few seconds. He sought the others and found Mark in a circle holding hands with their guests. His master was wincing in pain and he approached to place his hands on his shoulders. As soon as he made contact, the noise tormenting Mark traveled to his own mind and he held tighter, willing the noise to cease. He shouted over the din in his mind, "Stop! What have you done to him?" Paul grimaced, the pain becoming unbearable.

"Let go you fool!" The Other, and he sounded panicked. *"Back away RIGHT NOW!"*

Paul obeyed and yanked his hands to himself, The Other's terror filling Paul's mind, too.

"RUN, Paulie, RUN NOW!"

Paul scuttled backwards into the hallway and as he left the room, the noise abated in increments. He stumbled toward the kitchen, his arms pumping along the way to gain momentum.

"What's happening? Why am I running?" Paul shouted to The Other in his mind even as he fumbled in his pocket for the car keys.

"My priest has chosen the Carpenter. Come, I will help you escape. Take us away from here. Trust me and RUN!"

Paul needed no further instruction. He peeled out of the garage in the BMW and sped off the property. He had no idea where he was headed, but he would follow the advice of The Other. He would search Mark out again one day, but for now, he had to escape. And run, he would.

247

൦൭

"Dr. Corescu? Mark?" Tony asked and wiggled the doctor's hand. "Are you okay?"

Mark didn't answer. The excruciating noise had abated, but he still hadn't opened his eyes, afraid of what he might see and afraid of what he might feel. *Am I cured?* He sought Paul's mind only to be rewarded with dead air. He then peeked where he normally sensed The Other, but as with Paul, nothing pinged back. *Is he gone? Are they both gone?*

"Mark? How do you feel?"

That was Hope, her voice optimistic, so willing to believe a monster could be redeemed by uttering a few choice words. Mark hated to see her disappointed. What if there was no change? What then?

Tony asked again, "Dr. Corescu?"

"Yes, yes. Quiet," Mark shushed them, his voice too loud in his ears even though he had whispered a response. He still hadn't opened his eyes. The light from the library desk lamps were bright behind his closed lids. "The lamps, turn off one of the lamps."

Hope leaned over to the lamp nearest and switched it off. She then slid over to the couch and sat against him, her hand on his leg. "It's okay. It's going to be okay."

Mark released Tony's fingers to place his hand over Hope's, her skin hot to the touch. She smelled of roses and Mark frowned. *Nothing has changed.*

He steeled himself and opened his eyes. The room, lit by a single 40-watt bulb, was as bright as day to his vampire eyes. Nothing had changed.

"What? Is anything different?" Hope asked.

Mark offered a sad smile, studying the all-too-familiar aura surrounding her like a halo. He shook his head. "You are so beautiful, but no, It is all still there."

"But you *are* different," Tony asserted on Mark's left. "You're a new man. Children of God live by faith. Go out and live according to His ways."

"You're mistaken." Mark looked at the preacher, his gaze landing on Tony's lacerated arm. Because of Paul's rough treatment, the wound leaked blood that had dried in a grisly line to the man's elbow. The unmistakable sensation in his gut at the sight revealed his bloodlust remained as strong as ever. "Nothing has changed."

"No, *you* are mistaken." Tony closed his elbow. "You have a clean slate. Don't mess it up." He waited for Mark to look from his arm to meet his eyes. "I don't expect you to magically return to being the same man you were four hundred years ago, but you are a *new* man. You're a new creation. God will let you know when you sin. You might not feel it until you try to kill somebody—"

"I don't believe that," Mark interrupted, frustration in his voice.

"If you hold up your end, God will be your conscience. Listen to Him and He will tell you what you are to do. Trust me. Trust Him."

Mark stood and helped Hope to her feet. "I pray you're right Tony." He turned toward the door and Hope caught his quizzical look.

"He ran out." Hope gestured to the hallway. "He looked really scared."

"As he should be. I want you to leave immediately. Both of you," Mark warned as he left the room. He entered the study and clicked on the computer. His guests followed and remained quiet. As the computer powered up, Mark sat at the desk and ignored them. When they didn't leave after a few quiet moments, he urged them once more. "Go. Get out. I don't want you here," he cut his eyes to Hope, "either of you."

Hope's face fell and Tony frowned, but neither budged.

"Mark, I want to help you," Hope whispered. "I can help you through this."

Mark cleared his throat and turned, a dark look in his eye. "Hope, your sister Glorie aborted her babies. Your sister Glorie murdered her first and second husbands. Your sister Glorie is killing her three living children *right now*...poisoning them every day..." Hope's face froze, eyes wide and Mark finished. "It will be up to you to stop her. Call the police. Tell the children's doctor to look for poison, specifically household ammonia. She's slipping it to them in tiny doses."

Mark watched Hope's face for acceptance. Now, if she didn't turn and leave, he might never let her go. If he had to, he'd force them to leave. Mark hoped it wouldn't come to that.

◈

Deputy Sheriff Bill Coker slowed his patrol car to a stop beside the overturned vehicle. The medical personnel would be there in moments, but every second counted to the victims inside the car. The sedan lay on the driver's side, propped upon an immense landscaping stone and leaning against the rising concrete support of the overpass. Bolting to the upturned passenger-side door, he pounded on the glass, eyes fixed on the nearest victim.

The passenger hadn't been belted in, and she'd hit the windshield

249

hard. Now her quiet form lay across the lap of the driver whose hands still gripped the steering wheel. The deputy shrank back as he saw the bloodied knuckles of the driver. Were they both dead? It was an awful way to begin a shift, but as the approaching ambulance siren filled the night air, Deputy Coker heard a moan and a gasp for air. He leaned in the broken window on the passenger door as the nearest woman's fingers moved.

"Lady, help is here! You're gonna be okay!" Bill hollered over the clamor of sirens and made way for the medics to begin their work. Within minutes, the two women were extricated from the vehicle and secured onto stretchers. The passenger was whisked away in the primary bus. The driver was wheeled to the next with the sheet pulled over the face.

Bill's shoulders slumped and he trudged back to his car. Why did people insist on driving drunk? He'd gotten there as fast as he could. His friend John bounced the local bars and always called 911 when he suspected someone of being too drunk to drive. The news was going to crush the gentle giant at the bar.

"Drunken fools!" Bill mumbled as he reached his cruiser.

On the way to the hospital to follow up with the survivor, he phoned the bar and gave John the bad news. As he hung up his cell, he'd heard the big man's heart breaking.

ᘏᘏᘓᘔ

Hope stared at the back of Mark's head as he tapped away on an internet travel site, refusing to leave as he requested. When he huffed and stood, she backed to let him pass.

"Leave, now," he reiterated and headed into the hall.

Hope didn't buy it. She followed him to the stairwell where Anthony touched her arm.

"He knows where to find us." Her friend gestured for the front door. "Let's go."

"Mark?" Miserable, Hope stepped around so Mark would have to look at her. "Mark? What am I supposed to do with this information? How do you know these horrible things about Glorie?"

"Hope, go away, I've spoken my piece. Please leave."

The apathy in Mark's voice caused Hope to shiver. She turned to Anthony, her eyes filling with water. "Anthony, call us an Uber and wait on the porch..." When her friend didn't move she shooed him with her hand. "Please. Give me a second."

Anthony reluctantly turned and headed away. Once he was out of sight, Hope pleaded with Mark with more fervor.

"I believe what you said about Glorie. I won't let her kill those babies. Listen, don't push me away. I don't want to lose you. Not after all we've been through. Please…"

Mark locked his eyes with hers. "It is finished. I'm going home."

Hope took hold of his arm. "Home is where you make it. Let me go with you. We can start over."

"Hope," Mark lowered his voice, "I'm worse off now than I was before this night. Now, I'm a monster with no purpose and a lust that fills my soul. I'll kill you if you don't go now." Mark stopped without taking back his threat.

Hope swallowed hard, a challenge in her gaze. "I don't believe you. You're running away. What're you afraid of? You're stronger than—"

Mark cut her off. "The fantasy is over. I'll have the authorities after me soon. Paul and I have left a trail of dead bodies that leads directly to this house. I'm going to go home. You are no longer safe here; you're no longer wanted here. Hope, leave now." Mark jerked his arm from her grip and turned for the stairs. "I'll not ask you again."

Hope's chest constricted at the thought of letting him go. She chased after him and grabbed his arm on the third step. "Please, Mark, I can help you."

Whatever she expected him to do next, she was way off. Mark spun in her grip, taking her by her upper arms with hands like claws. Without meeting her eye or saying another word, he pulled her off her feet and pressed his lips against her throat. Hope screamed in surprise and then yelled for Anthony. As she kicked her feet hyperventilating with fear, she awaited the bite she knew was coming. What had she been thinking? To befriend and then challenge a vampire and expect to be safe in his presence? Hope stopped shouting and clamped her mouth shut, Mark's ragged breath on her neck, his hot tongue pressed against her skin, yet his teeth had not touched her. By the time Anthony reached them, she realized what he was doing. Mark hoped to frighten her, but was unwilling to bring her harm.

Hope opened her eyes to see Anthony punching Mark from behind, shouting with amazing authority. After a few more blows, Mark released her to tumble to the steps, and then pushed past Anthony and jogged up the stairs.

"Hope! Let me see! Are you all right? I knew we should've left. I'm so sorry!" Anthony had stooped to the carpeted stair and was pushing her hair away from her neck.

Tears coursed down Hope's cheeks and she shook her head. "He didn't hurt me, Anthony, he loves me." Hope shrugged off her friend's helpful touch and ran up the stairs after Mark, two at a time. "Mark!" she yelled when she reached the locked door that he'd disappeared behind.

Anthony was right behind her and he put his hand to her shoulder. "Please, let him go. He needs to go away and figure this out."

"But I can help him," Hope hissed, aware her behavior had grown irrational.

"Hope, I'm no better than the mythical monsters in your idiotic movies," Mark's saddened voice said through the door. "It's better this way. Listen to Tony."

"Mark," Hope sighed, "if the police come after you, I won't give you away. I'll never give you away."

"The police are after him?" Tony whispered, but Hope ignored him. She was still trying to cook up a way to stay with Mark. Couldn't he send for her later? Once he was settled wherever he was going?

"Mark," Hope said, now leaning against the cold wood. "Do you still think we're meant to be together? Or were we just brought together to have this messy night and call it quits?"

There was a pronounced silence in which Anthony started to interrupt, but Hope shot him a glance. Anthony was her best friend, sure, but he sometimes didn't know when to hold his tongue. Finally, the doorknob turned and Hope looked up into Mark's face.

"You need to forget about me." Mark touched her cheek and pushed her hair behind her ear, a sad smile crossing his face. "Get a life without monsters." He looked over at Anthony and inclined his head. "Take good care of her."

Hope didn't look at her friend, realizing with a heavy heart that Mark may still love her, but not enough to overcome his current spiritual distress. Their time together had been magical, but hadn't she also rearranged his entire universe?

"I'll go, but I love you and you know where to find me."

"You'll be fine, Hope Brannen. You have a brilliant life ahead of you." Mark pulled her head to his lips and planted a lingering kiss to her forehead. When he pulled back, he stepped into the room, preparing to close the door. "You have an amazing glow that I can see with my eyes. I'm not willing to do anything to dampen that spirit."

"Remember what I told you, Mark," Anthony said, peeking around

252

Hope's shoulder. "God is listening. You repented and you want to make things right. Just speak to Him. He will set everything straight for you. I am 100% confident in what I am telling you."

Mark offered a small grin. "I hope you're right."

"Mark—" Hope jumped into the room and threw her arms around his neck. "I'll be waiting for you. I know you'll call me. I just know it."

Mark returned her embrace. When she stepped back, he closed the door and the lock clicked into place.

Anthony touched her back. "Let's wait for the cab out front."

Hope nodded and clomped down the stairs to the foyer. She resisted looking back as they exited, and once on the porch, she stopped and faced the driveway.

"Anthony, I don't feel like it's over. I mean, he needs encouragement as he mends his ways. If he goes alone, before long, he'll be right back where he started." Hope spoke softly and closed her eyes at her morbid predictions. "Blood, death, misery—he'll fall back into the same pattern."

"You have to have faith, Hope. God can certainly rid that monster of his demons."

"I have faith in *Mark.*" Hope looked back as she spoke. "My inner voice is telling me I'm not supposed to leave him like this."

"That might be the enemy talking. The devil has a stake in this, too. Think about that." Anthony's compassionate words were not what she wanted to hear. "Just as you get clean, the devil would like nothing else than to toss you back in the mud."

His words stung and she clutched her arms to her chest. No matter how sound his logic or even his theology, she wanted so badly to have Mark with her.

"Go home, pray about it, and *then* follow your heart. Right now, we're both tired and scared and useless. In the morning, everything will be clearer."

Anthony finished as the Uber pulled up to the wrought iron gate. Hope clutched his good arm for support and he helped her into the backseat. Forlorn, she scanned Mark's house and her heart ached. She would probably pray about it, as Anthony suggested, but she had the answer. When the hubbub died down, she was going to find Mark, and no one would be able to stop her.

Satisfied with her plan, Hope rested her head on Anthony's shoulder as they sped down the dark street. Before they reached the highway, she fell asleep.

Forty-Eight

"Lord, if You are willing, you can make me clean."
Jesus reached out His hand and touched the man.
"I am willing," He said. "Be clean!"
Matthew 8:2-3

MARK WOULD LEAVE AT FIRST LIGHT. WITH A FOCUSED thought, he could travel almost anywhere, and now that he remembered his past, he decided to head for Germany. He had resources banked throughout Europe and stored memories of his favorite haunts. This wasn't the first time he had to leave a situation because the mortals came too close, but it was the most painful to date. Leaving Hope behind would scar him forever. Just then, the memory of her throat against his mouth caused his breath to hitch. What had he been thinking? If she only knew how close she'd come to death. He hadn't planned the move, rather reacted solely on instinct, something he hadn't done in ages.

By reflex, he wondered where she was and with no effort, in his mind's eye, he found her at home, pouring food in a dish for her cat. She'd grown sensitive to his ethereal intrusions and she looked up to her ceiling. Mark closed her out, vowing to not seek or contact her again. Leaving Hope behind was best for all of them. She had surely "rearranged his universe," and Mark would suffer the consequences.

He searched for Paul's telepathic signature and came up empty, feeling the void where he had kept his partner set apart. Paul was as far away as The Other, and although Mark needed to separate to find his way back to God's fold, he missed them just the same. Part of him had been excised and Mark resented the discomfort the process brought.

Mark clasped his hands beneath his chin to pray. It was time he reentered the congregation of the saved or rejoin the devil; choose a side. Centuries ago, he had been very close to his Maker and he recognized God's voice. Had the Holy Spirit actually departed when he accepted the gift of the devil in the cave or had He hunkered down to wait it out? Mark preferred to assume the latter. With his head bowed

254

and with the most sincere passion he could muster, Mark waited for the Lord to speak. He would wait forever if he had to. After all, he had eternity.

ಇಶಿ

Despite the short nap on the ride home, Tony tossed and turned in his bed, unable to fall asleep. He wasn't surprised. He still reeled with the scope of what he had seen and experienced in the past few hours. How could he fall into a blissful sleep and pretend it never happened? Moreover, how could he go through life knowing vampires were real? And were there more of them?

Well, there's at least one more.

Tony sat up in his dark room. The street lamp outside his apartment complex had blown days ago and not a slip of light spilled into his bedroom. He suddenly became aware of his vulnerability.

What if that crazy Paul Black comes here to finish me off?

Tony switched on his bedside lamp. After a new scan of his room corners, he spied his familiar red, leather-bound Bible on the nightstand. He lifted it with a sweaty hand.

I have nothing to fear. You pulled me through with barely a scratch.

Tony looked at his arm, blessed indeed that he came away with such a small wound. Add to that, Hope had been completely spared.

Thank God Corescu didn't bite her neck when he grabbed her on the stairs.

Tony thought about another desperate moment when Paul tried to drag him out of the library. Corescu ordered him to stop; something had come over the doctor then.

Didn't I see something in his eyes? Yes. God was working on him; correcting him, loving him, giving him hope of salvation.

Tony rolled off the messy bed and went to his knees to pray. Clearing his anxious thoughts, he raised his face to the heavens. He and his Master spoke a long time and when Tony finally crawled back into bed, he had accepted a new mission. It was going to be dangerous, but Tony would not refuse. He knew a lot about vampires and he knew his God. He was in good hands.

ಇಶಿ

Hope lay in bed, exhausted and crying. Rejected by Mark, she couldn't make herself face the truth; that it was over. Also, Hope couldn't ignore the irony that Mark's most threatening gesture, in fact, attracted her all the more. Those few seconds in his grasp, with his face

255

buried in her neck, thrilled her to the bone. She might have died, but the bottom line was that *she didn't.*

Hope looked at the clock. Where was her stupid sister? Glorie hadn't come home. She had tried Fran's cell, but got no reply. She had tried Glorie's and got only voicemail.

And what of Mark's solemn recounting of her sister's evil deeds? After noting the late hour, she flipped through her address book to call Jim's mother. There was no doubt what Mark said was true which meant Glorie would spend the balance of her life behind bars. What did that mean for the kids? Would they stay with Jim? Would they ask Hope to keep them? All of these thoughts scampered past as the phone rang eight hundred miles away in Maryland. On the third ring, a sleepy male voice picked up the line and grumbled a greeting. Hope composed her thoughts.

"Mr. Hershey? I'm sorry for the late hour, but it's an emergency. This is Hope Brannen, Glorie's sister." She waited for recognition in his voice and he finally woke up enough to realize who had called.

"Oh, okay, Ms. Brannen, something happen to Glorie?"

"Uh, not really." Hope scrambled for a coherent thought. "I have some important information about the kids. Are they okay?"

"Well, yeah, actually, they've been getting progressively better over the last few days. Seems they needed a vacation, too." Mr. Hershey paused to speak to someone on his end and returned to the phone. "Ms. Brannen, Mrs. Hershey wants to speak to you." The phone was handed over and Hope waited for the woman to speak.

"Ms. Brannen? Where's Glorie? Isn't she staying with you?" A strong female voice that Hope had only heard a handful of times filled the phone.

"Mrs. Hershey, Glorie didn't come home tonight, but more importantly, I found out why the kids have been sick." Hope barreled on so that she wouldn't be interrupted. "Glorie's been poisoning them. She's been slipping them household ammonia." A few audible gasps on the other end and Hope realized Jim's dad had picked up another extension.

"My Lord! Earl, that would explain what that doctor said yesterday when we took them to the pediatric center." Mrs. Hershey returned her attention to Hope speaking fast. "We knew the children's doctors at home were doing the best they could, but Earl and I decided to take them to the big guys in Hagerstown. They found tiny caustic ruptures in all three boys' throats and stomachs. They asked us if the boys had ever been into our cleaning supplies!"

Hope collapsed on her bed as she listened. When the Hershey's finished their rant about what a terrible mother Glorie was, and how God would get her back for trying to kill her children, they asked her where she got her information, as in, had Glorie confessed and where the hell was she. Hope thought fast.

"We're twins, remember? I'm afraid I know a lot more than that. For now, will you please contact the police? I'm sure they'll find all of the evidence they need in her house. When she comes home, I'll call the authorities on my end."

"We'll call them right now! Ms. Brannen, thank you, thank you. Thank God!" Just before she hung up the phone, Martha Hershey mumbled something to her husband and put the phone back to her lips. "Oh, and pray for the children. Pray for a complete recovery. And pray that Glorie will be brought to justice!"

Hope said she would and hung up. Lying snug in her own bed, fighting sleep, she recalled Mrs. Hershey's last words, and little by little, the entire horrible evening paraded past her memory.

Pray for the kids…
pray for Glorie…
pray for Mark…
pray for Tony.

Pray for …something. Hope was thankful she was safe. Never one to say much to the heavens, Hope lay on her back and watched her ceiling fan in the dark.

I hope this all works out. Amen.

It was the best she could do. Her mind was fried and she was dead tired. Hope fell asleep. She didn't hear the phone ring an hour later. On her iPhone, a notification blinked into place. In the morning, she would find a message from the Atlanta Highway Patrol and would have her answers regarding Glorie.

Epilogue

For God does speak—now one way, now another...
In a dream, in a vision of the night, when deep sleep falls on men
As they slumber in their beds, He may speak in their ears..."
Job 33:14-16

Black Forest *(Schwarzwald)*, Germany

MARK TOSSED THE KEYS ONTO AN ANCIENT OAK TABLE adjacent to the foyer and considered the space. Purchased at the turn of the Twentieth Century, the dwelling was as old as he was and smelled of moss and foliage. Finding no evidence of trespassing, Mark sighed and his shoulders drooped. He was home. Here he would rest, search for God, and perhaps even die.

As he stood in the damp front hall, he considered Paul. By the time he reached Europe, he'd finally been in contact with his wayward son. The boy was hiding in the lake cabin; alone, angry, confused and *very* hungry. Before Mark departed his mind, he sensed The Other, giving Paul bad advice and soothing with evil intent. Mark flashed back to himself, almost afraid the demon might sense his ethereal presence and attempt to latch on. No more, Mark was done with him forever.

Taking a tour of the old house, he looked into each room and then out the broken window of the dining area. The dense forest encircled the house and property for miles. With the stroke of the keyboard before leaving Georgia, Mark had bought two hundred additional attached acres to provide himself even more privacy. The untamed woods and impassable, eroded and trenched driveway further cushioned the estate from the world. The sun was falling fast and dark shadows filled the corners of the run-down residence.

A perfect place of solitude...

"A perfect place to rest," Mark said aloud, his voice reverberating to the high ceiling.

He returned to the great room where ruined furniture had been scattered like toys, fit for nothing but the fire. He found an overturned dining table, righted it and tested it with his hands before hopping onto its dusty surface. It bore his weight and he sighed. Mark regarded the tattered Hungarian-language Bible he held in his hands and read a few passages to himself. As if testing the waters, he then turned to lie flat. The table was six feet long so only his heels hung off the edge.

What do I do?

Of that, he wasn't sure, but he could no longer reside among the living. He would tuck himself away, study the Word, and seek God.

"Heavenly Father, I will wait for you," Mark said to the air, his voice soft. "I have no idea what You have in store for this old monster, but I await Your command." Mark clutched the Bible on his chest with both hands and closed his eyes. "I will lie here and wait."

Lie here and wait. Lie here and wait. Lie here and wait, he thought, his mantra soothing his spirit. Mark was hopeful.

So hopeful.

Hope…

Hope Brannen.

With effort, Mark again put the woman out of his mind and fell off to sleep. He dreamed of a brilliant white horse; free, clean, powerful, and perfectly whole.

END Book One

~ Please visit www.ellencmaze.com contact/newsletter
and sign up for her newsletter to
be alerted for every new novel release
plus giveaways!

259

The Corescu Chronicles
Continues with
Book Two: DAMASCUS ROAD

Tony Agricola is on a mission: pursue and attempt to redeem the newly-turned and ravenous vampire, Paul Black. But how do you subdue a creature a hundred times stronger or save one determined to remain as he is?

In danger at every turn of the vampire's whimsy and dodging two indomitable police detectives on their trail, Tony valiantly drags Paul to Germany to confront his master, Doctor Mark Corescu, who fled there to hide away from humanity.

Before the dust settles, Hope Brannen, madly in love with the doctor, arrives and puts her fists in the fight. Vacillating between the desire to be good and the lust for blood, Mark, Paul and Tony wrestle to the end, making the final result anybody's game.

Read on for a *Sneak Peek* from DAMASCUS ROAD...

260

Excerpt
DAMASCUS ROAD
Book Two of The Corescu Chronicles

The waiting was killer.

Paul forced his feet to remain in place. Fifteen feet away, secluded in the shadows of the alley, his prey leaned with her back to the slimy brick wall locked in a passionate embrace. Oblivious to her upcoming demise, the woman moaned with delight while her furtive fingers pawed her partner's pockets. Her happenstance paramour's focus kept him enthralled as he worked to disrobe his companion.

Paul bit down on his bottom lip, using the discomfort to distract his ballooning bloodlust. Two people at once, he really shouldn't; it would make the headlines. One hooker, page six. But this drug-addicted businessman *and* a lady of the evening, murdered together, the same night? Even in his less-than-experienced mind, Paul figured it best to avoid such print.

So, he waited.

Fingers twitching, stomach roiling, and his brain synapses literally misfiring and causing intermittent shock-like jolts, Paul stood immobile and worked to calm his nerves. It wasn't easy, he had no formal training; the one who transformed him departed before handing him the answers to such a life. Paul smirked; at least tonight he was aware of his activities. Too many nights since he had become a vampire, he would experience lost time, blacking out and awaking hours later, usually with a nameless stiff in his clutches.

Just as he thought his heart might burst from its pounding, the man in the shabby suit backed away from the woman, zipped his fly, mumbled a few drunken pleasantries, and ambled out of the alley. He shuffled past Paul hidden in the dark and disappeared around the corner to the sidewalk.

Paul flew into action. He'd waited so long, his urge to play with his food had all but dissipated. Instead, he grabbed the woman from behind as she counted her bills, jerkily stepping out of the shadows to seek new customers. With only the most basic thought, Paul plunged fierce fangs into her throat, flicked his head violently to the right to open the access, and allowed the sweetest liqueur to slosh past his palate and head to his deepest parts. Lasting less than a minute, another woman he didn't know breathed her last in his embrace.

Was this what his master felt when he ripped the life from his victims? Paul dropped the corpse to the ground and backed away. He'd never know what Mark thought when he judged them; Mark had abandoned him. Paul scowled and marched down the littered alley to the street. Tonight's meal satisfied, and with access to the full scope of Mark's wealth, he was living well. He'd be okay, and soon, he'd be reunited with his master.

It had been a good night, a clean kill, and unlike the last three occurrences, he remembered it all. Things were looking up.

Tony shook himself awake and rolled out of bed. Recurring nightmares had become commonplace since his stint at the Corescu mansion. Jogging to the bathroom, he splashed cold water onto his face and looked in the mirror. Repeatedly, the moment Dr. Mark Corescu sank his fangs into his arm revisited Tony in his sleep. It would be nice if God purged the image from his subconscious, but so far, He hadn't.

Tony's eyes fell on the half-used note pad and capless Motel 6 pen at his side. This lodging wasn't as nice as the first one he had rented, or even the second, but as his money ran thin, so did the luxury. If he didn't find the guy soon, he'd have to abandon the pursuit. Tony clicked off the lamp and lay back on the bed.

Paul Black, where are you?

Behind closed lids, Tony recalled details of the hunt so far. Corescu fled the country the day after their altercation, but the vampire's partner, Paul Black, was in the wind. Driven by a vague prophecy delivered by a stranger and a compulsion from the Spirit of God, Tony determined to locate him.

The vampire's estate had been put up for sale and the dozens of rooms of furniture had been sent to a storage facility. Thus, Tony found himself in a shabby motel in Atlanta, Georgia, two blocks from the climate-controlled Store-All where Paul signed for his master's belongings. Tony would get an address from the site manager tomorrow. Not bad investigating for a drop-out seminary student.

Tony sighed. It wasn't late, but he needed to focus. He'd been seeking the most dangerous of fabled creatures, fully aware he was an army of one. Tomorrow, he would discover God's will. If the Store-All manager refused to give out Paul's address, Tony would be justified in going home. God opened doors and sometimes held others closed. It was conceivable that God might use someone else to help save Paul's soul.

That would be okay, too, Tony mused as he drowsed. *I've seen enough blood and horror to last me a lifetime.* He chuckled, feeling no joy in the act, and finished his thought. *Even though I do have plenty of experience with vampires.*

A loud, metallic bell woke Tony with a start. He bolted upright and clicked on the lamp before he realized what caused the sound. Grabbing the receiver, he noted the time on the hotel radio/clock: 7:07 p.m.

"Preacher-man, did I wake you?"

The familiar voice sent chills down his spine.

"I've been thinking about you," the voice continued in an amiable tone.

Tony groped the bedside table for his glasses and fumbled them onto his face. Paul had been looking for him? Did he seek to finish him off? Tony cleared his throat.

"What a coincidence," he managed, smiling at his smooth response. "I've been thinking about you, too."

"I know," Paul replied, this time in a guttural whisper.

Tony rubbed the goose pimples that rippled his arms at the sound. The guy was as mischievous as he remembered. Tony hardened his voice. "Where are you?"

"Not too far away." Paul had resumed his normal tone. "I'm staying at Broadmoor Apartments on Union Street, number six. I'll leave a light on for you."

Tony didn't respond. Why would Paul invite him over?

Come to think of it, what did I intend to do when I found him? Take him fishing?

Even as the thoughts flashed across his mind, his eye fell upon his much-loved Bible. God would lead him as He always did.

"I'll meet you somewhere public," Tony said, tucking his dress shirt into his trousers. "I saw a mall nearby."

"No, it has to be here," Paul interjected. "If you want to see me, you'll have to come here."

Tony paused, hands on his hips, the phone pressed between his shoulder and ear. Inside, he sought a nudge from God.

263

"Look, I don't want to hurt you," Paul said, his tone sincere enough. "I was out of my mind last time you saw me. I'm much better now, honest."

God still hadn't spoken, but Tony decided to concede. "I believe you," he said with an audible sigh. "I'll come."

"Excellent, number six, see you soon."

Tony agreed with a grunt and shoved his wallet into his pocket.

"And Tony," Paul said, his voice soft again.

"What?"

"I've missed you," Paul whispered and was gone with a click.

Tony stared at the receiver in his hand. God would protect him, lead him, and tell him what to do when the time came. He had to trust. Tony grabbed his car keys.

I must be crazy.

Kneeling beside the bed, Tony bowed into his hands.

"Father," he mumbled, "You are the God who enables. Help me help Paul find you. You are my shield and my shelter. Amen."

Hoping that was enough, Tony grabbed his Bible off the dresser and walked to the door. Pray and proceed; it was all he could do. He allowed the door to lock behind him as he headed to his truck. Apparently, the nightmare was not quite over.

www.LittleRoniPublishers.com